THE LAST PIECES OF ME

A Novel

Lyn Groves

FairFarren Press

First printing, 2025

ISBN (paperback): 978-1-7643363-0-7
ISBN (hardcover): 978-1-7643363-1-4
ISBN (ebook): 978-1-7643363-2-1

Cover design by Laura Boyle

Editing by Laura Boon

There is forever a hollow place in our hearts
once we realize that darkness rings the campfire.
—Carolyn Hart, *Laughed 'Til He Died*

I am old enough to know that time passing is just a trick, a convenience.
Everything is always there, still unfolding, still happening.
—Sebastian Barry, *The Secret Scripture*

The web of our life is of a mingled yarn, good and ill together.
—William Shakespeare, *All's Well That Ends Well*

CHAPTER ONE

My name is Elise. This is my story. I should point out that my time left is limited, as death is knocking gently at my door. My advantage is that I know approximately when it might happen, and how many more summers I have left. I'm told it's likely just one.

This fact is of no great concern to me. Here in the nursing home, some put up a tenacious fight against the inevitable, but I have no need for that particular battle. At my age, death is a daily expectation, so I'm not afraid. All I need is a little more time to shape my life into something complete.

Having had opportunities to reflect, I'd like to lay claim to having lived a good life, or an interesting life, the kinds of things people say at a funeral about the deceased. Many moments in my past were undoubtedly good or intriguing; many others were delightful, some extremely painful, and I've experienced a range of universal emotions in between those two extremes. Mine is not unusual a reckoning in that respect, so perhaps that makes it simply an *ordinary* life. It will end neither well nor badly, fortunate nor unfortunate. I avoid using that circular proposition *It is what it is*. A word I prefer is *haluna*, which means, I'm told, *be at ease*. Two of the Filipino staff here whisper it to me every day, in gentle tones, with kind-hearted smiles. I *am* at ease.

So, with the future short, what I have left is my past. My time now is devoted to gathering together the scattered shards of my life, hoping to recognise and make sense of what they mean. Long ago, I lost the sweet gift of childhood innocence and have since fallen so far and too often from grace. I need to know if it's possible to overcome the tyranny of my own failings, to forgive others theirs, and locate those last, misplaced pieces of me.

It seems at times too hard a task, as my health and memory are increasingly unreliable. Some things I remember might not even be real, though they feel so. Recollections are often feather-like—fleeting, fluttering, warm, though disappearing quickly. A few are like rocks—bold, solid, and smooth—or else wedges of granite lodged in my stomach. But retrieving such events, sifting through my journals, musings and remembrances, and re-organising the past, is something I persevere with nevertheless. There's satisfaction to be found in locking together pieces of a life, in matching the shapes and colours, just so.

Fragments told by fragments of me.

CHAPTER TWO

I'll start near the beginning, since these are the parts I remember most clearly. The early days first—days of love and innocence. A time before the change.

I was born in 1938 in Bakersfield, Victoria. My earliest memory is of my grandmother's house, which overlooked a wide estuary and the sea. In the living room were two worn, green, velvet armchairs, and an imposing dark leather couch that retained the indentations of generations of both plump and bony buttocks. Large bay windows drew light in and turned gazes out. In summer, if I stood on tiptoes on one of the old armchairs, I could see the dots of ships on the horizon. Closer in were small fishing boats with nets trailing behind them, and up closer still, bright silver flashes of wing and fin breaking the water. At low tide, the bald, black sand shone with the slick of oil and stank of stagnant mud flats, rotting fish and tree roots.

Inside, a square card-table hunkered in a corner, but I was too young for card games, unless I was able to cajole someone to play a child's version with me. I remember willow-patterned crockery stacked in a glass-fronted armoire and a long, sturdy, oak dining table, the corner of which was dedicated to the piecing together of a jigsaw puzzle. The anteroom housed a clutter of antiques brought from Ireland, including an imposing mahogany sideboard cabinet, a writing desk, a grandfather clock, and an old Scots Pine rocking-horse, beautifully carved, which I was allowed to touch but not ride.

I remember too, the taste of hot, sweet porridge in a blue and white bowl, the warmth and tempting aromas of the vast kitchen, my grandmother's smile, the scent of the rose talcum powder that settled into her soft wrinkled skin, her generous, squashy bosom when she hugged me, the sound of a family's laughter and the hours I spent trying to solve the puzzle of the jigsaw.

• • •

Another memory. Happy or sad, sometimes it's easier to stand back and observe: I see the young Elise, my innocent self, walking with other little ones to view a rehearsal of the Easter Parade. We're accompanied by two nuns. Sister Mary Ignatius is a short, imposing woman of middle age, with arthritic fingers, an aquiline nose, and large, grey eyes often clouded with misgiving. From her belt hangs an extensive set of rosary beads that click as she walks, warning children of her impending approach. Sister Bernadette, by contrast, is young, tall and comely, with cornflower blue eyes, a timid chin, and lips that curl upwards. She wears rimless spectacles, through which she peers with optimism. But in the heat of this day her dark serge habit and starched white wimple make her uncharacteristically irritable while she's organising her charges into neat pairs.

'All right, children, stay in your twos. Straight lines please and no talking. Lift those feet! Who's that near the front who doesn't know what a straight line is? Follow me!'

We march cheerfully, untidily, over the small iron bridge that leads to Foster Park and pass the tall, brick watchtower, the purple-flowering tibouchina bushes, before turning into Westport Lane. We whisper. There's surreptitious shoving among those towards the back, until the older nun behind them blows a shrieking whistle.

Sister Bernadette stops the march and points. 'See those trees just there, children? Who can tell me what they are?'

I recognise them by their mild, minty scent.

'Gum trees,' a small chorus responds in unison.

4

'Yes, but you should say their proper name, Stringybark Eucalyptus, and the gum you see isn't gum, it's sap oozing through the bark. Those particular ones are…Freddy, pull your finger out of your nose right now.' She points again. 'And these trees, the ones here on the left? Anyone?'

Silence.

'Well, they're elms, and over there are oaks, and those ones in the distance, on the right, they're Canary Island pines…David Kowalski, stand to attention, right away! What's that you just put in your pocket?'

When we reach the endpoint, from which we're to view the parade, we stand in two lines, as directed, to form an arc along the side of the road. I secure a prime spot—centre-front of the large group. I bounce on the soles of too-tight shoes, peering in hope of being the first to catch sight of the floats. Children squint and squirm under a taut, scolding sky. A blanket of heat continues to build; wisps and sprays of white clouds dawdle from east to west. There's no breeze. I turn my face to a fierce sun, close my eyes and hum, while my companion, Susan, scratches at an elbow scab and whines.

Other pupils appear on the opposite side of the road. The temperature climbs. Fifteen minutes pass. Children stamp their feet into the dirt, boys kick dust at each other and teachers snap orders with ever-diminishing effect. Armies of persistent flies infiltrate school lines, but the swatting action of little hands hardly deters assault. Hot and sticky in my maroon school blazer and hat, I shift my weight from one skinny leg to another, and look longingly at the shade that beckons from beneath a nearby oak tree.

Then, from a distance, the tinny strains of Irving Berlin's 'Easter Parade' filter through the air.

Susan shrieks and grabs my hand, pulling me off the kerb. 'Look—here it comes,' she exclaims as the first float trundles into view.

> *In your Easter bonnet, with all the frills upon it,*
> *you'll be the grandest lady in the Easter Parade.*

A battalion of children surges forward. Sister Mary Ignatius appears to have a mutiny on her hands, though her censorious voice and the threat of her classroom cane soon restore some order. More floats appear, to clamorous clapping and cheers. It's a delicious blur of yellow and red balloons, blue crepe-paper streamers and tall white rabbit figures waving to the crowd.

Alison McVeigh asks which one is the bunny that comes on Easter Sunday. A few of the older kids nudge each other and laugh. Maurice Hartnell tells Alison that the Easter Bunny isn't real and, seeing the tears welling up in her eyes, adds for good measure that Santa is just someone's father dressed up in a red suit.

> *I'll be all in clover and when they look you over,*
> *I'll be the proudest fellow in the Easter Parade.*

The fourth float boasts a seven-foot-high plaster rabbit encircled by multi-coloured plastic eggs and surrounded by loops of white voile scavenged from Mrs Murray's discarded curtain material. Ten-year-old Barry Wilson sits on one side of the float to hurl at spectators small chocolate eggs that have melted into their tinselled casing. His actions result in more cheers and scuffles, dust, knees and elbows flying; treasures caught are speedily secreted inside pockets.

'This is not an occasion for greedy children to be thinking of themselves,' shouts Sister Mary Ignatius. 'You must reflect on Jesus and his sacrifice, on the true meaning of Easter. Wait with straight backs for the Resurrection Float. Christopher O'Malley, take that stupid look off your face and stand up straight.' Her cane whistles through its trajectory, orchestrated to stop three inches from the boy's nose.

> *On the avenue, Fifth Avenue, the photographers will snap us,*
> *And you'll find that you're in the rotogravure.*

Sister Bernadette's voice penetrates the animated crowd. 'Now children, you should wave to the people on those floats. Come on, all wave together. Jimmy Fuller, get away from the road at once! Jesus is *very* disappointed in you.'

I am enchanted by the next float—a gold and silver-coloured extravaganza, with Mariana Cirillo (whose dad manages the swimming pool) perched atop a spray-painted throne that's been constructed, somewhat haphazardly, from chipboard. Susan points to a sign which reads 'Bakersfield's Most Popular Gril', and there's some discussion about what 'Gril' might mean. Eric Moore suggests a fish. I think that blonde Mariana, with her blue dress and perfect white teeth, trumps the droopy-eared rabbits and the plastic eggs, hands down.

Oh, I could write a sonnet about your Easter bonnet,
And of the girl I'm taking to the Easter Parade.

Last comes the Resurrection Float with Mr Hennessy, who's dressed to represent a luminous risen Christ, but he's almost fifty and still unsteady on his feet after a knee operation and has to lean against the grey paper-mâché rock for balance.

Lena Wilenski, two years ahead of me, asks Sister Bernadette, 'Why didn't they get a younger person to be Jesus? That man's old.'

'Lena, you know perfectly well. It's because of the war, with so many men away.'

'Like my dad.' Her little face loops between pride and fear.

'Yes, like your father. Turn around now child, and wave to Jesus.'

Next is the deep rumble of drums. A bright red Chinese banner hurtles around the corner. Sister Bernadette glances at Sister Mary Ignatius, whose displeasure has etched another aggrieved line on her forehead.

Says the latter, 'But they've already had their New Year, their festival. The Council didn't tell me about this.' She turns away, her straight back giving off chill in the heat, and snaps out a *tsk* with, 'It's just not appropriate on such a solemn occasion.'

Sister Bernadette offers the retreating figure a raised eyebrow and a thin smile.

The next eight minutes are a haze of colour and noise; elaborately embroidered costumes, swirling banners, lion's heads with snapping mouths, petite girls performing a synchronised and intricate ribbon dance; the loud, tribal beating of drums and the red, green and gold of the snaking Dragon Loong, its mouth spurting great gusts of smoke.

The smallest ones are transfixed, some squealing with delight, others shrieking in fear, or gravely silent. I feel like a lynx, my tufty pigtails alert, preparing for the pounce. I laugh.

Sister Bernadette shouts above the music. 'See that, children? That's one of the oldest imperial dragon costumes in the world. The Chinese sent it over especially, so their people here can celebrate their New Year. The colours are beautiful, aren't they? Green is for harvest time, gold and silver are for wealth, and red, well, that's an important colour in China, it means luck and….'

She interrupts her lesson to yank Jimmy by the arm and push him back into line with a light clip across his head and a forceful tongue click. He grins, gap-toothed, at his younger brother, Willy, and peers around, ready to dart into the path of any oncoming adventure.

'But Sister, New Year's over, and anyway, my mum says that all Chinese people are heathens.' A wisp of mischief plays like dappled sunlight on Lena's face.

Momentary hush. 'Well, the…yes, they're heathens Lena, but they're also part of our community. They've been here for a long time, and we must be welcoming. Their ancestors did a lot for this town. You remember the lessons we had about the Gold Rush? Anyway, their new year is a different date from ours, and today it's just an opportunity for them to enjoy being with us all.' She stops and turns. 'Now Jimmy, if I have to tell you again, you'll be going straight home and I'll be calling your grandfather in. And you don't want that, I can assure you.'

'Elise, hey!' Susan shouts above the drumbeat, stabbing at the air with stubby fingers and pointing to the passing explosions of colour. 'Look! How come the dragons are wearing people shoes? See them?'

I can't answer, but I'll ask my dad.

As soon as the last flash of twirling dragon, the smoke and the final drum-pulse have passed by, we children are marched back along the street, in pairs, hand-in-hand. Limp remnants of the blue and white crepe streamers idle past us on a sudden desultory gust of warm autumn wind, only to be tramped into the ground by their tired, dragging feet. On the return trip, I'm paired with Caroline McHenry, a skinny brown-haired girl whose nostrils always house yellow crusts and whose knees are permanently imprinted with dirt. I try to loosen Caroline's grip as we shuffle along but give in to the anxious pressure from her hand; her fingers clutch and cling like tiny talons. In a moment of compassion, I offer Caroline an encouraging smile, but for the most part, I'm still lost in the realm of Dragon Loong.

• • •

I see myself a few weeks later, standing, distracted, at the base of the Anzac Memorial in the park by the main town square. I am holding my father's hand as he scans the names of the young men from around Bakersfield who served in the Great War. My father won't take part in the march on Anzac Day this year or any other year. He's brought me to watch from the sidelines, where we'll see a few old diggers who survived the horrors of that Great War, alongside those who've returned, intact or not, from the current one. Behind those will be fresh, eager recruits marching proudly into an uncertain future.

It's windy and warm. My feet hurt. I scratch idly at a scab on my knee and think back to the Easter Parade.

• • •

'Would you like a cuppa now, Mrs Harrington? You've had another big afternoon, what with those visitors and all the work you're doing with your books and such. What about a biscuit?'

I tell him, 'Thank you, dear, but I need to stretch my legs', so he moves the walker closer and helps me to stand. He pats my arm as I take a few stiff steps towards the corridor. He knows I'll be fine once I get moving.

'I'll leave your tea here then, shall I? When you come back, we can read something together if you'd like.'

Such a kind man. They are all, with one or two exceptions, exceedingly pleasant.

CHAPTER
THREE

Early mornings I'd wake to the clip-clop of the milkman's horse, the scratch and bump and creak of his cart on the uneven surface of our road. I'd run outside, barefoot in my pyjamas, to wave at Mr Mattaboni, a tanned and bespectacled man who delivered our perspiring bottles of creamy milk. He'd always tip his hat at me and smile. Dad said Mr Mattaboni's eldest son had died in Italy two years before, and that was a sad thing, and some people weren't nice to him, so we must always be kind.

My father would carry me over to the patient Clydesdale and I'd hold my palm out flat, as instructed, balancing on it a piece of apple or carrot retrieved from Dad's pocket, while the horse sniffed tentatively, testing my gift. I remember the damp and gentle exploration of the animal's wide lips over my upturned hand, the breathy snort from his nostrils when he took the treat, the tickle of his coarse hair as I patted his nose. I noted the stink of fresh manure and the earthy, friendly, sweaty aroma emanating from the horse's flanks. I'd wave to Mr Mattaboni as he made a whistle-click sound and gently flicked the reins to move the animal along.

Mr Collins, the iceman, came every fourth day in summer and once a week in winter. I'd watch from the front porch while he hefted a fifty-pound block of ice wrapped in hessian from his truck onto his damp shoulder, then I'd follow him and the water drips around to the back of the house, where my mother held the door of the ice-chest open and paid him his due coins. He was full of good cheer, always trying to coax a laugh from Mum and me with a joke or a phrase from a song. Mum would nod politely. I'd giggle.

'Dan Dan the Dunny Man' was a weekly visitor whose job it was to go house-to-house with his horse and cart and exchange full cans from the backyard dunnies for his empty ones. By the time he'd done his rounds, the collection on the cart might be slopping over onto the road, and the stench, well, even I—who loved most smells—couldn't handle that. But Dan, or 'Mr Poo', or whatever other name we kids invented for him, always whistled and greeted people as if he was bringing them flowers.

Mum told us with an embarrassed laugh that on one occasion, 'Dan' had opened the back flap of Mrs Wilson's outdoor privy to replace the can, without at first knowing she was perched on the wooden toilet seat above it. He just addressed her bare bottom with a cheery "ello, Mrs Wilson! Nice day, in'it!'

Our own outdoor dunny was a source of fear for me, sure as I was that snakes or redbacks were waiting to attack if I had to go there at night.

Another memory I have is of Dr Flynn, a tall, solid man, with a full head of silver-white hair, a darker, clipped moustache, and a reassuring smile. He made house calls from time to time, particularly if Marion had the croup and if Mum's onion and sugar syrup and the steam bath didn't work. Dad would say that Marion's barking, wheezing and coughing was enough to wake the saints, but Dr Flynn always put my sister right again. He'd peer into Marion's mouth and ears, listen to her chest with a stethoscope rubbed warm in his palm, remind Mum to put Vicks VapoRub on Marion's torso with a strip of sheet binding, and he'd leave a bottle of tonic, to help Marion sleep and to fix Mum's nerves.

'Call me, Mrs Brown, if you need me again. You can settle the bill next time.' But he said that every time. He would pat my mother lightly on the shoulder as he passed by her with his black leather doctor's bag before opening the front door. A last look back at Mum, at me, a flash of concern, then he would nod and close the door behind himself.

We kept chickens back then, sometimes ducks, and I saw them as pets and knew them by name. Dad occasionally beheaded one and it would appear stuffed and trussed on the dinner table. I'd lose my appetite.

'Don't be ridiculous Elise! Joseph, tell her to eat. She listens to you. Jeffrey—mind your manners. Hold your fork properly. Stop teasing your sister."

Home was safe, but school was my joy—the sense of belonging, the ordered structure of the day, the joy of learning new things. I liked some of the teachers and all of the noise—the rhythm and clatter of school bells, the beat of the marching drum, and the screams of children at play during recess or lunch. I enjoyed the simplicity of games of marbles, or Jacks, played with polished knucklebones from discarded lamb shanks, hopscotch and skipping, as well as the rough and tumble of chases, the invented entertainments that leapt the boundaries of the schoolyard and took us to exotic places.

Celeste Harris told tales of France because her grandmother had lived there, so we devised contests of endurance set against the backdrop of the Eiffel Tower.

Damian Balcescu boasted about once being lost in an enchanted forest in Romania and rescued by Robin Hood and his merry men, and though we all knew Damian was born in Tasmania, we were happy to act out the scenes with him. Damian, of course, chose to be Robin and Cathy Curtis always played Maid Marion. I longed to be Robin, but at best I was sometimes allowed to be one of the merry men. At worst, I was assigned the role of a tree, providing camouflage for an archer ready to attack infiltrators with a stick bow and arrow.

Terry O'Farrell took the role of Friar Tuck, though he insisted we address him as 'Try-a-Fuck.' We obliged, without knowing what it meant, until Father O'Halloran heard young Peter Simpson yelling it one time and gave him a clip around the ear followed by a swift boot to the backside.

Much of the play reflected what we understood of the real world, so we became adept at storming the monkey bars or the wooden carousel to gain control of enemy outposts and vanquish the Germans and Japanese. I was taught to be fearful of Stefan Hirsch in grade five—some suggested he was a German spy—but I also felt sorry for him. Other children whispered and pointed when he was in the playground where he sat, alone, eating strange-smelling foods from a tin canister while we dived into our brown paper bags to retrieve our staple peanut-butter-on-white-bread sandwiches.

• • •

Ah, how well I recall the scents, sounds and sensations from those days. I took pleasure in the textures of the wooden benches that lined the perimeter of the school courtyard; the faint pine odour of outdoors; the heat and grit of the dirt beneath my sandals in summer and the musty aroma of messy hair and grimy bodies straight in from play; the chalk dust in the classroom; the stained inkpot and scratchy nib pens, and even the patterns of the bird droppings at the bottom of the budgie's cage in the corner.

Sister Bernadette had sixty of us in the one room and we would all march dutifully to her drum. Her control was quiet but firm, methodical, encouraging, and I wanted to absorb everything she said. I was that thirsty for words. And for kindness. She *was* kind. Her reliability and her deep-set grey eyes were comforting.

'Grade twos, you should be on page twelve of your writing workbooks. Grade threes, you're doing the questions on page forty-five; Grade fours, finish up the decimal exercises from your maths textbook. All you children in the back row—out in the corridor and practise reading to each other. If everyone finishes by 10.30, you'll have an extra ten minutes at play time.'

I didn't like Sister Mary Ignatius, but she rarely came to our class. I hated being forced to read the illustrated books about the Christian martyrs, which contained depictions of the tortures and cruel deaths of various saints. We learned that the female saints had their 'virtue intact' when they died, and though we didn't understand the phrase, we knew not to ask. If intended to teach us about piety, faith and courage, these stories missed their mark, for me, at least. The only saint's tale I found palatable was that of Saint Francis of Assisi, who was kind-hearted to animals and always thanked his donkey for carrying him. Along with the gruesome accounts of martyrs were equally repellent but exciting fairy tales, myths and legends, all of which seemed to involve cruelty, abandonment, greed, wickedness, death. The world beyond my neighbourhood, as I saw it, was not a friendly place, and I had no desire to enter it.

Weekends and daylight hours not spent at school were used for playing outside with hoops or balls and makeshift bats, or trawling around the bush with the other kids in search of fresh adventures. The creek, which was forbidden to us, was a particular drawcard.

Nowadays, we'd be considered wild; I suppose we were, a little. We'd roam as a pack till dusk, run through the long dry grasses in vacant lots, thrilled to catch sight of any snakes as they slithered to safety under a woodpile or through tight spaces between rocks. Sometimes we'd spy them stretched out in the sun, oblivious to the thump of our feet or the raised voices that would normally alert them to our approach. Some of the slower snakes invariably suffered the torments of rough boys, who chased them with sticks, then poked and prodded until the reptile somehow found sanctuary. Unlucky ones—usually the smaller of the Red Bellied Blacks—might be caught, stomped on, stoned and strung up to die between the wooden slats of a boundary fence by the most daring and cruel of the boys. The rest of us studied frogs, lizards, crickets and grasshoppers, bees and flies; we imprisoned them in jars and fed them grass but they habitually died. We were hunters, tribesmen, warriors, conquerors. The world was vast and our thirst for discovery unquenchable.

There were occasional skirmishes, especially between the boys who would tussle and show off, though most of it was good-natured. We played like puppies, chasing, wrestling, growling, laughing. But as happens when children gather as a pack, we were sometimes cruel, taunting random strangers by pulling faces or whispering in their presence, or shouting litanies of scorn at any Protestant kids from the next street if they wandered into our territory. And although we laughed and mocked and chanted at anyone who was in any way different, most of us afterwards felt ashamed at having done so, judging by certain sideways glances and slight shifts in demeanour. But shame was short-lived and never enough to stop us from taunting someone else at another time.

My memory of most adults is limited. They represented a source for a drink, a biscuit, or a flavoured ice block during a break from play. Mrs Robinson made us 'spiders'—lemonade with a scoop of ice-cream in a tall glass, lapped up with the help of a spoon. There was no Mr Robinson around, but none of us knew why, nor did we care. She was generous, never irritable. But sometimes, from other adults, we could expect a sound verbal or physical reprimand (usually a brisk slap on the back of the legs) if we overstepped the mark.

I remember well the smells and sounds of the seasons: the salty, sweaty, fizzy, humid tang of summer; the crunch of the crisp, dry, crumbly leaves that lay over the sticky, vinegary remnants of fallen fruit in autumn; the damp, sweet rain, the smoke from chimneys and the strong mouldy-leaf aroma of winter; the heady grass and new-blossom fragrance of an optimistic spring. I also recall the intoxicating tobacco-and-smoke mix coming from Sid Sinclair and his clothes. Though he was only forty-something, he seemed ancient to us. He sometimes gave us a roll-your-own cigarette to share near his potting shed, even though he knew our parents would disapprove. As he continued with his gardening, he'd watch, chuckling, while we invariably coughed our guts up after the first drag.

And tastes: the delicious tangy assault that came with sucking up lime sherbet through a hollow liquorice straw; sweet and crunchy chocolate crackles scavenged from Eddie Thompson's mother's kitchen; cold, melting lemonade ice blocks that collected specks of sand at the beach; the rich gravy on a rare weekend roast.

'Meat-free Friday' meant we had fish and chips from the local chippy every week. After dinner, we'd kneel in a line facing the crucifix on the wall and take turns to say a decade of the rosary. Tuesdays and Fridays were for The Sorrowful Mysteries. Dad intoned his decade in a deep, musical lilt, Mum in distracted, hushed tones, Jeffrey mumbled sullenly. For my turn, I am sure I sounded prim and earnest while my mind was elsewhere. From a fidgety position stretched out on the floor, Marion contributed by mangling the Our Fathers or Hail Marys, stumbling through the words, punctuating them with farts and giggles, to the amusement of my father and ire of my mother.

On Sundays, we attended church. There was something appealing about the smoky, aromatic incense seeping from the thurible, the acrid burning of a hundred candles, the background fragrance of the multitude of flowers and the swish of opulence as the priest passed by in his heavy green and gold chasuble. Here, with the hypnotic flow of Latin prayers and soaring hymns,

I often disappeared into a kind of trance in which angels and saints played leading roles, some of them wearing my face.

I dream of all these senses now because, in truth, they've dwindled to almost nothing, just as my eyes have become paler and cloudier, creating a filter that makes my external world appear dim. I don't taste or enjoy food as I used to; my sense of smell is less acute. To compensate, if I'm not imagining different futures (limited though they are), I'm trying to remember those years when life was simply a saturation of the senses, lived in technicolour.

CHAPTER FOUR

Memories of the heart are an altogether different matter.

I have no anger towards my father anymore, though I carried it with me for far too long. He went off to war when I was just a toddler and returned a few years later—a shape in the doorway. He had a limp, alarming scars on his legs, and one arm permanently bent at the elbow. Then, after a few more years, he left again.

I'd hardly had time to really know him, but I adored him. At first, I was frightened by this strange man who'd shown up without fanfare one day, but he quickly won me over with his tricks with cards and pennies and his friendly, open face that was shaped a little like mine. He'd throw me up in the air (awkwardly, because of his gammy arm), sit me on his shoulders, and pretend to be a horse galloping around the yard, although his gait was more that of a camel—slow and lolloping. He tired easily. But any of his attentions made me squeal with delight.

My mother was less impressed.

'Get on about your business, Joe, and leave her be. She's to help me in the laundry and mind her sister. You've over-exciting the child.'

In Mum's presence, my father grunted responses and smoked heavily.

My brother Jeffrey was five years older than me. He was sullen, prone to attacks of asthma, moods, and slammed doors. He and Dad circled each other warily—Jeffrey's face full of resentment for the long absence, my father confronted with a pre-pubescent boy who'd grown tall and silent. Occasionally, they'd each drop their guard during a neighbourhood game of cricket on the unsealed road in front of our house. My father watched from the sidelines, kept score and gave a commentary. 'Come on boy! What a catch! Keep goin'!'

Jeffrey was chuffed by that.

But I knew I was Dad's favourite. My sister Marion, sweet and sunny as she was, didn't attract much of his interest. He'd not met her before he went off to war, since she was still in my mother's belly then, and when he returned, he seemed to regard her as something of a foundling, as if he'd forgotten his role in her conception. She was only two when they met. Loud noises made him edgy, and her sudden shrieks of exuberance or frustration would often prompt him to snap and bark.

'Does that child never stop? Quiet, yer hear me? For Chrissakes Lil, would yer shut her up? I can't bear the noise.' And he'd throw the newspaper down, struggle awkwardly to his feet and leave the room.

Then Mum would start, shouting to his retreating back: 'No need for language Joseph.' Then, 'Marion, stop that wailing, *now*! Jeffrey! Don't torment her. She's too young to understand. Elise, take your sister outside or read her a story or something. Just do it! Oh, get away, all of you!'

So Dad didn't warm to my sister, nor she to him. She sometimes hid her face when he approached, or clung tightly to my mother or to me. Dad's eye-roll made me giggle.

Time and again, he sat alone on the back veranda for long periods, smoking, maybe watching some distant element of his internalised battles replay in his head. At such times, it didn't pay for anyone to approach him but me, as I could charm him out of any dark reverie. I'd present my grubby-smocked self in front of his gaze, and when his eyes, the colour of melted chocolate, alighted on me, they'd lose their fixed stare and a smile would gather in the crinkled patchwork of his tanned skin. He'd swing me onto his lap, blow loud, snuffly noises into my neck as I wriggled and laughed, and tell me in the remnants of his Irish brogue that I was his *darlin'*. In such moments, I liked to hold his soft, leathery face in my hands and plant butterfly kisses on his nose and eyelids. I sometimes felt the weight of my mother's watchfulness glowering through the flyscreen door and would kiss his face the harder.

Dad entertained me with stories of heroes and villains, goblins and princesses, flying carpets and magic spells. When I learnt to read by myself, I'd grab a newspaper from his hands to demonstrate my expertise, and he'd laugh and tell me what a clever girl I was, his best girl, his one and only.

'You're just as smart as anyone else, better most likely Lisie! You go out there and get what you want out of life! No one's gonna give it to yer! Yer gotta grab it! And when yer do, come back and give some of it to me too, right?'

And he'd heave me up again on his lap and give me one of his awkward bear hugs that threatened to crush the air out of my lungs, though I cherished the love that came with it.

Regardless of his praise, I was learning elsewhere that blandness was considered a virtue, and to be anything other than ordinary was generally frowned upon, except when attached to sporting prowess. The nail that stuck out was hammered down. *Be humble. Be good. Be like everyone else. Don't get above yourself.* So I tried my best to blend in, to *be ordinary*, while allowing myself moments of confidence and certainty about my place in the universe whenever Dad looked at me, only at me, with a proud, delighted grin.

'How's my darlin' Lisie? What yer gonna be doing when yer grow up, eh?'

'I'm gonna be a pilot, Daddy, or a magician.'

'Atta' girl! Now, you'd better go in and help yer mum get tea or she'll be takin' the straw end of the broom to yer and the pointy end to me.'

We'd grin conspiratorially before I went inside to my mother, whose face wore a patina of tiredness and irritation. I craved her attention and would help with chores, stroke her hand, do anything to make her smile, just to see how it lit up her features. When that happened, her grey-green eyes softened. I loved basking in their sudden, tender warmth.

But being a child, caught up so much in excited play and reveries, I was unaware of the problems brewing at home. Dad's relationship with my mother became more strained: his demons kept him distant from her, her stilted politeness and disappointment made her a stranger to him. He took to staying for hours at the pub. Mum would regularly send a silent, fuming Jeffrey to collect him before Dad spent most of his pension on the grog. His absences were more palpable than his presence. After only a few years back home, not even my existence was enough to keep him there.

• • •

The week before he left, my father took us all to see a visiting circus. It was a rare treat, and rare that all five of us were out together.

'C'mon Lil, get yerself in the car. Right youse kids—pile in. We're off. Stop yer squabblin' in the back. If yer don't behave, we're not goin'.'

'Where? Where are we going?'

'I told yer, it's a surprise. Now shut up, all of yer, and let me drive.'

The battered old Plymouth Dad had *picked up for a song* managed about thirty miles an hour. Dad and Mum smoked in the front while we choked in the back, swaying and bumping against each other while our legs stuck to the hot, gummy faux-leather seats.

The circus remains a blur to me. All I remember are disjointed images, broken pieces of a different puzzle. We three kids running into the tent ahead of our parents; the ringmaster with booming voice and exaggerated moustache; chattering uniformed monkeys; elegant palomino horses; a small, woeful grey elephant; girls in sparkling leotards; clowns; trick cyclists; a high-wire trapeze act; jugglers; lions; and a bearded woman that Dad stated looked just like my mum's sister Helen. The crowd, the music, laughter, cheers, jeers, gasps, applause. And then screams and shouting when a lioness attacked the lion tamer, mauling his right thigh and knee.

Confusion

Animal roars

Blood

Long sticks

A bullwhip

Water jets

Crowbars

Chaos

I hid my eyes, blocked my ears, and cried. Mum shielded Marion with her body as they stumbled out. Dad pulled me towards the exit. When I turned back, Jeffrey was standing, pale, transfixed. The ride home is a lost memory.

Shortly after that, Dad left, and I cried. I howled and screamed and stamped my feet. At first, I blamed the circus, then decided I must blame my mother for his disappearance. I added to her misery with my sullen sulking. I refused to go to school, refused to do chores, refused to be kind, until I couldn't bear to see or feel the vibrations of loss emanating from her, or smell the defeat that floated on dust motes stirred by her slower movements throughout the house. Eventually—weeks, perhaps longer—I forgave my mother for my loss and hoped she forgave me for hers. I wrapped my arms around her aproned waist, pushed my face into her stomach and whispered 'I'm sorry,' and cherished the touch of her hand stroking my hair.

• • •

'Mrs Harrington. Mrs H! Elise? Are you awake? You looked like you were nodding off. Time for your medication. You'd be tired after your visitors today. Here, let me get you comfortable. Would you have that cup of tea? I'll help you sit up—here's a cushion for your back. There, that's the way!'

'Thanks dear. Yes, I did nod off for a bit.'

He's a nice carer, that one. From Sri Lanka, I believe. Beautiful smile, always laughing, in fact, and he has such thick, boisterous, happy hair. Can hair be happy?

CHAPTER FIVE

When Dad left us for the final time, it was clear he was gone for good; clear in the way my mother cried, brooded, snapped; clear from the peculiar flat emptiness left behind on his side of their double bed. The meals were smaller, the house colder and more morose. Cobwebs floated from ceilings. Mum scoured the newspapers for work. We saw through her translucent skin the emptiness of the shell she now inhabited.

But I paid scant attention to my mother's suffering. All that mattered to me was that home was no longer a place of pleasure and sanctuary. My despair revolved around the inexplicable loss of someone who'd adored me and treated me like a princess. Then there were the new embarrassments to be borne. Even though I'd always worn handmade or hand-me-down clothes for play, and second-hand uniforms for school, I'd never thought anything of it until Dad's absence, when this example of relative paucity became a new indignity. It was enough that some people pointedly whispered about our sudden abandonment, but I became fearful of the taunts that would ensue if a neighbour's child recognised her own discarded clothing on me.

Jeffrey was thirteen and whatever private misery he was going through he kept to himself, unless to express his anger and frustration by thumping me when I walked past. He specialised in 'burns'—grasping my arm and twisting his hands firmly in different directions, so that my skin pulled taut and stung. I'd shout or cry but my mother was always busy and out of earshot. If I took a swipe at him, we'd tussle, fight, kick like wild things. On the rare occasions I landed a solid punch, it did nothing to stop him. Since I was so much smaller, he'd always win through size, strength and will, but his chief weapon was spite.

He treated our mother with contempt. If she asked him to help with a task, he'd swear at her, slam doors, barricade himself in his room (a sleepout built onto the back veranda). Other times, he feigned deafness or simply refused. I detested him. The feeling was mutual.

Our sister Marion he ignored completely. She was the only member of the household who maintained a sunny disposition. She never asked when Daddy was coming home; she seemed to have anticipated his departure, was even pleased by it, since it meant she could make as much noise as she wanted to, without reprimand. The bright part of a day for me was listening to her immersion in simple songs, games and nursery rhymes. She'd chant and sing, clap her hands, jump or dance through a room, pull faces and break wind to make me laugh. Her magic failed to amuse anyone else.

So while Marion danced, Jeffrey brooded and I read, our mother searched for work, leaving each morning in her good dress and polished shoes. She found several part-time positions—long hours scrubbing other people's homes, ironing, and, in the evenings, cleaning the local presbytery. We were often hungry. Mum's parents in Mildura occasionally sent money, which Mum gratefully accepted, though with embarrassment. Sometimes they and Mum's sister Helen would arrive to look us over. Variations of 'I told you marrying that man would be the biggest mistake of your life, Lillian!' ricocheted around our living room and I wanted to stamp and shout and protect his memory and protect my mother too from their verbal assaults. But I only sulked in a corner, and poked out my tongue as they left.

Another mortification for Mum was to go begging for the guarded benevolence of the parish so we could stay on at our schools. But where once I had adored learning, now I'd joined some outer circle, one encased by stares and whispers. Days grew longer, lonelier. I didn't run with my old pack of friends after school—too many chores—and I minded Marion while Mum worked.

Jeffrey got a part-time job at the local bakery, became taller and crueller. Time passed, measured in my mind as grains of apprehension scattered upon a table. The monotony of depleted days. I didn't know then that things would get worse.

• • •

Books, musings and Mrs Robinson next door, offered sweeter consolations. In rare idle moments, especially if Mum was having a cranky turn, I'd visit her. She always seemed happy to see me. From the outside, her small, olive-green weatherboard house matched ours in drabness but inside, hers was a treasury of colour and light, bright furnishings and art works, fresh flowers from her abundant garden, knick-knacks and curios she allowed me to hold while she explained their histories. And books. Oh, she had so many! Often, there'd be a partially completed jigsaw puzzle on her mahogany dining table, and she'd invite me to help her place pieces while her ginger cat wound around our legs and purred.

Annie Robinson was a generous woman, gentle and softly spoken. She had a round face, short, straight, dark hair and mischievous eyes that changed shades of blue with the light. Though tall, she'd squat, stoop or kneel next to me to assist in any activity we undertook. She lived alone. Perhaps she was in her fifties back then.

'What'll we do today, Elise? Shall we try some more knitting? Or baking? Or what about we play chess?'

She'd taught me to play. I loved everything about her. I would shrug and grin as she continued.

'Oh, I need some help in the garden, if you're in the mood for getting your hands dirty?'

Whatever she suggested was enjoyable. She was the only adult who spoke to me as if we were on an equal footing, and she kept up a steady flow of conversation. She never got cross or flustered and—as far as I could tell—never played around with the truth. This particular day, we were on our knees on old towels, pulling out weeds and tending her vegetable patch with trowels and gardening forks.

'Just throw any snails in the bucket please Elise. They've been attacking my lettuces and taking bites from the marigolds. Perhaps we should cook the critters and eat them like they do in France! What do you think?' She grinned, making a show of licking her lips, and laughed as I grimaced.

We continued digging for some minutes, intent and quiet, before I took a hopeful breath. 'Can I ask you something, Mrs Robinson?'

'Of course, dear. Here, what do you suppose we should do with this old piece of pipe?' She held aloft a short, perished length of rubber hose, clicked her tongue and threw it over her right shoulder. 'That's for good luck. Now, what's on your mind, little one?'

I drew a breath again, for courage, and stared at my trowel, stabbing it at a patch of compacted soil. A throwaway query first. 'What happened to Mr Robinson?'

She was quiet for several moments. Her voice, when she eventually spoke, was matter-of-fact, though it contained a sigh.

'Well, he died after the first war, from a lung disease—it was caused by the mustard gas.' She expertly secured a toppling tomato plant with string, as she continued, 'Have you heard of that?'

'No.'

'It makes people very sick. It affected my Harry's sight, but the worst was his lungs. It's terrible to see someone in that kind of pain.' Her throat sounded husky.

I felt bad for having asked, but she went on. 'War's a dreadful thing, Elise. It really is. After they sent him home, I had him for only five weeks before he died. He used to have nightmares; night terrors they called them. He suffered terribly, but never complained.'

She used her fork to loosen more weeds, then paused and looked over at me. 'He was a good man, Elise. A brave man. We'd planned a whole future together, and then he was gone.' She shifted her position for a moment, as if sore, sniffed once, and continued with her gardening, her lean body working in a rhythm borne of habit.

We knelt close, almost touching, she planting seeds and me digging up more weeds, working in a companionable peace. I smelled the whiff of freshly turned composted earth. Tiny ants scattered. And I blurted out the words I'd rehearsed. 'Can you tell me about my father? And why he went away?'

Annie Robinson shifted back a little, looked straight at me, and cleared her throat once, twice, then said in her gentle voice, 'I don't know the answer, Elise.' She looked away, pressed more seeds into the soil.

I dug carefully, to avoid splicing a worm.

But she continued, speaking while we worked, her eyes focused on her hands working the soil. 'Wars can break people, Elise, no matter which side they're fighting on. We rarely talk about such things, men especially. My Harry didn't. Between the wars, there was real poverty, unemployment. A lot of those men, like my brother Bill, couldn't fit back into normal life, couldn't find work. Harry, Bill, and maybe your dad too, being injured and all, well, that would've been so hard, wouldn't it. And in time, people seemed to forget what those men had been through. All the fighting, the sacrifices, it all seemed for nothing. That's what I think happened, anyhow. No-one wins in a war. No-one.' She looked at me, her face open but tight somehow. 'They should teach you that at school Elise. It's important to know.'

A loud, sudden screech of a pink and grey galah made us peer up into the tall Casuarina tree. We saw the bird's wings flapping aggressively, beak wide open, as a yellow-eyed currawong watched from another branch.

Mrs Robinson coughed, stood, slapped the dirt from her gloves, brushed away a spider on her overalls, then stretched her whole body. I could hear the gentle click and pop of bones rearranged. We both drank from the flask of water she'd provided. When she knelt down again, relaxed on her haunches, she scratched idly at the soil with a fork before speaking.

'My brother Bill, he took up gambling after he got back. There's a lot of different ways people react to their troubles. I rarely see Bill now, and that upsets me.' She flicked an ant from her wrist. 'I know it's been hard for you and your family, Elise, and I'm sorry. But I can't really answer your question about your father. He'd have had his reasons I expect. Your mum…if there's anything at all I can help with, please tell her I'm just here.'

She removed one glove, wiped away a spot of dirt from my chin, looked at me sympathetically and sighed. A flock of black cockatoos appeared to the east, squawking their harsh tones in unison and flashing red tails. We watched their raucous passage.

'Will you look at that, Elise. What a spectacle! Aren't we privileged to see that. And that silly galah's sitting there in this darned tree! Did you know that Aboriginal Australians used the wood of the Casuarina to make clubs and boomerangs? Well, it's still used that way in some communities, I'm told. It's a very hard, dense wood. And it's playing havoc with my plumbing.'

Ten minutes later I was eating ice-cream in her spotless green and white kitchen, gazing at a vase of cherry-red dahlias.

• • •

Back home that afternoon, I summoned the courage to quiz my mother while she was ironing and I was curled into a corner of the settee on the far side of the room. We were alone. Jeffrey was outside trying to teach Marion how to ride a bike. We could hear his impatience and Marion's frustration.

'What a question Elise. How should I know? He left, that's all. Go and do your homework or help your sister, or something, anything.'

I persisted. 'Mrs Robinson talks to me. Mr Sinclair does too. They tell me about the war and lots of other things. They answer anything I ask about. Why won't you?' I stared at the worn carpet.

She snatched a pillowcase from the laundry basket and attacked it with the iron. 'Well, they shouldn't. It's all in the past. Why don't you spend time with people your own age, Elise? Like a normal child. Always scratching away at things that aren't good for you. Go on out and play or tidy the kitchen. Be useful. You can shell those peas before I start cooking. You're always so…oh! Just scoot!' The iron's prolonged hiss over the damp pressing cloth was my curt dismissal. I left the room.

I was used to filling in the narrow gaps between school, chores, homework, dinner and bedtime, so I mooched around for a while near the sleepout at the back, then coaxed Marion into the vacant lot across the road to meet Cathy Curtis and her little brother, Billy. We played hopscotch while Marion and Billy chased each other around the trunk of a black she-oak till we helped them to build a cubby house from branches. It was getting dark before I grabbed Marion and we ran inside. Mum sighed and rolled her eyes when she saw us both covered in dirt. I hurried to set the table.

'Clean yourselves up first, for goodness sakes. Look at your uniforms. I'll have to wash them again tonight. They'd better be dry by morning. Honestly Elise, I don't know what to do with you.'

Later that night, after dinner, Mum came into my room and sat, tentatively, on the side of my bed. Surprised, and afraid of what was to come, I dropped my book. Mum retrieved it, sat up too straight, hands tight in her lap, and caught my eyes in a brief, intimate glance before turning her face away. I swallowed. Marion turned over in her bed with a light, bubbly snore.

Mum must have caught the anxiety on my face. So as not to wake Marion, she said quietly, 'Elise, I'm sorry I snap at you. You just, well, you try my patience, and you say such strange things, and…I don't know, I suppose I should, but it's not easy to talk to you, when you ask so many questions, especially about your father.'

I waited.

She shifted on her perch on the bed, stared at her restless hands.

'All I can tell you is he was very different when he came back from the fighting, and he had, well, a lot of problems. He was…,' she took a deep breath, 'troubled. Unhappy.'

'With us? With Jeffrey? Me?'

'Not with any of you. Not even with me. It was a lot of other things.' She gave a brief nod towards Marion's form under her blanket. 'Come to the kitchen and we'll talk there.'

Barefoot and in cotton pyjamas two sizes too small for me, I followed her out. She made me a hot milk and busied herself with folding the tea towels and wiping down surfaces, over and over. While thus occupied, she spoke more easily about Dad, the war, and how he hadn't enlisted initially.

'He'd wanted to but was refused because of flat feet and being a railway worker—that was an essential service. But later, when everyone else was scrambling to do the right thing, he tried again, joined up and he was off fighting before he'd even been properly trained. He was in Malaya, then New Guinea, and he saw terrible, terrible things, Elise.'

Her voice wavered. She leaned back against the counter, arms folded, looked up to the ceiling with its dim light, and to the dark window above the sink. The kitchen was still, faintly purring with the quiet tick of the clock and hum of the fridge. She continued, looking down as she twisted a tiny loose thread from the sleeve of her blouse, her voice now matter-of-fact. 'He was sent home early because of all the injuries; there'd been shrapnel, explosions too, that all happened, and his leg…well it all damaged him, inside and out, you can't imagine, Elise. There was no work for men like him. The railways wouldn't take him on again, and he just took to the drink.' She looked up, straight at me. 'Because of what he'd seen, all the terrors of war, and because, well, because we couldn't seem to get along any more. It wasn't your fault. It was no-one's fault.'

She took my cup and rinsed it, turned back again to gauge my level of attention. Perhaps because I was quiet, and looking at her with appreciation, wide-eyed and expectant, she sat down opposite me and touched my hand across the small table for a fraction of a moment. She told me about Dad's father, my grandfather, a man I didn't know, an imposing giant of a man in photos, now long deceased. All I'd previously known was that he'd come from Ireland with his wife and six children.

'Oh I've no idea what year that was, but they had an awful time of settling in. People here were so set against the 'bog Irish'. That's what they called them in those days, didn't matter where in Ireland they'd lived or what they'd done. Anyway, things got better when your grandfather—Thomas, his name was—he set up a trading business. When they had more money, they bought that lovely house near Wonthaggi, you know the one.'

I nodded.

'Anyhow, after your father enlisted, Thomas disowned him. Never spoke to him again for fighting for the British, so that was hard. And your dad lost contact with his brothers and sisters. They'd all left home; some went back to Ireland. But that's by the by. Your father was a very sad and troubled man, and that's why he left.'

'Grandpa sounds mean.'

'Yes, he could be that; he was a hard man in so many ways. But you love your Grandma Kath, don't you.'

She stood, stroked my hair once in a distracted way, then kissed my forehead with more air than mouth. 'Now, get back to bed and remember your chores for tomorrow.'

Her kiss was a rare delight. And her telling me those things was special, but I didn't believe her when she said it wasn't my fault that Dad left.

I also learnt details of various men who went to war and never returned from Jeffrey, who enjoyed the shock value of graphic descriptions. Frances Pooley's dad bled to death in Greece when a grenade blew his legs off, and Stuart McKenzie's older brother, who'd parachuted from a burning plane, was stuck hanging in a tree and died of burns and starvation. Jeffrey was full of such stories, delighting in the blood and guts and drama they contained, and I don't know if they were all true. But back then, I'd still have preferred a dead father to one who'd run away.

• • •

I've had plenty of time to write, to gather these bits of my story, as we're in some sort of lockdown. All the staff are wearing masks, but thankfully, they're not insisting we do too. My granddaughter, Sophie, rang me yesterday to tell me not to worry, and she'd come in when she could, when she's allowed, to help me with my memoir. She calls it a memoir, but I'm not sure if it's not just the ramblings of an old lady with nothing better to do with her time.

CHAPTER SIX

After two years, our mother sold our home and we moved the eighty miles to Melbourne, where there was work in a jam factory that paid more than she'd been earning before. Our new place was smaller but more expensive than the one we'd had in the country. Mum gave or threw away much of what still linked us to my father, except for a few essential items of furniture and his favourite chair. She worked nights cleaning offices and took in ironing to supplement the factory job.

My memories of her during that time are of a woman distracted, crushed, quick to anger. Her stress and fading hopes infected us all. Jeffrey continued to behave badly, was obdurate and sullen. I withdrew into my world of dreams and books. Marion spent more time in the homes of others, presumably delighting a more appreciative audience. My mother's shoulders were habitually stooped, and her hands red from immersion in powerful cleaning agents. She smelt of burnt sugar and strawberries, and her pretty face carried a permanent frown. Sometimes I'd hear muffled crying from her room late at night.

Then she met Craig. He must have seen some of the beauty that was still there behind her strained image, or else he was quick to calculate another advantage. He moved in with us, and I noticed that my mother stood a little taller, spoke more confidently, and once again began to wear lipstick. He was, by some people's estimation, quite good looking, had sufficient charm and charisma to have attracted my mother, who was no fool, and he maintained a large network of friends and acquaintances. He was always quick with a smile and a joke. Smart too, people said—Works Manager of something or other, and hard worker, blah blah. You can learn a lot by eavesdropping. Things were better, for a while.

But the initial promise of a more comfortable life with him was short-lived. Problems surfaced. First and importantly, he was not my father, just a very poor substitute. He was large and imposing, with a dyspeptic disposition. A permanent knotty frown slid down the sides of his face, and he had thin lips through which he issued loud, insistent commands. I learnt, though, that it was his softer, quieter voice that carried the malevolence.

Whatever bargain had been negotiated between them, my mother remained the poorer for the deal. She worked just as hard and as long, resumed her scrimping with money and meals, and had little time for us. The smiles we'd begun to entice from her vanished again.

Jeffrey and I were finally united through our intense dislike and fear of Craig, who was strict and petty. He'd take a strap to Jeffrey for any minor transgression, while our mother chewed on her knuckles and fretted in another room. I don't wish to give further form or face or substance to the person who caused me pain and humiliation. Suffice to say, he had bulk and strength and a dark, sinister cruelty. He smelt of sweat and malice.

My main comforts remained books—when I could find them—and my fantasy world, where I was able to pretend that life was not as it was. Another consolation was the occasional visit to my paternal grandmother, who would have us to stay during school holidays, perhaps from a sense of obligation. Those things are what I remember the best from then—the view of the sea, the reflection of light on the glass of the armoire, the willow-patterned plates, the taste of porridge smothered with brown sugar and cream, and the benevolence and affection given to us by an old woman whose son, my father, had deserted us all.

• • •

Only my mother knew that I regularly wet the bed into my teens, and even then, she didn't know the half of it. She complained about the extra washing but never thought to investigate why the bed-wetting continued for so long. The 'special medicine' Craig gave Marion and me some nights—'to help you sleep right, but your mother needn't hear about it'—meant that I didn't always wake in time to stop my bladder. So I'd have been a smelly child, as we didn't bathe in the mornings before school, only at night, and then the bath water had to be shared. First Craig, then my mother, then Jeffrey, who'd thrash about creating a turgid pond of grey scum. After him, Marion and I bathed together. I hated sitting in their dirty water, so I stayed in the bath for as short a time as possible, barely enough to let the soap slip from one hand to another. Marion was oblivious and would sit longer, half-submerged, humming to herself and playing with a cracked yellow duck that wouldn't float.

From the outside, we probably appeared to be a normal suburban family. We attended church on Sundays, and gave money when the collection plate travelled from hand to hand along the burnished oak pews. I could sense a certain amount of discreet, embarrassed shuffling from my mother as she dropped coins rather than a note onto the plate. Anxious by nature, she cooked and cleaned and fussed, baked apple tarts for the school fetes, became prematurely grey and developed accordion-like lines around her habitually pursed mouth. Craig worked six days a week—something to do with engines—and I was glad for that reprieve at least. He wasn't much for talking, or listening. We followed the rules, did our homework and only occasionally played with the local kids. And we never tried to run away, as Bessie Johnson from the house around the corner did, though we each had reason to.

While on the surface I was pliable, and submissive, *good*, on the inside I carried a cauldron of insecurities. I could not shake off the Catholic burden of Original Sin and its corollary, guilt. The *hellfire and brimstone* style of religion was popular then, but it didn't stop many people from doing bad things to each other. The strain of constantly trying to be a dutiful child led me to retreat too often into the *reel life* that played endlessly inside my head. It became a habit, then a crutch. Over time, it caused me to withdraw, to hide and entertain imaginary friends rather than make the effort to find real ones. I could be strong, as long as I could replay the reel and savour the brightly-coloured pixels that masked my fears. I found a way to escape a confusing reality, and watch a different, less frightening existence unfurl on my screen, replaying events until they looked right.

• • •

I don't care to remember those nights my mother worked late with her cleaning jobs. I found solace in three things. One was the abundance and allure of the remote, winking stars I could see through my bedroom window, where the faded cretonne curtains didn't quite meet. Another was the fantasy world in which I immersed myself and conjured up an illusory happiness. The third was the regular congregation of large huntsman spiders that worshipped at the base of the little wooden crucifix nailed to my bedroom wall. My sister snored lightly while I watched to see if a spider might move. But the darker, malignant pieces of this part of the jigsaw—they've been discarded.

CHAPTER
SEVEN

How fragile is one's innocence! Its loss carved out a void in my heart. In moments of discomfort, confusion or deep distress, I escaped, imagining myself flying above the trees, floating in the skies and among the stars. Or wreaking vengeance on perpetrators in ever-creative ways. Or I withdrew into a nothingness, a place where I couldn't feel anything. Even now, I relay stories about myself as if I were someone else looking on, telling a tale of a girl I used to know.

• • •

'Elise. Stop your dreaming. What's the answer? Question ten—there! Right in front of you!'

The circus lights instantly dimmed, the heady smell of animals and straw receded, and the lion's roar was absorbed by the classroom walls. I felt the potent swish of Sister Conselata's heavy black cotton habit touch my bare legs, saw the dark, clinched cincture with its hanging beads and chunky crucifix tucked securely away and the blunt end of the wooden ruler hovering over my desk. I met the teacher's dark glare by staring at the starched white wimple that cut straight across her pinched forehead. Sister Conselata had a broad, pale face and the beginnings of sagging jowls, and the penetrating gaze of a nun long into her vocation. She reminded me of a brooding hippo-potamus, its face just above the waterline. The nun raised the ruler slightly, then tapped it rhythmically, impatiently, onto her left palm.

I could hear John Miller's mucousy snuffle behind me. Someone was whispering several desks away to my left. The edgy tapping of the ruler continued. A chair squeaked nearby. I stared at the page in front of me, calculating mentally while my breath caught on numbers inhaled at the back of my throat.

'Twenty-five percent, Sister?' I offered.

'Well, that's all very well, dear, but not correct.' She turned her back on me to face the rest of the class. A pause. Snickering from the front row. 'Who can tell me? You. Rose,' she said, pointing to the side.

'One third, Sister.' Rose's voice was timid. She so rarely received approval from the nuns; perhaps it was her red hair that irked them.

'That's right Rose, good. And you, Elise, would do well to pay a lot more attention in class. Now everyone, start the next exercise.'

Rose's mouth settled into a shy but pleased line. My cheeks burned as I lowered my head, tugging at my heavy wheat-coloured fringe. *I'm made of steel. I don't cry. Nothing can hurt me. Worse things have happened. I'm not here.* I stared at my ink-stained fingertips, pressed my pen into a desk-top scored over the decades by thousands of other bored hands, took a breath and returned to the circus tent, where I had control.

Sister Conselata moved to the front to write on the chalkboard. Pupils scratched answers into their workbooks with chewed lead pencils or they dipped sharp, treacherous nibs into black inkwells. Some continued to squirm in their seats, furtively picking inside noses or ears, jiggling bare legs or whispering. A large fly, stuck between glass and the raised wooden sash of the window, protested with furious, intermittent buzzing. The heat in the classroom became a heavy canvas that confined pupils whose restless bodies strained to escape. Leaves on a large kurrajong tree outside slumped. Cicadas screeched. The rhythmic scrape of a saw cutting into thick branches, back, forth, back forth, cut through the classroom air.

The lights reappeared, the plumed horses pranced and the elephant's trum-peting grew louder as it lumbered towards the tent. I smelt the sweaty, tangy animal scent, watched the striped mustard-yellow and black of a tiger padding back into its cage, its muscles primed for action.

• • •

Every week, Mother Thomas selected two pupils to set up the staff room table for the nuns' morning teas and lunches. She considered it a reward for good behaviour. I was chosen multiple times, and took pride in aligning, just so, the plates, cups, saucers and knives; the jars of lemon curd, jam and Pecks Paste; the glass containers of cheese and brawn and the bowl of oranges. Hovering on the periphery to tidy up, or just out of sight in the pantry, I sometimes overheard staff chatter. This is what my memory, such as it is, provides.

Sister Conselata started: 'Mother Thomas, I'm concerned about that new girl, Elise Brown, in my grade five class. I don't see her making any friends. Keeps to herself most of the time. She always off in a world of her own.'

'I wouldn't worry, said Mother Thomas. 'It's probably the move from the country, and she'd be missing her father, like a good many others.' The nun drank the last of her milky tea and put the cup down with care. 'Her mother told me his injuries brought him home before the war ended and he couldn't get any decent work. He just up and left the family, oh, a few years back. That war! So many lives lost, and the ones that return, they're never the same, are they?' Distracted, she shuffled through a spray of documents on the table. 'Must be hard on the family. They're quite new in the area, aren't they.' A brisk change of tone as she gathered her papers. 'Anyway, is she keeping up with her work?'

Sister Conselata pushed her chair away from the table and rose, her footsteps suggesting a walk to the open window. She coughed once. 'Well, she's diligent enough, there's no doubt about that. She reads well and always gets her homework done, but she's not concentrating in class. Seems like there's an older head on her shoulders than a normal ten-year-old would have. And to be honest, I'm not sure she's being looked after at home.' I heard the sound of the window sash being raised further.

'Oh?' The shuffled papers stilled.

'I've noticed she's often got bruises all over her arms and sometimes on her legs, more than you'd normally expect, even for an active child. She comes to school a bit unkempt, and she's jumpy. Nervy, you know? I think perhaps that's why the other children steer clear of her. She doesn't always bring lunch either, so the poor mite goes hungry unless I give her something myself. She doesn't like to be singled out though.'

'She's not one of the welfare pupils?'

'No.'

'Well then…'

I glimpsed tiny Sister Louisa sitting to one side, silent, sipping her tea like a little sparrow, peering over the rim of her cup. Her gentle voice: 'Elise's sister Marion's in my class. She's a sweet young thing. I'm told their mother works in a factory, and as a cleaner in the city too. She's away all day. The girl says that the stepfather comes and goes. I suppose the children fend for themselves a lot. There's an older brother in high school. I don't think any of the grandparents live in these parts.'

As the bell rang, Mother Thomas rose briskly with her sheaf of papers, and moved towards the door. I crept further back to stay hidden in the pantry.

'Just give Elise time to settle in. Keep an eye on her. Now, that Michael O'Malley from the orphanage, he's one to be worried about. He's got a touch of the devil in him and would try the patience of a saint.'

• • •

The large size of my new school and its population intimidated me. There were too many ways to get lost; too many groups already formed into which I had no admittance. I longed to be invited to join something, anything, be a participant in the random games and contests in which the other children were immersed. But I couldn't crack the required code, so I stood alone on the periphery and observed how people behaved and, importantly, learned what not to do. Quiet and watchful, I remained invisible and thus escaped the routine bullying I witnessed. I felt compassion for those whose struggles and mortifications at the hands of others made my own isolation and awkwardness more bearable.

Then there were the punishments meted out by the adults. I sat in startled, deeply uneasy silence, eyes averted, as Maria Jazinski was made to kneel in front of the class and apologise for not knowing her long division while blows from a cane fell on her back and shoulders. I said nothing then and nothing when Peter O'Dell told Christos Galanis that Father Hargety put a hand down his, Peter's, pants while he was getting ready for his altar-boy duties. Christos told someone else, so the story spread around the playground, eventually reaching the ears of those, like me, who studied life from the sidelines. A month later, Peter was sent to a state school and everyone said it was because he was a big fat liar. Father Hargety didn't have to leave, but altar boy numbers declined for a while.

Once, at a weekly assembly, little six-year-old Joey Winthrop received five hard straps to his bared bottom up on stage at the weekly school assembly, for (allegedly) stealing food from another child's satchel. Forced, along with a large audience, to be an unwilling and rigid witness, I lowered my eyes and placed a hand over each ear, to block out Joey's loud cries. I felt the sting of his humiliation, which must have been every bit as painful to him as was each well-timed thwack. The sounds of his disgrace and misery somehow aligned with my own and lodged in my chest. I tried to ignore the scratch and itch of the cloth scapular I wore beneath my undervest; it reminded me that I too was a sinner because my heart filled with burning hatred towards those adults who would hurt a child.

• • •

Family and school required that I attend regular masses, which for me were now an exercise in self-flagellation. Knowing God watched us all the time, waiting for us to trip up, made for a fear-filled existence.

'Every bad thing you do is a sin. Every bad thought you have is a sin! And whenever you sin, children, you're driving another nail into the feet and hands of Jesus. Look up there at that cross now,' Father Hargety barked from his pulpit. 'Is it *your* sin that did this to Our Lord Jesus Christ? Is it you who made him suffer?' and he gestured with a stern backward flip of his hand to the large crucifix behind the altar while glowering at the congregation.

People glanced with pity or indifference at the thin alabaster figure hanging crucified behind the altar. The priest would stare with intent into the upturned faces of the littlest of the children.

'You, and you, and you,' he'd shout and point. 'Is your heart pure enough to receive communion? Are you in a state of grace?'

We all kept our eyes lowered. But curious gazes might be turned on anyone who didn't later join the line of *pure souls* shuffling, heads bowed, towards the altar, to stand before Father Hargety and open their mouths like hungry birds as he intoned *'The Body of Christ',* and placed the wafer on each tongue. We murmured *'Amen'',* and tried not to let the wafers touch our teeth because our teeth were impure and since Christ's body was inside us now, through the wafer, we must treat it with the utmost reverence. But the wafer would get stuck on the roof of my mouth and it took a surreptitious effort to prise it back onto my tongue, where it sat, obstinate, until eventually it became soggy enough for me to swallow.

Receiving communion with a pure soul required a regular confession, so each Saturday I knelt inside the dark, closet-like confessional box, knees smarting on the single, hard, wooden slat. I would glimpse the profile of Father Hargety, or sometimes a different priest, through a latticed partition, then I'd bend my head, to appear prayerful and contrite, 'Forgive me Father for I have sinned. It's been a week since my last confession.' I invented sins because I couldn't think of anything I'd done wrong, except for not doing my chores, and for wishing Jeffrey and Craig dead. I knew that by declaring my sinfulness and saying I was sorry and promising not to do any of it again (an empty promise, as I enjoyed harbouring hateful thoughts), I'd be absolved by a quick but stern blessing and a penance of ten Hail Marys, and a few Our Fathers.

Sins at home were all around me. Craig demanded my mother's attention when he was home and was tetchy if she didn't have dinner on the table at six, or hadn't got his work clothes ready for the next day. She received a meagre allowance for the weekly housekeeping, and an almost nightly ritual in the bedroom. I'd hear the bed thudding against our shared wall until it reached a crescendo of hammering. Then things would go still and quiet, except sometimes, when I would hear my mother's soft whimpers or the nearby flushing of a toilet.

• • •

I'd lost my status as favoured child as soon as my father had left. Marion was the primary object of Craig's affection. For the first time, I experienced a brief pang of jealousy; no doubt I frowned through the screen door, just as my mother once had, when I saw Craig treat my sister with some fondness and light-hearted prattling. He sat in my father's chair on the back veranda—I hated him for taking that over as well— and told her stories and tickled her pink skin, just as my father had done to me. Although I didn't want Craig to touch me in that way, it would have been so much better than the slaps. And the rest.

Jeffrey remained hostile and uncooperative, watching sulkily from the sidelines too. Our mother tried her best to placate him and make him feel grown up and an important part of the family. He was fifteen by this time. Her efforts failed, as he essentially ignored her and focused on needling me.

'Hey Dumbo! Go get me some cigarettes from Mum's drawer, will ya? Before she gets back.'

'You're not supposed to smoke. She'll kill me if she knows I've gone through her things. Anyway, why don't you do it yourself?'

'Because I told ya to, that's why.' A thump with his elbow to my head or a sharply aimed knee colliding with my hip reinforced his words. 'Just do it will ya? Great sook! If ya don't, I'll tell Mum you were the one who broke the letter box.'

'But I didn't!'

'Who cares.'

He was careful to do such things only when Craig wasn't around. As much as Jeffrey's bullying hurt me, I was gratified to learn that he too feared the man. Jeffrey's eyes narrowed whenever Craig came into view; even just the mention of that man's name could make him flinch. Physically on edge, he was like a cat ready to arch, spit and scratch. I didn't then realise the extent of Jeffrey's displacement and the anger and resentment that seeped under his skin. And I didn't know what torments he too suffered in the quiet dark on nights when my mother worked late. Despite not understanding the notion of the enemy of my enemy is my friend, there were moments when we called a truce and left each other alone. It was helped that around this time Jeffrey discovered a talent for football and channelled some of his adolescent aggression and confusion into the physicality of the game.

During yet another altercation at home, Jeffrey, emboldened by his recent growth spurt and enraged at another unjust accusation, pre-emptively struck Craig with a fist. Seeing that he'd scored a minor triumph with his blow, under which a startled Craig staggered, Jeffrey strode out of the house and stayed away for two days. We never found out where went, but after he returned, he stood a little taller, a lot stronger. Mum ran her fingers through Jeffrey's hair, pecked him on the cheek, patted him on the shoulder while he ate his meal and gave him second helpings, all under Craig's scowl. Yet again, that man turned more of his attentions to me, in the dark, and I would try to escape into myself, into a different world, where nothing hurt, and angels floated with me. Sometimes I would wish myself dead. But I would submit to anything as long as it meant he didn't hurt Marion.

CHAPTER EIGHT

This is another painful episode for me. I'll step back a little, so I can tell it from a distance. I don't remember all the details, you see, so some is what I know and some is what I believe to have happened. While I can't be certain of its accuracy, there is truth within the tale.

• • •

Jeffrey and I were riding our bikes to school. It was my second week in high school and I was relieved to have a fresh start. I hoped my brother might even treat me with some respect, though on this morning he insisted that I was not to hang around him, ever. Not at home, nor in the neighbourhood, and definitely not once we neared the school gates. For most of the journey, he rode twenty yards ahead on the footpath while I struggled to catch up.

Eventually he stopped at a busy intersection and waited for cars to pass, straddling his bike and pressing his hand against a telegraph pole for balance—his well-practised *cool* pose. Over the previous twelve months, he'd perfected a swagger appropriate to someone in his last year of study, with a particular sneer that seemed to make him attractive to girls. He turned to me as I caught up.

'Once that red car there goes by,' he pointed, 'ya've gotta get across quick!' I watched the car speed past and turned back to Jeffrey.

'Now?'

'Go!'

I was still pedalling fast when I heard the squeal of brakes and a vicious metallic thud behind me. I applied my brakes so quickly that the sudden stop threw me over the handlebars and headfirst onto the pavement. Coming to, however many minutes later, I was fuzzily aware of being on the ground, and that someone, a man, had propped me up and was supporting me; one of his arms was loosely around my waist, while he held my head up with a firm hand across my forehead. My mouth was full. I leant forward and spat out blood and bits of teeth. My broken nose throbbed above the numbness around my lips. I reached up to address the pain that registered from a gash below my ear, now staunched by someone's thick handkerchief.

The blue Ford Prefect with Jeffrey's bike entangled in its bumper bars stood on the opposite side of the road. I couldn't see my brother, but a crowd formed near the car. I tried to call out to him but heard only a whimper and felt another gush of thick, warm fluid spilling from my mouth. My legs shook involuntarily, one knee oozed blood and the other was studded with spikes of bitumen. Saliva and blood dribbled onto my new, white school shirt.

Gradually, I registered a bigger crowd and the faint sound of an ambulance siren. My heart pommelled rapidly inside my chest; I was cold. My throat scratched whenever I sucked in air through split lips. My jaw felt stuck in a clamp. The legs of the man sitting behind me were splayed out alongside my own; he rocked me ever so gently, kept one hand on my forehead, the other still around my waist, repeating 'Shhhh, it's all right; you'll be right love.' And because of his soothing voice, his reassuring, firm hold on me, I *was* all right, for a time. A yellow Labrador approached, sniffed curiously at the puddle of blood and spit that marked the path beside me, and licked my shaking hand before it moved on to inspect a nearby tree. I was hazily grateful for the dog's brief attention. Pain attached itself intermittently. A light drizzle of rain fell on my hair and face and I closed her eyes, floated higher. From above, I saw Jeffrey being lifted into an ambulance, my broken bike lying on the grass and the two men who placed me carefully into a red Holden that followed the ambulance. I identified one of those who'd lifted me as Mr Brabic, the greengrocer, but the other was a stranger.

In that state between shock and dream, I imagined being part of the flock of black cockatoos that flapped slowly and effortlessly overhead. Their loud, mournful cries could be a lament or an invitation. I allowed myself to be carried away on the backs of the birds to some imagined place of tall mountains, thick green forests, lakes that reflected a sapphire sky, and wildflowers in astonishing abundance. I heard my father's voice: 'How's my darlin' Lisie? What yer gonna be doing when…? You're my best girl…'. The regular rhythmic swish of windscreen wipers became a metronome above a piano, a grandfather clock ticking in an elegant hallway.

• • •

Jeffrey's right leg was broken, along with his collarbone and two ribs. His extended hospital stay was both an accusation and a relief for me. As long as he remained there, he couldn't torment me, but his absence was another spoke in the wheel of guilt that I wore around my neck; guilt for having somehow caused the accident and thus his injuries. When he returned home, struggling with crutches made more difficult to manage because of his damaged upper body, his moods were even darker than before and his silences more leaden. A heavy, sooty gloom settled over the home and its occupants. Craig complained about the medical bills and shot accusatory glances at both Jeffrey and me. Our mother fretted and fussed, ran an agitated hand through her salt-and-pepper hair and tried her best to get all three children to focus on school and homework. The possibility that Jeffrey might fail his final exams became real, and that truth sat heavy in his eyes. He knew—reluctantly, stubbornly—that his time on his beloved football team was over. Now only Marion, though less sweet and sunny than before, could bring light into Mum's face, and then only rarely; any of her smiles were easily broken.

My injuries were mainly confined to my face. Splinters of smashed front teeth had pierced through the soft area between my nose and top lip, and though the doctor sewing it up had remarked in that jovial way doctors do when you're at their mercy that he'd have me looking 'as pretty as Elizabeth Taylor', the scar never completely disappeared. Some said it added interest to my appearance. Another scar, about three inches long, traced a snail's path along part of my jaw line below the left ear. At an age when conformity and perfection meant everything, the marks were my new symbols of isolation.

Because of these, I rarely smiled, fearing it would only draw attention to the imperfection near my upper lip, and I wore my wavy hair loose and wild much of the time to hide the silver line along my jaw. But uniform policy at high school demanded that girls with long hair wear it tied back or in plaits, so I always felt exposed. Now I hated the very idea of school when once, long ago, it had been my delight and comfort. But I accepted the disappointments and bore feeling alienated because I'd had so many lessons in stoicism at home.

When Craig whispered in the dark that I was no longer pretty, but 'would do', I understood that any reprieve my new ugliness might have given me was lost.

The rest of that year and the next became a jumble of endless trips to the dentist. Complete immersion into daydreams in the dentist's chair was the only way I could tolerate the discomfort and pain; the bright lights; the man's white coat and thick glasses; his stubby fingers that made me want to retch; and the high-pitched squeal of the drill. For Jeffrey, the signs of his physical damage eventually receded and he moved and walked and sulked as he had before, but the fall-out from the accident had further ruptured the household. Mum took in extra ironing and never complained about the steam burns she sustained while pressing someone else's clothes. Craig worked double shifts at the processing plant and made it clear that as soon as Jeffrey left school, he'd have to get a job to contribute to the mounting bills he and I had caused.

I sensed twin resentments from Craig and Jeffrey wafting towards me in bitter waves whenever either of them passed. The house grew more silent, with unvoiced accusations the shrillest, most piercing of all.

• • •

Thus, my Wonderland became my lone sanctuary. While the teacher's voice droned on and on, and the writing on the blackboard became jumbled and dim, my focus drew ever inwards. My fancies could take many forms.

I'm an actress in a black Valentina dress, or I'm an aviator in a brown bomber jacket, or a famous tennis player, or, or…

At other times, I returned to memories of my days of running through tall paspalum with my tight-knit group of friends. I'd summon the sting of the grass on my legs, the joyful shouts, the quiet, shared current of daring and excitement that signalled the thrill of another adventure. Anything to be away from the monotony of the classroom where the subjects were dull, the rules rigid, and the teachers often incomprehensible to me.

'What is all this extra nonsense, Hannah? Where did you get this information?'

'I looked it up in the encyclopedia.'

'Did I tell you to do that?'

'No Mrs Lincoln, but…'

'No 'buts'. Go to the library and find me the exact page you got this information from, now. What answer do you have, Debra?'

'Sorry Mrs Lincoln, I didn't get that one. I didn't understand it so I asked my dad, but he said….'

'You do not ask your father, or your mother, or anyone else. The homework I set is for you, not your parents. Understand? Everybody?'

A chorus: 'Yeessss, Mrs Lincoln.'

'Elise, what did you write for number seven?'

'I wrote what you said in yesterday's lesson, about the signing of the Magna Carta and all that.'

'All that?' A chuckle, a smirk. 'And what year was that?'

'Twelve hundred and fifteen, Mrs Lincoln.'

'Correct.' Her back turned.

Red brick, grey asphalt. Intimidating in size, easy enough to lose yourself in. I continued to observe school life from the sidelines. Alongside some dubious learning, the culture fostered fear and humiliation, orchestrated mostly by adolescent girls who were experts in games of exclusion. I was never invited to become part of any established circle. Girls with perfect teeth and obedient hair pointed, giggled or whispered as I walked past.

During most lunchtimes, while other girls primped and preened before the bathroom mirrors or smoked in the toilet cubicles, I assiduously avoided any reflective surfaces and read alone in the school library. I disappeared into *Anne of Green Gables*, imagined being a vibrant girl with fiery red hair, a smattering of freckles on a pale face, perfect white teeth, a spirited personality, loyal friends and no scars.

Also in the library, I discovered *Little Women*, and bold, forthright Jo March. Soon after that, *Jane Eyre* dominated my reading. There were always girls and women waiting quietly for me on the shelves. Some were daring, some were stubborn, some were just trying to make sense of the world, as I was. They were my companions when I had no others, and I devoured those pages full of fierce, flawed, beautiful lives.

In physical education classes, I'd get my name marked off the roll, loiter around the edges of the group—aware no-one would willingly pick me for their team game—then sneak back into the main building with a library book tucked into the waistband of my sports skirt. I'd spend the rest of the lesson locked inside a toilet cubicle, reading. Before whole-school sports carnivals, I begged off sick, developing a mystery ailment the night before so that Mum, reluctantly and worriedly, wrote a note to the form teacher, passed via a neighbour's child. Those days were bliss; I had the house to myself and could luxuriate in bed for hours with a book and my dreams.

But despite my now self-imposed isolation from the rest of the student population, I was at times drawn to other girls who, like me, were ostracised by the cliques. There was Stephanie, a plump, bespeckled and snub-nosed girl of fourteen whose only crime was that she was 'plain'. And Grace, thirteen, who was what they called 'slow' back then, and who beamed constantly and wanted to stand very close. And Loretta, twelve, whose mother had run off with Stavros, the Greek mailman, the year before; everyone knew about it and nudged and whispered when Loretta walked past.

Several times a week, at lunchtime, this bunch of outcasts collected near the library door or in the shaded area behind the assembly hall, where we exchanged wistful looks, sandwiches and a little talk. Somewhat passively, reluctantly, I was looked to as leader of the group, being neither too slow nor too plain, just different. My scars, which were healing slowly, were of mild interest. We exchanged gossip or invented stories about escaping to remote places, making our own rules. (I'd read but was unsettled by *Lord of the Flies*.) Generally, I only half-listened while the others communicated in a kind of haiku; I just played with my hair and dreamed about dancing with Gene Kelly.

• • •

Days at school were indeed painful, but my nights were worse. When I slept, I heard screeching tyres, saw some dark presence chasing me, that monster or Jeffrey looming close, my mother crying, and always, always, the sound and image of my teeth splintering. I woke every morning with my jaw locked, the sheets damp with sweat, and immediately thought that once again I'd wet the bed. That era of incontinence only recently behind me, it was hard to prevent the old stink of shame from assaulting my nostrils.

• • •

'Here you are, Mrs Harrington, here's your dinner! Nice lamb chop tonight, and some veggies. Would you like the television on? It's been another big day for you, hasn't it. That young lady who comes to chat to you, she's nice. The two of you seem to get on really well. Can I get you some more water?'

I nod and smile and tell her that 'that young lady' is my granddaughter. The staff here are pleasant, some of them patronising, but I don't mind. They have such a hard job. Aravinda, the man with the radiant hair and delightful laugh, is my favourite. He's always respectful and sweet, and he makes me chuckle. He says I remind him of his grandmother in Sri Lanka.

I get to see Sophie because she's wheedled her way around the restrictions. But Paul and Felicity and their brood aren't allowed inside. They can come to the window and wave. It's so hard to not be able to touch them. It all seems too strict, but I suppose they have their reasons. The radio and TV news make a big deal of this virus. It's caused a lot of deaths apparently, including a few here, though we only hear about them through whispers. I don't want to watch the news much anyhow. There's so much sorting and writing still to do, but having kept a journal for all these years makes the task easier.

CHAPTER NINE

The social worker, Alice, was a plump, fair-haired woman of middle age with florid cheeks and bifocal glasses that made her look a little cross-eyed. She had a warm smile over crooked teeth. She sat opposite my mother, who wouldn't look directly at me but stared, with fury, at some spot on the beige wall, twirling with agitation the gold wedding band that she still wore for respectability. Mum's voice was near hysteria.

'You have no choice, Elise. You cannot take care of a baby. You're not even sixteen! How would you look after a child? What work can you do? No one's able to help you. I can't do it, and,' a deep breath in, followed by a slow, vibrating exhale, 'oh, what will people say, Elise? This is awful, awful! You've brought shame on this family! I pray to God no one finds out! What am I supposed to tell Marion? She thinks…we've told her you're staying with your Aunt Helen. And what about your education? All that money we've spent on sending you to a decent school.'

On and on…not the first time I'd heard all this, and it wouldn't be the last.

I fixed my gaze outside, noting the thick white clouds gathered together in mute appraisal. Mum had never once asked about the *who* or the *how*, not that I'd have said, being still so confused about the nature of things.

Alice shifted in her seat, tapped the pamphlet she was holding, and glanced from fuming mother to dejected daughter. I dipped momentarily into the injustice of the accusatory words and tone from someone everyone knew was *living in sin*. When Mum's list of grievances finally wound down, we three sat in stillness while a wasp sought to escape through the half-open window. With the regular rhythmical ticking of the clock on the wall, I drifted off to a more familiar, comfortable place, constructing a fantasy around a boy from school, a beach party, dozens of friends: the music, the food, the sea, romance, the colours, the scents of salty water, warm skin and summer; the possibilities.

'Mrs Brown', the social worker offered at last, 'I think it would be useful if you give me some time to work through the things that need to be done from here on. So, um, I'll speak to you outside presently. Would you mind taking a seat near the reception desk? I just need to talk to Elise for a moment. I'll be right with you.' She rose in her chair to indicate the door.

I watched my mother move away with an upright, uptight, leaden shuffle, her back stiff and silent, straining to keep straight, her head wobbling slightly on an unsteady neck. The air pulsed with the bitterness of her swallowed bile.

• • •

Many women and girls were hidden away at the City Mission Maternity Home for Unwed Mothers (helpfully capitalised), and often considered on the outside to be little better than prostitutes. However, inside those walls we were treated charitably. But while the staff, which included many nuns of a compassionate order, were friendly and efficient, the dampness and grey confines of the place secreted an odour of quiet accusation. Thin layers of mildew and censure had formed on the walls over many years.

For me, the home was a welcome refuge. I'd joined an exclusive club, one where empathy presided. While the details of our stories may have differed, we boarders were united in our comfortable conformity to new rules and the lack of judgement towards others. Some of us were shy, some loud, some shared jokes, though I didn't understand the bawdy references I heard. I worked in the laundry, feeding wet sheets through a cranking wringer, ironing and folding linen, or chopping vegetables in the vast kitchen, washing plates, scouring cooktops. As one of the younger residents, I was shielded by the older girls and encouraged by the nuns.

The pains came without warning in my thirty-eighth week. A volcanic downward gush, before my sometime-ally Samantha pointed to a puddle on the floor. Sister George arranged for an ambulance. No one from the home accompanied me, but the driver and his attendant spoke to me reassuringly as I lay groaning and frightened in the back of the vehicle. Once more I felt like a pariah, the weight of my 'sin' almost as painful as the infrequent but unstoppable contractions. Fear wrapped clammy fingers around my throat while pain sent violent probes to encase my belly as I struggled to breathe.

Inside the hospital, someone whisked me into a cold and sterile preparation room, stripped and shaved me and left me alone to struggle to tie, with shaking hands, the trailing ends of a coarse cotton gown that gaped open at the back. Eventually a short, chubby nurse arrived, instructed me to lie on a plastic-sheeted bed and examined me with brisk, smarting intrusion. I winced, took a sharp involuntary breath, and was then helped up and escorted, half-crouching, to the delivery room. A curt nod directed me to a high bed. I grunted at the effort to climb onto it.

And though I tried hard to conjure up any one of my usual fantasies, the pain and indignities continued to accumulate; all means of mind-escape were blocked. Someone positioned my legs in stirrups and placed a mask over my face, roughly. I'd hoped for some relief from the agony, but no amount of sucking in the gas helped. I had no sense of time. All I knew was wave after wave of an internal earthquake that my skin and organs surely could not contain.

• • •

I need to step back a little from the telling. It hurts to write it, unless from a distance. The memory of it all…how much is real, or reconstructed, or now imagined? But I'll tell it as I remember it, the bits that are stuck in my mind and the things I wrote down, once it was all over.

• • •

With every order to push, I fought the contractions fiercely. I didn't want a baby; needed to keep it and everything that caused it inside; hidden, secret, unknowable.

More gas, the mask so jaggedly adjusted it cut into my mouth and made my eyes water, which was still nothing compared to the wrenching pain of my body being turned inside out. I screamed once—a high-pitched animal sound that I thought at first must have come from somewhere else. I took a deep breath and held it. For a moment, I had that serene feeling that always came whenever I slipped into my wonderland—a hint of being buoyed, floating on a calm sea, all being well in the world. Then the air in my lungs expelled in an almighty roar. Did someone just slap my face? The noises were from my childhood; a lion at the circus, chattering monkeys, an elephant trumpeting. Colours popped so brightly that I gasped. The lioness attacked and there was blood everywhere.

A nurse shushed and soothed me. A hand held mine tight. Then I heard a male voice say, 'Come on, let's get moving. Forceps! Looks like this one's not going to come out easily.'

Through time, through dense smog and concentrated pain, through a final expulsion of my being, I heard a small, forceful cry and then nothing more. I had a glimpse of bloodied mauve and white speckled flesh, before a nurse stepped across my view, while another left the room with what looked like a small armful of laundry.

Different noises came to me—a metal dish banging onto a trolley and two nurses speaking in quiet tones. The doctor's voice again: 'Let's tidy this up. That's quite a tear.'

I felt the tug and censure of his handiwork and turned my face to the wall. Tears escaped through my clenched eyes and slid onto the plastic-covered pillow. Had I cared at that point, I'd have been embarrassed by the poor job the blood-stained, rumpled sheet did in covering me.

Long after the mutterings and footsteps faded away, a young woman— olive-skinned, with strands of dark hair that escaped from her sanitised, white cloth cap—entered the room with a bucket which she pushed with her foot as she mopped at the various fluids on the floor. She looked somewhat like Mr Mattaboni's wife, Chiara, with a job to do. No smile. The air reeked of the metallic smell of blood and the sharp ethanol assault of disinfectant. I concentrated on counting my breaths, hoping they would cease entirely before I tallied fifty. Nothing that had ever happened before mattered, nor would anything again be of any consequence.

The room was empty. I was alone. My legs, still high in stirrups, were numb and blue; every other part of my body was cold, shivering. I was a piece of raw, bloodied and pummelled meat on display in a butcher's shop.

I opened my eyes again.

White

White

Bright

Empty

Cold

Cold

Room.

My feet were dead. I flexed my fingers. Movement in one hand, biting pins and needles in the other. The fluorescent lights above me stared; they too had witnessed my disgrace.

I want my mother. Mumma. Please.

One light flickered on, off, on, off, on, and after a while I closed my eyes, tilted my face towards the strobe effect and imagined the sun, its warmth over blue waters. I felt a soft hand stroking my face, my arm. The hand belonged to a young nurse who looked not much older than me. Her voice was gentle, soothing, her face a picture of concern.

'I'll get you properly cleaned up now. You've turned all blue and blotchy, you poor thing. My name's Anna. First thing we'll do is get you down from those horrible stirrups. Hold on, let me move you. Careful now.'

I couldn't feel my legs, but noted back pain. I was so overwhelmed by this show of kindness that I wept.

'Come on sweetie, no need to cry. I'll help you up and you'll be right as rain.'

Anna washed me down tenderly with a thin towel while her voice soothed, which only made me cry more.

Through shivering lips, I asked, 'Can I see my baby?', knowing I'd be refused. *I'm made of steel. I don't cry,* but I was unable to stop.

Afterwards, I remembered Anna's warm practical hands, her soft presence, her tenderness. Short periods of sleep did come; deep, leaden moments of exhaustion.

In the morning, I woke in a new room shared with two girls of about eighteen in the beds opposite. One was wearing the same shattered expression as I must have had; the other looked resigned, though a touch defiant. We avoided eye contact. I shifted uncomfortably and felt the abrupt pull and sting of stitches as I tried to swing my legs over the side of the bed. I needed to pee.

'You have to wait for a bed pan. You're not allowed up yet. Ring that bell, there, beside your bed.' The older of the two girls pointed.

At the bottom of each bed was a sign stating in large type, ADOPTION. I spent the next two days crying into my pillow and wouldn't eat. The nurses scolded, then tried to cajole. My breasts filled painfully with milk that seeped through my nightgown onto the bedclothes; the ensuing ache countered the emptiness of my gut. A brisk midwife applied cabbage leaves to my breasts and bound them with strips of tight linen sheeting, and told me, 'You'll feel better in a few days.'

Anna, the young nurse who'd been so gentle, came through at meal times. 'You must eat something, little one! They won't let you go home until you're strong enough'

So I obliged, though without appetite. But home? I had none. Before long, my ward companions left, empty-handed except for a small overnight bag. They each offered me a washed-out smile of acknowledgement before shuffling through the door.

Later, in the hospital administrator's office, the social worker, Alice, informed me that my child was a boy and the paperwork for his adoption was almost complete.

I whined. 'But I never signed anything. I don't want this.'

'Your parents did it for you.'

'They, no. They can't! Please. Please let me see him.' A broken, snot-filled wail, followed by hiccups.

'Elise, this was all agreed. We need to put the baby's father's name on the birth certificate. There'll be two certificates done. One's for you, and the other is an Amended Birth Certificate for the adoptive parents. We need the father's name for the first paper. Your mother said you wouldn't tell her. All right. But you should tell me.'

No, I can't.' My voice found the floor.

'You can't, or you won't?'

Once again, I shook my head slowly, to clear it, to deflect, to side-step. 'I didn't know his name; he was a stranger.'

Alice baulked. 'Well, I'm sorry, Elise, if that's the case. This is most unusual. I need to speak to someone. We'll have to find a solution.'

I don't know what ended up on the certificate. I went back to the City Mission Home, a temporary refuge until I could find somewhere else. The nuns were kind and helped me recover. In a few weeks, Samantha had her baby, considerably more nonchalantly than others had done, and afterwards suggested that she and I rent rooms together.

CHAPTER TEN

B ut I should go back a little. I'd kept my swelling belly a secret for as long as possible. Throughout the school day, I talked to the baby within, conversations managed inside my head, or sometimes on scraps of paper. I hoped that if he were a boy, he'd grow up to be a pilot, or anything that allowed him to escape my life, my world. If a girl, she should marry someone like Gregory Peck and get away, from this country, this town, this family, this mess.

This family? Well, it'd be nice to be able to say that they rallied round, but no, of course not. Jeffrey still lived at home, at age twenty; he'd have left much earlier but for the debt Craig kept reminding him he owed them since the bike accident.

When I could no longer hide what was happening, stinging wasps of questions and accusations attacked brutally but elicited no response from me. I waited for someone else there to confess but he didn't. My mother became almost hysterical each time she laid eyes on me so I stayed out of her way as much as possible, kept to my room and my books, journal and daydreams. My brother and stepfather remained silent and avoided any eye contact with me, often leaving the room if I came near. I tasted again what it was to be a pariah, but there was relief in solitude.

Only Marion, my dearest Marion, would speak to me normally and express joy to be near me. When no one else was around, she'd sit beside me, put her head on my shoulder, hold my hand or tickle my ribs as she'd done when we were younger. She knew I was in trouble but didn't speak of it. Some innate sense of decorum, plus fear of our mother's wrath, kept her from asking questions, even when we were alone in the bedroom at night. And I had no desire to tell her what had happened. She was so young, so innocent, as I wished I'd still been.

My condition must have been the worst in the long list of scandals attached to my mother. Having come from a *respectable* Methodist home, she'd been ostracised by her family for marrying a Catholic, a poor one at that, and Irish. Then later, having suffered the ignominy of being deserted by him, she now *lived in sin* with an atheist who drank. Having a pregnant fifteen-year-old daughter completed the anthology of humiliations for her. But to me, her outrage was hypocrisy. It had never been hard to work out that she'd married young because she had to.

The nuns at school surprised me. They were the only ones on my side. Though I had to leave school once my condition became obvious, they arranged a place for me in the Home and allowed me to finish my last term of study there. Except for the belief that I was abandoning Marion to an uncertain fate, I was relieved to get away and move in with girls who'd been judged guilty in the same way that I had. At the Home, an unusual sort of camaraderie developed between us. We all looked much the same with our plumped-out cheeks, self-conscious smiles and burgeoning bellies that stretched the fabric of our floral smocks. We busied ourselves with menial jobs and, for those my age or younger, continued with studies. Samantha— pretty, dark-haired, dark-eyed and eighteen—was my particular favourite. Her baby was due around the same time as mine. She'd make me giggle with her risqué jokes, though half the time I didn't know exactly what it was I was laughing at. Her sexual experiences were clearly quite different from mine. In the dormitory we shared at night, after we finished our twittering with the other girls, I could assuage my ever-present guilt and send myself to sleep by imagining being slim again and dux of the school, or by working out in the minutest detail what my baby would look like, how I would dress him or her, and what an impression we'd make promenading along Beach Road with my husband (his image yet to be determined) by my side.

I learned that circumstances forced other girls and women in the same predicament to take another route, seek an illegal solution, and likely pay the ultimate price. Whichever choice we made or had imposed on us seemed an impossible one to live with, or die for. In the Home, where we were safe, we created a new order, where our history, protruding bellies and uncertain futures were of no consequence to anyone else there.

After my son was taken away from me, his absence felt like a death, one I wasn't supposed to grieve. I never saw or even heard him, apart from that one instance of his brief mewling, the sound of an abandoned kitten. There was no acknowledgement of what had happened, no one to offer support or comfort, no congratulations or gifts or flowers. My belly, once so swollen and full of potential, returned to its pre-pregnancy state, while the stretch marks that had signified his rapid growth faded quickly because of my youth. My shame never did though. I was supposed to and did feel a need to repent for what had happened, though the extent of my culpability still escaped me. Guilt was my ingrained religious inheritance.

On the understanding that I was not to return to the family home (a letter from my mother, with words and tone that Craig would have provided), and with financial assistance from 'your Aunt Helen, so generous of her,' I moved with Samantha to a boarding house in a smaller town along the coast, where we both found work in a textile factory. Samantha bought a cheap ring and pretended to be married, so as to procure diaphragms and spermicidal creams. She'd either learned her lesson or really hadn't. She made jokes about never going out without her 'hat' on and would clown around in the bedroom and place the rubber dome on her head while getting ready to go out on a date. To satisfy my curiosity once, she showed me how to use them. Eventually, out of loneliness and because I was desperate to connect to people in any way possible, to feel cherished and accepted, I too slept my way around town. But I wasn't the slut that some people called me. I dislike that word anyway—it's harsh and there's no male equivalent. Slut, shag, slither, slam, slap, slash…Brutish words. I will, though, own promiscuous. I was that, for a time.

I had sex with anyone who asked me, and some who did not. I craved a soft kiss, a gentle touch, a proper relationship. I wanted desperately to believe in love, at least for a while. Hungry for something romantic, elusive, I'd have done anything to get it, and indeed did do almost anything. A man need only treat me kindly and I could be bought for the price of a Gin Fizz. Furtive fumblings in the back seats of cars, something quick against a garden wall, stolen moments in my room when the landlady was not around. Sex became a new drug, one that I might lose myself in, if only for a short while. It gave me a sense of power. Predictably, these liaisons didn't last long; I was too 'easy' and soon earned the reputation that could and did invite a pack, like sniffing dogs around a bitch in heat. Once, having missed the bus home from work on a winter night with rain imminent, I accepted a lift from two men, strangers. Instead of being driven home, I was taken to the basement of a partially built house in an otherwise empty street. I cursed myself for having been so stupid and prayed afterwards to a god I no longer believed in that there would be no missed period the following month. I hid the deep bruising on my neck and the scratches on my arms and legs and, after the blood came on cue some weeks later, I doubled my attention to the contraception that was available then, inconvenient and messy though it could be, and lay low for some time.

After any sexual encounter, back in my upstairs room where the smell of stale bread, burnt chops and boiled cabbage wafted from the landlady's kitchen, I'd lie in bed with a sense of deep regret in the pit of my stomach. I'd sift back through the scene, hoping to find evidence that the man I'd been with might have felt some genuine affection for me, and I for him. There were sometimes small, fragile nuggets of warmth, a belief that we'd exchanged something sincere and emotionally intimate, but really, I had to recognise the couplings for what they were—urgent, passionless interplays that just left me with a greater sense of self-loathing and hopelessness. Or if I was lucky, no feelings at all. The easiest thing to do was to dismiss any memories and return to one of the many romantic scenarios that were constantly under construction in my head. Those fanciful thoughts were enough to get me to sleep, though any dreams that followed were invariably of conflict and tension.

Many mornings, while I was in that half-state between sleep and wake-fulness, for a few moments it would seem as though the being that I inhabited was as innocent as an embryo. Then that worm of doubt would niggle away in some area of my brain. *Oh, it happened again.* Doubt would turn to revulsion. *Who was that? Do you even know his name? You stupid fool.* I tried to picture his face above mine. *Why did you do it? Oh Lord, I hope that diaphragm worked!*

It was easier, better, if I just pretended it all away. The evidence was undeniable—the sticky remnants on my thighs and the sting left over from intercourse without arousal. These I erased in a punishingly hot shower, then plastered a smile onto my face as carelessly as I did lipstick before going downstairs to the landlady's generous breakfast and her bright chatter.

For some perverse reason, I toyed with those few young men I dated who seemed to genuinely care for me, possibly because it gave me a sense of power, and power was exhilarating, even if only for a few moments. Feeling in control was a drug, though in reality my behaviour was out of control. In the end, somehow it felt that there must be something inherently wrong with any man who liked me. Sometimes, I'd be consciously cruel, provoke arguments, make him jump through hoops to provide proof of a fondness that I believed impossible. In these ways, I sabotaged any fledgling relationship, did or said something to hurt whomever it was and make him not care about me anymore because deep down I knew I was unlovable.

It was probably around this time that I really began to switch. The real world continued to prove too confounding and disappointing, so my dreams became my new reality. The fantasies allowed me to escape to a parallel universe. In my imagined world, I was perfect and completely in control. Mindless reveries and sex were potent anaesthetics, though I knew I was cheating myself by indulging indiscriminately in both.

• • •

Sophie, I hope you got the parcel I asked them to send to you. I do so much appreciate you helping me with my story. Please tell me if I'm not making sense. My thoughts can wander like lost sheep, which might confuse you. To me, early events still seem so vivid, but later ones, not so much.

I think my handwriting's getting worse, along with my memory. My neighbour in here, Jill, gave me a new voice recorder and showed me how it works, so I'll be mostly using that now instead of writing or typing. Jill says it'll ease the pains in my hands and wrists.

Here comes that lovely Aravinda with dinner. I wish you could visit soon; I'd love to give you a hug. But they're very strict. Of course, I long to see all the family, but I talk to your parents and Patricia every other day, though it's not the same. The only useful thing about lockdown is that I have uninterrupted time to keep going with this story of mine. I wonder who'd ever read it though? Perhaps your Mum and Dad might be shocked at what I've revealed. Maybe you should edit out the sex bits.

CHAPTER ELEVEN

On my way to work, I stopped at a phone booth outside the post office of a small country town, intending to call my mother, with the hope that she'd be alone and conceivably more willing to accept the call. All my previous attempts had resulted in the phone at the other end being swiftly replaced on its receiver.

'Hello?' A breathy, timid woman's voice.

'Mum, it's me. Please don't hang up,' I said in a fusion of fear and optimism.

I could sense the hesitation, a year's worth of what might be anger or disenchantment working its way into her intake of breath, to be transported along the telephone cable all the way to Niburu. But this time, as the line still crackled, there was no instant disconnect.

'What do you want?' The pulse of disapproval crept through the Bakelite mouthpiece, wrapped in her icy tone.

'Just to talk, Mum. I miss you and Marion.

'Elise, you can't call here. Your father...'

'He's not my father, Mum!' *Too loud.* A pause. 'Sorry. I just wondered if...I want...I wondered, can we meet? Please?'

Another hush, before a sigh punctuated the static. I allowed myself a few seconds of hope. Whispered, 'Please?'

I watched the slow progress of a blowfly as it climbed a few inches up one side of the sticky glass and dropped again onto its back on top of the faded, curling cover of a yellowing, outdated telephone book. The insect's legs waved furiously in the air until it righted itself with an outraged buzz and a flick of its wings, and repeated its slow, gluey ascent of the glass.

A further extended breath along the line, exhaled with deliberate caution. 'Where are you?'

'In Niburu.'

Surprise added a certain lightness to her voice. 'That's not very far away.'

'I'd catch a train, come to the city and meet you in town, or…'

'You know I can't do that Elise. I'm working.'

'But you still work in the city, don't you? We could meet for lunch.' Pause. 'I need, I mean, I'd really like to see you.'

'Why, what's wrong? You're not in trouble again are you?'

I imagined the handset steering determinedly towards its cradle. 'No, no it's not that. It's just, it's been more than a year Mum. Can't I come back, just to visit?'

My mother's voice was prim. 'You've made your bed Elise. You're a grown girl and you're obviously capable of looking after yourself. Besides, what kind of example are you to Marion?'

'She wouldn't care.'

'She doesn't know, thank God.'

'Okay, yes, but where does she think I am? She must wonder where. And why?' *Stop arguing! It won't help.*

'I can't talk now, Jeffrey's just arrived. He's dropping something off. I can hear his car.'

'Mum?'

'Elise, I have to go. Call me next week.'

The familiar clunk of the telephone. Dismissal. The clammy heat and stale stuffiness of the booth were oppressive and followed me when I opened the heavy door to leave. The conversation, though brusque on her side, left me with a small chink of hope.

Riding high on this, I sat on the bus with one of my co-workers, Philip, someone I'd only spoken to a few times. I knew he was about twenty-one, and a keen surfer; he was slim, with wide shoulders, sweet and gentle in his ways. He chatted on, about his new role in the accounts section, football, his plans for the weekend, his older brother's impending birthday party, and all the time, while I had my head turned to him, aware of his dark eyes, I smiled and nodded, while my mind rehashed the conversation with my mother. Then I drifted to thoughts of my father. I could no longer remember his face distinctly, only the sweet, earthy tobacco smell of him, the touch of his rough stubble where I used to stroke his skin. My throat constricted, so I thought instead of a wedding and white calla lilies.

'So, what about it?'

'Sorry?'

Do you want to go out sometime? Like to the movies or something?'

The scent of lilies disappeared. As I refocused, I noted Philip's not unpleasant smell of sweat and earnestness and his round, open face. His brown hair, flecked with light strips bleached by hours in the surf, was neither a crew cut nor greased back into a ducktail. He wore it parted on the side, but longer than most boys did. He reminded me of James Dean but without the scowl.

'Yes, all right. Sorry, I mean, yes, that would be nice. Thank you.'

When we began dating, I, with uncharacteristic restraint, delayed physical intimacy and exchanged only chaste kisses with Phil at my doorstep. Being *in a relationship* was still foreign to me and I didn't want to mess it up. Phil was someone everyone agreed upon: a *nice* young man—good manners, a hard worker, and *he's so clever to be studying at night school. An accountant!* He was considerate, thoughtful, often brought me flowers or chocolates, didn't pressure me for sex. "I'll wait till you're ready," he said, but this only sent me into a panic. I worried that he'd hear about me from someone I'd slept with before—it was a small township, after all.

But when this didn't happen, I let down my guard. After an evening together at the drive-in, a re-run of 'On the Waterfront', I accepted Phil's invitation to go back to his flat. The sex was better than I'd have imagined, no manipulation or games or control. Afterwards, we chatted of inconsequential things—light, unthreatening, unintrusive talk.

We became a *couple*; we met twice a week after work, and most Saturdays went to the movies or a football game. Sometimes I cooked him dinner in his flat, or he took me to parties; I liked his friends. After he obtained a position in an accountancy firm, and I got a raise at the textile factory, we celebrated with an expensive wine for which I hadn't developed a taste. I lost my frown and gained some weight, which people said was flattering. I met Phil's family, but told him nothing about mine. I thought that this must be happiness, but most nights, in the dark before sleep, a grey menace would creep in with the chill of the air, and I'd remember the whisper, "You're not pretty anymore, but you'll do."

• • •

Aside from factory work, there were few other avenues open to me in those days. Though I'd taught myself to type, and learnt basic shorthand, my first few weeks of secretarial work at a real estate office weren't at all successful. I was fired after sending out the wrong contract to a 'Very Important Client' and, I discovered, for not making the boss's coffee to his liking nor responding to his advances when I worked after hours.

My inclination was initially for teaching, where I might help children to avoid the same torments that kids like Joey Winthrop, Maria Jazinski and Peter O'Dell had endured. I also wanted to cosy up to all those books I'd not yet had a chance to become acquainted with. I wished for nothing more than to sequester myself inside a library and just absorb the learning that had seeped into the grey brick walls, to open textbooks that smelt of musty pages and years of shared knowledge. I couldn't afford to go to university or teacher's college, even if I had the right grades, and I knew nothing then about scholarships.

I investigated positions in a local hospital. Back then, they were considered the best training grounds for nurses, and the school qualifications I'd managed to obtain while pregnant were deemed sufficient for entry. Though my experiences hitherto in hospitals had been traumatic, I reasoned that something useful, noble even, might be achieved by working in such an environment. Plus, I needed to learn how to just *be* with other people, instead of living so often inside my head, where my wits still regularly went wool-gathering.

The job was demanding, and I worked hard, determined to impress even the most formidable of the senior nursing staff. However, no matter how compliant I was, and how much I tried to conform, there was always at least one matron or ward sister resolutely opposed to my efforts. Perhaps it was my oft-unruly hair that would fall out in defiant strands from its tight bun, or my shy, bland demeanour, or just the way I wore my starched blue and white uniform. I learned to let the unbending sternness and regular reprimands from the older staff roll over me. At night I constructed elaborate scenes of triumph over whomever had belittled me that day.

I wasn't the only student nurse who unintentionally brought disfavour upon herself. Anyone who found it difficult to conform, or questioned decisions or orders, or expressed exasperation, or yawned from exhaustion in front of the matron, found herself given extra bedpan or linen duty. Also unfairly targeted were trainees of a heritage other than Anglo-Irish. We were all constantly harangued about personal grooming and cleanliness, to the point where our hands were red and sore from the endless scrubbing with carbolic soap. In the early months, we learnt more about dusting lockers, emptying bedpans, cleaning basins and running errands, than we did about dressing wounds.

Learning humility was part of the training, and I was good at that. I recall the strict discipline, the hierarchical structures, the amorphous, gliding presence of doctors (those mysterious higher-order beings), the smell of floor polish and disinfectant and the idle gossip in the changerooms or stairwells. Even the driest of lectures in anatomy, physiology and nursing theory offered a reprieve, an ordered world set apart from the demands of the wards.

As in high school, I never entered the orbit of the favoured trainees, attracting instead the company of those who fell outside the mould. Sometimes, while working in the linen room or standing in line in the staff cafeteria, I'd be approached by a girl with sad eyes who sought an encouraging word and attached herself to me like a limpet. In truth, it was only pride that prevented me from doing the same to someone else. It cost me nothing to be kind. Besides, there was little time to forge meaningful friendships, given the demands of the job, and I was content enough to be only adjacent to belonging.

To satisfy my cravings for solitude and make-believe, I regularly visited the public library to borrow anything suggested by Miss Beneš, the slim, raven-haired, enthusiastic librarian. She recognised my thirst and introduced me to Iris Murdoch, Tennessee Williams, Steinbeck, Orwell, Austen, Dickens, Hemingway, Maupassant, Virginia Woolf….She even recommended I try to find some Nabokov, though *Lolita* was still banned at that time.

Twelve-hour shifts, textbooks and literary escapes made me less available to Phil than I'd once been. He remained sweet and attentive when we met up, and though I felt something like what I imagined love must be, I enjoyed my job and the worlds that literature created for me—bleak, funny, complex, exciting—I enjoyed these at least as well as his company.

The cracks in our relationship, when they began to appear, moved stealthily and silently, undermining what had gone into building us up as a unit. Increasingly, still lacking confidence in my appearance, I found it just too hard to believe that Phil could really love me. My fair hair was turning a mousier brown. I wasn't what people would call *buxom*, when the look of the moment was Marilyn Monroe. I was generally too self-conscious to smile because of the caps on my teeth, which I was convinced made me look like Bugs Bunny. There were also the scars—a very faint one near my upper lip, and a more pronounced zigzag along my jawline. If people did ever comment on my appearance, it was to say that I had unusual eyes—they were large and the colour of pale honey, with flecks of green and amber, making them hazel I suppose—similar to cat's eyes, some people said. I was lucky to have long eyelashes (a legacy from my father), pleasing height, plus thick hair and a slim frame from my mother.

At the Nurses' Home, it was tricky to stay out late if not working a night shift. Invariably, the nurses' comings and goings were the subject of concentrated scrutiny and fodder for gossip. Manners and morals were policed, and regular reports filtered up and down the line of command. I could usually spend a few hours with Phil twice a week, though often on those occasions, I was too tired to be good company. Increasingly, we found reasons to argue, and he must have noticed the distracted distance that clouded my normally direct gaze.

Phil began to spend more and more time with his mates, and there were girls who would beam luminously at him when we were out together. He mostly seemed chuffed to be the recipient of their attention, but other times looked embarrassed, depending on who'd bestowed the flirty smile. I wasn't sure if the embarrassment was because of being seen out with me or because he feared my catching him out for something he'd done.

Thus began the sabotage, initially in small, niggly ways. I could have let our relationship just drift along and eventually fizzle out, but no, I had to have the dramatic ending. Not in the vein of Emma Bovary of course, but more like Scarlett O'Hara.

'C'mon Elise, don't be crazy! I didn't mean anything by it!'

'Why did you say it then?'

'I was only joking.'

'Well, you're not being funny!'

'I thought…'

'You don't think, that's the problem! All it is with you is cars and beer and your friends and going to stupid football matches.'

'That's how I relax! It'd be different if you were around more often. You never have time these days, always working or with your head in a book.'

Phil moved to the window, folded his arms and watched the heavy rain form pools on the path outside his living room. The streets were slick with water; car tyres sent grey waves into the gutters. He addressed the world outside. 'You're not a lot of fun anymore, you know. You used to be able to take a joke at least.' He turned again towards me, arms hanging down, head lowered, eyes concentrating for a moment on a swirl of carpet before he looked up and said, 'Look, let's not fight! I'm tired! Can't we just sit? Talk?' He raised a hand to his forehead, rubbed it wearily, perhaps searching for the right words, words that wouldn't provoke further anger. 'Elise. Come on,' and he motioned for me to sit.

I refused and loathed myself for being difficult. 'Do you think I'm not aware of the other girls?'

'What other girls? You're being ridiculous.'

I moved towards him, and for a moment he might have hoped I would curl up in his arms and apologise, but I just glared at him, my arms straight and fists clenched, and I glowered with a sharp, intense stare that challenged him to contradict me. 'Don't think I don't know,' I said, my voice biting.

'*What* do you know?' There was a slight catch in his throat, his voice a little higher than it should be, and it confirmed for me that which, in fact, I'd only been guessing at.

So we argued, back and forth, first with Phil's protestations of innocence, then with my wilder accusations, countered by an angry admission from him and then his own false claims about me—his attack full of spite once defence had failed. I retaliated with an untruthful guilty plea to his charges, thrown down only to wound him.

Our voices grew louder, our stances more like boxers circling in a ring, with verbal jabs alternately pushing us further apart then pulling us both in for a knockout. I believed he was fighting a desire to slap me hard, and so dared him to do so. Foolish words, foolish behaviour—I knew this, all so unnecessary and unseemly—but right in that moment it didn't matter. There was power to be felt in the ring, to be an equal opponent who could thrust and jab and parry. Such power was, for the tiniest of moments, exhilarating. Before being able to check myself, I'd announced that I hated him, that I never wanted to see him again, that I was glad that he'd got someone else because, because, because…

I knew I was making no sense, knew that I was lying, knew this as soon as the words come out of my mouth, and saw instantly the damage they caused. His face registered a bristling, cavernous hurt, but it was all too late, and I was too tired and too wounded to change what was happening. I slammed the door as I left but it took an effort. Rage and the thirst to draw blood were immediately replaced by remorse and shame.

The following week was hushed and empty; more stillness than I ever wanted filled the space left by Phil. And there was no one to hold me, no one to block out thoughts of a presence hiding in a corner or looming out of the darkness. And I recognised, deep down, that Phil had never been the real target.

We made up again, as we had before, but this time Phil was justifiably wary and remote. He became the one pondering an alternative world, one that I didn't inhabit. Without understanding why I did it, I continued to needle and push, prod and poke, trying for a response that would match the drama and intensity and resolutions of my fictional world. This never came. By the end of another month, Phil, like Rhett Butler, frankly did not give a damn.

CHAPTER TWELVE

I remember life back then against the backdrop of a surge of interest in sports. The population was still buzzing about the country's success at the Olympic Games, held in Melbourne, that had not been without controversy: a boycott by China because Taiwan could compete as a separate nation; Egypt, Iraq and Lebanon withdrew following the Suez crisis. Several countries pulled out because of the Soviet Union's presence in Hungary, and when those two teams faced off in a water polo event, the match was ugly and literally drew blood.

Schools recorded a sudden jump in interest for swim clubs or track and field events. Parents rose early to take their future Olympic hopefuls to the pool, gymnastics class or athletics field. In my idle moments, which were few, I imagined being an Olympic gymnast.

At nearly nineteen, and in my second year of training, I still lived in the Nurses' Home, in cramped but clean quarters. I saw an increase in the number of sports-related injuries and did my best to calm traumatised children, recognising in their frightened eyes something of the pain and fear I had known as a child. I responded well in emergencies and had no crippling aversion to blood or trauma injuries. The work was hard, the hours long, the wages only adequate, and obedience and conformity were the norm.

Nursing was considered a vocation, not unlike that found in religious orders. But while I didn't yet feel that this was my natural calling, something in the routine and order and *fixability* of the work made it satisfying.

While I enjoyed the art of tending to broken bodies, it was difficult when a rotation took me into the neonatal care ward. The vulnerable flesh and form of crying or sleeping infants both repelled and fascinated me. I had only a fuzzy notion of the baby boy who had, just like that, slipped out of my body and out of my life in an instant. I tried to imagine how he might look now—what colour hair and eyes might he have? Was his face an oval shape, similar to mine? Was he healthy, happy, talking incessantly? Who loved him and who did he love?

In the nursery, surrounded by the pink, milky, peach-fuzz softness of the babies with their sea-shell ears, I'd place a protective hand on my belly and try to ignore the longing that manifested itself as a spasm. To avoid further agitation, I approached tasks with brisk efficiency, tried to lose myself in the unfocused stare of a swaddled, cocooned newborn.

And at night, when the wondering and the remembering and all the silent secrets caused the familiar upheaval in my stomach, I turned again to the consolation of imagination, far away from Niburu, from reality, from shame. I visualised many noble scenarios, like working in a makeshift hospital in Turkey, where there were hundreds of wounded soldiers lying on army cots, groaning, in desperate need of assistance. This one should have an amputation; that one needed so many stitches; the next one called out for his mother. They all need penicillin and comfort. It was cold and miserable outside; inside was a wet, musty smell, mixed with something like metallic sulphur, and the animal scent of blood and fear. We all heard shelling not far away and gunfire even closer, and saw ribbons of smoke. I helped a young soldier to his feet. Florence Nightingale had nothing on me!

I woke up from that thought and went back to work.

• • •

Outside of working hours, I fell again into the world of books for company. I admired Elizabeth Bennett, Jane Eyre, Amy Dorritt and Lily Briscoe: women of integrity and creativity who stood firm in their beliefs, were bold and assertive when necessary, and they would right any wrongs.

I imagined the garments worn, the plain woollen dresses or the high-waisted silk gowns decorated with ribbon and lace; saw the layout of rooms in intricate detail, and almost heard the ticking of clocks and the scuttle of minor characters around me. With stories of high drama, featuring Anna Karenina, Tess D'Urberville, Isabel Archer and other such protagonists, I'd rage against the injustices suffered by women at the hands of male authors, or I'd invent a twist to a happier ending. And have fantasies about a Darcy, a Rochester, a Vronsky, a Petruchio or someone new yet to be named. I so desperately wanted to feel the same fervour the characters did, would endure a tragic ending even, to experience those heightened passions, just once.

• • •

Having given up on the frequent pleading phone calls to my mother, I went through a period of stubborn refusal to keep chasing a prey so unwilling to be caught. I too could be cold and unforgiving. But eventually, on a whim, I decided to take a different tack and so wrote to her every month, outlining the pattern of my days at work, providing details of where I lived, inventing friendships and achievements I'd never experienced. I included brief notes for Marion but never received a reply, assumed Mum threw the letters away unread. I persisted with this for a year, gained a perverse pleasure from being mulish. When an envelope finally arrived with the small, tightly-formed handwriting I recognised, I was almost too anxious to open it. There were two letters inside, one from my mother, the other from Marion. Included was also a cheque for a modest amount that must have cost Mum months of sweat to earn. I skimmed Marion's note first; the handwriting was not at all familiar to me. The words conveyed a catalogue of minor events that filled the days of a normal sixteen-year-old girl and finished with extravagant declarations and a curly flourish: *We've all missed you here. I can't wait to see you again! Mum says you'll come and visit as soon as you can!* It was signed off with a red heart, a well-practised M', and a line of crosses underneath. I laughed, but then choked on a memory of the days of her innocence and her cracked yellow duck.

I turned then to Mum's message of conciliation, words that I knew would have taken an immense effort to write:

Dear Elise, I get your letters every month and like to read about what you've been doing. It's good news, you being a nurse, and I'm glad you like your job. It must be hard work but very interesting. I'm also glad you've made lots of friends there. I'm sorry I didn't write before, but life gets hectic, and I've just been very busy here one way and another. You might be surprised to learn that Jeff is married now. He lives out Blackburn way. It's a long drive but he's on a large property and he's married to Cynthia. She's a nice, pretty young thing. They're expecting later this year. Jeff's been given a management position which he's very pleased about. Craig's doing well too but he travels a lot with work. These past few weeks I've been able to cut back on my hours so I have a bit more free time.

Your grandmother Kath died, a while ago now; we didn't know how to contact you when it happened and anyway, I suppose you wouldn't remember her that well. It was sad, but she'd been sick for such a long while. It would be so nice if you'd find time to visit.

Love, Mum

My stomach fluttered and heaved. I felt a fierce gripping spasm in the centre of my chest and a constriction in my throat; grief for my paternal grandmother, whom I'd loved—the comforting bosom, the warm enfolding arms, the smell and taste of porridge in blue patterned bowls, the armchairs, the armoire, the sea....

I'm made of steel. I don't cry.

I wondered how a family, once broken, could ever find its shape again? Had I finally won the chance to redeem myself, to see forgiveness or understanding in my mother's eyes? Tears of relief and hope criss-crossed my cheeks. The shroud of accumulated losses—of innocence, of family, of my son and my sense of a place in the world—lifted, momentarily.

CHAPTER
THIRTEEN

The year I turned twenty-one, I completed my nursing apprenticeship and was on the way to becoming a registered nurse. I didn't date men but threw myself into more study and work. I experienced a new sense of achievement and purpose. I'd also found an access point back into my mother's life and, I hoped, her heart. I'd written back to her straight away, thanking her for the cheque and for contacting me. I followed this up a week later with a phone call. Since personal calls weren't allowed from the Nurses' Home, I used a phone box near the library, standing inside without any idea of what I was going to say. It was cold inside the booth, though that might have been my anxiety. A disoriented beetle hammered against the grimy glass panels. The smell of years of drunken urine within the confined space was strong. I called the number, not trusting myself to stay calm, so when she answered, it was hard to say more than 'Hello Mum.'

But her voice, unsurprised though tentative, was oddly reassuring. 'Hello Elise. Are you well? Marion's been asking after you a lot and we…I… thought, well I thought if you had some time off, if you came into the city, we could meet? Have lunch? I know it's a bit hard for you to get away, what with your work, but I've got more free time nowadays.'

There was something in the tone of her voice that wasn't familiar but it seemed to signal a fresh start. A thin shaft of sunlight through one glass wall of the booth felt pleasingly warm, comforting. After a few more minutes of polite and conciliatory chat, I replaced the handpiece with care, reassured by its satisfying click.

We'd arranged to meet outside Flinders Street Station on a Saturday afternoon. It was one of those Melbourne days when the temperature rose and fell sharply, unpredictably, while gusts of wind and light drizzle made people accelerate through the streets.

I saw her before she noticed me. She was standing in the middle of a surge of people buzzing around the station's exit. She looked lost, a reduced version of herself. Though it had been five years since I'd seen her, I recognised my mother by her old felt hat, the tilt of her head and the anxious shifting of her feet. She wore a brown woollen skirt and a yellow cardigan that had worn thin on both elbows, and she carried a coat that I knew was at least a dozen years old. Her stockings were loose, the bottoms gathering in small folds around her ankles, and her shoes old but newly shined. Her hair, what I could see of it beneath the hat, was now almost completely grey and her face etched with creases of concern, but when she saw me, the furrows disappeared behind a small, embarrassed smile and she let her eyes stare for a long moment at me. Up close, the greyish-green, smoke-and-moss tint of her irises was still striking, and I saw a welcome tenderness in them.

We embraced awkwardly by the steps of the station, with crowds bumping past us. Her shoulders were bony and thin, and her hair sparser than I remembered. She seemed smaller, depleted, as though a pinprick had released all the air out of her. Melancholy had settled on her like a cloak. The scent of lavender soap and talcum powder was so familiar that I wanted to cry, to bury my nose in her collar, but to do so, when I'd grown taller and she so much smaller, would have looked and felt clumsy. And such a display would have mortified her. We continued to stand self-consciously for a little longer, she a skittish deer and I a block of wood, nowhere near as calm as I pretended to be.

I managed 'Where would you like to go for lunch?' and we walked towards the cathedral, hands occasionally brushing together, and though there were words exchanged while we moved, I can't remember what they were. It was hard now to think of her as 'mother' or 'Mum'. Years and distance had given her a name—Lillian. And here we were, not quite matching steps as we walked, knowing everything yet nothing about each other. We stopped at a small, crowded cafe somewhere on Swanston Street; inside was close with the fug of heaters, damp woollens and wet umbrellas. While our lunch wasn't a great success—stilted, economical conversation, loud music, awful food—it was at least the beginning of a new healing.

• • •

After receiving a second, pleasantly worded invitation from Lillian, I again travelled to Melbourne, this time to the old family home in the suburbs. My anxiety grew as I got closer. The street was smaller than I remembered, though the house looked much the same—a compact structure of once-green weatherboard now faded into dull olive. A low metal fence guarded the front garden. The lawn was roughly mown, patchy, yellowed, and dead in places. Six camellia bushes struggled to provide cheer along the front of the house nearest the porch. Purple hyacinths in a pot gave off their potent sweet, spicy, earthy fragrance. It was August, the end of winter, and the curtains were already drawn against a cold sky. Smoke from the wood-fired heater inside curled and strayed from the brick-and-stone chimney, disappearing with a light breeze. The building sighed and shifted with an air of resigned abandonment.

I imagined its occupants battened down inside, awaiting my arrival with dread. My movements to undo the buttons of my coat and unwind the scarf from my neck were slow, as were my steps onto the porch. I noted the cobwebs that stretched from the edges of the front window to the awnings. An old paisley armchair, which I recognised as Dad's favourite from our previous home, sat stolidly in the corner, facing expectantly towards the street. Several tears in its seat cushion revealed some of the stuffing inside. The arms of the chair were grimy and the original bright colours of the fabric faded, now barely discernible. It was a gloomy and worn memory of a man once of substance. A ginger cat poked its head out from behind an empty pot, stared at me, then moved skittishly across the porch, leapt up and sprinted along the railing before disappearing behind the side fence. These details I took in during the seconds before I cleared my throat and knocked on the door. I stared for a moment at the large, lopsided metal letters on the wood panel above the door declaring 'Hill's View'. How long had that been there? And why? No hills. No view.

I heard light footsteps before someone yanked the door open. Marion—tall, taller than me, but still with dark blond hair—pushed open the screen door and said shyly 'Hi. Hello', then averted her eyes just a fraction before engaging me with a curious, open regard.

As I moved to walk through, Marion, pressing back to hold the door open, reached out a tentative hand to touch me on the shoulder. I took in the sweet, strange smell of her, like ripe plums. We grinned at each other for the longest moment as lost years fell away, and then hugged quickly, clumsily, before separating again. I heard cupboard doors being opened and shut in the kitchen, and the whistle of a kettle. Lillian came into view through the kitchen doorway. Her hair with large stripes of grey was caught up in a small bun. She wore a floral apron, carried a tea towel in one hand and tucked a loose strand of hair behind her ear with the other. Mother and daughter were swift in their mutual appraisement.

'Well,' said Lillian, brisk and efficient. 'You must be hungry. Come and sit down. I've made lunch. We have cake too.'

Unuttered questions hung in the air between us alongside her attempt at a smile.

• • •

I was relieved to see no evidence of Craig or Jeffrey, which made it all infinitely easier, almost pleasant, yet some awkwardness persisted between us. Lillian's voice, its timbre higher, a little quivery as she made small talk, indicated she still lived in her simmering state of fretfulness. She fussed with plates and cups and insisted on refreshing my tea, heaping sugar into it, though I didn't normally drink tea, and sugar gave me a headache. It seemed impolite, almost unkind, to point this out.

Marion, too, appeared ill at ease, unsure of how to behave. In the years I'd been away, she'd become a foreign version of the child I'd once held so dear. We followed the expected conversational path—the weather, my train trip, the neighbour's dog that had been run over the previous week, the latest news on the radio and so on—and in the inevitable lulls, we each concentrated on the sandwiches my mother had prepared. We filled the silence by chewing slowly and deliberately.

'These are tasty, Mum. And what sort of cake is this? It looks delicious. No, please, no more tea. I'll be sloshing all the way home.'

'Oh, but you're staying the night, surely? I've made up a fold-up bed in Jeffrey's old room, or we could put you in with Marion. We were hoping you'd stay.'

I placed my hand over hers on the laminated tabletop to ease its restless fluttering. 'Thanks Mum, but I won't be able to stop over. I've got a shift tomorrow.'

This was a lie and she doubtless guessed. Her small sigh, a rapid movement of her eyes towards the door, suggested so.

'I'll get the train back tonight. But thanks.'

While Mum's shoulders seemed to sag a little in disappointment, her eyes displayed, for just a second, a hint of relief.

I turned my attention again to Marion. She wore a dark green woollen skirt, and a white blouse that gaped a little near the buttons, where the fabric stretched taut over her impressive bosom. Her hair, still a thick, dark gold, was tied back in a ponytail. Her face was round and her skin luminous— clear, smooth, with just a hint of tan. She looked, she *was,* young and fresh, like a ripe peach.

I reached to touch her hand. 'So I heard you did well at school last year. You've started a new job? Clerical work?'

Marion's wide, expressive eyes turned away from her crumb-scattered plate towards me again. They were a shade of milk chocolate, similar to our father's. She spoke with spirit, her voice loud in the small confines of the room, stirring what I thought of as dead air.

She said, 'I really like it there. The people are so nice. And I'm going to secretarial school at night. They're even paying for me to do that. It's great!' She reached for another slice of cake. 'I can type really well, can't I Mum?' Specks of icing attached to her upper lip as she worked the food to one side in her mouth so she could continue speaking. 'And I'm learning shorthand.'

My mother's pride was evident in the way her face softened whenever she looked at Marion, in the way she attended to the crumbs from around her daughter's plate, and in her voice. 'She's with one of the top insurance companies. She was lucky to get in. And she's got a lot of friends at the night school, haven't you dear?'

A small part of me felt a stab of envy in that moment, seeing their solidarity, their unbroken history together, the small jokes they shared and the ease they enjoyed in each other's company. I thought too of the chances that Marion had that I hadn't, at her age, and I could feel the worm of this envy pulsing beneath my skin.

Despite this momentary lapse, the rest of the afternoon brought intervals of contentment, thanks in part to Marion, whose appetite for harmony matched her enthusiasm for food. After lunch, she took me into her room, the one we used to share. I'd been nervous, imagining it would still hold the stink of my shame. Now there was just a single bed, a lamp, several bright cushions, a small bookcase, and a desk covered by magazines, papers, a pen-holder, several unwashed mugs, and a solid Hermes typewriter. A large poster of Bobby Darin covered part of the newly-painted cream wall where the crucifix had once hung. On another wall was Elvis. She showed me her photograph albums against the background noise of Lillian clearing the table and washing up. The old copper pipes hammered in the kitchen as they always had. Once Marion had talked me through snapshots of herself with her seemingly endless stream of friends, she opened her wardrobe and brought out various clothes she loved and her new pair of high-heeled shoes. Her animation allowed me to relax and soon we were laughing over an absurd joke she'd recently heard. At one point, as we sat together, she put her head on my shoulder and poked me in the ribs, that familiar gesture I'd always treasured. I wanted to ask her questions, but not receive the answers I feared.

Our mother came to the doorway. 'Trevor's on the phone.'

Marion dashed out to take the call. I looked at Mum enquiringly. Her eyes reflected amusement. 'That's her boyfriend. She's been seeing him for a while now. Nice young man. He works at the car detailer's place in Templestowe.'

I waited, perched on the end of the single bed, running a hand over the bright blue chenille bedspread to smooth it down. I picked at a loose thread, discomforted once again, trying not to let in any memories—the agreeable or the terrible. Mum sat down next to me, interpreting my gesture as an invitation.

She picked up my hand with both of hers and held it in a surprisingly firm clasp, glanced at me, then spoke to the floor. 'Well, I'm glad you came. It's nice to see you.' She looked up then, directly into my eyes, studying me without wavering. It surprised me to see that frank, naked earnestness. I loved her the more for it.

'Me too, I'm…well, it's…it's good to see you. Thank you.' My eyes started to itch.

She took a breath. 'You know, it's been a long time, and, well, I'm sorry that things happened the way they did.'

'Yes Mum, so am I.'

Just then, the screen door at the back of the house creaked open then slammed shut. We both jumped. My mother sprang to her feet and smoothed down her skirt with some agitation. 'That'll be your…' She halted and avoided my eyes, though I was trying to send her an imploring message. 'That'll be Craig. He's back early. I'll just go and…' She left.

'Lil? Where are you?' A masculine interrogation under which the walls and the ceiling seemed to contract.

I waited in the bedroom. When Marion had finished her phone call—a conversation punctuated periodically with hoots of loud guffawing—she returned to suggest that we walk to the corner store, since she was in the mood for ice-cream. She also wanted to show me the new sports stadium.

'It's not far away. They used it for some of the Olympic events. You should have been here Elise. It was a fantastic time. All those athletes! Me and my friends, we'd go there really early or after school, and wait outside to try and catch someone famous to get their autographs. I got two. I'll show you later.' She grabbed my hand and pulled me up and to the door.

In the hallway, Marion called out to the closed kitchen, 'We're just going to the shops. Won't be long', and hooked her arm through mine.

As we hurried towards the front door, I stared ahead, waiting for a movement, waiting for someone to object. I heard a chair scrape and braced myself, but there was nothing more, other than the low murmur of a male voice, the sound of running water, and a cup meeting its saucer. Relief. Anger. Disappointment. Sorrow. An urgent desire for revenge. All these feelings converged in me.

Outside with Marion, after ice creams, I was a coward and asked her to tell Mum I'd had to rush from the shop to catch my train and would write next week.

•••

Afterwards, when I was back in Niburu, Marion and I spoke regularly on the phone, though we never stayed on for too long—distance phone calls were so expensive. Lillian wrote each month, and in our exchanges, we skirted around the corners of our little lives, filling our pages with details that would have been boring to anyone else, and expressing polite concern for the other. No doubt we were each supremely grateful for what was not said.

I met Marion once later that year in Melbourne, in a small deli near where she worked in King Street. She'd lost a little weight by then and sounded happy, comfortable and at ease with whatever was happening for her. While we waited for our meal, I asked, casually, 'How's Mum doing? She sounds a little stressed. Do you hear from Jeffrey?'

'Well, Mum's still working too hard, but you know that because she writes to you. I wish she'd do something else instead of those awful cleaning jobs, but she says they're saving to put new tiles on the roof. I think she just can't help herself. They've got the money, but she never spends any. Not on me at least, and certainly not on herself. You've seen her clothes! Jeff's wife Cynthia is pretty dumb. I can't stand her. She's not much to look at either, but she thinks she's something else. I bet their baby'll grow up to be ugly. We don't see them much because Jeff's always travelling around the countryside.'

'What does he do again? Mum told me, but I've forgotten.'

'Sales. Sells air conditioners or freezers or something. And he's doing some kind of trade too. Electrics? God, I wish we had some cooling at home in the summer. He won't get us one though.'

'And Craig?', the word ugly in my mouth. I avoided looking at her, turning gratefully as the waitress brought our food.

'Oh him, he's just like always.' Her voice low, she looked away and fixed her gaze on passersby outside.

Her statement did nothing to reassure me. I spooned some soup into my mouth, scalding my tongue.

'He comes and goes like Jeff. He's moved into some high-falutin' job now but that means he has to travel lots to different plants around the state. There's one in Coolaroo, another in Smithfield, I think.' Her voice dropped again in volume as she lowered her eyes and spoke to her plate. 'I prefer it when he's away. It's just easier. Mum's more fun to be around when he's not here, and I can do pretty much what I like when he's gone.'

Then she straightened up and waved her hand in dismissal before grabbing mine across the table. A taut expression crossed her face, before she slid on a mask of attentiveness. 'But I want to hear about your boyfriends. Tell me everything! I've met someone nice at the office. He's twenty-eight and really gorgeous, though he's just broken up with someone. I think he might even have been married before. Isn't that scandalous? Don't say anything to Mum.'

'What happened to Trevor?'

'Oh, Trevor. He was just too, I don't know, too young for me. I'm thinking of moving out with some girlfriends and getting a place away from here, closer to work. Can I have the rest of that bread if you're not going to finish it? Mum reckons I'm too plump, but she hardly feeds me anything at home. Guess what! Someone down the street got a television last week. It doesn't show anything except test patterns, but…' And on, and on.

CHAPTER FOURTEEN

In the hospital, I was making something of a name for myself as a competent emergency ward nurse and a useful person to have in the geriatric ward. I cleaned up their spills, dealt with their incontinence and managed their flights of fancy without complaint. I taught trainee nurses how to make beds with perfect tight corners, move patients without causing them pain, give injections, take blood, maintain charts, clean wounds, help set bones, soothe nerves, and all the other basic procedures that were now second nature to me. I moved up through the next tiers and gained some recognition from the senior staff, which occasionally translated into an overarching pleasantness.

I still didn't date anyone, just threw myself into the work, determined to prove that I could at least manage it well, and, at best, perhaps excel at something. I loved my job more than I wanted a complication in life. Certain doctors, even the married ones, would ask me out to dinner, or sometimes just suggest a hotel, or even an equipment room somewhere in the hospital, but I knew they'd already asked a dozen prettier nurses before me. Besides, I had no interest in returning to those sorts of regrets. And I saw from the swagger of those men that I'd be forgotten as a conquest by the following day. Over time, I'm sure many considered me haughty and aloof, since I kept to myself and didn't socialise after work. But if people commented behind my back, or ignored me, it didn't matter.

Much worse things have happened. I'm strong. I don't cry.

I moved into a different stale little boarding house within walking distance of work. The predominant smell here was of cigarettes, wet laundered sheets and burnt toast. Mrs Phipps, the landlady, provided adequate meals and a warm welcome, but the amenities were basic. An outdoor privy made night trips hazardous, and I had to share a bathroom with three other tenants. I frequently lost my battle with the stuttering shower and its rusty head that spurted erratically over the brown-stained bath, so I'd resort to washing myself instead with soap and a facecloth at the sink. I still had no close friends. Samantha had long before moved away. I heard she'd married and had another child. By and large, I found the company of acquaintances unfulfilling. I expect they thought the same about me.

Each night in my small, cramped room, which was stuffed to capacity with a creaking single bed, an upright chair, a desk and a huge mahogany wardrobe, my fantasy world kept me company. It helped to cleanse away the grimness and the grime, the wounds I'd tended, the blood and smells and puke and sadness and fear I'd been witness to that day. Despite drifting with little trouble into sleep, I still woke every morning with teeth clenched and a jaw that ached.

• • •

Within the confines of the white walls of the hospital, I enjoyed the routine and order that can be created out of chaos: the smell of antiseptic, the brisk chatter of nurses, the low murmuring of patients, the clatter of trolleys and hum of machines. Satisfaction came from the tasks, the lists, the fixing, doing, mending, soothing, listening. Now and again I'd see solutions, calmness or comedy where others perceived panic, see hope when others saw only tragedy. I was no Florence Nightingale but did my best and embraced being needed.

'Nurse, I need a bedpan!'

'Righto, Mrs Gladstone. Be there in a tic!'

'Nurse Brown, Doctor Macintosh is waiting for you in 12B. Have you prepared his patient for surgery this afternoon? Take these charts to him, quickly. And you're supposed to be getting the man in 6A ready to for X-Ray.'

'Yes, I...'

'Nurse!! A bedpan, please.'

'All right Mrs Gladstone, here I am. I'll just close the curtain for you. Here, let me help you onto this thing. Can you shift forward a bit? That's the way.'

'Brown! Get moving. Doctor Macintosh doesn't have all day.'

'Certainly, Sister.' I could move quickly but still idly imagine what it would be like to be Audrey Hepburn.

Little about the rush and clamour and stench of the wards bothered me. I let the bossiness of the senior staff wash over me and allowed the demands of patients who complained to go the same way. I practised a countenance of good cheer until it became real; I placated, cooed and winked, striding efficiently from task to task. The persona I presented was composed and confident, which gave relief to most of my charges and irritated some of my peers.

'And how are you this morning, Mr Carter? Ready to have a wash? Oh, I see you haven't finished your breakfast. Want me to help you?'

'Yes thanks, love, that'd be good, but only if you've got the time. I know how busy you nurses are.'

'Always got time for you!' I pulled up a chair and started to cut his fruit into smaller pieces.

'I'll have some of that cereal first, if you don't mind, love.'

Clive Carter's hands shook wildly, a permanent by-product of the lithium that he'd been prescribed on and off for the previous decade. From the birthdate on his notes, it was clear that he'd been only a lad, still in his teens, when he joined the military, and had returned after the war physically intact but mentally a wreck. Now in his forties, he'd just been told he had bladder cancer.

I settled into light-hearted chat as I spooned food into his mouth. Up this close, I could study his eyes. They were dark brown and troubled, set under bushy, grey-sprinkled eyebrows and a head of dark hair gone grey at the sides. I leant in to wipe a small dribble from the side of his mouth as he swallowed. We paused a moment to consider each other further.

He smiled and said, 'You're very kind, nurse. What's your name again?' and peered at my badge. 'Nurse Brown. Well, why don't you tell me something about yourself, Nurse Brown?'

I chuckled. 'There's not much to tell, really. I'd rather hear about you.' I wanted to stay linked to his eyes.

'Well, they're planning to cut my prick off sometime this week. Too bad I didn't get to use it much.' A pause. 'Sorry dear, shouldn't be rude!'

'Oh, they won't do that, Mr Carter. The procedure you'll be having is called a cystectomy. Didn't the doctor explain? It's taking a bit of your intestine and…'

He waved a hand in front of his face and spoke gruffly. 'I know what it is, just don't want it. The things they do to a man!' He took another spoonful of soggy cereal and mashed it thoughtfully before waving the next proffered spoon away.

I shifted in my chair and gave him an open face, always keen to hear other people's stories. 'Are you married, Mr Carter? Have you got family here?' I supported his head and neck as he struggled to lean back onto the pillow.

'Only got married eight years ago, bit of a late starter. Told you, didn't get to use my pecker for that long and now they're gonna fiddle with it! Oh, the wife's coming in later.'

'That's good! Any children?'

The gruffness was replaced by a wide smile. 'You bet! Two little darlins'! Two boys. Named 'em after me grandfathers—one's Harry and the other's Stephen.'

'Nice names! Bet they keep you busy then.' And I stayed chatting for a while, caught up in those eyes like softened caramel.

But there were also times when my confident persona crumbled a little. Or a lot. Working with babies—so tiny, so innocent, so vulnerable—that was hard. Seeing death on a regular basis didn't get easier either, just less frightening. Sometimes I'd tend a young child with a smashed shoulder or blood streaming from a wound to the head, and the fear in their eyes reminded me of things better forgotten.

My soft and soothing approach with the sick and healing wasn't entirely altruistic. Being busy, being useful, provided a distraction from demons that frequently gnawed away at my insides, images not easily dispatched by quiet daytime reveries. The dream world that had sustained me before, and which was still able, when combined with exhaustion, to rock me to sleep at night, was sometimes no match for the furtive scratching behind my breastbone.

• • •

But I was happy then, Sophie, mostly. I loved my job. It felt right for me. Of course I missed my mother, I missed Marion, and sometimes the bad, the sad memories attacked me, but books, a few acquaintances, my busy schedule at work, a vague keep-fit program, and my imagination and dreamworld all kept me from feeling too lonely. And I had my work; it was the thing that kept me going.

My memory is still very clear about certain events and the feelings accompanying them; they've stayed with me, and they still feel so real. I hope it all makes sense to you.

Did I tell you that two people died here last week from the virus? I just hope you don't get sick from being with all those patients. At least we can still talk on the phone. Thank you for all you do.

CHAPTER FIFTEEN

Life changed, and me with it.

Despite doing well with my job in Niburu, I'd become restless. When I found an advertisement for nursing positions at a large Melbourne hospital, I applied and was successful. I rented a room in an old boarding house not far from the hospital. Because I owned very few possessions, the move was smooth enough. I could borrow the landlady's bike to get around, so I toured those parts of the city I'd never had a chance to know, and often rode into work. The hospital offered additional on-the-job training, which I took up enthusiastically. Another plus was that I got along well with and respected my colleagues.

Shortly after I first arrived, I contacted the Children's Welfare Department, hoping to locate the adoption agency that took away my son. I was told they wouldn't provide information over the phone, and I'd have to come in person to complete the appropriate forms. On a beautifully warm Spring morning, I found myself in a straight-backed wooden chair under the indifferent gaze of a suited-up man not much older than me, who fiddled with his pen and blew his nose noisily into a crumpled handkerchief while I answered all his questions.

At the end of the interrogation, he said, 'This was a closed adoption, you know.' His voice was high yet censorious. 'Rules are changing, but at the time you had the baby, there were many more restrictions.'

'It wasn't so very long ago.' Resolution began leaking out of me.

'Yes, but the laws exist to protect the rights of the child and the adoptive parents.'

I noted his red cheeks that fed off his bluster, his officiousness. His fingernails, bitten short, caught my gaze while his eyes wandered to the wall behind me. The room was stuffy, the windows closed tight against the fresh air outside.

'I'm sure you understand Miss, ah, Miss…,' he mumbled as he scanned the papers on his desk.

I volunteered, 'Brown. Elise Brown. I just want to know something, anything, about my son, see if he's all right. And give you my details again, because I'm at a new address. In case they…in case he might one day want to meet me.' My voice cracked, the final sigh, another defeat.

'Well, I'll send these forms through and someone will contact you about the outcome, but for now, that's it. Nothing more we can do here.' His smile was between awkward and smug. He stood. 'Watch your step on the way out, Miss Brown.'

Moving through the doorway, I lowered my head to hide my anger. *Stupid arse! Holier than thou, with his shiny shoes and his shiny suit. And the way he said 'Miss'. Condescending bastard.*

• • •

I met Mark in the early autumn of 1960. We'd each gone alone to a darkened cinema, and were separated by several unoccupied seats. The film had a chariot race and gladiators—that much I can remember. And I know it was a Monday, my day off work that week. I also remember finding out after the film about the Sharpeville Massacre in South Africa. But in the dark, I was oblivious and content to be there on my own.

At one point the film reel broke and the lights came up. People took advantage of the pause to talk, stretch their legs and purchase drinks or ice-creams. I decided to duck out to the bathroom, but was in such a hurry, I tripped over the outstretched legs of the man sitting at the end of my row. He reached with his arm to help steady me as I lurched forwards.

'You okay?' His voice was solid, strong, like the bulk of him but not in any way threatening.

I nodded, embarrassed by my awkwardness, and hurried up the aisle. When I returned minutes later, he smiled and stood to give me room to pass.

'Sorry about before. These long legs of mine always get me into trouble.'

He had an open smile and a steady gaze. In brushing past him this time, I took a quick inventory: sandy-coloured hair, the dark eyes that seemed, in the dimming light, to be flecked with dots of amber, not unlike mine. Even when he sat down again, he was a tall presence.

Before I reached my seat, he patted the one beside him, leaned towards me with enquiring eyebrows, and whispered, 'Would you care to join me? Can I buy you a soft drink before the film starts up?'

And by then, aware that I felt so desperately, achingly lonely, I said yes. This time, I was bought for the price of a cola and a smile. We sat without speaking for the rest of the film.

Our courtship was swift, intense. Mark was a practical man, well-educated, with a sense of fun, and a straight-forward, no-nonsense way; he had a confidence born from privilege and luck, though not the arrogance that often accompanied such things. I thought him very handsome and intelligent, considerate and outgoing, and for these things I was both surprised and grateful. He seemed not to notice my flaws, although perhaps I'd become more adept at covering them. He showed interest in what I had to say, sought my opinion, introduced me to his friends and family with something that might have been pride, and was affectionate in public and private. I couldn't believe my good fortune. My real world had finally caught up with the fantasy one.

• • •

Mark had trained as a civil engineer. When we met, he'd just celebrated his appointment with the project management team of a well-established firm in the city. He was twenty-seven, bright, positive and full of ambition. I initially felt he was too much out of my league, but he was so convincing in his happiness around me—flowers, romance, and his natural *joie de vivre*—that it was easy to put those doubts aside. We spent as much time as possible together within the constraints of our respective jobs. His friends became *our* friends, and people commented on what a pretty smile I had, now that I displayed it more often.

I made an effort to befriend people at work, and my role in the newly-formed Nurses' Union also opened up a wider network. Finally I belonged somewhere.

Even Mark's parents seemed to quite like me. We usually visited them once a fortnight at their elegant home in Toorak, and while they were always welcoming and pleasant whenever we came, their smiles seemed to fall graciously from the lofty height of affluence. Other times we'd drive over to Richmond—a suburb that was heavy with factories, clinker brick duplexes and hard-working migrants from southern Europe—to pick up Mum and Marion and take them out for a quick dinner. On those occasions, with Mark beside me, I could cope with the possibility of seeing Craig from a distance, but he never showed up when he knew we were coming, and I was relieved about that.

'Why won't you introduce me to your father?' Mark asked once, after we'd dropped Mum and Marion back home.

'We don't get on. We haven't spoken for years. Anyway, he's my step-father. He treated my mother, all of us, appallingly when I was a child. He still controls her, makes her life miserable. I'm reading between the lines, but that's what I believe.'

He shot me a curious look as he eased the car away from the kerb. 'Why does she stay with him?'

I shrugged.

'Isn't it about time you made up with him? You said you'd gotten over a hurdle with your mum, whatever that was about.'

'That's different; she's my mother. I understand her better now. I told you my real father left when I was very young. Mum's had a terrible time since, and I don't know why she stays with that man, but I don't want to be anywhere near him.'

'You've turned out okay, haven't you? He can't have been that bad.'

Rain spattered on the windscreen in clunky drops and sprayed the road outside; the car's wipers scraped across the glass, leaving uneven smears of grime. The reflection of streetlights in the oily puddles on the road became my focus.

He studied me for a moment longer while I stared straight ahead, fixing my attention now on the squeak of the wipers. His voice was soft. 'Elise, do yourself a good turn, and let people *in* sometimes.'

I turned to look at him, but he was peering forwards through the back-and-forth of the windscreen wipers. The lights from an oncoming car gave him a pale glow, making him look almost ghostly.

'I'm sorry. There's just a lot of, a whole lot of history that I'm trying to forget. Between the two of them, Craig and my brother, they made things, well, vile. Honestly, I don't want to talk about it.'

Mark raised his hands momentarily above the steering wheel in a gesture of surrender. He knew my tone well enough to drop the subject, so he turned on the car radio. In a few seconds he was singing rowdily, purposefully out of tune, banging a rhythm on the steering wheel with one slender hand. By the time we returned to his flat, he'd coaxed much mirth out of me, and once we were inside, I lost myself in his playful, amorous advances.

This part of our lives together was always a delight. I was now particularly well placed to know about the latest in contraceptive measures, so it was a relief when Mark and I were able to abandon the unsatisfactory and unreliable condom or withdrawal method when the pill was made available that year. (My diaphragm had long since perished, unused, dried up and split in the bottom of a drawer.) Several months of exquisitely relaxed lovemaking with this new safeguard came to an abrupt end when I discovered I was eight weeks pregnant. When I told Mark, his face was a patchwork of shock, bewilderment and pride mixed with dashed hopes.

'You're not serious? You're on the pill. How could it have happened?' Dismay might have been behind his voice dropping an octave.

While I was to an extent now street-wise, cunning had never really been my forte, so in truth, deceit was the furthest thing from my mind. The idea of another child, even in these very different circumstances, terrified me. I was as bemused as he was.

After a long pause, I said, 'Remember how I was so sick after your parents' anniversary party? Perhaps it was a bad oyster at their buffet? I only just made it to the bathroom in time. Once we got back to your place, I felt fine, and we…'. My weak smile disappeared.

'So much for the new wonder drug.' His face, though somewhat relaxed, still held a hint of a grimace before he hugged me.

Thus it was that I never had my dream Grace Kelly-style wedding, and reality proved once again to be no match for my imagination. Our marriage was arranged hastily and performed perfunctorily in a quiet registry office with only two of Mark's friends as witnesses. In the few photos taken that day, I'm smiling nervously—Mark would say smugly—in my new yellow dress and jacket, and standing, on reflection, like an awkward, elongated canary, while Mark wears a tight smile and an air of resignation. His suit is crumpled to match his mood.

He moved out of his rented apartment and I out of my little room at the boarding house. His parents loaned us enough money for a deposit on a house and passed on some of their excess or unwanted furniture, all the while displaying tight lips and a censorious manner. They'd wanted more for their son, presumably someone of standing who came from a well-to-do family of some status.

Mark's sense of entrapment was clear in his increased moodiness, clipped speech, and silences that held weight; these all persisted for several weeks. It was not the best way to start a marriage. His suspicions about how he came to be in this *predicament* and what he saw as his thwarted ambitions, both personal and professional, inevitably altered our relationship. At a time when I might otherwise have indulged in a natural delight to be carrying this child, Mark's clear resentment during the early months of my pregnancy quashed any real joy, fostering instead a very palpable apprehension in me that something would go terribly wrong. I felt queasy and anxious, more linked to what my body remembered about pregnancy and birth than to actual morning sickness. I tried to economise, trawling around thrift shops for maternity wear and baby things, buying cheaper cuts of meat, walking instead of catching the bus to work. Mark worked longer hours; we dropped our weekly movie night. Mark's mother, Deidre, would ring every week, and if I answered, she'd often remind me in unsubtle ways how he'd so enjoyed his single status.

'Oh, he's still at work, dear? Poor boy. He used to have so much more free time. Always off playing tennis or meeting friends.'

But I didn't need Deidre to remind me that I always felt as if I was a disappointment to somebody, everybody.

Once again, I was obliged to hide a swelling belly, this time from my employers, but inevitably my condition became apparent and I was forced to leave that job that I'd grown to value. Then followed almost four months of waiting—waiting for Mark to further soften further and accept what was happening, waiting to meet this little developing being, and retreating once more to my Wonderland. The scope of my daydreams broadened. In these, I travelled the world, healed the sick in the remotest of areas, starred in *West Side Story*, sang with perfect pitch at the Metropolitan Opera House in New York or married a man who was thrilled at the prospect of a child. Back in the real world, I tried to please my husband by behaving as I read a worthy wife was supposed to behave. I created economical but tasty meals (served on time), read all the Good Housekeeping guides in magazines from the library, and ensured there was no clutter around the house. I wore make-up, did my hair nicely and left decision-making to him as Master of the House. This latter approach didn't work so well, since one of the things he'd admired about me to begin with was my independent spirit. Eventually we reached some version of a compromise: he let go of his resentment and became more interested in the idea of a baby and in my well-being; I regained his trust and more of my old spark and fire. The truce brought with it tenderness on both sides.

But I was bored. I shopped, cleaned, sorted and cooked, took walks to the library and the park, read with one hand propped protectively on my belly. And when not entering other people's fictional lives in books, I continued to indulge in my own expansive daydreams.

CHAPTER SIXTEEN

Phone calls from my mother, though more regular, were commonly short and succinct.

'Elise, I'm in Shepparton. Your Aunt Helen's had a bad fall. I'll put her on and you can talk to her. She's sitting up in bed and she wants to hear your voice.'

Sigh.

A few weeks after this, she rang again, this time from Adelaide. Her voice was calm, brisk.

'Your grandfather died Elise, I'm sorry to say, but it was a blessing in the end. He'd been ill for months, and, well, not himself. I had to arrange the funeral quickly; it was just a small service, a few neighbours and a cousin. Helen couldn't come, with her hip and all. I'll let you know when I'm back home. There's still a lot of his things to sort through. The place here is in such a mess; he was a bit of a hoarder, you know. Your uncle did his best to clean up, but it's different, isn't it, for the men.'

I knew they'd been estranged, on and off, for many years. I'd not really known her father, having only met him occasionally, but I have a vague memory of a tall, rangy, bald man with calloused hands that he rubbed vigorously against the skin of my arms and chucked me on the chin with determined grandfatherliness. I braced myself, not for the contact, but for the wave of forced cheer it was meant to summon. And he had a terrible cough from having worked in the copper mines in Moonta from a young age. My memory tells me it used to make him double over, barking like he might crack in half. The sound was sharp, brittle. It scared me and sent the adults in the room scurrying for a bowl or something else for him to spit into.

Her news reminded me of a school project I once had, for which I was to prepare a talk about all my grandparents and draw a family tree. I needed Mum's help with that. She told me then that her father's family were from Cornwall. All the men had been miners, going back generations, and her father had emigrated with a group of others hoping for better pay and conditions. In the library, I read about the conditions of the workers, which were hardly better than in Cornwall. The men had to work underground, 700 metres or more down, with shafts and tunnels that could stretch for eighty miles. I learnt that the local cemetery was full of hundreds of people, mainly infants and children, who'd died of measles or dysentery because of the poor sanitation and lack of fresh drinking water. There'd also been typhoid, cholera and diphtheria epidemics around Moonta in the 1870s. I remember that project so well! I worked hard on it, even as it made me sad and indignant.

But I digress. When I couldn't think of anything to say, Mum continued, unusually chatty. Liberated perhaps! 'You didn't get to know your grandfather, Elise, but I'll tell you. He was a Methodist, or claimed to be, and was very strict—far too hard on Helen and me and Bobby. You know, Elise, we had to fast every week, dress as plain as could be. He allowed no singing, nor dancing, nor music. Those men from the mines, they pretended to shun any form of gambling, but most were never shy of betting on the horses or the cock fighting. And he drank, and smoked, and didn't shed a tear, not that I ever saw at least, when my dear mother died of the tuberculosis.'

I was sad to hear that about Mum's earlier life and realized how little I really knew. I hoped the old man had, before he died, forgiven her for having first married a Catholic and then *living in sin* with Craig.

Two weeks later, I phoned her back. 'Hello Mum.'

'Marion! Where are you? I've been looking out the window for you for hours!'

'It's Elise, Mum.'

'Oh, I thought you…Well, you sounded just like her then.'

Heaven forbid.

She continued. 'I'm worried about her. She should have been here by now. I've got her dinner waiting. She usually calls if she's going to be late.'

'Mum, I've got some news.'

A pause. A long breath, which I imagined moved warily through pinched nostrils. 'Oh Elise.' The heaviness in that sound.

'It's good news, Mum. Mark and I are married. We're going to have a baby.'

'You're married?'

'We didn't want a big wedding, but we're happy with how things have turned out. Sorry we didn't contact you, but you were so busy with Helen and granddad and, well, it was just a very small affair, and,' my affability tripped out with ease. 'we're buying a house. Can you believe it? I hope you'll be happy for us.'

'When's it due?'

I hesitated. 'September.'

I expected to hear that old familiar grate of disappointment in her voice, but she surprised me then by sounding light and accommodating: 'Well, I suppose you'll be wanting some help when the time comes. Marion will help too. You know she adores babies.'

I hadn't known that; in fact I doubted it was true. 'Yes, yes of course. I'd appreciate that.'

'How are you feeling then, Elise? Are you well enough?'

'I'm over the nausea now. I'm filling out. We're both very excited.'

'Well, that's nice, that's good. Come and visit when you have the chance. Give my congratulations to Mark. I have to go, Elise, sorry! Marion might be trying to get through. I'd better hang up.'

'Sure. I'll call you next week, okay?

CHAPTER SEVENTEEN

My second son was born on his due date, and, unlike my first experience, this boy's birth was a time of joy and celebration. The labour was shorter and much less traumatic, the nurses who came and went, some of whom I knew, were thoughtful and efficient; the doctor was brisk, friendly and focused. The baby slid out of me in one final whoosh, blue and mottled, bloodied and still, then without delay set up a startled cry and shook his tiny fists at the room in defiance. Of what? The life to come? Surprise and relief overtook me and I reached for him greedily, placed him on my chest and stared with awe into his beautiful, speckled and bewildered face.

Mark, who'd waited outside, burst through the doors as soon as he was allowed to see us. He beamed, ecstatic; all the qualms and resentments that he'd let fester over earlier months disappeared as soon as he laid eyes on our now sleeping son. I felt his kiss on my forehead as he cupped one hand around the back of my head and gawped with astonishment at this little person we'd produced.

He laughed. 'Hard to believe it had all happened because of one bad oyster,' and kissed me again. The baby's tiny hand grasped one of Mark's own long, slender fingers. 'Paul. Paul James Michael, middle names of my father and grandfather.'

I was too tired, too relieved to object and had scarcely thought of names for a boy. No matter. I would name the next child, and the next.

Holding my child, my perfectly formed, perfectly innocent son, provided a well-spring of exhilaration. At last, I had something so innocent, so pure, so very much *mine*. But at the same time, I felt the tug of loss for my other boy, an acute ache that I'd never get to know and love him too. And the haunting shame and fear from earlier times returned for just a moment, scrambling through my innards.

'Elise? No need to cry. Come on now.' Mark hugged me and the baby, patted us, enveloped us in his warmth and pride, so that right in that moment I forgot to be afraid. Instead, I experienced a surge of relief, triumph, achievement and raw joy at the impossible fact of this new being. My son.

• • •

In those first weeks with the baby, I was almost too frightened to carry him for fear of breaking him. I'd reach out a tentative hand while he was sleeping in his crib to touch his tiny, pulsing skull, to check his breathing, to feel his heart beat. He looked so delicate but when I held him, my embrace was often tight enough that he squirmed and struggled and finally cried. He was the most perfect infant I'd ever seen. His skin, so like pink marbled satin, was yet to be filled with joyful plumpness. I loved stroking the softness of him. His face in repose was enigmatic, full of calm secrets, yet when he opened his large eyes, he appeared ready to reveal them all. He gazed up at me with such trust I sometimes had to look away. He smelt of milky warmth, lilac and innocence.

Lillian came to stay for a week soon after Paul's birth. She shopped, prepared the evening meals, tidied and cleaned the house and took over the seemingly endless loads of washing. She did these things efficiently, in a somewhat distant, preoccupied manner, as an employed housekeeper might.

'Mum, sit down for a bit. Take a break. There's no need for you to be doing everything. I can manage, truly.'

'You need your rest. I'll be gone soon enough and then it'll be over to you. Here, give me the baby, he needs to be burped.'

'No really, I can do that Mum, please.' The inevitable tussle over Paul began. Someone was always taking him out of my arms and telling me to rest. I grew weary of the advice offered by Lillian, Mark, both his parents, Mark's friends who dropped by, the district nurse, the neighbours and acquaintances who arrived with chocolates and flowers, casseroles and knitted booties. Much of the counsel was contradictory anyway. I was certainly tired, that was true, though I longed for a stretch of time alone with my boy so we could get to know each other, and I could keep him all to myself.

Nevertheless, despite small resentments at the intrusions, I appreciated the neighbourly gestures and all the help my mother gave, overjoyed that our relationship had improved so much. When the time came for Lillian to leave, I contrarily felt abandoned. Mark was back at work. The neighbours stopped calling by. The district nurse declared the baby 'bonny', informed me that I'd healed well, and didn't return. The house became close with the gathering warmth of an early summer. Looking around, with Paul lightly swaddled in my arms and sucking contently on his fist, I felt that each room had the stamp of a stranger. While the place was spotless, courtesy of Lillian, it still didn't feel as if it was my own.

When we'd first married, as well as providing funds to help us purchase the house, Mark's parents had again loaned us money, specifically to buy a new fridge, a lounge, a dining setting, and a double bed. Mark had selected modern Scandinavian designs, items with sleek, functional lines, not of a style I liked. I appreciated their generosity, but resented the uncomfortable chairs and the high, hard bed Mark had chosen.

Being a wife and mother wasn't what I'd imagined. The corners of Mark's easy-going nature as a bachelor had rubbed away. He developed a slightly brittle demeanour, except when he played with Paul, held him up in the air and chattered: 'My little man, my full-forward champ. Who's gonna play for the Hawks one day, hey?'

He looked at me was as if I'd become someone entirely new, someone distant and strange. He was polite, cordial and occasionally affectionate, but he turned his head away whenever I released a breast to feed Paul; turned his body away in bed when I tried to put my arm around him before sleep.

Over time, the physical intimacy that had been so frequent and enjoyable before the pregnancy became sporadic, merely a physical imperative for Mark when he was restless. Under his dispassionate eye, I grew self-conscious of my changed body, and embarrassed when rebuffed in my renewed, if timid, attempts to seduce him. Perhaps my role as mother, and all that accompanied it, supplanted all other identities for him.

I did my best to raise a healthy and happy baby. Some of it was instinctive, some terrifyingly strange. Paul wasn't a demanding child, but I was in awe of the mysteries encased in his tiny body. Most evenings, Mark and I rarely retired to bed at the same time. He watched television till late, listened to the radio or read newspapers, while I tried to get to bed early, anticipating another gruelling night ahead with a hungry, sometimes colicky baby, a snoring spouse, or my own night sweats produced by fearful dreams. Often, Mark found me curled up in exhausted sleep on a couch in the living room or on the floor of Paul's bedroom. Every day was a cycle of feeding, changing, settling, pacing with the baby, laundry, cleaning, shopping, cooking, tidying, walking Paul in his pram and anxiously checking his breathing. On the rare occasions that all chores were finished, I read, though had little energy for it. When I looked at the baby food I was cooking, straining and mashing, I imagined the inside of my head was just like that: mush.

When Paul was five months old, Marion visited for a weekend and Mark turned on the charm. He cracked jokes, affectionately patted me on the behind, held out my own and Marion's chairs before we sat down to dinner and helped in the kitchen while I washed up and Marion played absentmindedly with the baby. Her visit slipped by well enough, and without drama. I was grateful for the company, the extra pair of hands, though Marion was not practical or helpful, and soon became just another person to look after.

Before she left, Marion stood on the front veranda, holding Paul up and cooing to him. 'Aren't you just too adorable? I'm gonna miss you! You'll have all the girls swooning when you grow up.'

She called to me as I carried her overnight bag to the car, 'When can I come back and see him? He's too beautiful and I'm completely in love with him.' She held him out, well away from her, to avoid his drool, as she walked towards me.

I dropped her bag, took Paul from her fidgety hands and jiggled him as Mark strolled down the path smiling at Marion.

I said, 'You can come back any time, you know that. Hey, we have to hurry or you'll miss your train. Hop in the car while I get my things. Mark, take the baby please. Have you got the car keys?'

I manoeuvred the child into Mark's arms, noting with disapproval the cigarette dangling from his fingers, and hurried to the porch to retrieve my handbag.

Marion first extended her hand to shake Mark's but then leant in to kiss his cheek. 'Bye Mark. Nice to see you again. Your baby's gorgeous, by the way, just as handsome as his dad.'

Mark took a deep drag on his cigarette as he watched Marion open the car door. 'Bye now. Thanks for coming and helping. The baby's certainly taken to you. Make sure you come back; Elise could do with the company. Are you sure you don't want me to drive you?'

'No, here comes Elise. Bye.' She slid decorously onto the passenger seat, smiling at him through the window.

He blew out a smoke ring before turning to watch me as I drew near, and said, 'Are you all right driving?'

'Why shouldn't I be?'

'Well, don't be long. The kid's starting to squawk already, and he'll have worked himself into a state if you're not back soon. He'll need a feed.' He turned, cradling Paul, to move inside.

I spoke quickly, quietly. 'Can you not smoke while you're holding him? And can you please put that cigarette out before you go back inside? I truly can't bear the smell.'

'Yes, Ma'am.' He winked at Marion, balanced Paul in the crease of one arm, threw the butt onto the ground and stepped hard on it, once, rolling his eyes—an increasingly frequent habit of his—before moving inside. The door slammed shut. I could hear Paul's wail.

When I returned home, I found Mark sprawled on the couch in front of the television (another gift from his parents). Paul was on a rug on the floor in a sodden nappy, kicking his feet and staring at the garish pattern on a large green lampshade—Mark's choice. I knelt on the floor, deftly changed Paul, picked him up, carried him while depositing the wet nappy in the laundry, and returned to sit in an armchair.

Mark glanced over. 'You're not going to feed him in here, are you?'

'Yes, why?'

'Can't you do it in the bedroom? I'm watching TV.'

Incredulity added something thin and truculent to my voice. 'I'm not stopping you. This is where I usually sit. This chair's the only comfortable one we have.'

'It's just, it's very distracting, that's all. I want to watch the news.'

'I do too,' I said. 'I'm not getting in the way—I'm over here,' I waved at him, 'and we're not making any noise!'

On cue, Paul began to grizzle until I plugged his mouth with my nipple. He made small, contented gulping noises. Mark had turned his head away, chewed a fingernail, spat it out towards the floor, and stared at the television. The newsreader announced there was a new Prime Minister in France. I remained sitting, though doing so somehow didn't feel like a victory, so I focused on the soft sounds of Paul's suckling and snuffling. When he was full, I rubbed his back and carried him to the kitchen. I wanted him close, always. He gurgled happily in his carrycot while I peeled potatoes and set the table. Was this how it was for my mother? Unrelenting responsibility and chores day after day after day?

Later that night, Mark was propped in bed reading when I returned from checking on Paul for the third time. I made my voice sound casual as I undressed. 'You know you were flirting with my sister all weekend.'

He snorted a half laugh but continued reading.

'You couldn't have made it more obvious if you'd tried,' I said.

Mark lifted his head. 'What are you talking about?' His voice, weary, wary. Though his eyes looked perplexed, I sensed he was about to roll them in disdain.

The old Elise, the one who once baited and prodded and sabotaged until everything unpalatable she believed to be true about herself actually came true—that Elise backed off. I was married now, to a decent man. We had a son. I wouldn't rock the boat. Just let him be. I kissed Mark goodnight and in the early morning, unexpectedly, woke to feel his hand moving persuasively between my thighs.

CHAPTER EIGHTEEN

I was so wrapped up in my son, my beautiful boy, that there seemed little time or even inclination for the fantasy life that I'd always used; my comfort, my drug. But it was still there, waiting, tempting me in quiet moments with soft seductive tendrils and wisps of dreams where I had complete control over events and people. I tried to ignore the whispers that beckoned, just beneath reason, but wasn't always successful. When Paul slept and Mark was at work, I did my chores automatically—washed, scrubbed, polished, dusted, vacuumed, cooked, laundered—while imagining exotic places, meaningful friendships, a nanny to help, and an attentive Mark who adored me.

I moved around the house with soft footfalls so as not to wake Paul, and when it was all done, if there were spare moments left to me, I'd turn my mind over to ever more imaginings, often involving having power and influence and money and charm. Obviously, logic had no place in my daydreams. How trite and childish, how silly my thoughts were. Delusion, escape, addiction perhaps? Maybe all three.

Mark's parents, Bruce and Deidre, visited frequently, and sometimes his brother Adrian came to town from up north. Bruce was a lawyer. He had a treacle-smooth, confident persona and a deep, rich voice that could perhaps persuade a jury any which way he wanted. He was shorter than

Mark, with fair though greying hair and skin tanned from regular days on the golf course. His face, only a little lined, was still handsome, and I imagined, from his manner, that he might sometimes corner some pretty secretary or intern in his office and casually put the hard word on her with some measure of success. A position of power can do that to a person. Looking back, he was almost a caricature of a successful man from the fifties. A man of his time. When he kissed me hello at the front door, he'd aim for my mouth or linger just a fraction too long at my cheek, his aftershave a cloying reminder of other moments in another place, while his arm around my waist was just a little too tight.

'Darling,' he'd say in his velvety voice. 'You're looking especially beautiful today. Motherhood obviously agrees with you. And where's my little grandson? Is he awake?' The words stroked the air, easy and polished.

He'd go off in search of Mark and Paul but on the way, point to the corner liquor cabinet. 'I'll have a whiskey and ice with lunch. You know the drill, Elise.'

Deidre would trail in his wake, glancing around the room as she went, with an air of quiet reserve that folded neatly around her like a cloak. She was as stiff as her husband was smooth. I saw money and privilege sitting neatly on the bridge of her long, delicate nose whenever she turned it to look down on me. The set of her shoulders told me she believed her son could have done so much better; that I'd trapped her boy into a marriage that was beneath him. She'd glide into a room, let her gaze linger over the grey venetian blinds that lined the windows, so unlike the expensive damask curtains in her own home, and sit tentatively in a new linen outfit on the sofa, as if afraid it was riddled with germs, then plaster a smile on her face that was as thick and deceptive as her makeup.

'Well Elise, this is nice. Are you well?' She'd maintain a straight back, knees correctly positioned—crossed lightly at the ankle and with legs tilted to one side—her hands clasped together in a strained ball over her sculpted, tennis-toned thighs that stretched the fabric of her skirt. I would chatter inanely as a defence against her silent condemnation, offer tea and fresh-baked cakes which she claimed were 'quaint' and 'adorable', while I knew my awkward sponges were nothing compared to the delicacies that she purchased from the Jewish bakers in Ackland Street for her bridge mornings. Then I'd bring Paul in and she'd make a fuss over him, though at arm's length so her skirt wouldn't crumple or encounter a damp nappy, and her manicured fingernails wouldn't catch on a squirming baby's cardigan. I often wondered how she'd managed with Mark and his brother when they were young, but perhaps she'd been a different person then.

Adrian, though, was a pleasure to have in the home. He and Mark were close in their relationship and in age—just fifteen months separated them. Mark adored him. He moved through the world with a quiet wit and unassuming intelligence, always unfailingly polite, and so much like Mark in mannerisms. Whenever he visited, there was a gentleness to him, a generosity of spirit that lingered long after he'd gone. I liked to listen in when the two brothers fell into debates, about politics, current events, the latest in sport, anything. Now and then, I'd be drawn in, until Paul's cries or hunger called me back to earth.

• • •

Days dragged, months skipped. Domestic life had a rhythm. Feed and play with baby, bathe him, clean, tidy, laundry, push pram, shop, feed, tidy, play, rock, cook, clear, clean up, get baby to sleep, shower, do dishes, fold nappies, feed and play with baby again. This brought joy, purpose and exhaustion to my days. Along the way, major resentments I'd felt towards Mark's parents became small niggles, which in turn, developed into nuggets of gratitude.

Paul, at two years of age, grew into a sweet toddler with a sunny disposition. His tantrums were manageable, for the most part, and he was content to be held and entertained by just about anyone. He had chubby cheeks, a winning smile and large round eyes that were the colour of jade. We took turns to sing 'Green Eyes' to get him to sleep while he sucked his thumb and clung to a favourite scrap of material.

• • •

Every few months, I contacted the Public Records Office, only to be told each time that the courts still sealed adoption records. The Children's Welfare Department had morphed into the Social Welfare Branch, but the message at the end of the telephone was always the same. *There is no information relevant to your case that can be disclosed to you or to the adoptive family.*

The birth of my first child remained my secret. Neither my mother nor Marion ever alluded to it when they visited. I knew I should have told Mark long ago, especially given how changeable I sometimes became on the child's birthdate, but telling Mark would also mean revealing other details that were best left entombed. At times, though, the gnawing recollections and the nightly grinding of my teeth threatened to make the truths explode from my mouth.

Through our few years together, I'd tried hard to disguise the shame of my past, though it lay waiting, a slimy subterranean creature threatening an unpredictable, vicious attack. Mark had, early on, expressed some curiosity about my sexual history, but I assumed he really didn't want any details so I didn't give any, other than that I'd had only one serious boyfriend, Phil, before we'd met. That part was true. No need to mention the many men, some strangers, who'd been offered or simply taken the body I'd inhabited back then. He hadn't guessed about my pregnancy, perhaps because my stomach remained flat and my flesh still held its elasticity. Mark was equally vague about his own experiences and I didn't push for information. It was enough that we were three together, a happy, healthy unit. I couldn't, shouldn't ever, complain.

Though finances weren't such a problem, given Bruce and Deidre's generosity and Mark's rise through the ranks in his job, I wanted to return to work to keep up with the swift changes in my profession. There was also the monotony and routine at home, even with a child as placid and agreeable as Paul.

I'd tried to get to know our neighbours, and met regularly with a few women who had children of about the same age, but felt the weight of a new type of loneliness, and was troubled by my frequent lapses into dreamland. My ability to switch in and out between reality and Wonderland gave me less of a hold on practical concerns. Twice I'd left the gas of the stove turned on while I was outside pegging the washing and daydreaming about saving lives in Ethiopia. I once absentmindedly left Paul in his stroller inside a grocer's shop and was part-way home with my bag full of vegetables before I realised. (I'd been pondering the best treatment for intestinal perforation.) When I rushed back to retrieve Paul, he was playing happily behind the counter with

Yolanda, the shop-owner's daughter. His obvious contentment was the only thing that assuaged my guilt and distress.

At home that night, I scoured dishes in a sink of soapy water, chasing scraps of food and thought alike. Mark flicked through a magazine at the kitchen table. Paul, who'd been drawing on butcher's paper, threw down his crayons and ran into the living room in search of toys.

I shaped my words into a throwaway line.

'I've been thinking, you know, how it's important for me to go back to work when I can. I really need to keep up with the latest procedures, or I'll lose my skills.' I knocked a cup sharply, though accidentally, against the tap. My voice still light, I added, 'Besides, I'm going mad here by myself.' I caught my reflection in the kitchen window, pale against the backdrop of a navy sky, and recognised the stubborn set of my mouth. I turned.

Mark looked up. 'But you have your mother, and Marion, and that woman down the road, Jennifer someone, whatever her name is. We don't need you to go to work, at least not yet. And who'd look after Paul? He needs you here, at home.' He rose, looking through to the living room with a critical eye.

I followed his gaze and noted afresh the clutter of toys on the floor, nappies tiered on the clothes-airer and the remnants inside a discarded bowl of cereal on a side-table. Paul was stretched out in front of the TV.

I said with caution, 'I thought I could do night shifts, or work part-time, when you're here for Paul.'

'No, that won't work.'

'Why not? He sleeps through the nights now, mostly. All you'd have to do is give him a drink of water if he wakes up.'

Mark frowned at me but was unable to hold my determined stare. His stance—arms folded over his chest and his chin defiantly tilted—was language I knew well, along with the exasperation in his voice and tone. 'And how would you manage during the day with him if you've been working all night?'

'I'd be okay. *We'd* be okay. I just feel like I've lost half of my brain over these past few years. I need to be doing something useful, something I'm good at.'

'You're good at looking after our child. That's the most useful thing you can be doing.'

I returned to the sink and the dishes, wanting to scream that this wasn't enough, that I needed more than the clinging adoration of our son, more than his toys, trucks, toilet training, and the shallow conversations with other mothers in the park. I wanted to get back to a hospital. wanted to travel and see exotic parts of the world, wanted…more. I didn't know what. Just more than this. Without movement, without independence, the years ahead seemed to stretch interminably, promising little more than crushing responsibility, laundry, grocery lists, boredom, Paul eventually growing up and away. I spoke to my reflection in the window.

'You know how much I love you both, but I need my nursing, I need more in my life than this.' My hands gestured to the air, causing suds to fly.

His voice was tinny. 'Than what? You've got a family. Aren't we enough for you? We talked about having another baby. Have you changed your mind?'

I wiped my lathered hands on my apron, turned again to face him full on. 'No, of course not. We can have more, as many as you want, but later. Right now, I need to work, find my feet again, study and finish the course I started. I'm still young and there's plenty of time for more babies.'

'Well, I'm not so young.' He moved into the living room, picked up a sleepy Paul and carried him to his bedroom. I left the bedtime preparations to Mark while I tidied up. Twenty minutes later he was back, settling into to his armchair, no doubt hoping for a quiet night.

I joined him, sat near, determined to continue. 'You're not even thirty, for heaven's sake. That's not old.'

He frowned. 'Look, in a few years I'll be at management level. I don't want to be coping with the whole baby thing when I'm moving up at work and things get tougher. We can't put it off for too long, not if you want my help at home.' He shook open a newspaper.

I wondered what 'help' he was referring to, but kept my tone light. 'You *do* help me, yes. But it doesn't seem fair that you've got a life outside of the house and I'm just stuck here, day in and day out. I worked so hard to get my qualifications and now it seems it was all for nothing.'

'I'm not saying you can't ever go back to work, just not while Paul's so young, and when we'd agreed about having another one soon.'

'I didn't agree,' I threw back, darting around the room to restore more order. A well-practised art.

'You did.'

He always had the last word.

Sublimating my frustration was akin to swallowing a piece of cold potato that kept sticking in my gullet. The old Elise would have lashed out, continued arguing until I'd worn Mark down. Instead, I proposed a compromise. We finally agreed I could apply for specialist critical care training— though he warned (as I'd expected) that success wasn't guaranteed—and I'd attend evening classes twice a week. I'd do the practical component of the course on Tuesdays and Thursday if my mother was free to look after Paul. A neighbour, Therese, offered baby-sitting services for a small fee, so that might work too. And we'd try for another baby 'later'.

Suddenly the world became larger again and with it, my interest in things around me. Good and bad news punctuated the year. Aboriginal peoples gained the right to enrol and vote in federal elections; the government sold large parts of an Indigenous land reserve to a bauxite mining company. A visit by the Queen and Prince Philip. The death of the Pope. Valentina Tereshkova returned safely from space. Martin Luther King and Malcolm X energised millions with their speeches. A coal mine exploded in Japan. South Vietnamese soldiers shot nine Buddhist monks in Hue; a monk self-immolated in the streets of Saigon. Eighteen hundred people died in an earthquake in Yugoslavia. The Profumo affair. John Kennedy's assassination...

After I listened gravely to broadcasts on the small kitchen radio, I played the music of The Beatles and Bob Dylan on the record player and swayed slowly around the room with Paul in my arms.

• • •

I tell you about all these things now because my memory of them is still sharp enough, unlike the haze of just yesterday. It's important to me to get everything in order, you know, before I can't remember anything at all.

I hope it's not too tiring for you, dear Sophie, listening to my tapes and reading the scrappy bits of my journal, especially when you work so hard.

Your Mum and Dad and Patricia all came to visit through the week, but of course we can do nothing but stand and shout at each other through the window. I'm worried about your dad, Sophie. Is he all right? I'm sure he pretends to me that everything is fine. Next time you see him, ask him, please, and report back to me, truthfully.

You're such a treasure. Take care of yourself, won't you.

CHAPTER NINETEEN

The following eighteen months were full of promise. I was in a familiar hospital environment (though part-time), felt capable and in control and relished the interactions with patients and colleagues. I took pleasure in a new title—I was no longer poor, strange Nurse Brown, but efficient, capable Sister Harrington. Some of the same doctors who'd once seen me as only a harmless target, to be flirted with in idle moments, now kept a respectful professional distance.

Peace had broken out at home. Mark appreciated the independent, confident me far better than the woman who'd waited too anxiously for his arrival home every night. I made an effort to be a more stimulating conversationalist, always asked about his work and listened attentively to his tales of office politics, field trips and the latest reports of engineering achievements or gadgetry. I told him only brief snippets from my day, lest he become bored or jealous of my time spent elsewhere. I cooked his favourite meals, washed and ironed his work shirts, pressed his suits, kept my figure trim and grew my hair to the length he preferred. In the bedroom, I'd sometimes surprise him by behaving like the fantasy woman he'd once confessed to imagining, even when hampered by crushing tiredness or a lingering memory of blood and gore from hospital emergencies.

My libido had pretty much disappeared, but when required, I was certainly practised at pretence.

Paul was a delight. My work outside the home made my time with him all the more precious. He continued to pluck innocently at my maternal heartstrings and loved being cuddled, so there was no shortage of embraces to be exchanged. When I read to him, he'd turn the book's pages eagerly, pointing to pictures and repeating words and phrases that amused or intrigued him. Outside, he would chase insects, frogs and dogs and squeal at the sheer pleasure of running, even when he couldn't catch anything. Rain didn't deter him—he'd tilt his face to catch raindrops in his mouth or try to chase his shadow or grasp the end of a rainbow. His eyes, a little darker now but still peppered with that amazing hint of jade, remained focused on every activity. Whenever he turned them on me, his irises seemed to sparkle. Every day I thanked my good fortune for having such a beautiful, perfect boy, grateful that he was healthy and cheerful. And that he was mine to keep.

Lillian did her bit each week, ensuring our household ran smoothly. She'd enter the house with brisk efficiency, and obviously enjoyed her role as grandmother in a way she'd never been able to as a mother. Whatever the relationship with my stepfather, and whatever the disappointments in her life, she'd shake them all off with a vigorous flick of the tea towel and then tie on her apron.

'Now, where's my little man?' she'd ask with a laugh, while Paul hid under the kitchen table, or anywhere, giggling. 'Paul? Where are you hiding? Granny is coming to find you and then we'll bake some biscuits!' This more frivolous side of hers was certainly new to me.

Lillian appreciated Mark, was perhaps thankful that he'd taken me on, since she still no doubt considered me *damaged goods*. He always responded amicably to her presence. Her visits were short, just long enough to allow me my study time twice a week, and she always had a practical focus. Paul loved her. She adored him. We were all extremely appreciative of her help.

On the other hand, when Marion visited, she only ever stayed for a brief while, then left us with the mood slightly askew.

'All my friends are going to England, that's the place to be! So I'm saving to go. I can easily get a job there, you know. Everyone's told me they need secretaries everywhere! Did I tell you about Richard? No? We've been seeing each other for a few weeks. I'm not madly in love, so when I do go to London, it'll be…,' and on and on.

She'd slimmed down considerably and would have been marked as a real beauty, with her long, dark-blond locks, large brown eyes and clear complexion, were it not for the way she had of flicking her hair and a certain set of her mouth, both of which added an air of haughtiness. The sweetness and openness that had been so endearing in her younger years were absent. She'd play with Paul for a few minutes, then leave him to corner me to chat endlessly about herself.

I sensed something jagged about her, sharp shards of ice around the edges, and all of her empty dialogue did little to conceal the notion that inside she was merely staunching a wound that threatened to bleed out if she ever stopped and took breath. She was both flighty and intense, absorbed in her own little world. (I understood this was an ironic observation, coming from me.) Between her visits, we occasionally talked on the phone, but it was as if we were mere acquaintances. I could have poked around, tried to wheedle something substantial out of her and tried to understand what was behind that less-than-subtle transformation, but in truth, I was afraid to know.

For a time, I didn't visit my dream world, my Wonderland; there seemed no need. Jeffrey was married and there was no pressure from any quarter for me to see him. I rarely heard Craig's name—it was as though he'd never existed. (I wished.) My mother didn't speak about any aspect of her domestic life, only about her work and the few longer-term friends she now had. My past experiences, my troubles, belonged to another time and place. I was free of the ghosts. So I believed.

• • •

But the long tentacles of the past often seek us out. I was leaving the hospital gates one June evening, a time when the days are winter-short, cold and uninspiring, and was in a hurry to get home to Paul, who was in the care of Jennifer that day. A light drizzle of rain had formed. Passersby hastened over small puddles, their faces locked against the chill air. Car horns tooted. The air smelt of rust. Distracted by an errant scarf, and juggling a shopping bag with my satchel, I scarcely registered that someone was approaching me from the side.

A male voice. ''Scuse me lass, sorry to be troubling yer. But can yer spare me a minute?'

I glanced to the left and saw an arm extended as if to hold me back; the hand almost reached my coat but then fell to his side. He was about my height, an old man in an old coat, with a hat that had seen better days pulled down over his ears.

'Yes? Can I help you?' I said, thinking he might be one of the homeless men who regularly set themselves up outside the hospital gates.

'Lisie? It's you, innit?'

He took a step closer as I moved backwards in shock and stumbled over an uneven section of the footpath. His hand came up again to steady me with a surprisingly firm grip. I studied his face, its skin lined and drawn, with a dull sheen of illness and a patchwork of wrinkled regret. His dark, rheumy eyes darted over me, while his tongue edged along dry lips.

'I'm sorry, I don't know …,' I said.

'Lisie, it's me.'

That voice. Alarmingly recognisable. I wrenched my arm away, out of his grip, and turned to go, with no idea of what I should do. But he was by my side again in a moment, a sour smell of urine and beer accompanying him; his breath laboured, his movements agitated, and I couldn't yet bear to look at him again full-on, so I continued walking with him limping beside me. That limp. So familiar.

'I saw yer photo in the paper last month. You and some other nurses were at some money-raisin' thing for a new wing in the hospital or somethin'. I knew it was you straight away Lisie. There was a part down the bottom of the page that gave all yer names … Different last name now, but I knew. "That's her, that's my darlin' Elise!" I said to meself. Not too many girls with a name like that. Hey, can yer hold up a bit. I can't keep up with yer. Wait on a tic!'

I halted and turned, brusque in manner, not believing, not wanting, not willing to access any connection to this stranger and only a tenuous one still in my head to the man I'd once revered. His face was very tanned, bordering on florid, the lined skin stretched over prominent cheekbones while on his neck it hung loose in folds; his thin lips, when parted, revealed teeth only a little discoloured.

'What do you want?' The testiness in my voice surprised me perhaps more than it did him.

'I been staying not far away, just in the next town. I called the hospital to make sure it was you. I been waitin', hopin' to catch yer. Thought I'd just see yer. Can't we go somewhere, somewhere quiet, let you get to know your old dad again? There's a pub down the road.'

Drizzle turned to rain. I felt I was underwater already, under treacle, unable to breathe or focus, anxious to hold on to my present and not be drowned in a past that watched and waited and bared its teeth at me like some sly shark. Anxiety pulled me towards the bus stop, back to my son, my family, my safe world. Lost love and compassion kept me rooted to the spot.

But I looked straight at him then and hated him in that moment for having abandoned all of us. And especially hated the absence of him that had invited a devil into our home.

'I'm sorry. You've made a mistake. I'm not who you think I am.'

'Aww Lisie, yer might be all growed up now, but I know it's you. Yer can't fool me. I'd know those cat's eyes of yours anywhere. What happened there, near yer ear? Yer got a scar.' He reached his hand towards my face.

I ducked my head but was otherwise motionless, unwilling, perhaps unable at that point to look at him again. I needed to sit, even if in the rain, so I moved then to a section of stone wall by the street corner where I could prop myself up. I stared at my shoes for a long time, but was aware of him nearby, shuffling from one foot to another.

'C'mon 'Lis! Whaddayer say we go an' 'ave a drink just round the corner? Get outta this rain?'

Only because I thought I might vomit there in the street, I rose and began to walk with him, aware that my heart was thrumming irregularly and bile was rising in my throat. But soon I stopped and leaned over, one arm outstretched to cling to a lamppost as a stream of liquid poured out of my mouth and splashed over my white shoes. He must have stood back then, watched or ignored the evidence of my disorientation gradually seeping into the wet ground. Eventually, I was able to stand upright and take a deep breath. He was still waiting, edgy, hands now in his pockets, frowning. The rain splattered unevenly on and around us, stealthily trickling through my clothes.

'Elise, yer not well? I know it's a shock after all this time.'

His voice was the same, though a little gravelly. It broke my heart to hear it again. Memories, words, flashed through my mind: *'Atta girl Lisie … you can do anything yer want… you're better than most 'a them ding dongs… you're my best girl…'*

I searched his face again for the father I'd adored. His eyes were watery, his eyelids blinking fast over tiny red gossamer veins. I held his gaze for a long time and there was something beneath it that tore at me. I could see the regretful longing, the mournful searching, and finally, a trace of the man who'd once so entranced me. His velvet-brown eyes were a sorrowful, worn reminder of a now diminished man.

I don't recall why or how I accompanied him in silence for the few minutes it took to walk around the corner and down Murphy Street, but by the time we arrived at the hotel, we both knew I wouldn't go inside with him. The bus stop wasn't far away. I was full of the need to get home to my child, to my ordinary, shielded, secure life.

'I'm sorry, I need to catch the next bus. Here…,' I said, opening my handbag, searching for a pen or my purse. My hands were shaking so much, I abandoned the idea.

If I'd stayed, my father might have told me his story, tried to explain why he'd left and tell me what he'd done since. Possibly somewhere else, he'd started another family just like ours, and he might have told me about them. I was certain too that if we'd sat down together, he'd have asked me for money, made light of the pain he'd caused by leaving. I knew he'd had his reasons back then, and I had mine for leaving now.

In a moment of tenderness, I reached out my hand, touched his face gently—it was a tougher, rougher, more stubbled skin than I'd kissed and petted all those years ago—but then turned away and walked purposefully on, unaware of the traffic noise or the scattered rain. This time, he didn't follow.

I hated myself in that moment, and for many years afterwards, for being a coward, so callous, so cruel.

CHAPTER TWENTY

In the same week that Mark announced he'd accepted a job in Sydney, I discovered I was pregnant. For me, there was apprehension; for Mark, ambition ruled. The confidence and contentment I'd fought to achieve over recent years evaporated almost instantly. But time had made each of us uniquely stubborn.

'I don't understand how this could have happened. I've been on the pill since Paul was born.' I spoke with a hint of belligerence.

'Well, don't look at me. You're the one who's supposed to take it every night. Are you sure you didn't miss a couple of days?' Mark could barely contain his delight.

'Of course I'm sure! You wanted this, not me. Maybe you switched the pills for something else.'

He snorted gruffly, waved a dismissive hand, didn't deign to speak.

I glared. 'Well, you're the one who's been nagging to have another one, and you know I'm not ready, not yet.'

'Looks like you'll have to be, Elise. Do you honestly think I'd do something that deceitful, even if I could figure out how to?'

He speared his fork into his food which included a burnt lamb chop (my revenge) with more ferocity than was necessary, while I stared at my knife, assessing its possibilities, and absently moved the food around my plate.

Mark continued, 'Anyway, you told me yourself that none of these things is a hundred percent effective. Remember how easily Paul came about.'

I was silent a moment, a touch mollified. 'I suppose, maybe when I took those antibiotics, you know, when I had that infected finger?'

He kept eating and avoided looking at me, probably to conceal his amusement. Through a mouthful, he said, 'You're the nurse, you should understand how those things work!'

Irritation coloured my cheeks. 'Well of course I understand. Don't patronise me. Maybe I should have thought, but I didn't. It's just been so busy and I'm always tired. The doctor didn't remind me about antibiotics. He's the one who should've said something.'

Mark's face relaxed. He reached across the table, placed his hand lightly over mine, while I still gripped the knife. 'C'mon, it'll be all right. Paul needs a brother or sister. He's growing up too fast already. We'll be okay.'

I scoffed. 'Well, you might be,' and withdrew from his touch, adding with a thin, brittle laugh, 'We must be the most fertile couple on the planet.' My body unstiffened a little.

Mark grinned, then kicked my foot under the table, the sort of playful gesture that had been missing in our interactions of late. His obvious delight only made me more irritable. My initial instinct was to kick him back, hard. But I looked at Paul, who was playing absently with his peas and drawing patterns on the dining table with a finger dabbed in gravy, and felt that tug of longing. I couldn't imagine loving another child as much as I loved Paul.

Over the next few days, between anxiety, indignation and fledging gladness, I came to accept the pregnancy but the arguing continued.

'You didn't even tell me you were going to apply for that job. We should have talked this through. Don't you think I deserve a say in this?'

We were driving to meet Mark's parents for a picnic lunch at the beach.

Mark checked the rear-view mirror. 'Can we talk about this later? Not in front of the boy, and not at lunch either, please Elise.'

'But…'

'I didn't apply for it. It just came up. They approached me, and I had to give them an answer then and there, or it'd go to someone else. It's an opportunity for us, both of us.

'I doubt I'll get any benefit from it.'

'And it'll mean more money. There'll be a range of good schools for Paul.'

'The money's not important to me. We're doing fine just as we are. And you know how much I enjoy my job. I want to work as long as I can before this baby,' patting my belly.

He said, 'You'll work again, once we're settled, and the new one's old enough.'

'Then there's my mother—I won't get to see her. Mum won't be able to help out like she does here; nor will your parents.'

'Mummy, look at that bus? What's the name of the bus? Where's it going?' Paul's small fingers poked enthusiastically against the window, his head craning to see the vehicle as it sped by.

I turned to look at him and melted, as I always did. 'Yep, sweetie, I can see it.'

'Are Nanna and Pop on the bus?'

'No, they're coming in their own car and meeting us at the beach.'

'Will Granny be there too?'

'No, Granny's still busy. She's got loads of work to do. We'll go and visit Granny again soon, but not today. We're almost at the beach! You can have a swim first, then we'll have lunch. Won't that be good?'

• • •

We sold our home in Melbourne and bought a small, plain, three-bedroomed weatherboard house in what would later be considered an inner Sydney suburb. It was an older house, but quaint, and not too far from two major hospitals and an extensive park.

'It'll need more work, but it's within our price range and we can make it our own, in time. Don't look like that, Elise. I'll draw up the plans, find reputable builders, and supervise the whole thing. I have connections, the names of the right people.'

'When's all this work supposed to happen? There'll be mess, noise, chaos. Not ideal with a new baby.'

I had no job, had lost my colleagues, hard-won professional status, and much of the confidence I'd gained in the workplace. I'd also lost the security of my routine, the comfort and delight of having my mother back in my life. Even Marion was completely unavailable now, as she was working in England as an *au pair*. The spectre of loneliness approached, again.

But I had little energy to argue. There'd been endless sorting, packing, cleaning, supervising removalists and working through the checklist of the dozens of tasks required before doing the reverse in Sydney—unpacking, sorting, setting up a new life. And I had Paul. At almost four years of age, he was an easy child, biddable and sweet, delightful, chatty, with such eagerness for life in his open face and curious fingertips. His enthusiasm reminded me of my very young self, the happy, guiltless child I could barely remember.

We parents fussed and tussled over his affections. A typical evening might go like this:

'Come inside Paul, it's getting cold!' I'd call through the kitchen window.

'For God's sake Elise, he's just having fun. Leave him alone and let him play.'

'It's his dinner time. He needs a routine. Anyway, he's got himself wet and dirty. It's chilly out there.'

'He's a boy. He needs to explore.'

'Paul? Come in, sweetheart. Time for your bath and then dinner.'

And I'd turn to Mark with a satisfied look as the screen door squeaked and slammed and a blur of energetic limbs raced through the room. I didn't have time to tousle Paul's thick hair when he zoomed past.

'Ah, here's my fella,' Mark might say, as he scooped the boy up into his arms and tickled him. 'You can have your bath later. Wanna see some card tricks? Come in here with me' He'd carry the squealing child on his shoulders and bend to manoeuvre through the doorway, flashing a small smile of victory at me.

In fact, most days we disagreed—over the finances or the nature of improvements we should make to the house; about whether to send Paul to a government or a private school the following year (I was opposed to private schooling, on principle, but perhaps more so because Mark's parents were so adamantly for it); over Mark's schedule; my need for a job....

I'd become the whiney wife, the kind one often saw portrayed and ridiculed on TV, and I didn't like her but kept going. 'You spend so much time at work, Mark, and commuting. You're never here. And on weekends you just disappear into your reports or sports, or beers with your new mates, whoever they are. I've nothing to do with my days except housework. I feel more alone than ever. I wish we'd never moved here.'

'You should make an effort to meet people, Elise. Get involved in things, meet the neighbours. Stop nagging. That would be a start.'

The arguments created and sustained tension, but I knew by now when to stop, when to push, when to concede defeat, when to shrug, when to dream and when to put my head down at night on a martyr's pillow. So I tried to keep my mouth shut and focus on Paul and the new child within. Change happens as it needs to.

• • •

'Mummy, there's someone at the door!'

Paul ran past me and into the hallway as I heaved another basket of washing up from the floor onto the laundry bench. I heard a light but insistent knock on the frosted glass panel of the front door, and, as I moved towards it, saw the indistinct shape of two figures. Paul was already stretching up to reach the door handle.

'I'll get it, I'll get it Mummy.' He fiddled clumsily with the knob. He was dancing on the spot at the prospect of a visitor, his mop of hair bobbing, before he pulled the door open with a sudden wrench, and almost toppled over in the process.

Two women, who appeared to be just a few years older than me, peered through the wirescreen door and looked pleased to find me at home. One was tall, slim and elegantly dressed in a straight navy skirt and a white tailored shirt. Her fair hair was pulled up into a tidy bun. She smiled, holding up a plate with a tiered cake garnished precariously with strawberries.

'Hi, I'm Nancy and this is Gabrielle—Gabby.' Her voice was well-modulated, her tone direct.

I paid attention then to the shorter woman, whose dark hair fell in loose curls to her shoulders. She wore a shirt-dress, denim-blue to match her eyes, and bestowed on me a wide, generous grin, wiggling the fingers of one hand in a brief wave, before focusing on Paul, who was standing beside me, his hand clutching my skirt.

She bent down and spoke to him through the mesh of the screen. 'Hello you. What a handsome young man you are!'

He loosened his grip on me and mumbled a sticky 'Hello' through the remains of a biscuit in his mouth.

Overcome with awkwardness and a sudden shyness, and totally forgetting my manners, I nodded to them both through the mesh, offered my name, and hastily attempted a range of smiles before settling on one which I hoped looked friendly enough. I was inexplicably nervous.

Nancy continued genially, 'We both live across the way there on the other side of the street,' she gestured vaguely, 'and we've been waiting for an opportunity to visit ever since you moved in. Just wanted to welcome you and give you this,' holding the cake up to eye-level. 'I'd ask when the baby's due, but I won't, in case you're just naturally a bit fat.' She grinned. 'We've seen you waddling down the street.'

'Nancy! Stop it! You'll scare her away.' Gabby held aloft a bunch of deep burgundy dahlias, the stems wrapped in damp tissue paper.

I grinned. 'So sorry, please do come in,' opening the door and stepping aside to let them through. 'Thanks so much. It really is very kind of you. This is Paul, by the way. Oh, and I'm Elise.' Repeating. Nervous.

As they moved past, Nancy handed me the plated cake, smiled again and patted Paul on the head. He peered up at both women with what might have been admiration. I felt pleasure and apprehension simultaneously. I wasn't well-practiced at friendships and wondered what these might cost me. I also worried about the clutter they'd encounter if they came through into the living room, but they turned towards the kitchen as if they already knew the layout of the house. In a trail of perfume and exuberance, Gabby took a few steps across the carpet before returning to hold her hand out to a curious Paul. Though surprised, he took it willingly while Gabby escorted him into the kitchen, talking all the way.

She called back, 'Shall I put the kettle on while I'm here?' and then, 'Oh, I love your toy soldiers all lined up here, young man. How many have you got there?'

Once settled in the kitchen, I warmed to the two women straightaway. They cut and distributed thick, powdery slices of the sponge cake while I made the tea. Paul, intrigued, studied them from his chair, while they chatted and relayed anecdotes about the community that soon had me relaxed and laughing.

From then on, to my surprise and delight, they included me in their regular get-togethers, which involved an almost daily cup of tea once our collective gaggle of children were at school or settled happily into some game in the backyard. They also invited me to their weekly game of bridge at Nancy's. I'd never learnt how to play it before, but they were very patient, letting me watch and fumble while they talked bids and trumps and tricks with me and whomever they'd recruited that week to make up a fourth. To have been invited, included, acknowledged, instead of always being the one looking on at friendship from the sidelines… these things were uplifting.

CHAPTER TWENTY-ONE

Over the remaining months of the year, I watched my body expand and change with the pregnancy, but it held neither the apprehension and shame of my first, nor the joy and excitement of my second. My back ached constantly, my breasts felt full and painful, and my skin, previously supple and soft, felt close to bursting point, split into a crisscross pattern of long red and white stretch marks across my hips and belly. My gait slowed and changed; my temper flared. I disliked the new house and continued to miss the stimulation of my job. I didn't mind so much anymore that Mark spent time absorbed in work or in sport, as it allowed some respite from our almost routine bickering, though his absences brought a new loneliness into the marriage. There was also debilitating tiredness, relentless boredom from housework and additional concern for Paul's wellbeing. Was he happy enough, stimulated enough, brave enough to cope with the world?

In the long hours that I had to myself in the house, that old drug, my Wonderland, crept back in seductively, and took me to a more comfortable place—*always as corny as Kansas in August*—before I had to snap back to attention.

Mark drove me to the doctor's office when the pain in my back became unbearable. It was still six weeks before the due date. Although I'd asked that he wait in the small, stuffy waiting room, Mark was adamant that he should accompany me into the inner sanctum of the office. Soon we stood side-by-side, while a preoccupied, well-dressed male of about fifty perused notes at his desk. He was not the doctor I'd seen previously. I momentarily thought we'd entered the wrong room.

'I'm Doctor Moretti,' he said, looking up from beneath thick, dark eyebrows and smiling. I noted his long, straight nose, tanned skin, the receding hairline.

'Where's Doctor Kirkland?' I forgot to be polite. My voice was faint.

'Away…family thing; he'll be back in a fortnight. I'm filling in for him. Obviously!' He grinned, showing straight white teeth, and gestured for me to sit down. Then looked at Mark, 'You must be the husband!' and leant forward across the desk, extending his right hand.

Mark moved in to shake it, before sitting down on one of the two straight-backed chairs, too quickly, heavily, under an encumbrance of anxiety.

'Now, what can I do for you, Mrs Harrington?'

'Well, I don't know where to start, to be honest. I have a lot of back pain, and there's a pulling sensation, here,' gesturing to my ribcage. 'I've not felt it till recently, and I'm not sleeping very well.' I coughed. 'I'm worried there's something wrong.'

'What about your previous pregnancies?'

Dumbfounded silence, before I managed a squeaky 'What?'

'It says here that you've had two previous pregnancies, close to term, no complications. What was your experience with them? Did you have any of these issues, anything like the back problem, the pulling, with either of your other pregnancies?'

'Umm, I don't…'

'You'd have been quite young with the first then—what, in your mid-teens? Let me see…' He looked at the notes. 'Fifteen?'

My face must have flushed so deep a red, my breathing so loud and ragged, it prompted Doctor Moretti to hurry past us to the door and open it to call, 'Water, Elaine please. Quick!'

I could feel Mark's eyes on me but refused to look at him, was only able to grasp the corner of the doctor's desk and whisper that it was my back that had made me feel faint. A pulse thudded behind my ears, drowning all else, and I had the notion that I was being picked up by a wave and thrown against rocks. The doctor held the glass to my lips, and I tried to sip, but it dribbled down my chin and the front of my dress. I shook as he led me to a narrow bed in the corner. Its starched sheeting crackled while I tried to position myself, legs leaden weights, as Doctor Moretti assisted me.

'Just stay sitting up for a minute, have another sip of water, and we'll take a look when you can lie down. Here you go, here's the pillow…gently…'

A cautious examination behind a drawn curtain provided brief reassurance.

'The baby's in breech, which might explain your back pain. Don't worry—it should turn well before delivery. And if not, Doctor Kirkland will certainly do something to assist when the time comes.'

My brain and breath snapped into gear. Frantic now, I found my voice. 'An ECV?'

'Yes, if necessary.'

Mark's voice from the furthest side of the room was high, tight. 'What? What's going on? What the hell is that? EC something?'

Doctor Moretti talked to the curtain, calmly. 'An external cephalic version is a way of moving the baby into the right position for birthing; it's not uncommon. Perhaps the baby will turn by itself soon anyway. Up you get, Elise. Everything else looks fine.'

I don't remember anything more that was said. Mark and I left the doctor's office with a prescription for the pain, and a leaflet on sleeping positions I should try that might help ease any discomfort. The quiet space between us was sticky, congealed. On the way home, Mark beat his fingers on the steering wheel erratically, aggressively; I saw nothing but a smudged windscreen.

• • •

Mark held the front door open while I walked through with the draught of his frostiness. He went straight to the living room, where our neighbour's daughter, Molly, was minding Paul, curled up on the sofa with him, watching television. Mark thanked her perfunctorily and she, seeming to notice the frigidity that sliced through the room, scurried out without pause. Paul was engrossed in his program and didn't register our arrival. Mark followed me into the bedroom, where I was trying, unsuccessfully, to kick off my shoes. My reflection in the mirror showed a pale, pinched face as I twisted a hand to brace my back and sit on the bed. The cotton coverlet held a sudden fascination. I stared long and hard at it, blood thumping in my ears and saliva gathering in a gluey mass at the back of my throat. To think and to swallow proved difficult. How to escape?

I'm doing late evening rounds in Ward Seven with Doctor Carlisle.

Mark, leaning against the closed door, arms entwined authoritatively, stared at me. He said, 'Why did I have to hear about it this way? Would you ever have told me?' His words sounded muffled in the dead air between us.

The patient has vestibular disease, probably from a brain lesion, but I'd like …

He moved to pull me to my feet, his hands firm and insistent on each elbow. It was hard to focus on his face, his confusion distressing to see.

'I don't…Mark, honestly, it never seemed…'

There was nothing I could say in my defence, nothing that would soothe him, nothing that would take away the old, familiar stink of shame that burrowed into my chest. I was too worried for tears but leant my face in towards his chest and hoped for some response that might signify forgiveness.

Mark dropped his hands to his sides, turned and walked to the blue-upholstered chair in the corner near the wardrobe. He slumped into it with such force I thought it might splinter. His elbows balanced on bent knees clad in corduroy; his head was in his hands. If misery combined with bewilderment was a sound, it came in the expulsion of his breath. It was in the tautness of his hands, in their movements as his fingers scrambled through his hair, rubbed roughly at his eyes, then at the skin of his cheeks. Gradually, all motion stopped and he sat still, arms hanging slack between his knees but hands clasped tight. He stared for a long time at the carpet, finally looked up. A vein in his temple pulsed. There was nothing to read in his eyes—not anger, nor accusation. Nothing.

Then, leaning back, he spoke. Clearly, precisely, in a low tone. 'All right. Why don't you tell me everything.' A statement emphasised by its slow delivery.

• • •

These are my memories:

I'm standing in the middle of the room as if on trial. The softness of his eyes, those eyes that enchant me, has disappeared; now there's only ice. I've lost awareness of any backache; the energetic kicking of the child inside me takes over for a moment but then quiets. There remains a dull, rhythmic thump that accompanies the surge of blood to my head, behind my ears. I won't cry, but I also can't force my voice through a constricted throat. When it does finally come, it's little more than a whisper. I breathe deeply, start again, unable to control the tremor in my voice, and I begin pacing back and forth across the room like a frightened, caged animal. My hands are protective across my belly.

And I tell him the truth—that I'd been forced, though I don't reveal how many times, that I'd tried to hide the pregnancy, and by the time my mother found out, it was too late to do anything about it. That I'd been sent to a home for girls like me, to wait, to study, to work, and that the baby was taken away immediately after the birth, and I never saw him. I explain how I'd been banished, which was how I'd ended up in Niburu. I talk about the misery and shame and how I'd thrown myself into nursing instead of off a bridge, and that meeting Mark was the best thing that ever happened to me and I didn't want to lose him. That I'd wanted to tell him but there was never a right time, and the longer I left it the harder it became. All this is true. I tell him almost everything. I sit again on the bed.

He's still slumped in that chair, silent. His fingers are now entwined in a ball near his chin, and he leans forward, elbows again propped on his thighs. He chews on a thumbnail. His eyes move from my face to my belly to the floor. A low voice. 'Who did that to you?'

And here another tale settles over the first, weaves itself through my history to flesh out the details that can't, won't, come naturally from my mouth. 'It was some boy I didn't know. He must have followed me when I left school and he grabbed me. I was walking through that big park near where I lived, you've seen it…I tried to stop him, but I couldn't. That's the truth.' And it is the truth, just right then in that moment of telling, and as real to me as any other.

'Why didn't you tell anyone? Your parents? Why didn't you call the police?' His arms reaching outwards, trying perhaps to collect facts to make sense of it all.

It's impossible to answer, as I don't know. I understand only that secrets dig in and hide.

I don't think Mark believes anything I've said. By the time it's all out there, the truth, the half-truths, the lie, we're wrung out. He stands, moves towards me and reaches out a conflicted hand, but then drops his arm and leaves the room without another word. I lie down and cry until the contortions of my face and throat have no muscle left to cope. I'm aware that Paul is calling for me, and that Mark's voice is cold and abrupt with him. Then there's quiet.

The stabbing ache in my back grips violently again, as if accusing me. I rise, go to the bathroom for the prescription pills, then seek out Paul. He's in his room, flipping the pages of a book, looking unsettled. We cuddle, and I whisper that I love him, stroke his forehead and convince him to come to the kitchen, where I make him eggs and toast, get him bathed, ready for bed. We lie together and I read to him till he drifts off to sleep.

That night I dream of ruptured spleens, splintered teeth, Paul being pulled, hysterical, from my arms, with me equally hysterical and shouting at whoever is trying to take him. The assailant's face is never clear. There are other dark, determined faces hiding behind shadows.

• • •

For two nights following the disclosure, Mark slept on a fold-down bed in the room designated as the new nursery. He didn't address the topic again, but adopted a new, solid remoteness. On the surface, life had returned to normal. He stuck to his routine, left for work each morning, came home each night at the expected time and ate the food I'd cooked without comment. He continued his habit of reading work reports in the evenings, or watching television; he played with and told stories to Paul before tucking him in for the night. On the weekends, he mowed the lawn, kicked a football outside with our son, wandered to a friend's house for a beer and a run-down on the latest cricket or football scores, or helped Clive Bolcher tinker with his Holden FX—any number of things to keep himself occupied, legitimately absent in body and spirit. He remained civil, politely distant, sometimes smiled vaguely at something I'd say. Always, he avoided the crushed velvet dejection in my eyes while his own reflected sharp pinpricks of disillusionment.

After that moment, when I'd been so exposed, when memories were being forced back in and then out of my body like an invasion of locusts picking everything bare, I'd believed Mark would leave me. I knew his distance was deliberate and necessary, and I must do my penance. I immersed myself ever more completely in the vocation of child-rearing, hugged Paul tight, never complained, performed all the household chores mechanically, scrubbed and polished and shone so that a visitor could see their reflection in any surface, should they care to, while I took care never to look at my own.

When Mark returned to the marital bed (the fold-down being too uncomfortable and besides, anger and disappointment both need nurturing), he slept with his back turned, a silent, impenetrable wall between us, while I lay on my side and rested a hand on my belly to soothe the squirming, impatient child within. And sometimes I hummed a song to myself and thought about how nice it might be to meet Paul McCartney.

And then, just like that, his frostiness thawed. He kissed my cheek before leaving for work every day and brought library books home for me; he complimented me on the dinners I'd prepared and even rubbed my back solicitously when we got into bed. I waited for a comment, a reference to The Issue, but none came. It was strange to be forgiven for something I hadn't caused, but I was thankful.

CHAPTER TWENTY-TWO

Our daughter, Patricia Michelle, was born in February after a quick but excruciating labour. Doctor Kirkland didn't arrive in time for the birth, though the midwife ("Call me Beth") managed me well. No one else paid me much heed in the delivery room. I took the loosely-wrapped, startled child into my arms and checked her over. Everything was where it should be. Still mauve and mottled, she had very little hair, just a few patchy tufts dark and slick from the birth. Her little face was pointed and pinched, as though she was both puzzled and infuriated at being thrown out of the womb without consultation. She cried vigorously, her face turned dark pink, and her fingers, long and slender, curled into tight fists. I looked to see any family resemblances but couldn't. She didn't display any of the placidness Paul had when he'd first emerged, but I was enormously relieved that she'd arrived and was evidently healthy. After I'd finished examining her, and Beth had cleaned, checked and weighed her, I put her to my breast, but she kept turning away, wanting to feed but not wanting me.

'You need to hold her this way.' A young woman whose name tag identified her as Nurse Morris prised my baby away from me, resettled her into a different position and pushed her tiny, vulnerable head towards me again. This only elicited louder cries from my infant wonder.

I snapped, 'I know how to do this, thank you!' and brushed the nurse's hand away.

Nurse Morris' brows shot up, she blinked and bit back a retort as Beth came into view. They both kept busy with afterbirth procedures while I continued to coax Patricia to suckle. After several more minutes of trying, I was able to placate her enough to promote in her a fitful interest. But then she'd pull back and squirm, making a face as if to say 'That's disgusting', and mewl like a kitten before latching on once more.

'She'll need to be in the nursery before change of shift,' said Nurse Morris, using a tone I knew well, the officious, censorious manner that some staff adopted with patients. I ignored her and directed my speech to Beth.

'Can I keep her here for a bit longer? My husband must be outside somewhere and he should see her first, before she goes anywhere.' Patricia sneezed once and went to sleep in my arms.

'I'll go and find him. No, actually, you can go, Nurse, while I finish up here. Look for Mr Harrington.' Beth smiled as Nurse Morris clomped out through the door on thick ankles wedged into bright, white shoes.

'She's young,' my hero Beth the Midwife whispered, nodding towards the door, as she lifted Patricia from my arms and placed her in the tall, transparent crib. 'You can keep bub with you for a little while. She's healthy and gorgeous. Congratulations!'

I relaxed under her ministrations and allowed pride and contentment to erase any lingering soreness and exhaustion. I watched my perfect new infant sleeping, stroking her when she squirmed or whimpered, and took in the miracle of her.

Mark came to the hospital about an hour later, after I'd been moved to the ward and was dozing, with Patricia beside me in her tiny cot.

'Well, a girl hey, that's wonderful! Let me take a good look at her.'

He moved to the crib and bent his head down close. 'She's beautiful! Just like you, Elise. Sorry I didn't get here earlier. Work, you know...' He continued to stare down at Patricia, making all the right clucking noises.

I noticed his shirt was crumpled and sweaty. There was a small, dried stain on his trousers near his fly, and the eyes beneath his sandy hair were evasive. I didn't ask where he'd been, but I smelt the beer on his breath and a faint hint of perfume when he bent to kiss my cheek.

Then he settled comfortably into the pale blue armchair near the window, hands cradling the back of his head, elbows wide, legs lightly crossed. Perhaps a hint of smugness infused his face. I'd no energy or will to be combative; at that point I hardly cared where he'd been or with whom, so I just smiled, and yawned. He didn't stay long. For this birth too, there were no flowers.

•••

Patricia's arrival signalled a truce of sorts. Mark was chuffed to have a daughter and to have produced the 'perfect pair' that everyone congratulated him on. He doted on both children, enjoyed spending money to buy Paul bigger toys and more books, and Patricia an expensive but impractical layette, something she'd grow out of in a few months. He'd always relished the kick of big city living and found it easy to make friends and acquaintances, to build networks (always the charmer), and fill any perceived voids in his life. When my body returned to something like its previous state, he became more physically demonstrative—casual hugs in the kitchen before work, frequent lovemaking at night in ways that were new to us as a couple. Perhaps he was measuring me against the person who wore the gentle floral scent of Arpège, still faint on him after his late nights at the office. At least whoever she was had good taste in perfume.

But I kept my mouth shut about that. Played the docile, undemanding wife. Betty Friedan would have been ashamed of me. Ironically, it seemed that the portion of himself that he still withheld from me was the part I most desired. If only he would look at me with the same intensity and interest that was evident whenever he engaged with other people. I wanted access to his thoughts, not just the routine ritualistic pleasantries we exchanged or the physical explorations he made at night. I made sure to check any new diaphragm, used with all the right accompanying creams, and as soon as I could after weaning Patricia, took the pill as well. Our children were my treasures, but I didn't know who I might become if we added a third to the mix and having children became my whole *raison d'être*.

Paul started school and arrived home every afternoon full of excitement and chatter. Patricia was a beautiful but fretful child who hardly ever slept. I loved to hold her; she would, in calm moments, gaze at me with dark, serious eyes and give a brief smile. She smelt of orange blossom and determination. I was always weary, so between chores and the business of mothering, was often caught napping. But if the phone rang, it could be an invitation for a cuppa. It was one solitary ring if initiated by Gabby, two if by Nancy. My signal was three-rings and I knew they'd come over if the timing was right for us all.

'Got the kettle on Lisie?' Gabby might say as she bustled through the door with some treat—freshly baked biscuits, a pile of magazines or some baby clothes her daughter had grown out of. She was generous by nature, in thought and deed.

'Here, Lisie, put these scones out—they have to be eaten. I baked them this morning.'

But some days, I noticed a bruise on her arm, or a scratch on her neck. On one occasion, she arrived with her ring finger taped in a bulky bandage.

'Oh you know me, girls, I'm just a klutz. Caught it in the door. Terribly clumsy.'

Nancy and I exchanged glances, but Nancy would divert.

'Patty still not sleeping, 'Lis?' Nancy might say, moving to the carrycot and tickling the baby's cheek. Then she'd turn and look me over. 'Well, you could do with a decent long nap, even if Patty doesn't need one. Why don't I take her home after this and let you have some time on your own?'

'Oh, Nance, please just call her Trish, or her full name. Patty reminds me of cupcakes. Anyway, she'll need a feed soon.'

'Then do that now while we're having our tea, and we'll see what happens. If she sleeps, fine; if not, I'll take her with me for an hour or two and tell her one of my stories. She'll be snoozing in no time.'

And they'd always make themselves at home in my kitchen, chattering and clattering while setting cups and saucers on the laminated table; they'd forage in my cupboards for snacks, fetch milk from the refrigerator. In time, I learned to make myself just as comfortable in their homes and to reciprocate their kindnesses in any manner of ways.

I didn't know why they were so generous, why they picked me to befriend. But I was grateful. I so enjoyed being part of their alliance and having an entrée into that precious, colourful and comforting world of female friendships. With Nancy and Gabby, I giggled and chortled, and it felt so good, so *clean*, to share in moments of pure fun and joyfulness, to experience great *head-thrown-back* guffaws. It brought back the pleasure and sense of play and innocent recklessness that I remembered from childhood games. Such a contrast to the carefully measured smiles that so many people dispensed by the half-spoonful.

Getting to know their families was important for us all. Paul found excitement in the ready-made cartel of playmates he had in Nancy's and Gabby's children. Mark found easy companionship with their spouses.

Nancy was married to Jack, a navy man who was at sea for weeks or months at a time. He was a charmer, pleasant and easy-going, funny, and a dab hand with anything mechanical, so was a much sought after Mr Fixit. A handsome man too, tall, navy-neat and the kind who could have had a girl in every port. Maybe he did. They had three children—two boys and a girl. Their boys were close in age and carbon copies of each other, both being fair-haired, blue-eyed and inclined to be boisterous, but kept in line by Nancy's no-nonsense parenting. The daughter, Rachel, was darker, quiet, timorous, an example, you might say, of someone frightened of her own shadow, though seemingly content to live in the shade cast by Nancy's dynamic personality.

Gabby's husband, Frank, managed a hotel and worked late most nights. He was prematurely bald, had a broad smile and was an engaging conversationalist, always quick with a joke and on top of the latest in politics and sport. He and Gabby were easy-going with their four children—two boys, two girls—who were pleasant and usually polite and sensible, though, like all siblings, they had their skirmishes. We heard one of the boys was rough with other kids at school.

On weekends, along with others in our little street community, we'd often get together for a barbeque or card games, or to help one another with some home improvement project. There was real pleasure in being surrounded by such genial company. When I mentioned, just casually, that all the rooms in our house needed painting, Gabby organised a working bee to take place over a couple of weekends. Moving in convoys from room to room, Jack sanded and applied undercoat to the skirting boards, Frank and Mark tackled the ceilings and cornices, while we three women did the walls.

Patricia dozed or observed the activity curiously from her cot in the kitchen, agreeing to be fed and changed every few hours. If she squirmed fretfully or cried, one of the older kids would take her out onto the back porch and jiggle her around, sing to her, plug her mouth with a dummy or bottle until she settled.

The back yard filled with children; they played any games that required action and screaming, and we all stopped mid-way through the work to eat pies, sandwiches, ice-cream. I don't remember how it started, but on the last afternoon, when we were outside cleaning up, Nancy began flicking paint from her wet brush at Jack, who retaliated, only his spray hit Frank. Before long, we took what was left in the paint tins and randomly threw globs of colour at each other in a mock fight. The children, surprised and charmed by our antics, soon transformed it into a game of *stealth and smear*. By the end, all of us were wet, covered in splotches, streaks, smudges, shades of white and blue, and doubled over with glee. Rachel was laughing so much she peed her pants. Paul, gobbets of paint stuck in his hair, his cheeks and legs daubed and speckled, ran whooping in circles around the clothesline. No-one was spared as a target, so by the end, we all looked like clowns. Mark and I hadn't shouted or cackled with such merriment in all our time together. I remember that day very well, so attached am I to that singular funny moment and the freedom we all had. Back then.

CHAPTER
TWENTY-THREE

Mark had missed being conscripted for compulsory National Service because of his birth date—selection was as random as that. But in August, six months after Patricia was born, he entered the house with a buoyant step.

'I'm changing jobs,' he said, dropping his work satchel onto the kitchen table and displacing some vegetables I was about to chop. He extracted a beer from the fridge and kept his back turned while he opened the bottle and took a brief, determined swig.

I listened out for Paul. The television was on so he'd be splayed on the floor in front of it. Patricia was due to be fed soon. I proceeded cautiously.

'Okay. What is it?' Contrived indifference struggled in the muscles between my shoulder blades.

'It's with the Royal Aussie Engineers. Army thing. Starts in six weeks.' Another swig before he looked squarely at me. 'I have to do some training.'

'Training for what?' I focused on the rhythmic chop chop chop of vegetables, the knife directed firmly by a wrist fused in fury.

He turned away again, his hand loose around the neck of his beer bottle, and strolled over to the living room door.

'Tell you later,' he said without a backward glance, then walked through to greet Paul. I heard in his voice that steady, warm, tender tone he reserved for his children. 'Hi there tiger! What've you been doing? Come outside before it's too dark and we'll kick the footy around, okay?'

'Daddy!' The noise from the television abruptly stopped and I could hear Mark's resolute footsteps alongside Paul's excited scampering. The back door slammed.

Patricia set up a wail. I turned off the pot of boiling water and hurried to the baby's bedroom.

Over dinner we kept things light, engaging with Paul's chatter and Patricia's cooing and babbling.

'How was your day?' I said, the same question posed in the same way, at much the same time, every evening. I concentrated on the meal, the scrape of cutlery against plate.

'Pretty good.' His standard response, monotone and predictable. 'How about yours?'

'Okay', I said, determined to be pleasant.

'What did you do?'

'The usual, you know. Chores. The baby. I took her to the clinic this morning for her vaccination. She was so good; didn't scream at all. Saw Gabby later. Did some shopping. Paul's made a new friend at school, haven't you sweetie?'

Paul's head was bent over his plate; he picked bits of vegetables out of his casserole, examined them suspiciously before sampling them, piece by small piece. Part way through, he looked up again with pleasure at my question. 'Yes, and his name's Alec and he can do this!' He demonstrated a karate move with his arm. Fork and carrots fell to the floor.

The banalities ran their course while Paul continued to play with his food, even though he was keen to get back to the television. Later, Mark volunteered to take over the routine bathing and story-telling, thus avoiding the inevitable discussion, while I nursed and paced with a colicky Patricia. Finally, in bed, propped against the pillows, we talked, each assessing the chances of a safe passage through turbulent waters.

His voice was twenty degrees below petulant. 'I've told you many times that I want to try something new, stretch my wings a bit.'

My voice was agitated, annoyed. 'But why the army, for God's sake? That's not *you*! That's not what you want! You're an engineer, you fix things.

There's a bloody war going on and you want to become part of the machine that supports it? You know where I stand on all that. Besides, you've only been in this job for a year, even less than that.'

'Yes, and I'll come back to it. They're giving me special leave, a government-sponsored deal. Means I'll do some training, some travel, but come back to the office here at intervals till the end of the contract. It'll be like I'm doing two jobs, and the pay will be much better. Excellent, in fact.'

'But I don't understand. Where will you be working? Training for what? What sort of job is it?'

He paused. 'There'll be some short-term stuff in Vietnam.'

'What? No. Mark, you can't go there. It's stupid. You've got a family now. You can't go. It's dangerous and…' Other emotions took over. My face contorted, scrunched and ugly, and I turned away, reached for a tissue on the side table.

'I won't be out on the front line, Elise. They need engineers to advise on roads and bridges, water management, things like that.' He didn't mention then about having to penetrate minefields, locate and help disarm booby traps. He didn't yet know those risks himself, though he would soon find out.

'Anyway, you know Pete's over there. I couldn't say 'no' to supporting him and his mates, now could I.'

I turned to face him again, the movement twisting my nightdress tight over my hips.

'Pete who? Your cousin Peter?'

Mark lay back on the pillow with his arms behind his head. I punched the soft part of his inner arm, harder than intended, and he flinched b ut continued to look at the ceiling.

'You'll go to a war that we shouldn't even be in because of some half-baked sense of obligation to a cousin you've spent about five minutes of your life with?'

He yawned, then frowned at me. 'It's not like that, Elise. Anyway, I know a couple of other fellas going too. We'll all be looking out for each other. You should be proud I'm going to be doing something for our country. And for us. Look, with this we'll be able to afford someone to look after

Patricia a few days a week if you do really want to find a job. That'd make you happy, wouldn't it?'

His tone was light, glib. He continued trying to placate me, his voice smooth and soothing; he touched my shoulder, began to massage it, while I stared at the wall. I didn't have the will or energy to continue arguing that night. He cupped a hand over one of my breasts.

'Don't!' I pushed his hand away.

He leant over, kissed the skin that stretched taut beneath my collarbone, stroked a nipple and moved his hip against my frosty side. Then he turned my head, kissed my mouth, not noticing or perhaps not caring that my lips remained clamped in a thin line of exasperation. His hands moved over me, and it disturbed me to find that I could feel so much anger and so much desire in that one moment.

From then until he left Sydney two months later, he was a different man. Excited. Reckless. Passionate. Channelling all his energy and focus on his impending adventure. Or as I saw it, his escape. But when we said our goodbyes at the airbase, unexpectedly, his eyes filled, briefly, though he said nothing while I clung to him. We were a couple drowning, creating a dance of desolation. Paul wrapped his arms around Mark's legs and howled. Patricia smiled and hiccupped in her pram. A photographer snapped us just as I turned to leave, my no doubt distraught face focused on manoeuvring the children through the diminishing crowd. The photographer asked for our names, and I gave them, summarily, absent-mindedly.

CHAPTER TWENTY-FOUR

Of course I saw very little of my mother after the move to Sydney. She wasn't comfortable speaking on the phone, and even less at ease with the idea of getting on a plane. In the letters we exchanged and during our occasional phone calls, she wanted to hear about the children and always asked after Mark. There was usually an update about Marion, sometimes Jeffrey and his children, but I'd have tuned out by then. She was vague about her own life, vague about everything in fact, and I wondered if older age had brought with it the beginnings of dementia, or whether it was a general melancholia. Perhaps both. Once, I travelled to Melbourne by train with the children to see her—a long and tedious nightmare of a trip, with my own two kids whining and complaining the whole way, and other people's children either screeching, being sick, or running up and down the aisle in pursuit of an elusive ice-cream trolley or a toilet. The carriage smelt of urine, vomit, stale food and turpentine. Even with Craig absent, my brief visit back to the old Melbourne house raised prickly spectres, so I was glad to go home. Home. Sydney! How much I'd initially resisted that move, but I was grateful now.

The next time I saw Lillian was when Mark organised for me to fly down on my own while his parents travelled to Sydney to mind the kids. Mum and I spent most of that visit in Shepparton with her sister Helen, who'd mellowed and proved to be a marvellous hostess, generous to a fault, and sensitive to the fact that we, Mum and I, also needed time to ourselves. We walked a lot, talked and enjoyed companionable silences while the one important topic remained buried.

Marion returned temporarily from overseas and visited Sydney a few times, but our lives were too different. I sensed a new coolness and abruptness in her, no vestiges at all of the sunny little sister I'd once known. Family members grow apart, I knew this, but I was sorry there was no genuine connection anymore. Her beautiful face had developed frown lines and she wore those pursed lips that can suggest either disapproval or private pain, perhaps both. Her voice had lost its youthful, exuberant character; she'd also succumbed to the fashion for exaggerated make-up and a dark-dyed, blunt, both of which gave her a severe look. My bright, light-hearted sunflower of a sister was lost.

• • •

Without Nancy and Gabby, I wouldn't have coped so well over those next few years. I'd picked up how to be a better parent from watching both of them, and settled somewhere between Nancy's more clinical, regimented approach and Gabby's casual hands-off style of child-rearing. We were all pretty much tackling it alone. Nancy's Jack was deployed on short naval stints around Vietnam, Singapore, Hong Kong and the Philippines. The busy hotel that Gabby's Frank operated in the city became home to a stream of American and Australian soldiers on R and R leave. With the opening times of the bars extended to 10pm, he rarely made it home before midnight.

In such circumstances, we women developed an even closer camaraderie and enjoyed independence in our respective households. I confidently paid bills, balanced the budget and ran a household more or less capably, with all its maintenance requirements, while raising the children, albeit haphazardly at times. We looked after each other's kids, car-pooled for the school run if the weather prevented them from walking, held joint kids' birthday parties, baked treats, worked out rosters for school fete stalls, helped out if anyone was sick, and protected each other from news reports of war fatalities, storms at sea and drunken brawls in the city.

Who was it that wrote about life being partly what we make of it, and the rest by the friends we choose? I'd chosen well. Or they'd chosen me, and I was the lucky one.

Nancy had polio as a child and always walked with a slight limp. Now she needed a cane and the housework was harder for her than it once was. Gabby and I would routinely go over to pitch in. Despite Nancy's protests, one of us could easily distract her with chatter and tea while the other whisked through a room with broom, mop, duster or vacuum cleaner. In those days, it wasn't considered interfering, as it would be now. Back then, it was just normal. Neighbourly.

We were there straight away to help support Gabby when her oldest child telephoned to say, 'Mum's bleeding and it won't stop.'

I found her in her bathroom, crouched over a bucket in a corner, trying not to get blood on the mat as she suffered a miscarriage. Nancy called the doctor, got Gabby into bed, and placed thick towels between her legs, while I shooed the children outside and cleaned up. Shortly afterwards, Frank tripped down the stairs at the hotel and was in hospital for two weeks with a fractured lumbar vertebra. Gabby was still recovering—weakened, distracted and unmotivated—so I tidied, made sure the beds were made, and packed school lunches while their four children did their chores before school. Nancy cooked meals for them and organised for her brother and a few of his mates to manage things at the hotel for as long as Frank was bed-bound.

There was a time too, after one of Mark's trips home, when I had a very early miscarriage and my friends rallied around me, cajoling me through my period of conflicted emotions. These included extinguished hopes, guilty relief, and despair over another child lost to me, plus the disappointment that comes to all of us when our bodies don't behave as we expect them to.

We three friends also saw each other through the various mishaps that befell our children: Paul's sudden asthma attack that had me stay overnight with him in hospital; Patricia's broken ankle when she stumbled down the back steps; Gabby's daughter's fractured arm when she fell out of a tree;

Nancy's boy who nearly impaled himself on a broken section of their back fence as he climbed over—he'd bled profusely by the time one of the other kids alerted her. We formed a complementary team: with my medical and practical skills, Nancy's calm, no-nonsense approach, and Gabby's positive energy and heightened compassion. It was as if we exchanged and absorbed the best of each other. I felt I belonged.

They could make me laugh, help soothe any upsets, and I believed the person they saw in me was someone they genuinely liked. But as open as we were when together, we each held onto secrets. We confided in each other, certainly, but there were things that were never discussed, even when their roots were evident. Nancy's youngest, Rachel, a quiet, serious girl with dark hair and brown eyes, clearly held one of her mother's secrets. Nancy's eyes were a bright, deep cobalt blue, and Jack's a much softer, gentler shade, like washed-out denim, so you might have assumed that Rachel had been adopted but for the fact that in every other way she was the image of her mother. If Nancy was concerned about this, she didn't show it. If Jack was aware, he didn't show it either—his interactions with Rachel were the same as with his boys. He was protective and kind-hearted though stern and regimental with all of them if he deemed it necessary. In my view, he was a fine man.

Gabby's secrets…well, I'm sure there were several, but over time you couldn't help but see small welts or bruising on her arms, a scratch on her face, a broken finger, occasionally a black eye when she'd yet again 'walked into a door' or 'tripped over something'. Sometimes her voice on the end of the phone became brisk, even officious, if Frank had come home extra late the night before. 'Sorry, can't make it today! Got a bit of a headache. I'll be fine tomorrow.' And a few days later we'd see her wearing thicker makeup. The face she presented to the world was one of eternal sunshine and who were we to question that? We should have, though.

• • •

During this time of Mark's extended absences, I continued my search for my first-born son. I needed to believe that losing him to a new life had been worthwhile and that he was with a good family, had grown to be a healthy and happy teenager who might, someday, want to meet me. While still living in Victoria I'd made the annual pilgrimage to Melbourne's Public Records Office to speak to staff who refused to make my records public. In Sydney, I wrote letters every few months, always eliciting a response along the lines of "We regret to inform you that no information can be provided to you at this time."

But persistence eventually brought results. A thick envelope arrived, containing a letter requesting I complete the details and return the attached bulky forms. The laws had changed, along with the name of the department, and my request had been reviewed. Perhaps my file had become an irritation, my regular communications making it tiresome enough to prompt someone to want to stamp it "Case Closed".

Several weeks after I'd completed and returned the paperwork, I received a typed response on official letterhead, which stated that the adoptive parents had agreed to the department providing basic information about my son, but with the proviso, within their rights, that no address or other contact information be released. The letter read in part:

'The child you placed for adoption in 1954 is called Simon. His parents wish to inform you that he is doing well at school, is good at sports, and has many other interests. He takes piano lessons and enjoys reading and football. They do not wish to provide a photo at this time.

'His parents also advise that Simon knows he is adopted, but to date has shown no interest in locating or being put into contact with his biological parents. They are willing to provide updates on his progress, but do not wish to be contacted by you directly. We ask that you honour their wishes, keep your enquiries to a minimum and utilise the appropriate channels for any further queries. Please note the new address and phone number for such enquiries below.'

I read and re-read the letter, tracing its words with my finger, memorising, hoping, trying to conjure flesh and blood from the pages. *Simon... Simon...*

the word eased itself onto my tongue, gave him shape and substance, plumped out that tiny mewling being that had been bundled away from me like an armful of laundry. I tried to imagine him, fourteen years old, perhaps with fair hair and contented eyes. Maybe a taller version of me. Well, he was smart, had musical abilities. I wondered about the people he called Mum and Dad; what they did with their lives? Where did they live? How I might find out more, meet him, hold him? The idea of this Simon, *my* boy, dominated my thoughts; I imagined a tearful but joyous reunion before sleep finally claimed me.

• • •

I was more and more drawn to watching Paul and Patricia ever more closely. Paul had his distinctive ways and his own temperament—a contented disposition and a certain jauntiness in his step that suggested the same sort of optimism that Marion once had. He had Mark's features and frame; he'd grown tall for his age and was lean and lanky. A kind, thoughtful boy, he was creative, inventive, affectionate. I delighted in hearing him sing or hum quietly over his homework, his expression a study in concentration. He made friends easily but lost them too; children can usually sense vulnerability in others, and thus be ruthless. Paul endured my subsequent overprotectiveness with good grace.

Some people said that Patricia looked more like me, but she reminded me a little of Jeffrey, with her small fine features every so often set in a scowl. Her earlier fractiousness was also reminiscent of what I remembered of him. She was tall too, had Mark's long fingers and feet, his smile (when she allowed it) and his beautiful honey-coloured eyes. I'd stare, drink her in, and feel a rush of adoration and affection, but as much as I loved her with the same fierce intensity as I did Paul, she seemed determined to fend me off. By the time she was two years of age, she'd evolved into a tight little ball of resistance. Getting her to agree to be bathed, fed, dressed, undressed, cuddled, read to, put to bed—all these things required persuasion, bribery, guile. I joked to Mark and my mother that Patricia had been born with the word 'No' stencilled inside her forehead and this was her life's mantra. There was nothing simple, straightforward or readable about her gaze. She measured out her charms carefully, deliberately, in the same way she tipped water into the tiny pink floral teacups of her tea set. And a sense of complexity and deliberation was associated with almost every one of her movements. But she grew, and the tantrums tapered. When she allowed herself a smile, her face became a miniature blossom opening full to the sun, and my heart would shimmer. When Paul or I could make her laugh, that laugh that was a sound so light, joyous, unfiltered, those were blessed moments indeed. Whenever Mark returned, she readily attached herself to him, followed him like a puppy and pushed Paul away from him so she could own him. I loved that she felt that close connection.

In my daydreams, I'd try to imagine all three of my children together, playing, talking, having a picnic with me, with Mark, by the river. In these stolen moments of reverie, Mark was back for good and we were one fine, happy, united family.

• • •

The truth is. The truth is…I don't exactly know what the truth is anymore. I've lived so long in my imagination and have been so long sifting through memories, that today it's all become jumbled and I don't always recognise what was real, what was lost, what was discarded in anger and what was hoped for but never achieved. Not all the puzzle pieces seem to fit. I remember very well the things that were important to me, but trying to remember the time frame—that's more elusive these days.

Sophie dear, you've been so very kind, but you're busy and the hospitals are in crisis, so I won't burden you further. The nursing home people have found me a lovely volunteer who's available to transcribe stories for me. He starts next week. I'm sure he won't be as efficient as you've been, but I'm pleased, nevertheless, and determined to get all this tidied and finished. I'm not getting any younger, am I?

With love, always, dearest Sophie. Take care of yourself.

PS I spoke to your mum last night, and to your brothers and sister. It was lovely to hear they've all recovered from this wretched virus. Just you be careful, darling, especially as you're in the thick of it. A lot of staff here have succumbed, and three more residents have died this month.

Last thing—tell your father he's not to keep driving over here just to look at me through a window. He's busy, and it's way too far for him to come.

CHAPTER
TWENTY-FIVE

My future floated in wispy dreams in my head. My past was selectively buried. My present was fortunate enough—cemented friendships and an established routine with the children made life easier. But I heard little from Mark, was apprehensive about his safety, and panicked whenever there was news of another casualty in Vietnam. I needed him home. Though competent enough in managing the household alone, I missed him terribly. Now I better understood my mother's vulnerabilities as a single parent.

Over that time, Mark returned every few months on 'recovery leave', always a little richer in wealth but more broken in spirit and a lot less sure that what he was doing was right. But he wouldn't give it up. When home, he could be more absent than he was while overseas.

'I'll be in the garage, got a project I want to finish,' or 'I'll have a bit of a drive along the coast road, need to clear my head. Be back in time for dinner.'

While he paid the children plenty of attention when he was home, he became emotionally distant with me, and his libido all but disappeared. I recognised his depression and begged him to give up the job. His argument always came back to money, citing how much better placed we'd be to pay off the mortgage, have holidays, or eventually get the kids into university.

I found part-time work as a community nurse 'fill-in'; the flexible hours fitted well with the children's routines. The kids grew taller. Paul developed a nervy twitch just as Patricia seemed more comfortable in her skin. I thought my heart would burst from loving them both so much.

Lillian wrote regularly, the tone of her letters ever warmer over time. She was always interested in the children's welfare and expressed delight that I had a career of sorts. She mentioned neither Craig nor Jeffrey, and wrote sparingly about Marion's activities, which primarily seemed to involve parties and travel. I responded promptly, either by letter or a phone call. Mum still didn't trust the mechanics of a telephone, so our conversations were often stilted, despite our filtered warmth and familiarity crossing paths down the wire. I offered to book flights for her to Sydney, though my motive wasn't altogether altruistic since I knew she'd help with the kids.

Mum initially sounded horrified. 'How on earth do those aeroplanes stay up, Elise? I can't imagine how they fly with all those people and suitcases. And the food! I can easily catch a train.'

'No Mum, that'll take far too long.'

'I'll think about it.'

Perhaps it was also her fear of being away from all that was familiar, or of spending more time alone with me, especially if aspects of our shared past could conspire to emerge and wound.

Finally, I took the manipulative route. 'You should be much better acquainted with the kids, Mum. Paul loves your company, but Patricia scarcely knows you. They're growing so quickly; it'd be a shame for all of you to miss out.'

That worked. She acquiesced graciously, even with enthusiasm. Motherhood might never have suited her very well, but being a grandmother evidently had its charms. Her subsequent visits always began with her stating, 'Well, Elise, I had to work really hard to keep that plane up in the air.'

She'd become both my mother and my friend.

• • •

My women friends and various neighbours continued large in my life.

Nancy was always a woman to speak up, which was one of the many things I admired about her. She'd been a teacher before having children and was a powerful voice in the Teachers' Union. For years she was a member of the school board and the local council. But though she planned to return to work after Rachel started school, Nancy never quite made it.

'I want to study, use my mind, do some good. Besides, I don't particularly like other people's children, except the ones around here, some of them, anyway. I couldn't stand being stuck again in a classroom all day with smelly, cheeky kids.'

Despite limited opportunities for women at that time, she enrolled in an arts course, though we learnt that her attendance was patchy. Always on the lookout for a cause, she became a champion for social justice. When I first knew her, she regularly joined protests at the university campus to support Aboriginal land rights. She added her voice to the feminist movement, burnt her bra (one of them, anyway) and carried 'Abortion: Our right to choose' banners in Martin Place. She'd attended vigils in Centennial Park after John and Robert Kennedy and Martin Luther King were assassinated, joined peace marches holding a 'Ban the Bomb' placard, and joined a 'sit-in' at a proposed nuclear power plant site in Jervis Bay. At home, she engaged in local issues, frequently harassing the council about the removal of trees in nearby parkland or penning irate letters to the newspaper about the potential mining of Colong Caves.

Gabby and I kept an eye on the children whenever Nancy deemed it necessary to join the fray. I admired her passion and her willingness to *stand up and be counted*, though she sometimes backed up her ideas with rubber-band logic, elastic facts, her steely intellect and a disarming grin.

Jack was less impressed. 'You're such a nutty left-wing rat-bag, Nancy. It's unbecoming for a woman. For anyone. Tone it down, will you? You're an embarrassment.' But then he'd smile and move outside with his beer, and she'd chuckle and keep talking.

She was loud in her condemnation of conscription, and despite her limp, marched eagerly beside the many who were then expressing their opposition to Australia's involvement in the Vietnam War. One night, I caught a brief glimpse of Nancy on a TV news bulletin; she was standing fearlessly in front of mounted riot police, supported on one side by a young, bearded student and on the other, by an elegantly dressed man in his fifties. They were chanting 'We don't want your effing war' and she'd lost her cane in the mêlée. Her face as she looked up and yelled at the officer on horseback was a picture of excited defiance.

Police arrested Nancy during a May Day Parade one year, though it had started as a peaceful gathering and she claimed to have merely been distributing anti-war pamphlets for Save Our Sons. As she told it, there'd been a stoush with a small group who'd called her un-Australian. One man tried to tear up her stack of pamphlets. She recounted the events for me, leading with her indignation:

'Leave those alone! Just take one and read it,' she'd shouted at the man responsible.

'This parade is about workers' rights—you don't belong here. Go back to your hippy commune, you useless bitch. You should be working and paying taxes, like the rest of us.'

'Why aren't *you* at work then? Ouch! Get off.'

The man's wife had stepped intentionally hard on Nancy's foot, shouting 'Communist harpy!'

The man added 'Deadbeat! You're a terrible example. Why aren't you at home looking after your children?'

'I yelled back, Elise, of course I had to. Think I might have used the F-word. Tomasz—you know, from church—he backed me up.' Then Nancy grinned. 'I only flicked my cane at the woman, but somehow it drew a little blood, barely anything, honestly, and then we were in the middle of a brawl. The officer who arrested me was ever so polite. He escorted me to the police van and helped me in. Very courteous he was, smiling all the time. At the station, he let me call Gabby so she could pick up the kids from school. He made me cups of tea, helped me fill out the paperwork. He was such a sweetie, Elise. Asked polite questions about my family, held me there for the requisite hour, then let me go with a smile and a warning to stay out of trouble. He was a few years younger than me and quite handsome. And he had a brother in Vietnam, so....'

Gabby was the opposite of Nancy in almost every way—generally the peace-keeper, who kept her views very much to herself, unless it was an issue that involved any of her children, of whom she was exceedingly protective. Her kids seemed mature for their age, a little distant but polite enough most of the time. Gabby was an organiser, efficient, practical, methodical, and thus able to help coordinate her friends' lives. She kept the books for the hotel business in order, was active in the school canteen, and convinced me to volunteer with her at a charity shop once a month. She was compassionate too, intuitive, a good listener, and a great foil to Nancy's more forceful approach.

I wished Gabby would assert herself more, especially with Frank. Bruises still occasionally appeared as odd-shaped smudges beneath her make-up. I tried to talk to her about it, but she was always defensive, dismissive, even angry if the topic ever strayed into that territory.

When Gabby appeared with a split lip one time, Nancy confronted her and threatened to call the police, but she denied any problem. 'Leave off Nance. You don't need to involve yourself. Just leave things alone. Elise, you too. Stop trying to change me.'

'Gab, we're trying to protect you. Why are you protecting him?'

'Nance, I'm not. It's not what you think. He's a good man.'

'Rubbish. No-one who does those things is good. You're scared to leave, I understand, but…'

Gabby turned to me again. 'Can you pick up the kids from school today, I don't feel well.'

'Sure, but…'

'Just please, leave me be, both of you. You don't understand. And you're not to say anything at all to Frank, ever. Hear me? I'll never speak to either of you again if you do. It'll just make everything worse. Don't say anything. You're the only true friends I have.'

It was clear that while she was easy-going, generous and kind with all others in her life, Gabby was unable to be those things to herself. And she was very, very stubborn. Even Nancy backed down. At that time too, I was so preoccupied with Mark's latest visit home, I allowed my response to Gabby's issue to drift.

CHAPTER
TWENTY-SIX

Those tentacles of the past once more reached out to intrude. I received a brief letter, hand-written, signed by a Louise Parry, stating she wanted to meet me to discuss 'a matter of some importance'. I was initially inclined to throw the letter away, but curiosity got the better of me and I left it on the kitchen table while I went to rescue Patricia, who was yelling at the back door about a lost shoe. While I was attending to that, Gabby sailed inside (we rarely knocked in those days), and I could hear the whistle of the kettle starting up. She waved the letter at me when I walked back in with a hiccupping and snotty Patricia trailing behind.

'What's this all about then? You don't mind me looking, do you? Who's Louise Parry?'

'No idea.' I reached for an old, battered biscuit tin and passed it to Gabby.

'So why is she writing to you, and what's so important?'

'Again, no idea.' I sat heavily, holding Patricia's hand. She whined, clambered into my lap, and pretended to attack me with the shoe. I grabbed it and dropped it to the floor, whereupon she struggled to get out of my arms and escalated her whine to a shriek. The promise of a biscuit placated her and she sat still, observing, waiting. Gabby foraged and passed one to her, then placed the letter on the table between us.

CHAPTER TWENTY-SIX

'Well, you're going to ring her, right? There's a phone number there.'

'Oh, it's probably some charity thing, asking for money for something or other.'

'Call her.'

'No.'

'Then I'll call,' and she rose to go to the phone in the hallway, letter in hand.

'Hey!' I couldn't move fast enough to stop Gabby; she held the handset and was dialling the number as I reached her. She handed the mouthpiece to me and took Patricia from my grip, walking a few paces away to tickle her, which prompted a giggle.

I froze when I heard a woman's voice answer with a tentative 'Hello?'

I took a breath. 'Mrs Parry?'

'Yes?' A nervous, high inflection. 'Well, it's Miss Parry.'

'Ah, I'm Elise Harrington. You sent a letter?'

Silence.

I spoke again. 'What is it you want exactly?'

I heard an in-drawn breath at the end of the line. 'I'd rather talk to you in person, if that's all right.' Her voice had an unaffected quality, though she was forthright, as though the words had been well-rehearsed.

'Well, I'm not arranging a meeting if I don't know what it's about.' I matched tone for tone.

'It's…it's regarding Mark.'

'What's happened? Is he all right?' Alarmed, I stared at Gabby. She moved closer so she could hear too, but retreated when I waved her away.

I tried again, my voice an octave higher. 'Tell me what's happened? Is he all right? Is he hurt?' A host of tragedies played out in my head.

Another moment of quiet on the line, then the sound of static and a deep intake of breath. 'Mrs Harrington, I haven't seen Mark for, well, quite a while, so I don't know where he is or anything. I just need to talk to you about something. I met him, you see, late last year.'

'And?' My chest was doing triple thumps and I had a terrible urge to pee. Paul slid rowdily through the front door and though I saw his mouth moving, I heard nothing of what he was saying. Gabby, puzzled, grabbed

Paul's hand and whisked both children into the living room.

A new note crept into the voice at the other end. Arrogance? Or was it prudence? 'I'd really rather not talk about it on the phone. Can I call around to see you?'

I replied, 'No. I'll come to you.'

• • •

Nancy and Gabby both offered to go with me, but someone needed to watch over the younger children, so it became a choice between having Nancy's forthright steeliness accompany me or Gabby's quieter, gentler demeanour. Whatever it was I would hear, and I already knew what it would be, I thought Gabby might at least be able to calm my nerves before and after the meeting.

After settling the kids with Nancy, we left in Gabby's Austin and drove slowly through steady traffic to a suburb close to the sea. Several wrong turns later, we found the address, but stayed in the car for several minutes, trying to guess at the manner and number of occupants inside the house.

'Well, it's big.' Gabby offered.

'Quite old though, by the look of it.'

'Would that be solid brick or brick veneer? I don't like the colour.'

I managed a short snort of laughter. 'Gab, we're not here to talk about bloody bricks! Look, let's just turn around and go home. I don't think I can do this.'

Gabby twisted in her seat and stared at me for several seconds. 'Listen, I didn't drive all the way out here just to turn around and go back. Whatever she has to say, we'll hear it and then we'll deal with it. It might be nothing. Maybe she's his cousin or someone he worked with. Maybe she borrowed some money from him. Maybe he borrowed some from her. Come on lady, get out and start moving. I'm coming in too.' And she pushed open the car door and darted around to my side, grabbed the handle and yanked it open. Gabby seemed to be morphing into Nancy.

I stood up reluctantly, fighting nausea.

Gabby led the way through the wrought iron gate and along a short path that bordered a small garden of well-tamed lawn, bright philodendron, hydrangeas, and a few straggly rose bushes in need of pruning. The air was sticky and humid, and the smell of meat cooking wafted through the nylon curtains at one of the front windows.

I stopped at the bottom of the five steps which lead to the front door. 'Gabby, I can't,' then leant over, hands on knees, staring at the ground and breathing hard, a sprinter who'd lost the race.

Gabby, almost at the door, stopped and turned, determination hardening her features.

'Elise! What's wrong with you? There's nothing to be afraid of.' A tender pause. 'You'll be okay. Knowing what this is all about will be better than not knowing anything. You'll talk to her, we'll leave, then we'll do whatever you need to do after that. Come on sweetie.'

Gabby extended her hand towards me, using the other to knock on the door, twice. When it opened, a short man, possibly mid-fifties, with a stocky build, stood squarely within its frame. He wore casual trousers, a loose short-sleeved blue shirt and held a cigarette between fingers of one hand. His expression was one of curiosity, wary but friendly enough as he sized us up.

'Yes?' His voice was a pitch higher than his bulk suggested.

Gabby spoke. 'Does Louise Parry live here?'

'Who wants to know?' With a noisy nasal intake of breath, he stood a little taller, as his voice found a lower register. "She's inside." Ash from his cigarette fell to the floor before he took a long drag. He squared his shoulders just a fraction and blocked any glimpse of what might have been behind him.

I stared down at my feet, agitation still fluttering beneath my breastbone.

Gabby hesitated then began in a rush. 'We, well, we spoke to Louise on the phone, on Tuesday.'

Just then, a female voice and footsteps on the timber floor grew closer. 'It's okay Dad, she's here for me.'

Something about the tone reminded me of Marion. Youth. The artificial bravado.

The man turned and looked at his daughter, grunted and shuffled side-ways to make room for her to pass him. He stayed for a moment longer to watch we three women grouped together in silence before he spun around to re-enter the house. He moved with surprising speed, given his bulk. Louise looked curiously at both Gabby and me.

'Sorry, I wasn't expecting two of you,' Louise said in a small voice, apologetic rather than accusatory. 'Actually, I wasn't expecting you until later.' She avoided eye contact but indicated the chairs on the veranda. 'Can we sit out here please? There's not, I mean, the place, inside, it's pretty full, um, busy, with people, you know, at the moment.' The boldness less bold.

As she and Gabby moved towards cane armchairs that had seen better days, I scrutinised the woman: she was little more than a girl, perhaps no older than twenty. Her blond hair was tied in a thick rope of ponytail that hung part-way down her back. Her bright green dress, dotted with white daisies, complemented her fair skin; the style was old-fashioned for that time and rather loose, conservative. Gabby sat down first while Louise turned to smile nervously at me and again gestured towards a chair. It was with that turn that I had confirmation, in the swelling of the belly that the flowing fabric of the dress didn't hide.

Louise sat forward in her seat and faced Gabby, taking a few deliberate slow breaths while her eyes darted from ground to garden and back to Gabby. 'Mrs Harrington, I...'

Gabby held up her hand. 'No, not me,' she blurted, and turned her palm and wrist towards me. Such a graceful movement, I thought. Nancy would have probably already pummelled the girl before now.

Louise, embarrassed and flustered, let out a tiny 'Oh,' then turned quickly in her chair to face me, but the movement must have caused her some brief discomfort. Her hands first moved protectively to her belly, then grabbed the sides of her chair. Her knuckles were white.

• • •

I thought I'd be angrier. I thought a lot of painful things in the moments between seeing Louise for the first time and then sitting down on the scratchy furniture. I wanted to be enraged: with Mark, with the girl. But seeing her youth and beauty and burgeoning belly, this took me to my own stolen years, when I was even younger than Louise and had no one on my side. I could hear magpies trilling in the trees, thought I detected a cinnamon-scented bush—grey myrtle perhaps—somewhere near the veranda. I observed the abundant tendrils of mauve wisteria destroying the timber fence at the side. The base of the chair on which I was sitting was devoid of a cushion, so thick strips of cane dug into my thighs and buttocks. My queasiness disappeared.

She was staring at me, with such pretty, wide hazel eyes, and was plainly nervous. I shifted forward, leaned towards her and reached over with both hands to pick up hers. They were soft, unadorned, and trembling. She flushed and looked over to Gabby, unsure of what to make of me, and let her hands lie limp in mine.

My voice belied all the contradictory feelings that had unsettled my insides. 'Louise? Please look at me.' She turned her face towards me again, tears threatening. Any courage she'd mustered before we arrived and in the first minute of our meeting had disappeared.

I tried again. 'I need you to tell me the truth. That's all I want. Is your baby Mark's child?'

She stared out into the distance. A tiny, almost inaudible response. 'Yes.'

'If you're sure then, what is it you want from me?'

A hush followed, punctuated by the shrill whistle of a myna bird. A tear not wanting to be noticed, a private tear that first resisted momentum in the inner corner of her eye, soon marked a transparent trail down Louise's cheek, while her bottom lip quivered. She bit it hard, trying to keep it still. 'I'm sorry,' she said. Then she was crying big, bold waves.

Gabby stared at me, raised her shoulders and hands in a small gesture of helplessness before retrieving a folded handkerchief from her bag. She passed it to Louise, who took it and covered her face, weeping into the cloth. I caught sight of the man dallying inside the front doorway.

My soothing, practical nurse's voice spoke again. 'Louise, will you tell me what happened, where you met, how long this has been going on? I need to know. Is it money you want?'

She shook her head, raised her gaze, eyes red, face blotchy. Yet still beautiful.

I'd deal with Mark later.

• • •

Nancy and Gabby thought me a cold, cold fish because I hadn't screamed, cried, cursed, howled at the moon after Gabby and I left Louise's home. There were reasons why I didn't want to put on a public display. Passivity had become my default mechanism. I held things together, stared ahead through the windscreen during most of the trip home while Gabby tried to talk about what had happened, but then also fell silent. I escaped for a bit, going to that other place inside my head in order to tamp down any emotions, whatever they were. *I'm made of steel. I don't cry. Worse things have happened. Nothing can hurt me.*

By the time we arrived home and I'd collected Patricia from Nancy's house, picked up Paul from school, gone through the motions of setting out their afternoon tea, got them to tell me about their day's activities, cleaned up, supervised backyard play with their friends and prepared dinner, it was almost as though nothing of note had actually occurred. But I wouldn't fool myself for long. When Mark strode through the front door that evening, I watched him with careful eyes, trying to fathom how he'd been able to live his own parallel lives so effortlessly, and by then my heart had shattered and scattered into sharp pieces. I said nothing.

Grief is bold. It is unkind. It is cunning. It is relentless. I put it with the other lockboxes of trauma, inarticulate rage, guilt, and shame that I'd kept hidden for so many years in a dark, heavy place somewhere inside me.

CHAPTER
TWENTY-SEVEN

Each time Mark returned from Vietnam, it was with the promise that the next deployment would be the last; he'd say that things over there were escalating and implied there'd be a withdrawal soon. He acknowledged there'd be no real victory but couldn't bring himself to quit. His eyes were dull. His silence on the dangers, losses and atrocities, on both sides, prevented me from pushing him to talk more. It was enough every day to see the horrific images relayed via television. Mark refused to watch any news, preferring to spend his days reading novels, trashy things he'd pick up at the airport, or go on long walks or runs, gulping in a different air, one not tainted by the smell of cordite, diesel, shit, decay and destruction. He listened for old, familiar sounds to defeat the nightmare of the *whop thwop thwop* of helicopter rotors, or the numbing quiet preceding a mortar shell.

I heard this from various sources that he'd sometimes stay in Frank's pub and drink alone for a few hours, avoiding conversation with Frank or anyone else who tried to catch his eye. When he arrived home in the evenings, he never appeared to be drunk; he'd fall into our routine, kiss my cheek, ask about my day, check on the kids and unfold a newspaper he carried tucked under his arm but which he never read, merely turning its pages. While I cooked dinner, he'd talk for a short while with the children, though Paul seemed not to trust the bulk and forced cheer of his beloved father and might say he had homework, or he'd rush out for more time with friends. It was different with Patricia, who craved Mark's attention. Seeing them together, this time I was the one watching with envy through a speckled flyscreen while the man I held so dear, the damaged man out there, picked up our daughter and swung her in the air and made her squeal with delight. As a father at least, he functioned well enough.

We took the children for occasional holidays to Frazer Beach, a few hours' drive north of Sydney, where we stayed in a caravan park. Once there, Mark would dive recklessly into waves and swim for hours, returning exhausted. We'd walk along the beach, holding hands, saying very little, before he'd sprint off along the sand, trying, I supposed, to outrun his demons. I'd lose sight of him and eventually have to take the children back to the caravan for dinner. At night we'd often eat fish and chips while perched on large boulders by the shore, throw scraps to the loud and aggressive sea gulls, and when the kids were asleep in the caravan annex, I tried to repair the man he'd become. I did it in the only way I knew how, stroking, soothing him like a sick child while he sweated and tossed and cursed in his dreams. Sometimes during the night he'd initiate sex, but it was empty, rough and quick, or too soon abandoned by him in exasperation.

Back home in Sydney, two nights before he was to return to Vietnam, he glanced at me, then at the children—all of us seated at the dinner table—and said, almost inaudibly, 'They're killing women and children over there. And women and children are killing us. We don't know who the enemy is.' And then he turned his face away. 'I'm supposed to be an engineer, Elise. This isn't what...' and lowered his head.

Paul stared at his father then at me. I leaned over to stroke Mark's hair as he slumped further forward.

'You don't have to go back! It's not as if you're in the regular army. And you still have your job here. You have us. We need you here, Mark.' I inclined my head towards the children, who were listening with tight faces and troubled eyes. They'd never before been witness to their father's vulnerability.

'Only a few months more, then I'll be finished.'

'You keep saying that. It's been too long. We don't need the money. We need you.'

Patricia began kicking the underside of the table and rocking her chair back and forth. Food from her plate had spilled onto the floor. Paul slid noiselessly out of his seat and headed for the living room. For once, Mark didn't insist that the children wait and finish their meals. I wiped Patricia's hands mechanically with a napkin and sent her after her brother.

'It's not the money. I just have to do it, finish what I started, support the guys.' His voice cracked as he held out his hand to grasp mine. 'Otherwise, everything I've done up to now, over there, will have been for nothing. Those men I saw, those boys lost, it will all have been for nothing.'

That night in bed he clung to me and wept, until there were no more tears, then his body sought and must have found something life-affirming in my touch. Afterwards he slept like a dead man.

Each time he went away, I wrote him long letters, giving him the details of our ordinary lives and the children's progress and growth. These letters were perhaps the most open and honest I'd been with him in our marriage, but I wondered if he ever received them all. For every three or four letters I sent, there'd be one short dispatch from Mark, often heavily redacted, assuring me he was safe and asking that I give the children extra hugs from him. Though his messages were brief, there was a rawness and honesty to his words. Over this distance, we'd become the friends I'd always hoped we'd be again.

• • •

While Mark was away, I bought a dog from the animal shelter, for security as much as company. He was an adorable pup, part Collie, part Kelpie, and initially very timid and cautious, but he grew into a contented and loyal member of the household and a fierce protector, particularly of Paul and Patricia. The children named him 'Samson', which suited him somehow, and he soon learned to answer to it. Amazing what good company a dog can be. He'd follow me everywhere when the kids were out, sit by my feet and gauge my moods, listen if I was talking to the air, put a paw or rest his chin on my knee if I seemed troubled, nudge my hand for a pat, run around in circles when the children arrived home, and always make me laugh with his antics. Walking him every day, rain, hail or shine, gave me energy and focus.

Two months before the end of the year, Mark was back home for good. He knew nothing about Nancy's involvement in the latest moratorium marches and hadn't anticipated the hostility, verbal abuse or social exclusion directed at veterans by some in the community. There was no heroes' welcome. The public mood had changed. Instead of blaming the government, people blamed individuals who were easy to spot with their army crew cuts and dead eyes and the bewilderment etched on their faces.

Mark returned to his old firm, though by then most former colleagues had moved onwards, upwards, or out. Thus, he was generally regarded as a newcomer, an outsider. Many of his co-workers were young, some not long out of university; they wore a certain arrogance in the tilt of their chins and walked with a confident swagger that belied their lack of experience. Typically, he might hear:

'Hey Mark, killed any gooks lately?'

'Got a grenade there in your lunch box, mate?'

'You listening, soldier boy?'

'Fuck off Spencer.'

'Or what, Harrington? You'll set a booby trap for me?'

Snickers, chortles, idiocy, cruelty.

Before long, Mark applied for other positions, began networking, and secured a good job with a new firm on the North Shore. His spirits eased, a little.

'Elise, I've been thinking about…if you want to get a new job then maybe you should look into it. Especially now Trish's ready for school. We could get a sitter for after school.'

We were in the back garden, I muddy from sweeping wet leaves, he glistening with a sweat brought on by the savage pruning of a fig tree. I stood straight, both me and the rake stiff with anticipation. 'Really? You're happy for me to do that?'

'If you want to.'

I grinned. 'Oh yes! I'm sure there's work at the Royal. It'd be perfect. It's not so far away, and they're desperate for medical staff.'

CHAPTER TWENTY-SEVEN

'Well…,' he smiled.

I dropped the rake to one side and jumped over the pile of leaves to lock him in a clammy, mucky embrace.

• • •

To be working again gave me a sense of coming home. I had a routine I understood and could predict, a team to be part of, and though there were new approaches and techniques to learn, the environment was familiar, comfortable. Doctors were less aloof than I'd remembered. More women had become surgeons and men had entered the nursing profession.

Post-Traumatic Stress Disorder wasn't commonly recognised as a disorder back then. I knew that Mark had real problems because I saw similar signs in other men who came through the hospital wards with physical ailments and broken spirits. Men returning from the war were offered counselling, but in those days, many would have considered it 'unmanly' to take it up. I thought of my father and his comrades, who'd been told they had *shell-shock* or *combat stress reaction*, or even *a lack of moral fibre*, and were simply sent home to rest and buck up. Whenever such memories of Dad surfaced, a twist of guilt would manifest in the restlessness of my muscles.

At home, the children grew, changed and thrived physically. But Paul was quieter and less vocal, less ebullient, than he used to be. Some days he'd drag his feet getting ready for school, and though I tried to find out what the problem was, he'd just clam up, avert his eyes and walk through the front door with his school satchel slung gawkily over his narrow shoulders. I could see from the window how he hunched while he walked, unless a neighbour's child joined him, and then he'd lift his head and there'd be a noticeable and lighter shift in his step and I'd breathe a little easier. Several times I asked his teacher if he was being bullied, but she gave a variation of 'Oh goodness no, Mrs Harrington; I wouldn't let that happen,' and laugh in a nervy type of way that didn't reassure me. I knew the signs.

Patricia, at almost five, was tall for her age but could be clingy and sooky at times, or charming or aloof when it suited her. I was never certain which of these she'd turn on for the moment. She was selective in her choice of friends and I observed that for her, two was company but three a crowd, so any of her social gatherings at our house were quiet and usually held in her room or the garden. Her favourite pastime was watching television, as she had little patience with reading and not much interest in toys. She was energetic and physically well-coordinated, so I encouraged her to take part in outdoor activities, and spent hours with her, throwing balls back and forth, playing hopscotch or cricket and helping her build things with Mark's cast-off wood.

I taught her to knit, thinking it would be a good bonding experience for us, but inevitably she became frustrated at dropping a stitch, or was bored, and would run off to ride her small bike or climb into the jacaranda tree in our backyard. She and Paul could sometimes play well together, but the age difference gave them disparate interests. I didn't fret about her, as she seemed so self-sufficient. I adored her just as much as I did Paul, but she was always, well, just her own wonderful, independent, extraordinary, beautiful, challenging, defiant self.

CHAPTER TWENTY-EIGHT

I could never find the right time to raise the issue of Louise Parry and her pregnancy with Mark, such was my relief that he'd returned home permanently, and besides, I thought the revelation would cause him more pain and panic. Though he'd seemed to settle once he found the new job, he remained locked in his torment, easily became moody and distraught over trivial things. It felt wrong to bring up something that might crush him, crush us. In truth, we didn't find much to say to one another as he wouldn't talk about the past few years, so, on the whole, I continued to flirt with my flights of fancy and keep busy.

While he worked, slept, ran miles, built a new shed at the back of the garden, and sometimes talked to Frank, Jack, and other neighbours, I played the dutiful wife, carried on with my routine, donned the nurse's uniform, mothered our children as best I knew how, attended school concerts and volunteered at community fetes. Sometimes I'd have to collect a bloodied and tearful Paul from school after yet another scuffle. On weekends, we'd go to the beach or have a picnic in the park, or I'd invite a horde of local kids over to play, or any number of other parent-type things. The days passed.

Eventually it happened by accident. We'd agreed to take the children to the zoo on a Sunday, though Mark was snappy, tired and red-eyed after a sleep disturbed by nightmares. A day that had begun sunny and clear turned cloudy and drizzling; gusts of wind sent scraps of newspaper to play in and over the trees. Family groups sought shelter in the souvenir shop or cafe. Mark was determined that we should continue our walk past the various enclosures and pressed on while Paul dragged his feet and Patricia grizzled. Mark's subsequent fury was completely disproportionate to the situation, with those demons bottled inside him that had nowhere to go but out to the ground and the sky, his children and his wife, and the startled strangers hurrying by. I took hold of Mark's arm and tried to pull him towards a shelter but he shook me off angrily, his face a grimace. He shouted something unintelligible, a hoarse sound from a place of deep anguish, and raised his right arm, the palm of the hand flattened as if ready to strike. For a second, I flinched, anticipating a slap, but he dropped his arm and shook his head, just as Patricia's high wailing reached a crescendo. She'd grabbed hold of my skirt and was looking up at me imploringly. I stroked her head as rain drops plopped on and around us. I stared at Mark. Paul was behind him, rooted to the spot, his small fists clenched, his face a collage of anger, fear, defiance and bewilderment. We all stood perfectly still, a brief tableau of misery and quietness before I became aware of the change in temperature and the animal noises—an elephant trumpeting, a Friarbird squawking, the low whoop from a gorilla almost vibrating through the humid air.

And just then Louise hurried by with a pram.

She struggled with an umbrella that threatened to turn itself inside out in the gusting wind; she was leaning forward with it to shelter the front of the pram. She was close but hadn't yet seen us. Nor did Mark see her initially. It must have been my intense observation of Louise that caused him to follow the direction of my gaze. When I next looked at him, it was like observing a balloon deflate. He stared at Louise, at the pram and at me, while truth settled heavily on his face, followed by a look of alarm as he turned to grab hold of Paul, who ducked and ran over to me, jostling with Patricia to hold my hand. Despite the fact that I was shaking inside, I gave a weak smile to the universe, stunned, amused and horrified all at once, then instantly ashamed that I'd seen anything at all funny in the situation, even if just for a moment. His face ashen, Mark turned abruptly and strode towards the exit. Patricia started crying again at Mark's retreating body. I lifted her up, settled her on my hip, and stepped closer to Louise, who had halted, flustered. She dropped her umbrella, flapped both hands in annoyance, and let out a series of frustrated grunts. Clouds darkened and fiercer raindrops splattered on us all.

I reached out my free hand to steady the pram. 'Louise, let me help you.'

Startled, she turned. Recognition gradually registered on her face. 'Mrs Harrington!' That soft, tentative voice. I suppose that's one of the things that Mark fell for. 'I'm sorry, I didn't see you.'

'It's okay. Here, you pull the cover over the baby and I'll hold onto your things.' I set my daughter down, retrieved the umbrella and lifted Louise's bag away from her shoulder to stop it swinging.

Her lips settled into a thin line while she re-organised the pram, checking, with great deliberation, on the child within its confines. The path was almost empty now and we were both soaked, as was Patricia, who'd stopped crying and seemed to be enjoying the experience of being pelted with the rain. Her fingers again clutched the fabric of my skirt. Paul stood a little apart, holding his hands over his head as if to protect himself from the downpour, but watching us with both curiosity and concern.

Louise wore a pale green jacket over a pair of cream slacks that were wet and muddied from the knees down. She was thin, her face a little drawn with frown-lines etched on her forehead and damp hair now plastered closely to her skull, but none of that could disguise her youth, beauty and freshness. She dithered, seeming not to know what she was supposed to be doing except to keep control of the pram.

I pointed. 'Over there, where there aren't many people. You can wait it out until the rain stops.'

And without thinking, I hurried along beside her, with Patricia bobbing next to me, Paul trailing somewhere behind, until we reached the entrance of the reptile enclosure where the overhang shielded us from the increasingly heavy rain.

Patricia kept repeating, 'Where's Daddy?' and tugged once more on my skirt.

There was one other person with us, a short, stocky man in overalls who stood under the eaves and whistled, with his hands in his pockets. He nodded towards us and recommenced his tune. Louise and I waited side by side in the shelter and stared out, until she turned to me.

'Mrs, ah, Mrs Harrington. I wanted to thank you for all your help back then, you know, before the baby came and afterwards, you know, everything you've done to help.' She smiled nervously. Her teeth were white though not entirely straight.

'That's, um…,' I waved a hand dismissively. 'How is she?' I asked, pointing to the pram.

A full-tilt smile lit up Louise's face in an instant. 'She's beautiful! Her name's Emma. Would you like to see? She's grown such a lot.' And she went to pull back the protective cover over the pram but then checked herself, perhaps not at all sure of the protocol when you meet the wife of the man with whom you've not so very long ago had a baby. I wasn't sure either.

• • •

On an impulse, as the rain eased, I leant over to kiss a startled Louise on the cheek. Then 'Goodbye' seemed sufficient, and I hurried with the children to the ferry terminal at the bottom of the hill, hoping to find Mark waiting there. I was disappointed, then alarmed, when he wasn't.

With both children tired and irritable, it seemed too challenging a task to climb the hill again, pulling them along. I bought a bottle of soft drink at the kiosk—too sweet but all they had—and took a swift gulp before passing it to Patricia, who fumbled, dropped it and watched, fascinated, as its *Passiona*-yellow contents glugged slowly out onto the rain-soaked cement.

Paul yelled at his sister then turned and ran towards the end of the pier. He was fast. While sprinting, he looked back once over his shoulder, as if daring me to follow. I hauled my reluctant daughter along, screaming his name and terrified that he might fall into the roiling water. A middle-aged woman in a purple raincoat grabbed Paul's arm and steered him away from the edge of the pier, looking around for the negligent mother.

Guilty as charged. 'Here! I'm here Paul!' Out of breath.

I continued, with Patricia's hand in a firm grip, and waved with my free arm. Just as we got closer, I tripped and skidded on the wet timber planks to land with force on my back, knocking the breath out of my lungs. Patricia, still attached to my hand, was also whipped backwards but landed across the buffer of my torso. A surprised grunt escaped her, but she was unhurt and curiously unperturbed by the fall. She extricated herself and sat beside me in a puddle formed by the dip of the timber. A deep frown played across her forehead as she leant in towards me, exploring my face with her fingertips. 'Are you all right Mummy?'

I struggled to sit up and pull her close. 'Oh my darling, are you okay? Are you hurt?'

A brisk examination, a cradling of her head in my hands, and kisses to the damp skull. A searchlight stare for Paul. An awareness that my coccyx was tender and my left ulna might be cracked. Deep breath. I moved again gingerly. Where was Paul? I screamed his name. Over and over.

Fix all this Elise!

Paul. There. Stationary. Alive.

Patricia. Unhurt.

Mark

Paul

Patricia

Mark

Fuck all this!

Paul ran back along the pier, all regret and concern, and scooped a protective arm around his sister while he tried to pull me up. His tears were barely noticeable through the rain. A young couple helped me stand, joined by the woman who'd rescued Paul, while Patricia scrambled to her feet without a whimper.

A chorus of voices:

'Can we do anything?'

'Do you need a doctor?'

'The hospital?'

'Are you sure you can walk?'

'We should get an ambulance...'

I felt the cold seeping into my bones, a numbness spreading across my hips.

'No, thank you, I'm okay; I'll be fine,' I mumbled, as I bent with discomfort to enclose both children in my arms. 'It's okay. We're all okay. We'll be fine.' I said this mainly to convince myself.

The Samaritans hesitated, looked at each other; the older woman put a hand on my shoulder. 'Do you have a car somewhere? What about a taxi? Shall we call a taxi?'

'No, the ferry's almost here. It'll be quicker. But thank you. Really. You're most kind. Come on kids, can you see the ferry coming in? It won't be long.'

And I walked gingerly back along the jetty, giving Paul coins to buy two ice-creams from the kiosk while I dealt with a soaked and cold Patricia, who now grizzled mechanically, watchful through her tears. Strangers looked at me with pity, or annoyance. The ferry docked, discharged its human cargo, and we boarded, squelching and cold. Once inside, I settled Patricia into my lap, rocked her gently and stroked her hair while the ice-cream dripped pink and white onto our clothes. The vessel filled while Patricia's sounds became a tiny whimper as she drifted, loose-limbed and floppy, into sleep. Paul, silent, grave and miserable beside me, placed one hand solicitously on my arm. I kissed his hair and told him 'I'm sorry.' He sighed and leant his head against me, closed his eyes and dropped the ice cream. My elbow and knee throbbed—bruised, scraped and oozy, but not broken.

We were wet. I was aching. We were all confused.

• • •

When we finally arrived home late that day, variously tired, sore, regretful, irritable and anxious, Mark was in the garage, hand-planing wood he'd bought for some new project or other. He'd have heard my footsteps and the opening of the door, but he kept his back turned, so I went inside, got the children sorted for their baths, changed into dry clothes and cooked spaghetti. Routine was a welcome distraction from the damage of the day. Samson provided some gentle relief to me and the kids with his playfulness and affection.

Mark continued with whatever it was he was doing out there well into the night while we three ate our dinner inside. The children bickered. I chewed my nails. I suggested to a reserved Paul he could watch some TV while I read stories to an alert but pliable Patricia. After I'd settled them into their beds, I cleaned the kitchen and bathroom, laundered the clothes and awaited what was likely to be a troubling showdown.

But when Mark eventually entered the house and took a shower, there was no space or energy left in either of us for hostilities. He no doubt wanted to avoid the topic of Louise and my expected wrath, and I didn't want to see Mark diminished further by a war of words and conscience with me. Perhaps we were both cowards. When we finally met late that night in the bedroom, we carried on as if nothing had happened. I swallowed painkillers and nursed my self-pity and self-righteousness until sleep melted into me.

CHAPTER
TWENTY-NINE

What remained unsaid between us over the ensuing years was bigger and more painful than anything said. Mark returned from work at the same time each night, withdrew more into his garage projects, spent less time interacting with the children and even less pursuing any physical or emotional intimacy with me. I still worked at the hospital and took a full-time position as the children grew. Occasionally I sent a little money to Louise for the baby but never saw her again. Perhaps it was an altruistic gesture, but if I'm honest, maybe it became an attempt to buy her silence, to separate her existence, and her baby's, from our marriage, which was loving but increasingly strained.

Our children inevitably felt the tautness in our relationship. While there was no violence between us, physical or verbal, nor any directed towards them, their simple quest for love and security, together with their observations of the empty spaces, the razor-like wariness that grew between Mark and me, shaped their behaviour. Paul moved from victim to bully, and I was often called to the high school to hear details of the latest incident.

'Mrs Harrington, we've called you here again because Paul instigated another fight today.'

'But he says he was provoked.'

'That's not the way we see it. He's to go home and calm down and write a letter of apology to Christopher. It's the second time this term, Mrs Harrington, and we can't have that kind of thing going on here. If he's not careful, there'll be a suspension. Or expulsion. And you should know, he's been caught wagging history classes. We can see he's a bright boy, Mrs Harrington, but this conduct won't be tolerated. And besides, he's starting to fall behind academically. The reputation of the school, Mrs Harrington...'

In the car on the way home, he'd beg me, 'Please don't tell Dad. Please!'

'But why's this happening, Paul? What's got into you? You've never been like this.'

'They...' Head down, tears only just held back. 'I don't know.'

I'd try to extract some further explanation from him, but he'd close down. I knew it stemmed from pain and confusion, and I was ill-prepared to explore those depths. I skirted around the issues later with Mark, but he just stared at me, jaw set in that way he had, gave a shrug and expected me to deal with it. So I'd be on the phone to other school parents, deeply apologetic, then remind Paul of the rules, the expectations, and his victims' pain, give him hugs and reassurance and encouragement or, sometimes, frustrated reprimands. I sought help from Gabby and Nancy, since they had boys and would know what I should do. They urged, in varying measures, opposing strategies.

From Gabby, for example: 'Be patient. Get him to talk about his feelings, but don't talk about yours. Reward him when he does well. Make him get a hobby. Help him with his homework. Don't bother Mark with this.'

From Nancy, statements along these lines: 'He needs more discipline, Elise. And consistency. Set boundaries, but don't over-react if he misbehaves. Ground him if he gets into more fights; take away his weekend privileges. Get Mark to deal with him.'

Given their different parenting styles, I pursued an assumed middle road.

Patricia...well, on the surface she was a little angel. She was doing well enough at school, and she'd grown out of the squirming, shrieking, stubborn individual she'd once been. But underneath, there was a quiet, unsettling quality to her. She'd be happy, relaxed and playful one moment, then disappear into a fugue-like state, becoming either robotic or dismissive in her interactions. On my insistence, our GP examined Patricia systematically, distracting her with his soothing chatter, a stethoscope and his smile.

He concluded, 'She's as fit as a fiddle, Mrs Harrington. There's nothing to worry about. Children go through stages similar to what you've described. But if you're really worried, I suggest you see a guidance counsellor at school or a private clinic, whichever you feel comfortable with.'

He gave us a warm, encouraging smile and led us to the door, patted Patricia's shoulder and said, 'Bye, little poppet!'. She grinned at him and held my hand as we left.

I dutifully took her to the school counsellor, who interviewed me while Patricia stayed outside with a classmate. Jane, a petite woman of about forty, had close-cropped brown hair, a disarming smile, and spoke with a strong Scottish accent. She asked general questions about Patricia's health, her habits, behaviours, school performance, our family composition, etcetera, then she called Patricia in to join us.

I remained silent, apprehensive, as Jane in gentle tones encouraged Patricia to tell her about school, how she felt about her class, homework and so on. I fretted, thinking our daughter's frequent disappearances behind blank eyes paralleled my own tendency to hide inside a fantasy life.

I received no answers at that appointment, but two weeks later, Jane called me in again.

'I've had a look at Patricia's schoolwork, and sat in with her in some classes. I can see she struggles with reading and writing, spelling too, but don't be alarmed—it's clear she's a very bright and capable child, creative too. Her verbal fluency is excellent. I don't think she's dyslexic, so...'

Startled, I interrupted. 'I don't know what that is.'

'Oh, now, don't be worrying. It's probably not that. It's a condition not widely recognised here, you know, but there's a lot of research happening in the UK now. The word itself might sound scary, but it just means that the brain processes reading in a different way. We won't know unless there are more tests, but with a little help, those specific communication skills can be improved. I'll go through some strategies you can use.' She picked out a leaflet from several on her desk.

I nodded, half of me numb, the other half unnerved, as she continued with a cheerful countenance, 'I'm surprised her teachers haven't mentioned it, Mrs Harrington, but I'll get them on to it straight away. If I were you, I'd be speaking to them directly too, just so they know you're aware of Patricia's reading problems, and you expect results from them. I'm not saying she does have dyslexia, just that she might. It would be great if you could spend a bit of time with her on any homework, read with her too, regularly, and check she's sounding out the words correctly.

'Phonics, that's the thing! Needs reinforcement. And praise, lots of praise and encouragement. And patience. Oh, and it would help too if you could organise her space so she has plenty of books available, at the right level of comprehension of course, and a comfortable spot where you can read aloud together, for pleasure, not just for homework. Do you enjoy reading, yourself, Mrs Harrington?'

'Oh, yes!' I said, shifting uncomfortably in the chair.

'Well then, she already knows what a fabulous pastime it is, if she's seeing that you appreciate a good book!'

She hesitated and sought my gaze. 'Please don't take this the wrong way, my dear, but can I ask, are there any problems at home?' A pause. 'Is Patricia sleeping well?'

I nodded.

'Here then, dear, take this information sheet and I'll give you some others.' She rifled through her top drawer and drew out a thick folder. 'Sometimes a change in sleep or eating patterns, or showing more restlessness, or becoming withdrawn, or even more clingy, any of these can indicate a child who's not coping well with stress. Are *you* feeling on top of things, Mrs Harrington?'

Her delicacy, her warm approach, her charming accent, led me to lower my head and struggle to locate a handkerchief.

• • •

I doubled my efforts with both the children, taking them to the local library every Saturday morning, where we'd each select a variety of books. At home, I read Patricia's choices with her, and found language, phonics, rhyming and sentence-building games, which she seemed to enjoy. But being a social butterfly, her interests remained less with written words and more with her friends. I queried her teachers about possible dyslexia, but they knew as little about it as I did, and just reported that that her school work was 'satisfactory', but that she should pay more attention in class. Perhaps, as the doctor had suggested, it was just a stage in my darling girl's life.

I encouraged Paul to invite different schoolmates over on weekends, but he resisted, so when he revealed a yearning to learn tennis, I found him a spot at a local tennis club for weekly tuition, and he initiated practice sessions with one of Nancy's boys. I implored Mark to spend time with Paul on weekends; to take him to football matches or go bike riding with him—anything to fill in the gaps for my sweet boy. Over time, Paul gained a little more confidence, made more friends and fewer enemies and his grades improved again.

CHAPTER THIRTY

Mark never truly recovered from his traumas. Physically he was intact. But the essence of him, the shape he moved from room to room, had been hollowed out. He became a scarecrow, full of shadows and straw and empty spaces. He tried hard to be the husband and father who'd left us, but that man was lost somewhere in a muddy, vicious place where he'd witnessed the impact of rifle power, grenades, booby traps, ambushes, mines and bombs. He'd seen indistinguishable body parts, animals and human; mothers who mourned dead babies, children howling for parents vaporised before their eyes; the fear and despair on both sides of the conflict. And he had smelt the stink of war—rank, stagnant, greasy water, kerosene, gunpowder, napalm, melted flesh, decomposition and treachery.

He didn't talk of it. I knew a little at least, from seeing television footage, hearing radio interviews, reading the newspapers and listening to the stories of the wives of other broken, empty, muted men.

Mark was more an echo of himself than substance, but now mellow in his own, shattered way. The characteristic male brittleness which could attach to boys and men, in this country, and at that time, had been sloughed off, so he projected a different perspective on the world, a gentler one, a softer one, but a much sadder, wiser and more fragile one.

I was reminded of other shapes that had stood in doorways. Allowed myself to remember my father when he'd returned, broken in body and spirit, from a different war. I understood that man better now, grasped a little of why he'd left us. Knew that he'd loved me before the drink drowned his capacity to feel. "My Lisie, you're my best girl." I cried for having abandoned him, that one important, unrecoverable time.

I also had a fresh respect for and understanding of Lillian, who'd been witness to the splits and splinters, the heavier artillery of war, that can ripple or blast through a family. I knew she too indeed loved me, in her own apprehensive, timid way.

Then the blurred silhouette of another man entered my thoughts, a hated cactus of a man who'd watched and lingered and moved stealthily through my bedroom doorway at nights while my mother worked. *I'm made of steel. Nothing can hurt me. I don't cry.* That was never love though he tried to claim it as such.

But enough of those thoughts. Mark's shape and shadows were my priority; they took form and dismissed the fearful spaces that the other had once inhabited. Through Mark's hollowness I was made whole again. I had purpose. I worked to tame his demons. Thus, we grew. Our tempestuous dance of earlier times, the aggravations, the doubts, the irritants, the questions, the pretence and the lies, they all evaporated. I knew again what it meant to love him. This peace lasted a brief while.

• • •

'What the bloody hell's going on, Elise? Where are those papers I put here? For Christ's sake, will you stop tidying up my things when you know I'm working on something?'

'I only…'

A door slammed. A gate creaked. A car horn blasted. Another day in paradise.

The children grew wary of him, kept their distance. I tried to soothe with words, distractions, sex, any of which sometimes worked, but more often caused him further stress.

He once admitted to having tried marijuana and heroin during his time in Vietnam: 'Everyone was doing it—it was just experimental, temporary.'

I thought his moods were linked to that. News would filter through to him of people he'd known in Vietnam who were permanently disabled or had fallen headlong into drug addiction or had committed suicide. When a report appeared in the media linking Agent Orange to brain dysfunction, various cancers, and birth defects in children, Mark completely fell apart. He stopped going to work, barely ate, and became paranoid.

One afternoon, Lesley Harris from a few doors down called me at work to say that he was kneeling on the road just outside her house, blessing the cars that honked and veered around him. It didn't take much persuading after that to get him to see a psychiatrist, after which he was hospitalised for several weeks, followed by a long, slow recovery at home. Because of what they deemed to have been a psychotic episode, he was heavily dosed with Librium, Clozapine, Valium or whatever new treatment the doctors wanted to trial. He slept. Awake, he was a zombie. We all hated to see him so shrunken, foreign. I desperately wanted to help him reconnect with the world and tried to get him to eat regularly and exercise, to heal, but I had to attend work, to cover his lost income.

Gabby, Nancy and other wonderful friends arranged a roster of people to help with the children, and to call in on Mark throughout the day, though he seemed, they said, largely unaware of their presence while they chatted, made him tea or set out the meals I'd prepared. They told me he generally stayed in bed or sat slumped on the couch with the television on, a newspaper open on his lap, hardly blinking, not registering what was in front of him. None of us knew how to deal with PTSD back then.

During this time, Mark's father, Bruce, died suddenly of a brain aneurism. I remember shuffling with Mark through the airport, the children subdued on either side of us. I remember:

a church

a coffin

a crowd

flowers

music

singing

tears

speeches

the wild choreography of a bird trapped inside

Mark's mother Deidre, crumpled and sodden

Mark's brother Adrian, tearful but strong

Mark, a ghost, clinging to my hand

the quiet family home in Toorak denuded of Bruce's vitality

then the flight home

Mark wraithlike and shuffling, the children boisterous and argumentative.

• • •

Within six short weeks, Deidre moved to Sydney to assist with Mark's care and rehabilitation. She was still dealing with her grief from the loss of Bruce, and devastated by Mark's illness, but she wanted to help, saying often that she couldn't bear to lose another loved one. Desperate sorrow had filed down the brittleness I'd thought was her way, and in all things, she was gentle, efficient, and practical. She rented a small house just a suburb away from ours, so we saw her on an almost daily basis.

She offered to have the children stay overnight with her on weekends, no doubt to help distract them and assuage their sorrow as much as to provide her with company. Paul, since home had become like a parched landscape with little sound, submitted graciously to her grandmotherly affections. Patricia also enjoyed the attention she wasn't getting much of at home. I was failing at motherhood and felt indebted to Deidre for her timely intercessions.

Mark's tall, once athletic body was now bent over with fatigue and stress. His sandy hair was streaked with premature grey and untidy with inattention. His beautiful eyes regularly looked fuzzy and confused. Alarmed at his fragility, his gaunt frame and features, I'd stroke his forehead, talk about everyday things and try to entice him back into the world he'd known before the war. I moved around him with gentle care and soft murmurings, demanding nothing, and would climb into bed at night to gather him into my arms. I would anchor my leg over his to draw him even closer, and rock him until he fell asleep or pushed me away. And always, always, my heart ached for him.

Paul and Patricia, having witnessed some of their father's lowest moments, were clearly distressed, but over time they learned to deal with his moods through a combination of gentleness and wariness. The only light that came into his eyes was when either of them entered the room. Then his mouth would shape itself into a tremulous smile; he'd open his arms to one or the other of them and invite them to sit with him. He'd ask Patricia to tell him about her day and show him her artistic creations, get Paul to talk about school, or sport, or whatever was going on in the neighbourhood—anything to hear the voices he loved.

In this way, little by little, the children returned to their old ways of being around him, though they saved their arguments, their shouts or complaints until they were out of his earshot. And so Mark, my Mark, our Mark, stirred, softened, connected—a cocoon opening.

But then there was me—with my own peculiar history, my own way of dealing or not dealing with things. Though I now rarely disappeared through the Looking Glass to Wonderland, there were other means of escape. For a few short months I hid my worries behind drugs obtained by easy craft from the hospital. Mainly Diazepam to deal with stress, or amphetamines to keep me going during a long shift. Sometimes alcohol at home, just a glass or two, to help me sleep. I justified this because I knew some hospital staff were using marijuana, cocaine, Fentanyl and various inhalants, so I believed my helpers were, by comparison, harmless. Funny how we kid ourselves this way. Either I'd move almost robotically through the day, glassy eyed, slow of voice and movement, or I'd approach tasks feverishly, glisten with sweat, bounce around at work and later pounce on the children at home with questions and hugs and declarations of love. They were not amused. I lost weight, often felt nauseous and had tremors, and knew I wasn't functioning well in any sphere, work or home. I'm not proud of this part of my life at all.

In time I edged away from my 'helpers', the uppers and downers, because I saw how my oddities and mood swings were affecting the household. Paul's facial twitch had become worse. His mouth and eyes could convey confusion or pain, though outwardly he remained placid, cooperative, and loving, especially with his father. Patricia's moods sometimes resurfaced, but she was good-natured, kind and bright in Mark's company, and helpful to me with household tasks. Mark's own attempt to return to a semblance of his former self was slow but encouraging. I knew I had to let go of my props. It wasn't easy, but my guilt, pride and stubbornness helped direct me through.

• • •

Paul, Patricia and Deidre, weaving magic through the force of their disparate personalities, gradually drew Mark away from his ghosts and back into a world of practicalities. Where I'd often failed, they could cajole him into eating more, talking more, paying more attention to the things that had previously interested him. They'd busy themselves around the house, read him judiciously selected items from the newspaper, and encourage him to eat the meals Deidre and I cooked; they could entice an occasional laugh with a store of jokes, talk about their days, walk with him in the garden, sit with him through football games on the TV or keep him company in his workshop. My admiration, respect and love for our children was limitless, and my regard for and appreciation of Deidre grew and grew.

Mark's brother, Adrian—similar in height to Mark, single, good-looking, as introverted in temperament as their father Bruce had been extroverted—also regularly visited from Newcastle. His presence had a revitalising effect on Mark and they spent a lot of time together either in the workshop, talking and making vaguely recognisable things out of wood, or sitting inside watching sport, enjoying a beer. Adrian appeared comfortable in my presence and was a good listener. He persuaded the kids and me to engage more again with our community and take our lives back during Mark's recovery.

It was Adrian who convinced Mark to access the counselling and 'networking support' being offered to military personnel and former contractors. Initially reluctant, Mark eventually agreed to attend the therapy but refused to go to the regular social gatherings organised for veterans and support staff when I suggested it.

'It'll just keep bringing everything back. I can't do it.'

'How about you talk to Ben from around in Smith Street? He knows the organisers. He'll go with you if you want.'

'Elise…don't!' Shaking his head. Looking at the ground.

'Just a try out?'

'Stop! No. I can't *do* it, I said!'

'Talk to Adrian, please?'

And he did. They spent hours on the phone each week.

Between the loving ministrations of his children, his mother and brother, my own efforts and the therapy sessions he attended, Mark was eventually well enough to get back into the workforce, initially on shorter hours and with fewer responsibilities. With time, effort and determination, he regained a degree of equilibrium and much of his physical health and athleticism. My relief was intense, exhilarating, a touch of madness. I could place the darker memories of his traumas into imaginary boxes, tied securely with black ribbons, and bury them.

Mark no longer lingered in doorways but walked into rooms with a purpose, chatted about his co-workers, laughed at some silly story on the television. He stopped flinching at the bark of a dog or the slam of a car door. He drove with confidence and regained a sense of independence. He started making plans again; small, practical things as well as bigger pipe-dreams, and spoke with the droll humour I'd always loved. He became again the brave, honest, handsome and smart man I'd fallen in love with. Our time together, our conversations, were tender, affectionate.

'I know I haven't said it,' he said once, his eyes averted, focused instead on our dog Samson instead of me, 'but you stayed. You didn't give up on me. Thank you.' Then he kissed my forehead, stood back, and said, 'You changed your hair.' He reached out to touch it and added, 'It looks really nice.'

My response was as honest as I've ever been. 'Of course I stayed! Silly! I love you—that never stopped, even when I didn't know what to do, how to help. I can't even begin to imagine the hell you've been through. Come here.'

• • •

But sadly, ironically, inevitably perhaps, the ebb and flow of normal life—with its external irritations, its ordinariness, the humdrum and banal—competes with energised loving and compassion, meets limitations, forges new paths or repeats habits. By and by, Mark's regained health saw a slight disconnection in our coupledom. With a major crisis in decline, there came a slow return to the taking of the other for granted, a resurgence of forgotten aggravations, a sameness. Though loving and forgiving of each other, we limped along together over the next few years, finding fault, as couples can do, over mundane, stupid things, but both of us also now more willing to concede, compromise, bite tongues, avoid squabbles. Acceptance replaced passion. A new, quiet love emerged to wrap us in foil.

CHAPTER
THIRTY-ONE

Nancy asked to meet Gabby and me at a local wine bar—7pm sharp. She'd also advised our respective husbands to take on parenting duties for the evening and not to disturb us barring an impending death. It'd been many months since we three had met without interruption or distraction. At this juncture in our lives, we were always busy—Nancy at a Rape Crisis Centre, Gabby as a receptionist in a dental surgery, while I continued nursing and studied part-time.

The wine bar was darkly lit and only partially full when I arrived. Wisps of exhaled smoke played in pockets of the room. A Bob-Dylan look-alike—tall with a stringy build and a mop of curly hair—was perched on a stool near the bar, plucking at an acoustic guitar and doing a good job of emulating the singer's unique voice, the gravelly rise and fall, the flat vowels, the moody melodies. He had a following of four young women and two men, who'd arranged their stools in a semi-circle to face him; they regarded him through the dimness, moving fingers or feet in time with the jerky rhythms, occasionally passing comments back and forth.

Nancy and Gabby were already at a corner table in a booth, drinks lined up—each a lethal-looking yellow concoction in a highball with ice. Nancy wore her signature dark trouser suit, her once long fair hair now darker, peppered with grey and cut in a short, stylish fashion. Her walking cane—this one an elegant ash wood with a brass handle in the shape of an eagle—stood propped against the wall beside her. Gabby appeared fresh and younger somehow, in a flowing red skirt, a white cheesecloth blouse and sandals. Her longer dark hair, still with its natural curl, fell to just below her shoulders. Current and past stresses had briefly released her.

Nancy scrutinised me as I walked towards them. 'Lisie, what've you done to yourself? You look like a nun. What's with the boring clothes and flat shoes? Not to mention your hair. And you, Gabby,' turning to her, 'please— your outfit. I wasn't going to say anything, but since I'm on the subject, are you thinking of moving into a commune?' She laughed and gestured inclusively. 'Could we three be any more different? Look at us.'

I tucked away a few stray strands of hair that I'd hastily twisted into a messy plait, smoothed down my grey skirt, and grinned. Gabby greeted me with a broad smile and shifted on her bench-seat to allow more room. Nancy contemplated each of us again, then picked up her drink, took a sip, shook her head at the taste and put it down. Then smiled at us both and waited, drumming her fingers on the table between us.

I spoke next. 'What's this all about, Nance?'

'Just thought it was time we got together again. I see so little of you both these days. Plus, I have things to tell you.'

'Ok, go ahead.' Gabby took a sip of her drink, blinked fast several times and drew her head back. 'Whoa, that's strong! Is it going to be some kind of confessional session?'

Nancy raised her glass as a salute to us both and nodded. 'Bottoms up girls. We've got business to attend to.'

We settled back and exchanged thirty minutes of pleasantries—updates on our various spouses, collective brood of children, a selection of familial successes and dramas recently witnessed or experienced, our work and other commitments.

'Right,' said Nancy eventually, with a gesture to the barman for a second round of cocktails. 'Here's the thing. I'm leaving Jack.'

I glanced at Gabby, then at Nancy. Studied her hard. Gabby scoffed on a syllable, but a look from Nancy stopped her short. I'm sure confusion must have settled on my face, before I too decided it was a joke and waited with a half-smile for the punch line. Nancy's demeanour didn't change.

'I'm serious. If you'd both just stop that goofy grinning for a minute and just listen, I'll explain.' She took a deep breath and a deeper gulp from her glass and began. 'You know what Jack's like, the life he leads. He's away more often than he's ever here. So we don't have what you'd call a typical marriage, whatever that might be.' She glanced around at the patrons in the bar, then back at us.

'To be honest, since I've been working in this job, I just get so *incensed*. I hear all this shit about men and what they're capable of. Don't get me wrong, I like men, I've got two beautiful sons, and male friends, and Jack of course. He's decent, kind, always worked hard, been a good provider. I care for him a great deal, you know that. But I need space away from our set-up. I've met someone else I care for too.'

Gabby waited a moment. 'Who? Is he someone we've met?'

'No, and it's a she, not he.'

A hush of disbelief descended on the table. I leaned back against the booth's cushioned support. Gabby snorted and fidgeted with her bag, before staring across the table with astonishment.

Nancy's loud laughter drew attention in the bar.
'Look at you both. You're like those clowns at a fun fair, with your mouths wide open.' She did an exaggerated imitation, picked up a few pea-nuts from the centre bowl, and tossed them across the table. 'Here!'

Gabby ducked her head, located my hand beside hers and leant forward. 'Nance, you're not serious! That's just…well, it's…I don't know what it is.'

'Look, it's not that I'm suddenly attracted to women, so you needn't think that you're in any danger. It's just that I'd rather live by myself. I've pretty much lived that way anyway. I've brought the kids up on my own, been the disciplinarian, made all the big decisions. And I realised well before I met Cheryl that I just don't need the physicality of a male. Or the emotional distance they create. I already get my emotional needs met by my female friendships.' She smiled, raised her glass again, first towards us, then swept it out towards a broader world.

'And I imagine that if I have any libido left, which I almost certain-ly don't, the idea of physical intimacy with a woman isn't unappealing.

Someone soft and considerate. Who needs all that frantic poking and humping? Cheryl's become a friend, a good, generous friend. I like her, a lot. I'll be staying with her, at least for a while, until Jack comes to terms with things. And I haven't…*We* haven't slept together as such, yet. Maybe won't ever.'

My voice was soft, competing only with the low music weaving around us. 'So you've told Jack?'

'Yeah. He's hurt, livid. Of course he is. I hate that he's miserable, but I can't go on with the way things are.' Her gaze dropped.

'What exactly is wrong with the way things are?' Gabby's voice was terse.

Our friend eyed her intensely. 'I just told you Gab, I'm tired of doing it all, without any help. I want a life back. And I'm pissed off with men in general.'

'So you're leaving Jack just because you hate the men you hear about at work?' Gabby snapped.

Nancy rolled her eyes and ignored her, turned to me with eyebrows raised in query. 'And you? Got your penny's worth ready?'

'It's not my business Nance, but…the kids?'

Her voice faltered as she responded. 'They've been aware for a long time that things haven't been right. I think it'll be a relief to them if there's a change. They're old enough now to understand. They'll be upset initially, but…,' and she let that hang in the air.

Gabby, still wide-eyed, opened her mouth to speak but Nancy put her hand up to shush her. 'Gab, my dear, dear friend, before you make any more pronouncements or try to talk me out of this, just listen. It's my choice. We each have choices. And let me say, honey, I'm exceedingly worried about you. Quite seriously, if we're being honest—and I hope we'll all be honest here. Let's lay everything on the table.' She hesitated, her hands firm around her half-empty glass, and lowered her voice. 'You should have left Frank years ago, Gab. He's been a right royal bastard, everyone knows it. You deserve so much better than that, than him. If not for your own sake, at least for the kids.'

She leant across the tabletop to clasp Gabby's hand, which fluttered and pulled away, then continued, without malice. 'Your boys will marry and think it's okay to treat women the way Frank's treated you, because that's what they've grown up with. And your Susie and Linda, if they marry, they'll expect to be hit, because you are, and you do nothing.' Her tone softened. 'Gabby, I'm honestly concerned for you and your kids. We have been, for a long time, but you never let us in.'

'You're not being fair!' Gabby glared at Nancy, dropping her eyes to the floor, her chin quivering, before turning to me. 'Is that what you think too Elise?'

'Well…'

'Because we all have skeletons, don't we?' She took a long swig of her drink, smacked her lips theatrically, nostrils flared.

I mumbled, 'Yes, we do. I don't think any one of us is perfect, or in a perfect relationship. I've never claimed that.'

Gabby bristled. Her dark pupils dilated. 'Since we're being up front here Lisie, thanks to our friend here, why didn't you ever confront Mark about his affair, his baby with that woman?'

Nancy interrupted, 'Gab, we're talking about you, not Elise.'

'Shut up, Nancy, I'm not talking to you.' Gabby persisted, staring at me. 'Why didn't you leave him?'

I shrugged, squirmed and glanced out towards the other patrons, before a sense of obligation made me turn back to Gabby and hold her gaze. My voice was resolute. 'He was broken, more broken each time he came back from Vietnam, and I didn't want to make him worse. And I love him. That's why.'

'Not so broken he couldn't impregnate that pretty young thing.'

I flinched, frowned, pondered. 'I wasn't able to fix him. I didn't want to use that situation with her, with Louise, to grind him into nothing. He's been through so much. I know how hard it was for him. We've all seen what war can do to people, even if they're not on the battlefield. To the men themselves, to the families.'

Nancy leant forward, patted my arm, her firm touch conveying support. 'You don't need to tell me that, love, but Mark still has a responsibility to that poor young woman and to the child; at least a financial responsibility if nothing else.'

'I sent her money when I could.'

'Yes, you did, and you're extraordinary for doing that. But her child is a half-sister to your own kids. Surely that counts for something, some recognition? You can't just pay someone off to keep them quiet. The kid's a person, not a lay-by.'

I felt my face prickling, mottling, and shifted on the bench again to stare at my friend. Perhaps my voice came out more aggressively than I intended. 'Okay clever pants Nance. What would you have done?'

Nancy held both hands up in surrender but her tone was light. 'Ah, you've got me there! Maybe I'd have killed Jack and poisoned the woman. Look, what I'm trying to say to you, my two best and most wonderful friends, is I think we've all been limping along in marriages that haven't served us at all well. And I think, I *know*, we all deserve better. I'm doing something about my life. Maybe you should both consider how unhappy you want to continue to be for the rest of yours.'

Gabby sat back, flushed with the effects of her second cocktail. 'It's not as bad as you think. Frank's not like that anymore.'

'Gab, how many times has he hit you over the years? Did you think we never saw your bruises and misery? Any time we mentioned it, you'd make excuses, "I ran into a door," or some such clap-trap. You lied to us. But it was our fault too. We were irresponsible, negligent not to challenge you; wrong to let you put up with this for far too long. I'm so sorry.'

Gabby glared and opened her mouth to speak before her body mutely retreated behind crossed arms.

Nancy leant back. 'Come on ladies, I'm guessing we've all been fucked over by men in one way or another. That's why I'm giving up on them, at least for the moment.'

We were all quietly absorbed in our own thoughts as yet more drinks arrived. I wasn't used to the spirits in the cocktails and my head spun; I noticed that Gabby's face had reddened and her eyes were narrow darts of resentment.

Her voice rose, a brittle edge to it. 'It's not as bad as you're making out, Nance. And despite everything, I love Frank. And I love my kids. That's why I stay. He's provided for the kids. He's always worked hard.'

'Bosh! That's not a good enough reason. How could you love a man who hits you? 'Love'. What does it mean anyway? You're sacrificing your own happiness, Gab. Is that love, or martyrdom? And you're not protecting your children by staying. You must realise that.'

The music had stopped, the crowd that had gathered while we'd been drinking momentarily thinned; the only sounds were low chatter, background traffic noise and the clinking of glasses. Gabby remained silent, stared around the room, tears apparent in her eyes. A barman wiped down nearby tables. Cigarette smoke curled around the light fixtures, creating a pale haze.

Nancy reached out for Gabby's hand again but turned to me. 'Elise? What about you?'

'I'm not miserable, Nance. Truly. I love my family, love Mark. He's a great father, a kind man. He's just not capable of functioning so well at times. He'll...'

'Interesting, isn't it, that we've all used a version of "he's a good man" tonight? And there's that word *love* again! What do you mean when you say it? Isn't it more like loyalty, or pity? Or laziness because you can't bear to work out what you really feel? Or are you, both of you, just terrified of being alone, being lonely?'

I was silent for a moment, hating the confrontation, wishing to be home, or inside my Wonderland. I felt lead in my stomach. Took a breath. 'Look, okay, things aren't always fabulous with Mark, he's been messed up. They all were, those men, those boys. Anyway,' I hesitated. 'Everyone's broken in one way or another, aren't they? Aren't we?'

My friends watched and waited.

I continued, 'I've been...well, there're things that we've all had to deal with in life. I'm trying to focus on the positive, not on what's missing in the relationship. He's doing his best. It's so much better now than it was when the breakdown...'

Nancy glanced around the room, shook her head wearily.

I insisted, 'He *is* better Nance. Anyway, it's not always about the man, the men, and what we blame them for. Sometimes it's what we demand of them. Sometimes, look, I'm no saint.'

They both stared at me enquiringly.

• • •

I'd wanted to tell them about my past, but in that moment, I couldn't. I believed I'd never let those secrets out, so deeply were they buried. What they did know had been wheedled out of me previously with a few wines in this same bar a year previously. I'd had a short liaison with a doctor in my third year back at work. *Doctors and nurses*—such a clandestine cliché. But it wasn't physical intimacy, just an emotional fling, a friendship that had a frisson of something else, something potentially bigger. I justified it at the time by thinking of Mark's brief affair, but in truth, it was the attention that hooked me in.

James was a reserved, thoughtful man, attentive and easy to talk to. There was laughter too, which was missing then at home. He was balding, had an aquiline nose, a slight gap between his front teeth and a disarming smile. His attention was flattering and, for a while, exciting, but as soon as things started to become complicated, and he wanted more, my guilt took over, and we agreed to finish it (whatever 'it' was.) My other *liaisons* remained locked in my imagination, accessible whenever I stepped through the Looking Glass. These idle fancies seemed harmless enough, but I can see now that they drew me away from my family, who needed much more of my attention than I gave them. If I'd been more available to them, more focused, understood their needs, been a better mother, a kinder partner…but all I saw were my failures. The effects of past traumas, that darkness beyond the campfire, had shrunk my world, caused me to collapse into myself and often be oblivious to the real world around me. I deeply regret that.

Nancy, on the other hand, wanted to save the world single-handedly. She'd been so caught up in all her causes over the years that she was unaware of how her hard-line views and frequent political and anti-religious browbeating had affected her kids and their friends. She spent more time and energy attempting to deal with society's ills or other families' problems than her own. I know she loved all her kids, but she believed they were old enough to sort themselves out without her help. One son was expelled from school for selling drugs. The other was just plain embarrassed by his mother and by his life in general, though he rarely got into strife, except for the time he drove Nancy's car into a tree and spent weeks in hospital. And then of course there was the open secret of Rachel's paternity. I couldn't have been the only one to have noticed the eye colour, and I thought from the way Rachel would often avert her gaze that she was well aware herself of being different. In her teens she'd become even more introverted; Nancy worried that she, Rachel, was becoming anorexic.

Gabby's way of dealing with the trauma of her violent abuse was to placate her demons with possessions or status, and for that she needed money. She worked hard to hide it, but inevitably there were days when she'd move between friends and neighbours to borrow an amount 'until pay day. I'll give it back to you, soon as I get it, promise.'

As a consequence, the circle of people she could run to became less well populated. We thought once she began full-time work, she'd be able to sort out her finances, but it just got worse. Gambling, shopping, stealing—that's what we assumed was going on. Her kids stopped being polite, stopped wanting to see their friends. Her eldest boy slapped Gabby on one occasion; she didn't tell us, but we heard about it through our own kids. Another son went a bit wild—drugs, drunken brawling—while one of the two daughters took up religion of the evangelical kind and seemed to me to be a bit loopy with it. The other daughter was pregnant at sixteen and moved in with her boyfriend's parents, never speaking to Gabby again.

For all our flaws, I loved Nance and Gab dearly and knew they loved me. We were all just messy people living messy lives.

CHAPTER THIRTY-TWO

I have an old photo of my mother in a white bathing suit, standing with my father at a beach. She's beautiful—glorious long chestnut-coloured hair that's tumbling past her shoulders as a few strands float in an apparent breeze. She has shy breasts, a small waist, toned, lithe legs. She's leaning in towards Dad, her bare arms slender but muscular. And she's looking up at him with a confident smile. He's in a dark pair of bathers, standing up straight and tall, looking self-assuredly into the camera. He's handsome, with a full head of straight fair hair, is lean and sun-darkened; he has a cigarette in one hand, an arm around her shoulder. They fit well together. The photo shows me she was happy once, strikingly pretty once, and I seek to find beneath her now wrinkled skin, beneath the years of worry and sorrow that have marked her, the woman she'd been before grief had made a mask of her features. I valued her the more now for everything she'd lost, and for her courage to face one more day, again and again.

Having overcome her fear of planes, and with our financial assistance, Lillian visited us more often in Sydney, though on one occasion she declared, 'I've worked hard all my life and I'm ready to retire. I've a little nest egg put away, so you shouldn't keep sending me money. You've been very kind, but please, I can manage.'

With retirement, she found both opportunity and inclination to cultivate personal friendships and she was happier, in a muted way, than I'd ever known her to be. I liked to study her, to recover early fond memories. Each time she came, she appeared slightly more frail, but still stood tall, proud. Her grey-green eyes held a pleasing fire. We'd relax into each other's company and chat without barriers. She adored being with Paul and Patricia, savouring the chance to make up for lost years. They enjoyed her company too; it also cheered Mark whenever she arrived. He remarked how much he appreciated her no-nonsense approach; how she showed sympathy without pity, generosity without fuss or expectation. It felt good, he said, to be seen just as a man, not an invalid. I took this on board.

During one of her visits, she revealed that she'd left Craig, and I whooped with delight.

'How? Why now? But that's great news! Tell me everything.'

'It was time, Elise, long overdue. I've got a place in a hostel. Just temporary, mind, until everything's been sorted.'

'Come live here, Mum.'

'Don't be silly, Elise, I wouldn't impose like that. I've got plans. But thank you. I've been to a solicitor; he's helping me get things organised, and said I could soon move back into the house and be able to manage perfectly well.'

I knew that tone and was relieved to hear a new confidence and contentment in her voice. She refused to go into further detail, so I dropped the interrogation, and was thrilled on her behalf.

A few weeks after that trip, she phoned one night, quite late. Her voice was steady, calm. 'I'm just calling to tell you that Craig died yesterday, Elise, but there's no need for you to come for the funeral. He'll be cremated. I want it all done as soon as possible. It's expensive for you to fly down, so don't. You've got your work and the children and Mark to think about. I can manage. Jeffrey will help organise things.'

'Mum, I …'

'I'm fine, Elise, honestly. Don't fuss.'

She didn't sound upset. Nor was I. The tears that welled up in me were of release, the banishment forever, I hoped, of that frequent furtive scrambling beneath my breastbone.

• • •

A few weeks after that phone call, Lillian called again.

'Would it be alright if I came up to see you all? I won't stay too long.'

'Mum, it's always fine if you want to stay. We'd love to see you. When? When can you make it? I'll organise to take a few days off.'

She arrived on a Sunday. Mark picked her up from the airport while the children made colourful cards and a bright poster as a welcome. As soon as she was through the front door, she threw her arms around Patricia and Paul, then gave me a brief pat on the shoulder. Mark took her small case to the study, where I'd made up a camp bed, then he called out.

'I'm going to help Jack with a motor. See you later.' A door slammed, jauntily, I thought.

Mum and I shared a light embrace before she drew back. 'Now, let me help you in the kitchen. There must be something I can do.'

She was calm, more than I'd known her to be, and we'd found common ground in our joint love for the children, in each discovering the lighter side of the other, in the small joys associated with sharing the mundane—gardening, preparing meals, baking cakes or shopping together.

'Oh Elise, I couldn't possibly wear this. It's just not me. And it's so expensive.'

'Mum, you can't go around in those old things you've brought up. You look like a bag lady.'

'I do not.'

'No, but this colour is great on you and the cut suits your shape. Come on, let me buy it for you. And we'll take that skirt as well. We can have a look at some new shoes for you while we're here.'

One afternoon, while the children were still at school, we sat together in the back yard, toasting our bare legs in the sun. I noted that Mum's limbs were still strong and toned. We drank tea and ate generous serves of the lemon slice she'd baked. I brushed crumbs from my skirt onto the ground.

Samson, much older, grey now around the muzzle, walked over stiffly, licked my bare foot, then turned in compact circles a few times, scratching at the grass before flopping down, panting with the effort. He looked up at me through cloudy eyes before resting his head on his front paws.

I reached to scratch his ears, then turned to my mother. 'Mum, you look really well, very good actually. Better. New lease of life?'

She grunted, shifted in her chair, and was silent for a long time, before leaning forward to grasp my hand. She looked right *into* me, her eyes suddenly pained and stripped bare, tears collecting.

'My child, I honestly didn't know what he'd done to you. And I'm so, so sorry. If I'd known, I'd have gone to the police, had him arrested. Taken you all away from him.'

I stared, mute, before we clutched at each other, moved awkwardly into a new embrace, tighter than we'd ever been able or inclined to do. We sobbed together for what seemed a very long time.

Finally, we let go. I breathed heavily through snot and tears, wiping at these inefficiently, before I was able to speak. 'Who told you? How did you find out?'

'Marion.'

'When?'

'A few months ago, on the phone one night. She'd been drinking. She does drink a lot these days, it's a worry to me how much. I'm anxious about...' She halted. 'Elise, I didn't...,' and stopped again.

I was afraid to ask, afraid to know, but said, 'Did he ever touch Marion? Hurt her?'

Hesitation. 'She says not, but she saw, she heard. You shared a room after all.'

I struggled before my voice could find a way out. 'He drugged us, Mum. Many times. I don't know what he used. It made me nauseous, almost paralysed.'

She flinched, recoiled, her hand flying momentarily to her mouth, as if she might vomit. 'Elise—no!' She stopped to swallow what might have been bile. Her voice now vehement: 'I wish I'd killed him before anything so terrible happened. I should never have let him in the house.'

She stood, circled the chair and stared at me, her eyes red, her face grim. 'It's all my doing, Elise. How can I ever make it better? How can you forgive me?' Then she scratched fiercely at her dress, her chest, her arms; fresh tears cascaded down her cheeks. 'Why didn't you tell me, darling, when it was happening?'

She'd never, ever called me 'darling'. I swallowed hard, touched by her endearment, but disgusted by a memory, exhausted by having all this out in the open, in the air, in our faces. My voice was low. 'He threatened me. Said he'd kill me, or you, or Marion. I tried to tell you, without having to say the words, what he was doing, but I didn't understand what was happening anyway. In so many ways I thought it must have been my own fault.'

'Elise! If anyone's at fault, it's me, for not knowing, not guessing. For letting him into our lives. He was a bastard, an animal!' Her hands covered her face again as she sat.

I'd never heard her swear before, even mildly like that, and reached to stroke her head tenderly, before a queer kind of wrath consumed me, making my body shake, my voice hiss and spit. 'The fault was all his. *His* sin, Mum. Don't you dare take that on.'

But just as quickly, it was gone. My fury unexpectedly deflated and my tone changed to one of pity. 'Mum, you and I, we have to move through this together. And be glad it's all over.' A surge of something else ran through me, perhaps trying to make sense of it all. 'What about Jeffrey? Has he ever told you anything?'

She straightened, wiped her nose with her sleeve and brushed at her face, her voice still unsteady. 'He doesn't ever say much, you know what he's like. Well, you don't know actually, do you? He hated Craig. There were the beatings, the strap, early on. Jeff's such an angry man. Always has been, really. But he's been good to me, Elise, still sends me money from time to time, though I tell him not to, and he always checks up on me. He's a great dad to his kids.'

I scoffed. 'I don't know where he'd have learnt that.'

A long pause. 'Yes, I suppose you're right there.'

A magpie strutted past our feet, sending up a long melodious serenade to its fellows before plunging its beak into the moist earth and extracting a small worm. It flew off into the listless, tangled green foliage of a neighbour's peppercorn tree. We watched as a tiny male wren, wearing the brightest and purest of blue coats, landed delicately on the lip of the birdbath, checked his surroundings with a nervous twitch, dipped his head to drink, fanned his little tail delicately, then disappeared swiftly on a gentle waft of air.

I turned again to my mother, still holding her hand tight, and cleared my throat. 'Mum, did Craig hit you?'

Lillian's head dropped; she stared at the ground. 'Sometimes, yes.'

CHAPTER THIRTY-TWO

'Why didn't you leave straight away?'

Her face lifted. Her voice became louder, almost indignant. 'Elise, be sensible. Women didn't leave back then. What would I have done? Where could I go? Three children to support.'

'Oh Mum, I wish…oh I'm so sorry.'

She sat up straight again, smoothed her dress. Used her brisk, 'let's get on with things' tone.

'I'm the one who's sorry. He ruined your young life, and tried to ruin mine. He was a pig, and I'm glad he's dead. If I have to go to prison, so be it.'

I looked at her quizzically. When she spoke, hesitancy created a mellow softness in her features, though a wary smile played on her lips. She kept her face slightly turned away and said, 'Elise, you remember when I called you after he died?'

I nodded. 'Yes.'

'I didn't tell you how it happened, did I? Except that he fell in the garden?'

I didn't want to talk about him but nodded again. 'You said he'd been up a ladder.'

'Yes, he'd been pruning that huge tree at the back, that London Plane tree. It's always been such a nuisance, sheds bark like mad, and makes me sneeze in Springtime. And the roots spread everywhere.'

'Mum! Just tell me what happened?'

She turned to look straight at me, eyes glassy, her breathing, her words, her tone all even. 'I'd gone there to collect the rest of my clothes, bits and pieces I'd left behind. He wasn't happy about it, but I reminded him it was *my* house and he had to move out, quick smart. He knew I'd been to the solicitor, so I had all the papers that proved the house was still in my name. I told him if he tried to stop me, I'd go to the police, tell about his violence, tell them everything. What he'd done to you.'

My heart hammered against my ribs. She looked away. Her hand clawed at her neck, one finger yanked on the collar of her blouse. A swallow, a sigh, before she turned back to me, her eyes resolute, hands clenched now.

'Elise, here's the truth. He didn't fall from the ladder. He'd been digging and was walking towards the house with that mad face on him, like he always had. I was scared of what he might do. I stood at the kitchen window thinking I should leave before he came inside, then I saw him clutch at his chest and he made a peculiar noise, sort of a strangled sound. His face turned almost purple. That's when he fell down.'

I waited, dizzy with disquiet. She held my gaze, direct in her resolve to continue.

'I wasn't able to remember the emergency number for ever so long, Elise. I don't know, fifteen, maybe twenty minutes…? I had a cup of tea while I thought about it. He wasn't moving at all. And then I called the ambulance.'

A brief hush before her slippery smile slid from shy to sly, moved on through a grimace to a look of defiance, and finally a wry smirk crept around her mouth. This, together with her matter-of-fact tone with all she'd just said, caused in me an overwhelming but brief wave of laughter.

I was simultaneously stunned and relieved by her revelation, and then, like Macbeth's witches, through more tears and snot, boil and bubble, toil and trouble, we began to laugh together, cackle outrageously. All our secrets exposed, hers and mine. We clasped each other. I felt her regret and relief pulse through her breastbone and into mine. Then, unlocked and sober, we stayed in encoded silence for several minutes, the muted sounds of a healthy garden soothing us in their own way.

She stood then, arms crossed near her waist, and looked at me. 'I want to ask you something more, Elise.'

'Yes?'

'The baby you had. Was it his? Craig's?'

I blinked rapidly, to keep the monster away, then nodded, flushed. The body remembers what the mind works so hard to forget.

She asked, 'What was it?'

My voice croaked. 'A boy, Mum. I've tried very hard to find out about him.'

Mum was silent, reached for and squeezed my hand, then whispered, 'I'm sorry, so sorry. If I'd known…'

'Don't, Mum, let's not talk about it anymore, please.'

Staring me down, she sighed. Sat again. With my eyes half closed, I caught the chirrup of birdsong, the crawk of a frog and the hum of a lawn mower. I slapped at a mosquito on my calf, startling Mum.

She mused, 'Elise, I hate thinking about what you three children went through, and how you're all living such separate lives, none of you together anymore. Do you think you'd ever want to see Jeff again, meet his kids? They're nice children. And he's not like he used to be.'

I stared at my feet. 'I don't know Mum. So much has changed. Jeffrey and me, we were never close. I just don't know. Not right now, at any rate. But I'll stay in touch with Marion.'

This seemed to please her. We drank our cold tea, watched the sun move slowly behind the distant hills and gathered our things to go inside. There were sounds of hunger coming from the kitchen—cupboard doors opening, a fridge door slamming, the clunk of a plate on the table, Patricia shouting at Paul: 'Leave *me* some!' Then Mark's voice, deep and calm and reassuring.

My shock at what Mum had just revealed had ebbed, while the lesser part of my character cheered for what had happened. Perhaps I'd have done the same; certainly I'd have been tempted to ignore his plight. But right in that moment, all those years of hate and anger towards that man lifted briefly, guardedly, from my shoulders. I confessed to her then how I'd seen my father those years before and how I'd just walked away, leaving him there in the rain, perhaps penniless, perhaps homeless. And how I'd regretted it ever since. Hearing this clearly caused her pain; sorrow seeped from her pores, and I tended to her fresh tears as a mother would a distressed child. We were both exhausted.

A moment of stillness and composure, before we turned our attention to a noisy Patricia, who'd run, breathless, into the garden, screaming with delight, 'Daddy's home!'

CHAPTER THIRTY-THREE

Simon entered my life in tiny scraps, as a paragraph here or there over the years from his adoptive parents in response to my regular enquiries via the agency. They provided no photos of him, so my imagination filled in the gaps between the words on paper to create an image. Lines like: 'In high school and doing well…has a sister and brother…gives us great joy…thank you for placing him in our lives…'

On good days, I felt relief and gratitude that he was happy, well looked after and had such amazingly well-adjusted parents. On not-so-good days, I was a touch resentful, empty. But those feelings would pass. I just felt the need to see him, hold him, and tell him I'd wanted him from the moment he slid out of my body and into someone else's arms.

Eventually more information arrived. Two letters, in fact, snug inside an official envelope on which my name and address were typed in capitals. I ripped it open, expecting it to be something from the bank or tax office, so was surprised to read, 'Wish to advise… Simon…adult…accompanying letter… continue to direct correspondence through this office until such time…'

Simon's note was brief, two paragraphs handwritten in curly, confident strokes. He said he wanted to know his heritage and asked if I'd send him a photo of myself and his biological father and provide our medical histories.

His tone was forthright, mature, I thought, though a little cool. No mention of us meeting, A week later I'd written twenty-odd drafts of a reply but sent nothing before I combatted my fear of showing Simon's letter to Mark.

I picked my time. Mark had, not long before this, settled into another new job and received a promotion. He was in better control of his emotions and continued to see a therapist. His world became more expansive to him as time passed. Paul and Patricia had the usual ups and downs of youth, but on the whole, they knew instinctively to be generous in spirit to their father, to give him latitude while any of their teenage angst or defiance was generally directed at me. But like most children their age, they colluded with their friends to enjoy a life outside the home. When they were both out one Saturday, I began to rehearse the narrative, without having any idea of how it would end.

• • •

Mark came in from the garden, sweat staining his T-shirt, his forearms thick with dust. He glanced at me before heading towards the bathroom.

'Make me a cuppa, will you, hon? Just hopping in the shower.'

I mustered a quarter-smile, trying to ignore the lurch in my stomach, and turned to the kitchen. A cup I removed from the cupboard shook in my hand before rattling onto its companion saucer. *Breathe. Breathe.* As the kettle reached a boil, I stood with my hands tightly around the top of a chair, knuckles white. *Breathe. Breathe.* I felt the sudden weight of the two letters in my pocket. By the time Mark re-entered the kitchen, bare-chested, skin damp and clammy and hair still wet, with a towel over his shoulders, I was steadier, a little more resolute. This had to be done.

I poured the tea, and sunk onto a chair, its back straight and stern against my shoulders. I gestured to the other chair. Mark sat with a slight grunt, turned a quizzical eye on me.

'What's up?'

I put my hand over the hidden papers, traced fluttering fingers over their folded creases, looked down at the other hand that lay trembling on top of my right thigh. And considered not proceeding.

'Come on Elise, I haven't got all day. What? What do you want?'

So I drew the letters out with care, slid them across the table towards him, and leant back again, clasping both hands together in my lap.

Mark stared, puzzled, at the folded offerings, frowned, glanced at me and opened the few pages. He read each letter without haste in bewildered quiet. Then sat back in his chair with the same sense of heaviness that I'd felt moments earlier, and stared intently at me.

I was caught in that stare, in the accusations and questions contained therein, but whispered rapidly. 'I contacted the adoption agency a long time ago. I wanted to know if he was all right, to learn something about him.'

'And?'

My voice rose in volume and croaked as I looked straight at him. 'His parents, well, the mother I guess, sent a few details through the agency, maybe twice a year. Never any photos, but they told me his name and how well he was doing and all those kinds of things. I just needed to find out he was okay, Mark. I won't... it would never be...I'd never expect to meet him. I just...'

Mark pushed the letters aside, glanced around the room, ran one hand through his hair, drummed the fingers of the other on the table for several seconds. He shifted his weight uneasily and avoided looking at me for several more seconds. Then he cleared his throat, twice. His own hands were trembling. Weariness modulated his voice. Or was it anger? He spoke with care, each word weighted.

'I thought there were no more secrets between us. Why did you hide this? I hoped you'd gotten over all that business. I've done what you wanted Elise. Never asked more questions. Never held it over you.' His hurt manifested in a constriction of voice.

I tried to speak but the air remained empty. He continued, a little louder. 'What do you expect the kids to do? Invite their half-brother over, and we'll all live happily ever after?'

Defeated, deflated. Nowhere to go but on the attack. My voice rose. 'What about your secrets, Mark? I never asked you the big questions either, about her, and your daughter.'

I placed both elbows on the table, put my head in my hands and stared at the swirly grain of the wood before looking up again. I'm sure my face was flushed, so hot I felt in that moment. My tone was weary too. 'I can't ever "get over" losing my child. You really have no idea, do you?'

He rose—a curt movement that caused his chair to scrape harshly, almost tipping over. He glared at me, turned and walked out of the room. But I knew I had to see this through to the end, whatever that was, yet keep Mark on my side and not send him back to that place of emptiness he'd been trying so hard to fill with things substantial and good.

So I followed his trail of indignation and injury to the bedroom, where he'd thrown his damp towel onto the floor and was standing at the window, staring out onto the streetscape. A car trundled past; a horn bleeped; a stray dog dawdled through the front garden, stopping to lift a leg on a low white viburnum. The scent of lavender through the open window seemed to mollify Mark's sour stance. I hoped so. I walked up behind him and gently placed a hand flat against his back. Though he flinched a little, he allowed me to rest my forehead against his spine and encircle his waist then with both arms. I nestled into his damp warmth, the sinew and muscle and tautness of him, then spoke into his skin, my voice soft and muffled.

'I'm sorry. I don't want to hide this thing anymore. But I never knew how to tell you. Simon…he'll always be a part of me, even if I'm not part of his life.'

I leant back then, to create a triangle of space between us, my voice deeper, energy returning, and spoke directly to the curve of his back. There was safety in that.

'I've thought about him every day since he was born. I've always felt as if a piece of me was torn away. There were things about it that I never wanted you to know, that I never wanted to face, and I thought if I told you, you'd hate me as much as I hated myself. And you're right, I didn't consider what I'd have to say to the kids if Simon came, if I found him. I've been selfish. I don't want to lose you, any of you.'

He turned then, placed both his large hands on my shoulders, ran them firmly along my upper arms while his breath evened out. I could hear the effort it took, the noisy intake of air in his nostrils. I tried to synchronise my breathing with his, find some accord. His face was set while he observed me curiously, still standing at arm's length to keep a distance between us. I almost anticipated a slap and leant back a little, straining against his grasp, bracing myself. But his voice when it came was low and soft.

'Elise, I have to ask you again. I want the whole story this time.'

We moved back into the kitchen, a comfortable, familiar zone, though not necessarily safer, in my thinking. I sat. He stood. For a while, we each avoided each other's eyes. I could hear a radio from next door through the open window. My mind took me temporarily, ridiculously, to Spain. *Dark hair, a red dress, Flamenco dance, that distinctive guitar music from Andalusia.* I travelled anywhere when cornered.

Mark picked up a cup from the sink and examined it closely, turning it over in his hands as he leaned back against the counter. He raised his eyes and I saw a tick of discomfort flick over his face. We both started to speak.

'Mark, I never…'

'Were you ever going to…?' He gestured for me to continue.

'I never wanted to make things harder for you, after all the…after everything you went through, over there, and afterwards. You were so…'

'You don't have to try to protect me anymore.'

He replaced the cup slowly, gingerly, as if as concerned by its fragility as I was of his own. Then he joined me at the table, sitting opposite, arms crossed. The muscles in his bare upper body flexed once, just slightly, as if for battle. And I looked at his chest and his strong hands, brown from the sun, a few small scars marking the knuckles of his right hand. I noted with surprise that some of his chest hair had turned grey. There was a slight scent of the soap he'd used still clinging to his skin. Then he spoke again.

'I want the truth, Elise.'

'Yes.'

'No secrets.'

'No.'

'Okay.'

He exhaled, leaned back in the chair and glanced up at the ceiling, then looked at me again with a steady, trusting gaze, those honey-amber eyes piercing any armour I might still have worn. The rhythmical tapping of his fingers on the table between us became a loud invasive thrumming, matching the music on the radio, and I closed my eyes. *The stomping of fla-menco dancers…*Why did I go to these strange, distant places when stressed?

'One thing I want you to tell me, Elise, is who's the father? You said he was a stranger but is that true?'

The word, imprisoned for so long, was out of my mouth before there was any chance to obfuscate. 'Craig.'

I don't know which of us was the more surprised. Mark moved forward, reaching his hand across towards me but then pulling back; confusion picked its way across his features.

'Craig? Him? Your stepfather?'

I was aware of a creeping itch on my face and neck, of my skin burning.

I knew the shame I wore was not a deserved mantle, but my body wouldn't give it up. Fear, like an insect, burrowed under my skin. I nodded and stared down at my lap while Mark stood and moved wordlessly to my side, one hand cautious on my shoulder. I continued to avoid his face but was aware of his bulk, the maleness and separateness of him.

Soon we were both standing, arms awkwardly encircling each other, my cheek against his chest. His hand moved then, to stroke my hair, while my tears traced a path on his skin. Then he was crying and I became the soother. Our movement together from the kitchen to the living room became its own slow, sad waltz.

We sat on the couch, eyes averted, while my fingers twisted into knots and my lower lip suffered from my biting. Mark ran a hand through his hair again and had a look on his face of devastation or disgust, emotions which settled miserably into his slouched shoulders. He looked up.

'I'm sorry Elise. I never…I should have guessed, or asked more questions.'

'You couldn't have. I never told anyone back then.'

'Not even your mother?'

'No. Well, I tried to, when it started, but whatever words came out of me, she didn't understand, or believe; it was just too hard to articulate. *I didn't fathom what was happening, so how could I explain it to anyone else?* Besides, he always said he'd hurt her and Marion, kill them, or me, if I ever spoke about it to anyone. But she found out, eventually, not so long ago in fact.' The truth, so long unaired, sounded almost false to my ears.

'How old were you, when…when it started?'

'Oh Mark.' *I'm made of steel. Nothing can hurt me.* A deep sigh. I closed my eyes. 'I was very young. Not quite ten.'

He turned his face, covered a sob with his hand. We let the ensuing quiet, the stillness, muzzle emotion, and bring a small degree of composure.

'Marion—did he…?'

'I hoped, prayed she was safe. But I can't be sure.' Remorse made an ugly grimace of my face. 'I hated leaving her behind.'

'You didn't go to the police?'

'I told you. He threatened to hurt my family! I didn't know how he'd do it, but I believed he could and he would.'

'What about your brother? Did he know what was happening?'

I slumped back, so very weary now. 'Not all of it. I often thought maybe something horrible was happening to him too. But truly, I was never equipped to do anything to stop it all. I was a child. Mark, please, you can't tell the children about any of this. Promise me!'

His voice, rough, fierce, 'Where's the bastard? I'd like to kill him.'

I began to laugh in that moment of pain; a loud, breathy snort that made Mark baulk. I said, 'My mother already did, in her own way.'

He stared. And as I continued, the lack of emotion in my voice must have appalled him, as it did me, on some level. 'Craig was having a heart attack; he was outside when Mum saw him from the kitchen window. He'd gripped his chest, and she watched as he fell. Heard his moans, and saw his legs spasm. But she says she moved in slow motion, unsure what to do, then finished her packing and waited for a full twenty minutes before calling for help. She even made herself a cup of tea.' I shook my head. 'Who knows if he'd have survived if the medics had come earlier, but he was certainly dead by the time they arrived.'

In calmly stating the facts as relayed to me by Lillian, I'd felt a perverse sense of justice. There was nothing whatsoever left to say. Mark looked horrified.

CHAPTER
THIRTY-FOUR

Marion still worked in the UK, doing something ambiguously described as an administrative job. She travelled to Europe for holidays, and eventually saved enough money to return to Australia for a brief visit. I looked for but couldn't see much now of her youthful allure. A fashionably skinny face and frame had replaced her earlier beauty and soft curves, but she seemed to inhabit this new body uneasily. She spoke with a slight British accent, seemed to be trying to cultivate a sophistication that sat self-consciously on her small-town disposition. She stayed a week with us, essentially ignoring her niece and nephew, and tried flirting with Mark, who was oblivious, and spent a lot of time talking about or attending to clothes, nails, hair and make-up. It was an effort to engage with the adult Marion or connect her with the sister I'd loved so much. We never spoke of the past.

Jeffrey—well, very little news ever filtered down to me about my brother. Mum told me he'd divorced, was living somewhere near Albury and saw his children every second weekend. She didn't hear much from him, but he wrote occasionally, including cheques from time to time, which she'd told him not to send but they kept coming. He was generous in that way. Marion said that she'd written to him many times, but he rarely responded. I guessed that he clung tightly to whatever grudges he still held about growing up in our family.

Our children were teenagers and growing up and away from us.

Paul, a young boy in manner and years, had gone through a tough time transitioning from primary into high school; the bullying behaviour left him when he encountered taller and stronger boys, and I initially worried that he would again revert to being a victim. But he gained some status by offering his completed homework to less capable students in exchange for cigarettes or an hour of friendly companionship on a tennis court.

By fifteen he'd developed an interest in science and mechanics and spent many evenings poring over text books and devising experiments using household products or pulling apart radios, cameras or an old TV and reassembling them. Towards the end of his last year of school, when he'd turned seventeen and was working part-time stacking shelves at a supermarket, he bought himself a battered old Holden Kingswood, with a cash donation from us, and had a bevy of girls his age or younger swarming around him.

I'd mess up his hair and make jokes about the magical pull of his unique, beautiful eyes—comments which either annoyed or amused him. His circle of friends was still small, but he appeared to be happier in himself than he'd been as a younger teen. He'd often be outside with Mark, engrossed in the workshop projects they'd devised together. Initially, Paul was the one who planned, instructed and executed with Mark assisting. As time passed, and Mark grew stronger, those roles reversed again. They were a good, solid team.

Patricia was fourteen, in some ways wise for her years, but also captive to her adolescent hormones. She didn't walk, she flounced, and reminded me of Marion in that way. She too developed a skinny frame, and with it a brittleness that added emphasis to her sharp, protruding bones. While Paul was still young in conduct and temperament, and was usually happy to allow me to ruffle his hair or give him an impromptu hug, Patricia kept herself at a polite distance physically and emotionally. She tolerated my embrace but looked relieved when I let go. Her conversation was habitually monosyllabic.

'How was school?'

'Fine.'

'Do you have any homework?'

'A bit.'

'Tell me about your day.'

'Mum!' An exaggerated rolling of the eyes.

'But I'm interested in what you've been doing, how it's all going.'

'It was fine, okay?' And she'd push herself away from the table or the sofa or the bed, exit the room and busy herself with the phone or her homework or an urgent visit to a friend. Her previous diagnosis of mild dyslexia hadn't held her back, and though she struggled at times with text books and assignments, she used her stubbornness and determination and excellent memory to keep pace with her classmates.

I'd scrutinise both our children, drinking them in. Paul was tall; he had thick, dark hair, fair skin, and those extraordinary green eyes full of truth and promise. His face was shaped like mine, but his smile and mannerisms were identical to Mark's. They both had a way of tilting their head to one side when concentrating and a dimple on one cheek when they grinned. Paul had filled out after his gawky adolescence, developing muscles and carrying himself with more confidence. He had a calm and gentle manner, was witty, observant, honest, kind, though at times secretive. I laughed inwardly at any of his small acts of rebellion, silently cheering him on. And my heart ached with love.

Patricia was in many ways similar to Mark in mannerisms and in height, though she was more angular. Her little ivory-shaded face, sun-kissed with light freckles, could appear stern, and she often hid her smile from me in a way that suggested she was either embarrassed by her teeth (which were, in fact, perfectly white and straight), or she thought a pout was more appropriate to our relationship. But when she did smile, she created magic. Her eyes were an intriguing shade—dark honey with little flecks of lighter brown. She wore her hair long; it was a chestnut colour, thick and wavy, as my mother's had once been. She was very smart, generous with material things, independent, stubborn but curious. She *noticed*. And absorbed. I saw hesitance, vulnerability and defiance in her movements, and my heart ached with love.

By now, my Mark seemed to have shed many of his demons. He grew a moustache, filled out his gauntness with increased exercise and second helpings of food, and practised his best estimation of a smile that he perhaps believed might do well enough in the new world he inhabited. But he never stood quite as tall as he once had. I saw in his movements a resolve and determination, but also defencelessness, and my heart ached with love.

• • •

Very occasionally, I studied my form in the mirror, and tried to ascertain who was staring back at me. It wasn't often that I got to clinically observe myself naked. The reflection showed a woman of middle age with shoulder-length brown hair that was still thick although it had a touch of grey at the temples. My face was round but had long ago lost the softness and naiveté of youth. My eyes were an unusual colour, difficult to classify, and variable with the lighting. Some days they were a mix of grey and green, occasionally leaning towards hazel with a very slight butter-yellow fleck. No sign of the melted chocolate-brown of my father's eyes. Tense narrow shoulders. Gravity was working on my breasts but they were still high and had attitude. My waist was small but thickening, and my hips narrow, in line with my shoulders, which gave me a boyish look. I had long, muscular, practical and efficient legs.

If I ever stayed at the mirror long enough to ponder, I could sometimes see the face of the happy, chubby five-year-old who adored her dad and was adored in return. Or the eight-year-old on whose face much of life's confusion and fear had begun to settle. Or the ten-year-old who'd learnt to hate school, distrust anyone in authority, and tremble at shadows. The bewildered, pained child of twelve who was petrified of life and still wet the bed. The terrified girl of sixteen who gave birth to a mirage, and the needy eighteen-year-old who had no idea why she did it but opened her legs for any young man who gave her attention. If I looked with intent at what I saw in the mirror, my heart, just sometimes, jolted with compassion.

But more often the shutters of shame, confusion, anger and embarrassment reappeared. I'd hurriedly dress, and go back to sleepwalking through my daily existence.

• • •

My memory of detail from some of those years isn't so good anymore, and I'm a bit confused about the chronology, but more pieces of the jigsaw keep falling into place. David, I'm especially grateful that you're typing these latest musing for me. It's so kind of you. Now that they've shown me how to use Zoom, and the internet here is more reliable, it's been a great bonus to be able to see you on screen and chat as we have. When we've finished this project, you and I, I'll put it together with the material my granddaughter has sorted for me. But my daughter is the one who convinced me to do this, so I'll give it all to her when we're done.

CHAPTER THIRTY-FIVE

Time galloped past me. Past us. Simon, my first-born, my lost and found son, who had come to me on slips of paper over time, was almost thirty by the time we met. He'd suggested a cafe in a town roughly half-way between his city and mine, so I caught the early train and had time to fill in before the noon bells would ring out from the church on the hill. Nerves fluttered and collided like small birds inside my chest. I didn't think I'd be able to eat anything in his company without throwing up.

His letters and very occasional phone calls had given me a sketchy outline of his life. His voice suggested a private school education. Good at sport, keen on rugby, he said that university had been 'a bit boring but useful'. He had a good job—something in the public sector—and was engaged to a teacher. His mother was in good health; his father had developed prostate cancer but was in the clear.

He wanted to meet me because, he said, 'I'm curious to see what you really look like. The photos don't show much. Are there any medical issues I should know about?' I sensed a certain arrogance and affectation in the way he'd relayed this. It made me feel as though I would be a specimen under scrutiny, to be disposed of instantly if I didn't measure up.

I arrived early, and paced the streets, rehearsing what I thought might be logical and acceptable answers to the questions I anticipated would come. As I neared the church, its interior beckoned, promising a sombre, reverent familiarity, and I was struck immediately, inside the entrance, by the old smells—burning wax, smoky incense, sweet chrism oil, aged wooden pews, fresh flowers. But the altar and pulpit, the desolate Stations of the Cross, the dark, forbidding confessional box, and the agony conveyed by the crucifix all repelled me and I left.

My steps led me back to the cafe. I entered and surveyed from inside the doorway. It was a large space, filled with noise and bustle from a lunch crowd. Workmen hunched over hot meals, their laughter mingling with the hum of conversation from friends swapping stories. Young mothers bounced their babies on their knees as soft coos and chuckles crossed the tables. School kids wagging their classes gossiped and slurped milk shakes. A kind of unified contentment made the space feel full in all the right ways. At 11.58, with an urgent need to pee, I made my way to the bathroom where I glimpsed the ghost of my sixteen-year-old self in the mirror over the basin. Tears threatened. *I'm made of steel. I don't cry.* I left the room.

And there he was, sitting at a table in the corner, browsing the menu but glancing occasionally towards the main door. I stood partially hidden behind a shelving unit to study his profile. Short, mid-brown hair with a side-combed fringe. Seated, he appeared to be of medium height. His clothing was casual, neat, unremarkable—a pale-blue short-sleeved shirt, tailored black trousers and black leather shoes. When he turned his head to scan the area, I felt I was looking into a slightly distorted mirror. Somehow, it settled my nerves.

He rose when he caught sight of me walking towards him and adopted a tight smile. A hand hastily brushed back some invisible stray lock from his forehead. He was a little stockier than I'd first supposed but awkward in that young and eager way, almost like a foal finding its feet. Not so arrogant after all. He held out his hand to shake mine—his grip limp and clammy—before sliding back onto his chair, a little too vigorously. The table shifted against his sudden movement and a glass threatened to topple while the menu dropped to the floor. As he bent to pick it up, I wanted to touch his head or his shoulder, anywhere to make a connection, but I resisted. He fumbled with the menu again and sat up straight, glancing everywhere but at me. I supposed that a similar shock of recognition had thrown him completely. I felt a rush of a maternal *something* and grinned as I sat opposite, reaching my hand across to cover his shaking one.

I began. 'You're not working today, obviously. Not needed at work?'

'I took the day off and went to Bowral to see my, my family. It's only a short drive from here.' His voice was deeper than on the phone. His brief glance at me gave nothing away.

'How is your dad?' I asked.

'Better now. The surgery went well.' He looked towards the counter. 'Should we order?'

• • •

I tried hard not to keep staring at the young man opposite me. Thirty years of wondering, imagining, hoping, and he was nothing like I'd envisaged. I didn't hear most of what he said, just kept peering at his mouth and sensing a subdued voice somewhere in front of me that must have belonged to him. I felt as if we were both underwater, my eyes not able to see through a blur of remembering. Eventually my muteness hung awkwardly between us, and I had to strain to understand what he'd been saying, asking of me. I saw that his hand had long since slipped from underneath my own, and his fingers now tapped nervously beside his cup of coffee. When had he ordered that? When had it come? I looked down and saw my own cup, filled to the brim with tanned milkiness. I raised it carefully, hands shaking.

'I'm sorry. I just can't help staring at you. You're so...beautiful.'

Simon squirmed, looking around to see if anyone had overheard. He glanced back at me, cleared his throat, picked up his coffee and scanned the room again as he took a large gulp, almost scalding his mouth before he spluttered with an embarrassed cough.

A cash register sang. Children's voices rang out. I heard a light bell-ring from the kitchen. I noted jars of honey that sat in amber brilliance on the shelves behind him.

'My mum,' he began before pausing, perhaps to gauge what effect those words might have on me. I hoped my face remained impassive. 'She said not to ask you too much; not to ask why you gave me up, because she said that's not relevant. But I'd like to understand.'

I was surprised at his bluntness. *Straight to the point! Cheeky even.* Then I said softly, wistfully, more to myself. 'I never got to hold you. I didn't want to let you go.'

He waited, watched.

'I wanted to keep you. I very much wanted that. But I was so young, and people convinced me that I wouldn't be able to look after you, that it would be impossible. They insisted, and I couldn't fight back.'

Clearing my throat, I said in a louder voice. 'I'll tell you whatever you want to know, in time, but for the moment, I'd much prefer to hear about you. Whatever you're comfortable telling me; things that weren't in your letters that you'd be willing to share. And then I'll try to answer your questions.'

He nodded. I studied his eyes again, though he didn't hold my gaze for long. They were a very light brown, like the honey in the jars on the shelf, with a faint tawny ring around the irises. There was something else in his face that I preferred not to acknowledge; an expression, or the tilt of his forehead, a familiar set of the mouth perhaps, that might take me back to darker times if I let it. So I focused on the timbre of his voice, which became fuller, rounded and more resonant the longer he spoke.

We ordered food and he talked more fluidly then about his work, his family, his siblings (also adopted), his fiancée and his plans for the future. Much of it sounded rehearsed, though he spoke with enormous affection about his adoptive parents and with pride in his career. His aim was to become a diplomat. I couldn't help but think of the little boy who was inside there somewhere, behind the grown man I studied.

'How old are your other children?' he asked. 'You never said in your letters.'

'Paul is almost twenty-three and Patricia's eighteen.'

I noticed a flash of something that looked like annoyance or perhaps pain cross his face before he quickly realigned his features. Then he asked the inevitable question: 'Tell me about my father. His name's not on the birth certificate I've seen. Where does he live? I want to meet him.'

I'd prepared myself for this and answered with surprising calm, 'I'm sorry, Simon, but he disappeared from my life. I can't give you details, because he wasn't someone I knew well. It wasn't a relationship as such, not something I wanted to pursue. It was so long ago.' The pulse in my throat sped up.

A new expression, something like disgust or disappointment, perhaps both, flickered over Simon's face. 'He doesn't have a name? You won't tell me, or you didn't know it? Well, where did he live?'

His tone stung me. 'I don't know. He was just someone who….as I said, it wasn't a relationship. I only knew his first name. I'll try to answer any other questions next time, if there is a next time?'

He nodded, while the tilt of his mouth indicated uncertainty.

I continued. 'I can tell you about my medical history in a few words though. I'm disgustingly healthy.' I waited for a smile that never came.

The conversation progressed, though strained, with Simon alternating between false cheer and moody silences, while I tried my best to convey to him a sense of my years of longing and regret without sounding melodramatic.

Finally, I stood, and said, 'Well, my train leaves soon. Thank you for organising this…,' I gestured with both hands towards him and back to myself, was annoyed at my lack of eloquence.

We parted company at the station. As we said goodbye, he held out his hand to shake mine, but I hesitated a moment, before pulling him towards me into a tight, clumsy embrace. Then I promptly released him and walked away before he could see my face.

I never got to hold you.

CHAPTER
THIRTY-SIX

By then, of course, we had to tell our children that they had a half-brother. Patricia had turned eighteen in the spring, was still living at home, but had an active social life. She'd done pretty well at school, through sheer will, had mellowed considerably; she routinely socialised, often slept over at the home of friends. She worked part-time at a fast-food outlet while investigating other job options. University didn't interest her.

Paul was living in a group house in the inner city while he finished his last year of chemical engineering. University and shared house arrangements had ironed out his nervous twitch. He had a lovely girlfriend, Felicity; he or they usually visited us every fortnight.

How do you tell your children that you're not exactly who they thought you were? We enticed them to join us at home for a 'special' dinner on a weekend. I'd made the house look as cosy, homey, as *normal* as possible. When they arrived, we exchanged the obligatory parental hugs, which Paul accepted happily, Patricia endured.

'Here, sit down, honey,' Mark patted Patricia on the shoulder, pulled out a chair for her then turned to punch Paul lightly on the arm. 'You too son, take a seat. What's your drink? Beer?' He sounded as nervous as I felt.

'Yeah, okay, thanks.' Paul scraped and thumped into the seat, as young men tend to do, to accommodate their energetic bulk. He brushed his fringe away from his eyes, staring at me steadily with that frank, open watchfulness I adored.

'Mum? What's up? You don't look well.'

I forced a laugh, rather too loud. 'Oh, I'm fine; we just wanted to have you both here together, that's all. You're always so busy.'

I rose from the table and started moving pots around the stove, dishes around the counter, not sure what I was doing or how the dinner would actually appear. My hands shook.

Patricia volunteered, 'Want me to help you?'

'Ah, no I'm fine thanks darling. Just…just talk to Dad and I'll get things moving.'

'Can I have a coke please Dad?', she said.

Mark looked relieved to have an excuse to rummage through the fridge.

Routine family questions, answers. How to get to the point? When? While I served a too lumpy lasagne, we spoke of this and that; I've no accurate recollection of all the preamble. We ate and chatted and joked, while an undercurrent of panic passed back and forth between Mark and me. Then I was assembling dessert (I don't remember what), and Mark was frowning at me. He stood, pacing a little, nudging me with his elbow when he passed. I placed bowls on the table, forgot spoons, fetched them and sat again. Mark stood opposite and nodded at me. I froze. Paul and Patricia began to eat, Paul glancing with amused suspicion at both of us. Finally, Mark took the initiative, since I wouldn't.

'Mum and I have something we want to talk to you about.' He took his seat again, uneasily.

The children exchanged a glance. Patricia put her spoon down in a slow, deliberate movement and leaned back in her chair, arms folded, eyes narrowed. 'What? Are you getting divorced?'

Mark choked on a half-laugh and glanced at me, raised his eyebrows, tilted his head.

'This is hard,' I began. My ears were ringing. I closed my mouth, blew air through my nostrils, thought hard to recall what I'd practised a dozen times. Words jostled.

'I should have told you both about this a very long time ago.'

I looked at each of them in turn, my elbows on the table, hands fidgeting, then glanced over their heads at the clock. Paul had stopped eating, eyes apprehensive. Patricia scowled.

Breathe in. Exhale. Hands in your lap. Lift your head. Say it. My voice wavered but I made it come out. I spoke to the clock.

'When I was very young, just sixteen, I had a baby, a boy. My mother, step-father, and a social worker made me sign papers to put him up for adoption, and I never saw him. He was taken away straight after his birth, but he got in touch with me, and we've met.'

I looked down at locked hands on my lap, kept my eyes to the floor. My cheeks flushed; a snail's path of brine tracked slowly to my chin. 'I'm so sorry I never told you. I was too ashamed.'

A vacuum. When I raised my eyes, Paul was leaning back, his chair teetering on its back legs, his eyes wide with surprise or curiosity. 'A brother. Cool! What's he like?'

Before I could answer, Patricia stood abruptly and strode to the door, her shoulders rigid with fury. She turned back to glare at me, and spat out 'I hate you.'

The barricade slammed shut.

• • •

Soon, Patricia found work with an accountancy firm, started a Business Studies course, made plenty more friends, moved into shared accommodation, acquired a boyfriend (a serious but pleasant young man with large teeth), and was out doing what I could only imagine teenage girls were supposed to do with their lives.

Already enjoying her independence, her interludes at home tapered right off after the news of her half-brother. Eventually, Mark and Paul were able to coax her out from her place of hurt and indignation, though I'm not sure how they did it, given her legendary stubbornness. She questioned me about my story, reluctantly at first, and then with genuine interest. I told her only the barest of details, emphasising my youth and immaturity, and invented the 'who' and the circumstances. Another truth located deep within another lie. I didn't want to sully my darling girl with the ugliness that had been Craig.

We were in her old bedroom, both standing by the window, aware of a wind that had picked up; dark clouds threatened a storm.

'Mum! Sixteen's so young. Two years younger than I am now.'

'I was very naïve, Trish, and so very frightened. By everything. I couldn't have kept the baby, not at that age, and with Grandma being so upset with me.'

'She should've helped you Mum, not sent you away like that.'

'It's the way it happened, in those days, to a lot of girls.'

Patricia's chin quivered as she opened her arms wide for me. I stepped into them, and felt her tears, warm and plentiful, in my hair, on my neck. I cherished the smell of her—that wonderful citrus fragrance of her skin, the woody-daisy scent of her shampoo—and noted again how innocent yet determined she was, and how strong she'd become. Oh how I loved her.

• • •

Simon and I continued to exchange letters, and we met several times when he travelled to Sydney for work. Once, he brought his wife along. She was a striking brunette named Chelsea, compact and athletic-looking, with large blue eyes, a confident chin and a firm, friendly handshake. She seemed to help Simon relax and gave him a warmth that'd been missing on previous occasions.

I wasn't surprised to learn that he was right-leaning politically and had generally conservative views, which suggested that I wasn't off the hook with him, not yet. He was still unsure about me, wasn't yet ready to be introduced to his half-siblings or Mark. I had to accept that we were, essentially, strangers, united only by some similar features and a moment in time I'd prefer to forget. Our emotional connection was loose, delicately balanced. But I was chuffed when he called to tell me I was to be a grandmother, and grateful for the photos of the grandchild that appeared occasionally.

Mark didn't interfere in any of this; in fact, he pushed me to keep in contact with Simon. I often wondered if he ever thought about trying to meet his daughter with Louise. He'd never spoken to me about Louise or the child, except once, perhaps to expel the rest of the secret only half un-covered. We were walking home from a visit to an art gallery when he took hold of my hand, cleared his throat and said, without looking at me, 'I want to explain something. Since you've told me the truth, you know, about the past, you should know about Louise, how it happened.'

He steered me to the nearest bench. We sat, both still looking ahead.

I protested, 'I don't want the details, Mark. Spare me those, please.'

'It's not that, not those kinds of things, but how it happened. During the war, you know how messed up I was. Whenever I came back, I couldn't face you; you were always fussing, Elise, always worrying. I could sense your anxiety every time you came near me. And I just didn't know how to talk to you about what I was feeling. It was like *your* worry became the big issue and that started leaching something from me. I felt smothered by everything. I'm not trying to blame you, Elise, of course that's not what I mean. It was just,' he broke off. 'With Louise, it was just something that happened. Oh fuck it. Okay.'

He took a deep breath. I braced for the details, though already knowing the basics from Louise.

He said, 'I met her in a bar one time I was back on leave. We started chatting, got along. She was sweet and,' he paused, 'uncomplicated. We met again a few times over a couple of weeks, I left to go back, over there, you know, and never saw her again. Honestly Elise, I had no idea she'd gotten pregnant, until that day at the zoo.'

Those bare facts were as much as I needed to hear. And I believed every word.

While I didn't expect we'd see Louise again, every so often, when I checked the *Births, Deaths and Marriages* registry and the Census records for any information about my father—unsuccessfully, which cut deep—I also occasionally searched for Louise's name. Over time, I discovered she was married, with two more children. Her daughter, her child with Mark, would be about seventeen by now.

CHAPTER
THIRTY-SEVEN

Life has funny ideas. Comedy. Coincidence. Fate. Tragedy. Farce.

The doorbell rang while I was emerging from the bedroom one evening, not quite fully dressed, aware the waist of my pantyhose was cutting an uncomfortable line into my midriff and my hair was unbrushed. Patricia was temporarily back living with us due to rental problems and I heard her call 'I'll get it', so I finished buttoning my shirt and started towards the kitchen. I heard my daughter's customary hard yank of the door, her offhand 'Hello?' and a young woman's voice asking if Mark was home. I turned but couldn't see much of the figure in front of Patricia, other than a halo of fair hair, a tan handbag and the lower half of a pair of jeans.

Patricia turned to look at me, then swung around again and spoke to the girl. 'Dad's not home yet. Do you want to talk to my mother?'

The voice hesitated. 'What time will he be back?'

Patricia again turned to me. 'Mum! Can you...?'

Hurriedly running fingers through my hair, I moved towards the front door, curious, as Patricia slid away and bounced into the living room. She'd been bouncing a lot lately, which was cheerier than flouncing. I assumed it was because of the new boyfriend.

The woman before me was actually just a girl, pretty in a rather fragile way, and too small for her large bag and over-sized checked shirt. Her wavy hair was pulled back into a loose ponytail, with golden wisps escaping near her ears. A smattering of light freckles danced across her nose; a small red mark near the corner of her mouth suggested the remnants of a cold sore or a pimple. This all added to a projection of youth and breakability.

I smiled at her and opened the screen door. 'Yes?'

Her eyes widened at the sight of me, and she turned as if to walk away, then faced me again. 'I'm Emma Williams.' Her voice was low, almost a whisper.

'I'm sorry. I don't know....'

I moved to get a closer look.

'Do you want to come in? Mark should be home in about thirty minutes.'

'No, I....' A feathery voice. Soft. Hesitant.

'Is there something I can help you with?'

She lowered her head and I saw that her hands were trembling. A single bead of perspiration had made its way down the side of her neck and disappeared into the collar of her shirt. She fumbled inside her bag and drew out a white envelope which she hastily handed to me.

'Can you please give this to Mr Harrington? I have to go. I'm sorry.' And she turned and walked swiftly down the few steps to the path and was gone before I could call her back. Her likeness to Louise hit me. I also saw something of Patricia in her build and in the way she walked. The name Emma fell into place.

• • •

When Mark arrived home, tired and slightly out-of-sorts, I was reluctant to pass on the letter, so I waited until after we'd had dinner, and Patricia had left with Gabby's daughter to meet a friend in the city. Before he moved to settle in front of the television, I placed a hand on his arm, fingers tense.

'Here,' I said, my voice a pitch lower than normal, and passed him the envelope. 'A girl dropped this off for you earlier this evening. She wanted to see you, but she wouldn't wait.'

Mark turned the envelope around in his hands, looked at me, puzzled, and began to tear it open. 'Who was she? Did she say what she wanted?'

'No, but…I think you need to sit down.'

I moved my hand to his shoulder as he unfurled the single page and read. I waited. He stared at me, remained standing, silent.

'She said her name was Emma, Emma Williams. Her mother is Louise.'

He was confused, flustered, and shifted his body, turned towards the door as if to escape. His brow furrowed; he blew air through his lips, rocked back on his heels, then slumped onto the edge of the couch and read again.

It seemed that the past was determined to bark and grasp at our heels all our lives, but I made my voice calm. 'I haven't had any contact with Louise since she married. I just didn't twig about this girl today until she was walking away, and the name, her first name…'

He was still re-reading the note. I tried to decipher some of the words from an upside-down vantage point but saw only a dense forest of small loops. Mark held it out to me and let his arms drop between his knees, clasping both hands together as if in fervent prayer, knuckles straining.

'Bloody hell!' And he stared at the wall, as if seeking answers in the wallpaper that refused to appear.

I skimmed through the letter.

'Dear Mr Harrington,

I am Louise Williams' daughter and I believe that I am your daughter too. My mother told me recently how she'd only known you for a short while and I was conceived during that time. She told me you were married, so she didn't pursue a longer relationship with you. She also said that you didn't know she was pregnant when the relationship finished, so I certainly can't blame you for not being a part of my life.

But years ago my mum contacted your wife and she told me that they met and your wife sent Mum money for a while, which was very kind.

Mum has been married to Graham for fifteen years. He's been a wonderful father to me and I love him very much. So does Mum. But way back, she did some research and found a newspaper photograph from a long time ago of you and your wife and children. You were saying good-bye at the airbase, before you went to Vietnam. This was taken before you'd even met mum, but she came across the photo afterwards, in some archive, and kept it, to show me when she thought I was old enough. And she said the photo was to remind her that you already had a family so she wouldn't intrude.

I'm only writing because I think all children have a right to know their father, and fathers to know their children. I'm moving to Newcastle soon and wanted to see if we could meet before I go.

Yours sincerely,
Emma Williams'

There was an address and telephone number. I realised with a sinking feeling that we'd need to schedule another round table with our children, and I felt a lurch of apprehension for them. *'Oh, and by the way, did we mention you have a younger sister too?'*

'She seemed very nice,' I said lamely. And touched his arm again, lightly, while thinking how ludicrous, quirky, confusing and magnificent life can be—far more so than the trite, silly fantasy world I still sometimes created for myself.

● ● ●

I imagined happy family scenarios where Simon and Emma would be welcomed without a fuss and we'd spend wonderful Christmases and birthdays together, mistletoe and angels, and on and on, la de da.

But on the flipside of every fantasy is a nightmare. It occurred to me that if we didn't tell our children, a consequence could be that our Paul might one day unwittingly meet Emma, fall in love, have sex, create a catastrophe. Highly improbable, but not impossible. In the end, Mark reluctantly agreed that we had to tell them.

So, another family dinner was arranged, with Mark this time uneasy, apprehensive, as I paced around the edges, worried he was still too fragile, hoping he'd be able to pull all the pieces together afterwards.

Patricia brought the food to the table, crunching on an apple as she set down individual plates. 'Are we waiting for Paul? He's late.'

My voice controlled, tight, as I played with cutlery. 'His new job's pretty demanding. But he should've left work by now.'

'I thought computers were supposed to help ease a workload, not increase it. Maybe he should have stuck with engineering.'

'He's on better pay, he reckons, and he enjoys the new environment.' I kept my eyes down.

Mark opened a beer, poured it too quickly into his glass and watched blankly while foam slopped onto the tablecloth. I hovered on the sidelines, wiped absentmindedly at the damp spot with a dishcloth, retrieved some napkins from the sideboard. We all turned at the sound of the front door slamming shut. Paul entered the room hand-in-hand with Felicity who, true to her name, embodied happiness, expressed through her warm dark eyes and smile, her calm and breezy personality. She was tall, like all of us, had mid-brown hair, a smooth olive complexion, slender limbs and a slight lisp. She was always a welcome guest, though unexpected that night. Mark stood, flustered again, knocked over the rest of his beer, extended his arms weakly in greeting, coughed, excused himself and left the room.

I stepped up.

'Felicity, how lovely to see you! I didn't think you'd be able to come tonight', I lied. 'Here, sorry, let me set a place for you.'

Paul hugged me. 'Sorry Mum, I should have let you know.'

I beamed, a haphazard movement of my mouth, patted his cheek and turned to kiss Felicity. 'Absolutely fine! Delighted you're both here. Paul, could you mop up that beer? And help yourself to one. I just have to go check on something. Make yourselves comfy.' I made a rapid exit.

Mark was sitting on our bed, head in hands, depleted. 'What'll we do?' His voice was quiet, strained.

'Maybe it'll be easier with Felicity here. Or if you want to, we'll do it another time. Or maybe we just don't do it at all?'

He shrugged, baffled, then took a sharp breath, stood quickly and squeezed my hand before returning to the dining room. Food somehow made its way to our plates, and we began our dinner, garnishing it with counterfeit gusto and bonhomie. Emma's name wasn't mentioned. They all left afterwards in gentle bemusement, assuming, I supposed, that we were just older and more senile.

Mark contacted Emma the following week and they arranged to meet in Hyde Park, where for an hour they walked, talked, found a teahouse nearby. Later, he relayed the gist of their conversation to me, in a light tone with a hint of indulgent surprise. 'She's very mature for her age, Elise. I like her. She says she doesn't want anything from us and wouldn't impose on me, on us. I think she just needed to meet me to see what I'm all about. She said Louise wasn't aware we were meeting, and wouldn't approve yet, but Emma wants to see me again, when her mum's okay with it. Louise is married, she's got two other children. Emma says the father—his name's Graham and of course she calls him Dad—she says he's a really nice man, a good father.'

He stopped. Mused over what he'd just exclaimed. Looked momentarily defeated, guilty.

In an attempt to move him back into the moment, I piped up, with careful enthusiasm, 'Yes, she told us some of that in her letter.'

'I know, I know, I'm just, well, all over the place. Excited. Worried. My heart's hammering.'

I nodded, paused. 'Are you going to tell the kids?'

His lightness vanished. He ran the fingers of one hand across his jaw, leaned back, closed his eyes and frowned. Let out a long sigh.

'I don't think they're ready for another story like this.' He paused. 'I don't think *I'm* ready. Besides,' he gave me a forced, rueful smile, 'they'll never come here for dinner again if we keep doing this.'

As it happened, Mark took each of them out separately and broke the news to each of them over a few glasses of wine. He told me later that this time it was Paul who became angry and upset, blasting Mark for his infidelity, more loyal on this occasion to me than he was to his dad after my earlier revelation. To his credit, Mark made no excuses, pure in his repetition of how sorry he was. He emphasised that he and I had worked things through, and he'd said to Paul, "Your mother forgave me. I hope you can too? Emma's your half-sister, and none of it was her fault. So, can you? Son, I love you."

It took time, but eventually Paul managed to look his father in the eye again, and they eased back into their former relationship.

Patricia, who'd always adored her father and believed he could do no wrong, apparently was more sanguine when told. I heard that her response was along the lines of "That girl who came around that day, she's my sister? I don't want her living with us. Does Mum know? What is wrong with you two? How come you haven't divorced? Honestly, you're both as bad as each other." But she'd punched his arm then hugged him, while shedding confused tears.

When I heard that, I wished I'd developed the art of forgiveness as readily as both my children had.

• • •

Despite everything, Mark and I managed somehow to continue as a couple, were comfortable in ways that we'd never been before, or at least not for a long time. Perhaps I'd grown up, finally, just a little. And Mark was a more equable, more generous version of himself. Sometime, I don't know when, it dawned on me that we'd stopped arguing, stopped expecting too much of each other and stopped taking too much for granted. And while that might have left us little to talk about in our everyday lives, there was also then no need for blame, quarrels or recriminations. The things we did convey were loving and gentle as we explored a new dimension to kindness. That old flamenco dance of ours, which once was passionate but could also be wild and destructive, had turned into a graceful waltz.

• • •

Time shrinks behind me, it shrinks ahead of me, and I worry that I might not beat it before this story gets told. Many details have tumbled and jumbled into a loop rather than a linear pattern. Somehow, David, all those early years are still so very clear. But recent things, no. I can barely remember what I did yesterday. Does it matter? Does everything I've told you make sense to you?

This wretched virus isn't going away. I've seen so many pitiful things happening here. Sickness. Loneliness. And death is never very far away. The staff have been magnificent, even when there are too few of them to cope. They're very good to me. And when I'm not working on this project with you, David, I have a few friends in here to keep me company, if you can call it 'company' when you're sitting five metres apart, and all of us wearing masks.

I hope you are well. I look forward to our Zoom chat next Tuesday.

CHAPTER
THIRTY-EIGHT

The 'happy families' picture never did quite work out for everyone, though Simon occasionally called to fill me in on the growing family he and his wife had produced. He invited me to Canberra to stay with them on a few occasions. I went once, but it all felt a bit strained, though I did appreciate the gesture. His three children with Chelsea were badly behaved, rowdy, bumptious, spoilt and not nice to be around.

'You're not our real grandmother.'

'Perhaps not, since you already have two others. But I'm related.'

'How?'

'Your dad will tell you one day.'

'I don't like you.'

'I don't care if you do or don't.'

'I don't like this dumb game you brought.'

'Too bad, that's all you're getting.'

They were all practised in eye rolls and the poking out of tongues, but only when their parents were out of the room, so I was equally adept at doing the same. I didn't feel grandmotherly though perhaps I should have tried harder to tolerate them.

Simon finally expressed a desire to meet my family, but by then I didn't think it was a good idea. Maybe I was just resentful it had taken him so long to reach that point. But they all eventually agreed though, out of curiosity if nothing else, so a gathering at the country property belonging to Simon's parents was arranged for a weekend. The home was a huge farmhouse, set on about forty hectares of land, with access gained via a wide avenue of Dutch elm trees. An English cottage garden, replete with deep blue campanulas, fragrant honeysuckle, lavender, hollyhocks, peonies and roses, encircled all sides of the main building, and was maintained by an intricate irrigation system, as was the large expanse of lawn. Early autumn gave a golden tinge to the surroundings. There were several guest cottages, two tennis courts, four sleek horses in a fenced-off paddock, enormous rainwater tanks, and a dam half-full of water. Perhaps even a partridge in a pear tree somewhere.

We pulled up in front of the main house in our dusty Ford Falcon and were greeted politely by Simon and Chelsea and ushered inside to meet his parents, who took turns to fling their arms around me, around all of us, without reservation.

His mother, Mary, petite, with hair the colour of birch bark streaked elegantly with grey and cut into a bob, had a broad smile and a tinkling, bell-like laugh. She kept stroking my hand and peering intently at us all. Bob, her husband, was a little stooped, almost bald, with bright, canny grey eyes and a loose-lipped grin that revealed perfectly straight, perhaps false, ivory teeth.

Our hosts escorted us through several large living spaces, each with a stone fireplace at the ready. A huge modern kitchen gleamed and sparkled, its surfaces bare except for one tall vase of meticulously arranged flowers— blue and purple delphiniums, with white hydrangeas providing a collar around the rim of the vase. A centre island was home to an impressive set of chef's knives and an enormous bowl of fruit.

Mark whispered, 'Is someone getting married?'

'Shhh.'

Our family of four was led to one of the guest cottages, which had two bedrooms, a kitchenette and a compact bathroom. Inside, with our small overnight bags grouped self-consciously in a corner, we wandered through the space before taking turns to shower and smarten up for the festivities in the main house.

It turned out to be a late birthday celebration for Bob, who was not particularly well but very graciously put on a good show for the attendant crowd, made up of family, various friends and local residents. I'd have certainly brought a gift had I known about the birthday. Time passed with no trouble as we proceeded from afternoon tea, accompanied by a loud, off-key 'Happy Birthday' and assorted children spitting on the cake as they blew out the candles, to a stroll around the property followed by pre-dinner drinks, then an impressive dinner. It was akin to being at a distant uncle's funeral, with everyone except Simon's children on their best behaviour, and all of us smiling and trying to say the right things.

After the feast of prawn cocktails, a rack of lamb, roasted vegetables and pavlova, Mary cornered me near the bathroom, her voice lowered. 'Thank you so much for coming, Elise. It's so good to finally meet you. Are you alright? You look a bit peaky. I just wanted to say thank you, thank you for giving us Simon. He's an absolute joy in our lives, along with his brother and sister. We're very proud of them all. You can be proud of Simon too. He's a wonderful man, a thoughtful son. Now, you must come and talk to…'

Her arm around me steered me solicitously towards the living room, where glasses of port were being served.

I *was* proud of him, though a little torn, conflicted and relieved, but also just happy that he'd found such loving parents, a good home and stability; all the things I could never have provided for him. When we parted company early the next morning, Simon hugged me, self-consciously, and shook hands with Mark and our children. I saw that while what Simon and I had was fine, perfectly fine, it would doubtless never be anything more than this. At most, we were casual acquaintances. My heart flipped once, twice.

In the car on the way home, Paul spoke first. 'Sorry, Mum, no offence, but Simon's a snob. Such a big-head. Is there anything I should like about him?' He paused. 'His wife's nice.'

'No point in judging before you get to know him better.'

'Do we have to?'

'No, not if you'd rather not. Besides, he's almost a different generation to you both. But honestly, thanks for being there with me, all of you. It must have been hard.'

Patricia laughed. 'Yeah, it was weird. He's a bit snooty but Chelsea's okay. Their kids are revolting. Bob and Mary seem sweet. What about their place? They must be loaded.'

Mark remained silent but attempted to fix a smile on his face.

Simon wrote a pleasant letter afterwards, expressing appreciation for our attendance at the get-together. His formal tone suggested that he wasn't overly anxious to go through it again. I'd desperately wanted everyone to like each other and get along, so I kept looking for ways that they might all bond, but it wasn't to be. Simon and I continued to exchange occasional letters and phone calls, but the span of lost years, of not knowing each other, kept him respectfully distant. I never did tell Simon the details of his paternity, just let him (and Paul, and Patricia) believe he was the result of a brief encounter with an acquaintance whose whereabouts were unknown. That might have been very wrong of me, but I didn't think it would help any of them to learn the truth.

Emma and Mark, well that was a different story. For several months, they had contact by letter or phone. She told Mark she was desperate to meet us all, and that Louise was by then 'Okay about us getting to know one another.'

She arrived on our doorstep once again, this time with shorter hair and a more assured step. I liked her at once. In fact we all did, and I'd see the pride and delight on Mark's face as he watched his three offspring chatting and laughing and sparking off each other. She visited a couple of times a year, went out on the town with Patricia and would sometimes join Paul and Felicity for a movie or dinner at a local pub. Occasionally, they'd all come to our place for a meal. We weren't *The Waltons,* but it was very sweet and companionable. I was happy for them all, especially for Mark. He was as relaxed and contented as I'd ever known him to be.

● ● ●

My search for my father was largely unsuccessful. Over and over, I replayed our last encounter, picturing his watered-down chocolatey eyes, the gravelly voice, the 'I been waitin', hopin' to catch yer', the pathos and the touch of his hand on my arm. I revised earlier memories too. 'You're just as good as anyone else; better, most likely Lisie. Yer gotta grab life. And when yer do, come back and give some of it to me too, right?'

And I knew I wasn't a good person, was ashamed I hadn't gone back to give him anything, not even a hug or smile. When I finally found a death notice, tucked away in a rural South Australian chronicle and dated two years previously, I wept—for taking too long, for being too late, for failing to understand or forgive and for failing to show that I had indeed loved him so very much, in that very short span of time we'd had together. Who'd arranged his cremation? Did anyone go to his funeral? *Was* there a funeral? If so, I should have been there.

CHAPTER
THIRTY-NINE

Time unravelled. Moments cascaded.

Mark found his vitality again. He kept the draining emotions in check, countered sentimentality with rationality, read and made sure he kept abreast of current affairs, social and political issues. We'd sorted out a companionable and loving way to be together and I assumed we'd continue into a peaceful old age. He was looking forward to retirement a few years hence, had travel plans for us and big ideas about moving into a more modern home. In the interim, he enjoyed his work, as I did mine.

Returned soldiers finally received an official Welcome Home parade, but this recognition had a negative effect on Mark's mental health and brought the nightmares back. Then he became ill, first experiencing headaches and nausea, then respiratory problems. He'd never been a heavy smoker, and doctors were at a loss to explain the underlying cause. Some medications worked for a while but then a different health issue would arise for him.

There'd been increased attention in the press about the effects of Agent Orange, with calls for the government to provide compensation for those who'd developed cancers after their service in Vietnam. The medical fraternity was initially reluctant to recognise the link, and my own research provided no clear answers.

Everything escalated rapidly.

Mark's various illnesses caused him considerable physical and mental discomfort. His nightmares became more frequent. Sometimes he lashed out at me verbally, frustrated and confused. Doctors prescribed anti-depressants. Over time, he began to forget simple things—the date, the street where we lived, sometimes even the names of our friends. Some days he was more placid, the newer, rougher edges were sanded away, and we all thought we had a glimpse again of the affectionate, loving husband and father we knew. But over time that changed.

It was heartbreaking to see the effect that his increased fogginess and subsequent mental distress had on him; to witness the slow and insidious slide of a once proud and good man into someone with a quick temper and a shuffling gait. The light from his intense, beautiful eyes shut down whenever he became lost in a forest of tortured thoughts, his new internal battlegrounds.

Our children made their visits home less frequent—it hurt them way too much to see their father that way. But Emma, stoic, loving Emma, insisted they be there as much as possible to support both Mark and me. Paul and Patricia would hover, worried, distressed, oozing helplessness. Emma, when she was able to stay, brought with her a determined smile along with her natural charm, patience and grace. Mark responded well to her voice and stared intently at her, but some days, he couldn't work out where she fitted in his life.

Felicity and Paul married in a quiet ceremony inside the Botanic Gardens, with only immediate family and a few friends present. A calm spring day, a lush lawn, a shady fig tree and the harbour view were the only props required. Felicity was stunning in a simple ivory gown, her dark hair long and loose she carried a small bouquet of red roses, white peonies. Paul's navy suit stretched taut across his shoulders while he fidgeted during the service, his smile a curious mix of pride, delight, concern. He'd glanced back at a thin, hunched Mark, who sat between Patricia and me, each of us holding one of his hands. Emma was behind us with a young man we hadn't yet met. I noticed she patted Mark's shoulder from time to time. It was a period of lightness and controlled joy inside months of disquiet. I remember:

Yellow wattles and crimson bottle brush

The scent of lilac

CHAPTER THIRTY-NINE

Birdsong
The delighted couple
The smell of the ocean
A Schubert Serenade for violin, relayed through tinny speakers
A sea breeze lifting the hem of my skirt
Mark's cough.

• • •

Then came the diagnosis of cancer—a primary in the bowel, a secondary in the lung. Surgeries followed but gave no cause for optimism. The children and I agreed that we wanted Mark at home for as long as possible. I morphed into Nurse Harrington at home, functioning with efficiency and practicality, managing his personal care and his morphine. I chatted, plumped his pillows, read to him, massaged his feet and shooed away friends who stayed too long or whose presence made him agitated or tired. I encouraged him to eat, washed him, tended to his bedsores. So long as I didn't have to think about the future or about loss, I managed.

Yet after visitors left, and his medications were administered, the messes cleared, the bedpan emptied, everything scrubbed clean and the children farewelled or tossing in their old beds, only then did my nursing persona disappear. I'd crawl into bed beside Mark, hold him, careful to avoid pressing against the places where hurt plagued him. I'd sing, hum, whisper, recite poetry and tell him how much I'd always loved him. I would stroke his forehead, kiss his dry cheek, listen to his laboured breath and cry soundlessly, until both our pillows were damp.

Some days, exhausted, I'd just sit in a chair by our bed, observing the dust motes that floated lazily in the sunlight streaming through smudged windows. Tiny specks lifted occasionally with my anxious breath, or his exhaled pain; they settled on our bare arms, on our averted faces, or on the indifferent furniture. In the last days, I rarely left his bedside, an uxorial sentinel, reading aloud, holding his hand and mouthing comforting words but still at times wandering mentally to another place—such an old habit; anything to avoid facing the sorrow of his pain, my imminent loss. One of the children might drift in and out but I wasn't much aware of their movements, how long they stayed, nor even of what they said. My grief was selfish. It was blinkered, bold, unkind, cunning and relentless. It was total.

• • •

This is so hard to retell. Bear with me. All of this period is hazy, and I'm tired today.

After Mark's death, after the funeral, which I have blocked from my mind, a thick, prickly blanket of desolation settled on me. Despite the barbs, I wanted to remain beneath it, hiding, wallowing in my sorrow, suffering for my loss, a prisoner of pathos…but someone ensured that the house opened up again and curtains were pulled back, the world allowed in. Various friends arrived and departed, Paul coaxed me out of my bed, Mark's bed, for longer periods. Food mysteriously appeared on the dining table, cooked meals turned up in the fridge. Patricia helped me dress each day. Emma's voice carried down the hallway. The kettle boiled for endless cups of tea. Nancy and Gabby were often there, always dependable, patiently waiting until I was ready to live again.

And when I was, it became my turn to nurse each of the three children through their grief, their own earthquakes. It took a long time. I carried my own sorrow as quietly as I could, trying not to let it spill into their days, but it was theirs that troubled me most. We had lost the same person, yet I could see how mourning had tracked its own private route into each of them. I wanted to gather them close and somehow absorb their pain, but they kept it tucked away, just out of my reach. And I was too tired to press. The weight of my own sadness was enough. Still, I watched, and worried, and hoped that time, or love, or something gentler than heartache, might begin to soften the edges.

CHAPTER FORTY

I need to hurry. Time is a demanding taskmaster. I'm feeling so much older. Well, I *am* so much older. Simple words are often elusive, and I know some days I don't make much sense, even to myself. The staff here are so understanding and patient, with me, with all of us.

• • •

Paul secured a good job with an engineering firm in Brisbane. He and Felicity had a baby, and I cried tears of joy whenever I was able to visit them.

'Charlie? What a name to give a baby! But he's gorgeous. May I hold him? Oh, such a bonnie boy! He has your olive skin, Felicity. And your smile.'

Patricia travelled overseas and met her Aunt Marion briefly in London. 'She's nothing like you, Mum, and I think she's an alcoholic.' On her return, she moved to Adelaide for a job with an advertising company. I cried then too, for this new separation, my family further splintered. Tears for all occasions. *But I'm made of steel. I don't cry. Nothing can hurt me.* My armour was gone. I do cry. Life hurts.

Mark's mother Deidre lived on well into her nineties but with dementia, to the point where she couldn't recognise the people she knew best. Nevertheless, I continued to visit her in the nursing home, as did Mark's brother Adrian. The children did too, whenever they were back to visit me. My compassion for Deidre was immense, now that I had seen the woman behind the mask, behind the stiffness and elegance of years past. She, like all of us, was not immune to grief and vulnerability.

Adrian would also drop by, stay for dinner, and speak fondly of Mark, their bond and their lives before I'd met them both. He reminded me so much of Mark, though he was a shyer, more introverted version, and I valued his presence and his counsel whenever he came by. He became a kind of brother to me, one I'd always wished I'd had.

Jeffrey sent me a postcard once, out of the blue. Marion had given him my address. On the front was a sketch of a koala on a surfboard and the name Hardy's Beach at the top. On the back, a scribbled message and signature that had smudged in transit. I wondered how he was he faring? Should I try to track him down? I did, eventually, and we exchanged a few superficial letters that would never fill in the huge gap of the lost years, nor the emotional abyss. He'd married again. From the children of his first marriage, all boys, he now had four grandchildren. He'd worked in a trade most of his adult life—electrical work, plastering, a bit of carpentry—but had retired. His back had 'given out' and it continued to cause him pain. His handwriting was tight, as if laboured, suggesting to my imaginative mind a still-repressed fury. What unspoken terrors might he too have suffered in the night, all those years ago?

Marion wrote to me occasionally, though her letters were as flighty as she'd been the last time I'd seen her, with their light tone and frequent use of capitals and emphatic punctuation.

'Hey 'Lis, remember those RIDICULOUS clothes we all used to wear? They're back in fashion, and they're even more TERRIBLE! The young ones don't know how to wear them. HILARIOUS.

She'd married, divorced, married again but never had children ('I don't see the point'). She'd enjoyed a brief career in the tourist industry, followed by a period of study then a short, unsuccessful sojourn in some type of certificated social work. Later was an interlude in retail. Now of mature enough years, she seemed stuck in adolescence. I often fretted about what horrors she too might have endured under Craig's patronage after I'd left the family home. But that thinking would send waves of guilt over me, so I tried to push such wonderings aside.

My mother, very old but still with all her wits about her, eventually died of a stroke. My tears at the small funeral in Richmond were intense; wracking sobs of tenderness, pity, remorse and regret. I missed all of her—her mossy eyes, her hard-won smiles, the touch of her work-rough hands on my skin, her funny and gentle way with Paul and Patricia. I missed what we'd built up over time and missed what we might have been to each other if all those early years had been different. But I was grateful too, for the solid relationship we ultimately achieved.

The funeral gathering filled only a few rows in the small crematorium's chapel, with its timber panelling, skylights, high windows and straight-backed chairs. Patricia came with me; she'd really loved Lillian. Felicity was too heavily pregnant with a second child to travel, and naturally Paul didn't want to leave her on her own.

Marion was still abroad, but Jeffrey turned up with one of his sons. He looked so much older than his years, stooped, and I noticed his limp as he walked into the chapel. His once thick, black hair was now a grey, patchy fuzz. His eyes—in my memory so steely, full of derision and challenge—were glassy, the irises encased by Saturn rings of physical or emotional pain. Or both. A checkerboard of responses played across his face when he caught sight of me. He sat tentatively on his chair, leaning forward at one end of the third row, avoiding further eye contact. I thought about how much I'd once hated him, for his meanness, his moodiness, his taunts and cruelties, but mainly for the fact that he'd sometimes been a reluctant witness to the shame and pain inflicted on me by Craig, or else urged to be an unwilling, fumbling, snivelling participant. I thought about the times when Craig left me alone but I could hear the muffled pleading or raw, throbbing silences that then came from Jeffrey's room.

I sought forgiveness from my mother, in her plain wooden coffin covered in pink-streaked calla lilies. I recall their creamy, clove scent, the drone of a bee, the deep voice of the funeral celebrant and the occasional cough of a woman I didn't recognise who sat across the aisle from me. After the service, Jeffrey and I hugged for what would be the first and the last time in our lives. And we parted, finally united by a grief that was, this time, pure and uncomplicated.

• • •

I remember an occasion when I was sitting on my bed, twisting a handkerchief around my fingers.

'Nance, I need to see a counsellor, a shrink, someone, anyone. I'm not coping. I'm anxious all the time, and I miss Mark. It hurts. Here,' pointing to my chest. 'I miss him. And I miss my Mum.'

'I know, sweetie, I know you do. I'll get the name of someone you can see, if you want me.'

'A woman, I think; I couldn't bear to spill everything out to a male, unless he's kind, and understands. God, I feel so *guilty* all the time.'

'Why, love? You've done nothing to feel bad about!'

'I don't know exactly.' My voice struggled, commandeered by grief. 'All the things I didn't do that I should have done, the things I did that I shouldn't have, with Mark, with the kids. I wasn't the best wife. He deserved better. And I've not been a good mother.' I slumped forward, head in my hands, staring at the ground.

'Tosh! That's nonsense.' Nancy patted me on the shoulder and passed me a clean handkerchief as she observed the neglected living room, then pulled me up to a standing position. 'You're going to have a sleep now, while I tidy up and get some food organised. You're far too skinny my friend. I'll check the cupboards to see what you need. And I'll ring around for some names, a professional you might want to talk to.' She pointed to my head and then her chest. 'And you can always talk to me, or to Gab.'

I nodded obediently, head down, shoulders curved into a stoop, and moved with little haste towards the door, turning to whisper, as Nancy followed, 'Thank you.'

A fortnight later I was in a waiting room staring at the neutral, aloof walls covered in diplomas and other credentials, and at the receptionist who looked about twenty and had very short, purple-dyed hair and a white shirt that was stained at the collar. She was busy inspecting her mauve fingernails and talking on the phone. I tuned out, escaping briefly into another time, another work environment, where I was the one in charge—calm, confident, happy—and when Mark was alive and healthy and the children still young, secure and waiting for me at home. Was there ever such a time when all those stars aligned? There *had* been such times. Had I cherished them then, as I did now? The waistband of my pantyhose had rolled up uncomfortably and bit into me.

My eyes were drawn back to a poster of *The Book of Kells* on the pale blue wall above the receptionist. On an opposite side was a print I identified as *The Annunciation*, though can't remember the artist. *Oh, please don't let her sprout commandments at me.* The lighting in the room was soft. There were bright green artificial plants in strategically-placed pots.

A door opened and a small, slim woman with short, greying hair nodded at me, raised an artfully drawn eyebrow. 'Mrs Harrington? Elsie?'

'It's 'Elise'.'

Peering at the notes in her hand, she said 'Oh, of course, *Elise*. Come on in please. I'm Diane.' She stood aside to let me pass into the inner sanctum. Her breath had a hint of plums, not unpleasant. The walls here were powder-blue too. A deep red cyclamen decorated a side table. We took our seats—a straight-backed, beige swivel chair for the counsellor, a deep brown leather armchair for the client. Actors, props, lighting—all predictable but comforting.

A few questions in and I was on my guard. *I shouldn't have come; I shouldn't be here. I'm not crazy, just full of grief, and I'm lonely, fractured, broken. That's all.* But I provided an outline of my recent history; the bereavements, the anxiety, the sleeplessness. Then before I could stop, I spat out the facts about Mark, my mother, my father Joseph, Craig, Jeffrey, Simon. The words—escapees—flew and battered against the walls. Diane's face remained impassive. Somehow, in me, there were no tears.

I added, 'I daydream too much. It's an escape route for me, something I've always done, but now it seems to be taking over again and happening much more frequently. I feel very foolish about it.'

'What kinds of daydreams? What do you think about?'

'Just silly, trite, impossible scenarios.' I described some, assuming all the while that Diane was inwardly laughing.

She made notes on her writing pad; her legs were crossed elegantly beneath a navy skirt of modest length. She tapped absently with the end of her pen before asking me a few more questions. The clock on the desk counted down our time like a faint metronome.

She said, 'Elise, your waking dreams, the way you describe them, they're vivid and colourful. You have a good imagination. Some might call it a dissociative disorder, which isn't unusual, especially after trauma. But it's obviously not stopping you from functioning normally.'

'But it *is*. I don't think I should continue working anymore. I can't afford to make mistakes in my job. And I'd be lost without my work.'

'What you're feeling seems a normal response to a series of abnormal events. After everything that's happened, you need rest and time to reassess. And the opportunity to be kind to yourself, after everything you've been through. Let me read you something that I'd like you to think about.'

I grimaced in protestation, but I remained silent while Diane retrieved a ring-binder from a bookcase, and leafed through the pages inside.

'Ah, here it is.' She pulled out a single sheet. 'Perhaps it might help you see things in a new way. It's written by a specialist in childhood trauma. He says,' and here her voice modulated as if delivering a talk in to a lecture hall: "Your trauma isn't only about the painful events you experienced. It's also about the ways you had to emotionally shut down in order to feel safe. That might include being disconnected or separated from parts of yourself. Perhaps at the time, those behaviours were actually smart and necessary strategies and your best efforts to find love and protection in an unsafe environment."

There's more, but here, take it with you, Elise. Read it for yourself. And I'd suggest you see your doctor about the insomnia and your depression; maybe there's something you can take to help with those things.'

Diane leaned forward, her voice still earnest. 'But in the meantime, perhaps you can write about your feelings and your sense of self. Elise, remember, we don't always honour our present if we live in the past or the future, or always in our imaginations. It's important to focus on what's happening to you right now. Okay? I'd like to see you again in another week or two, if you feel up to that.'

Diane checked her watch as her smile trickled loosely into her neck. I looked down, chastened, embarrassed, relieved, exhausted.

We stood. She smiled at me sympathetically, almost tenderly, her eyes steady and warm. 'Goodbye, Elise. I'll see you again soon.'

I hesitated, awkward, unsure whether to speak, shake her hand, or run. As we walked towards the door, she placed a gentle hand on my shoulder, saw me through, and closed it noiselessly behind me. I nodded at the purple-haired receptionist, who still had a phone attached to her ear, and settled the weighty bill that appeared over the counter top. I decided not to make another appointment. I had Nancy and Gabby. And besides, *I'm made of steel, I don't cry. Nothing more can hurt me.*

• • •

But I did read the printed sheet Diane had given me many times, and kept it; I have it still. I returned to see her, just once more, and opened up even more then, disclosing my few remaining secrets. I confessed to the remorse and self-reproach I had for never reporting my abuser, my rapist, when I'd gained adulthood. I revealed the guilt I'd felt for using sex as a bargaining chip, and for choosing risky, promiscuous behaviour as a form of control. I admitted that I'd desired power in relationships, and, once acquired, had used it poorly. I told Diane of my cruelty towards Phil and my father, and of the many times since then that I'd chosen passivity over honesty in a desperate need to be liked.

I'd never before peered into that black box of memories for fear of what might crawl out—self-condemnation with jagged, razor-sharp teeth, a scratchy voice of regret, and the fragile version of myself I'd buried long ago. Diane reminded me again that my negative emotions and behaviours were a response to trauma and abuse. She believed I'd used my fantasy world to escape, to ignore the suppressed rage and shame, and to mask the ache and the fears. All clinical observations, perhaps textbook babble, but there was logic and truth in it. No hiding anymore. I saw in myself a mess of a human being, but a courageous, relieved one too.

It surprised me that I'd told it all to a virtual stranger—a new form of the confessional box but without the penance. Understanding myself better though, didn't equate to immediate forgiveness of self. That's when I resumed journal writing. Perhaps I could write myself back into *being*.

CHAPTER FORTY-ONE

Time continues to concertina. Recollections of events are like random cards pulled from a deck that's hidden inside a magician's sleeve…

I can't recall exactly when, but the government eventually acknowledged the role of Agent Orange in the development of various serious illnesses in Vietnam veterans. A compensation scheme trickled down to surviving Vets with specific cancers, or to their widows. Between that and Mark's work pension, his years of saving and my own, together with owning our home, I was comfortably enough off, but some days the endless, inescapable loneliness persisted. Gabby and Nancy were still there, my reliable collaborators, our gang of three always mutually supportive, but time began to play games with us all.

When we got together, we'd talk about our children, grandchildren, the weather, the television shows we watched and our various ailments. We'd buoyed each other through our individual illnesses—Nancy's breast cancer, Gabby's hysterectomy and diabetes, my heart problems and bad back. We reflected on the perils of being older but laughed about the less worrying complaints—the bunions and hammertoes, the arthritis, the incontinence that might accompany a sneeze—and exchanged local news or gossip.

'Marcie's daughter's house burnt down in those fires, did you know?
They had no insurance.'

'Yes, she told me. How on earth…?'

'Did you hear Eymen was killed in a car accident? He's the young
Turkish boy from the next street. Only eighteen.'

'Such a terrible loss! Poor Mrs Polat.'

'Lovely family.'

'Another cuppa?'

'Simon's wife's, no, not his wife, his daughter, she's my granddaughter;
she had a third miscarriage. I think they'll have to stop at two children.'

'Who's Simon? Remind me?'

'He's my son, the one I had way back, you know.'

'But that's Paul.'

'Paul's my second boy, Mark's and my son. I had Simon very young. I
told you that.'

'Oh, that's right.'

'You never told us that, about Simon!'

'Yes I did. A long time ago.'

'Oh yes, true.'

'What about that awful shooting down south? Wasn't that shocking?'

'Rachel told me that all the young ones have vibrators these days.'

'What's that got to do with a shooting?'

'What's a vibrator? You mean one of those chairs that shakes? An inclin-
ator? Isn't that a chair that goes up and down stairs with you?'

'Gabby!'

And so on. Harmless, inconsequential, binding. And always the healthy
laughter, at ourselves and each other.

I was lucky to have other wonderful neighbours as well, many families
of European immigrants who've styled their homes and gardens in ways
that reminded them of their roots and their desires; dreams that origin-
ated in places like Greece, Hungary, Serbia. They always invited me to
their huge family parties, and they'd drop by with hearty lamb dishes or
luscious sweets ('You're way too thin Elise.'), and generally kept an eye
on me, the house and the garden, offering help in so many wonderful,

generous ways. Made me feel special, though underneath it all, I didn't think I deserved that.

● ● ●

Paul and Felicity regularly visited with their expanding brood. Charlie had grown and was a happy, handsome boy who reminded me of Paul at that age, with the lovely jade eyes and placid temperament. Their second child, Archie, was chubby, dark-haired and full of smiles and energy. Later, they had a third baby; they named her Olivia, and she was the sweetest little angel. She had Down syndrome, soft hair, an enchanting smile, curiosity and such infectious eagerness to participate in all things. And then their fourth child, Sophie, arrived, quiet, thoughtful and imaginative. She became a nurse, and is now a doctor, if I'm thinking straight. I hope I have the order of them right.

My Paul seemed content, was cheerful and loved his job with an engineering/tech company, whatever that is. I've never fully understood what he actually does, though he has tried to explain it. Felicity, always so smart, taught geography. She was easy-going and funny, a picture of efficiency, a great mum, and so patient. They were a well-matched couple, and proud, capable parents, and their children were delightful. So this was how families were supposed to be. I loved them all.

Patricia tried to coincide some of her visits with those of Felicity and Paul, or Emma, but I enjoyed it more when I could have her to myself. She opened up with me then. She had a good career in marketing; it sounded overly busy but I knew she was competent and very creative. She mixed with a large circle of friends, male and female, and enjoyed occasional holidays in exotic places like Vanuatu, Bali, the Maldives. The fractious, brittle, pouty little girl she'd once been now moved elegantly, conversed smoothly, was calm, confident and allowed a touch of humour to crinkle the skin around her eyes. I loved her dearly.

They all missed Mark, and occasionally teared up when his name was mentioned. We saw less of Emma, but she stayed in touch, and she and Patricia often spoke on the phone.

Simon has all but disappeared again from my world, popping up maybe once every two years or so. He moved out of government work and into the banking sector; must be a high flyer. Recently I saw on the television there was a Royal Commission into misconduct in the banking industry, and since then, his phone voice has been brusque and defensive. He divorced that nice Chelsea and remarried.

Once, maybe eight or ten years ago now, I took a bus to Canberra for Simon's sixtieth birthday party, which was, naturally, full of people I'd never met before, but he was attentive and sweet to me, as was his new wife. Gail, I think her name was. Simon even acknowledged me in a speech he gave, which I thought was unnecessary but very kind. His once obnoxious children had grown through their rude childhood years and gauche, graceless adolescence into pleasant enough adults.

Simon became, well, he was a different man; in truth, we barely knew each other. He rarely visited, had a new, busy career in that organisation he worked for, the one he moved to after the banking thing. He was still quite handsome and had a good heart, but as he grew older, I saw traces of his father in him and so it suited me that we saw less of each other. When we did meet, it was likely from a sense of duty rather than any real affection, so I didn't press for more. He was all big teeth, confidence and smooth charm, and he'd successfully erased any trace of my genes from his face. But I loved him, I suppose, for all that. Or is it that I loved the *idea* of him?

• • •

My loneliness must have been evident. That, or else it was my age slowing me down. Between them, my children hatched a plan, suggesting I rent out my home in Sydney, and stay with Paul and his family in Brisbane for six months, in the granny flat attached to their house. I could help out with their children; it would give me a sense of purpose, plus precious time with them all. For the rest of the year, I'd stay in Adelaide with Patricia. She has a large, modern apartment which boasts white walls, raked ceilings, a view of the city, and comfortable furniture.

'Plenty of room, Mum,' she said many times.

'It's very good of you darling, so kind, you and Paul offering like this. But I don't want to get in the way. You've got work, your friends, a full life. I don't want you to feel obligated. I'm fine, darling. Truthfully.'

'Mum, you know me well enough to see that I've never done anything out of obligation. I honestly want you stay with me. Say *yes* for my sake, so I can keep an eye on you. And Paul and Flick definitely want you there too. It doesn't have to be forever. Just try it out, Mum. Don't be stubborn, not over this. I know you're lonely there without Dad.'

'I've got Nancy and Gab and a few others.'

'Yes, but you're not spring chickens, any of you. You can't be propping each other up the way you used to. What if you had a fall?'

'Darling, I'm not that ancient. Yet. But you're right, it would be lovely to be with you. I miss you, miss all the family. So, thank you. You're so....' My voice cracked, just a little. 'What would I do without you and Paul?'

'And Flick.'

'Yes, and Felicity.'

• • •

So that's what I did, for a while, leaving behind all that had been so familiar. Paul and Felicity were thoughtful, and solicitous. They ensured I was comfortable, kept me company in the evenings and tried to prevent loneliness from creeping under the door to my flat. Sometimes I thought they fussed too much. They insisted I saw doctors and dentists regularly; they introduced me to their neighbours. Only occasionally did I slip into my fantasy world—it was familiar, entertaining, required no effort, and was so much nicer than what was on the television.

'Hey Mum, lost in space again?' Paul clicked his fingers near my ear and grinned. 'Where do you disappear to?'

Next door lived a large, loud, lovely Vietnamese family whose parents had been refugees in the seventies. Some of their relatives had settled in Germany, France and Canada, and they visited occasionally, along with some extended family still residing in Vietnam. When the windows of my downstairs flat were open, I could hear a beautiful, vibrant song, an excited medley of soft and sharp sounds, or loud and riotous, and delivered with great affection. I'd listen, nod to myself, smile, and celebrate their connectedness.

I loved spending time with my grandchildren. I'd often wake to the sound of them racing up and down the stairs, could hear them inventing games just like I used to do: storming the invisible barricades; shouting or arguing with passion; sharing secrets and chatting on the phone or outside with friends. Sometimes they called out to me, asking my advice on some issue, wanting me to take them to the movies or the pool, or bake their chosen treats. Olivia was my special favourite; I shouldn't say that because of course I loved them all. In that environment, I learnt to smile again. I got such delight in seeing that my grandchildren were living their natural succession, and I was a part of that too. I bought a set of blue and white willow-patterned bowls and made them porridge with cream and sugar for breakfast. We played card games and I helped them with jigsaw puzzles. I embraced the ordinary, the mundane, and was grateful.

For the other half of the year, I lived in Adelaide, a beautiful city. Most days I'd walk down by the river, feeds the ducks, and watch dogs and children play on the grass. I wandered through parks to enjoy the vivid mauve of the jacaranda trees, visited the local library and read, or sat alone in a cinema and savoured an ice-cream, immersed in new images on a screen.

I kept Patricia's apartment tidy, cleaned the floors, did the washing in a new machine that whistled and chirped and blinked with lights and cherished the smiles from my daughter. Most evenings I'd cook; once or twice a week Patricia might take me to a new restaurant to sample the latest food trends. Sometimes on weekends we'd drive to a winery or go to a movie. Occasionally Patricia invited me into her thoughts; she'd chat about her work or plans, and this was the best of times—such moments touched my heart. Contentment settled more comfortably on my shoulders.

CHAPTER FORTY-TWO

Much as I adored my family, I didn't want to become that old parent who needed constant attention. Nor did I want to get in the way of Patricia's new romantic involvement, or have Felicity complain about her mother-in-law's increasing deafness and bouts of confusion. Or alienate the grandchildren. I imagined an aged version of Amanda Wingfield waiting in the wings of my future if I continued living with my children.

Besides, I wanted to be back in Sydney, close to where Mark was buried and where my friends had lived their lives entangled with mine. I moved back into our old home, pottered in the garden, met up with Nancy and Gabby and any of their kids who happened to be passing through. I enjoyed the clatter of teacups and the Arnott's biscuits (we didn't bake much anymore), the companionable talk and shared moments of quiet.

While I was still reasonably mobile, I sometimes flew back to Adelaide to help Patricia. She and her partner, a very pleasant man who I think was called Derek, had produced a baby through IVF just after Patricia's fortieth birthday. The child's name escapes me today, sorry to say. It's something a little weird, though it sounds mellifluous, seasonal; perhaps it's Summer or Willow, both nice names, and she's the prettiest little thing, with chestnut hair just like her mother's.

Patricia has taken to parenting way better than she ever took to being parented. Very competent and nurturing. She's blossomed, bloomed. Sometimes her softness turned its attention to me and she'd pat my shoulder or my cheek as she walked past and say lightly 'Love ya Mum.' I miss her a great deal, but we talk on the phone almost every day. They all tell me I'm too old and frail to travel, so Patricia flies over two or three times a year with Summer or Willow or whatever the little one's name is. Sometimes Derek (I think I have that wrong) comes too.

Paul seems to have no trouble finding new jobs in engineering or I.T. or whatever it is he does. He and Felicity eventually moved down from Brisbane back to Newcastle to be closer to me, so they visit when they can and that's lovely. I'm so grateful for what they do for me. Their children are adults now and I think I have a great grandchild or two, but I don't get to see much of that generation. They all have busy lives. They're content, or seem to be, and that's what's important. Paul calls me regularly but my hearing is going and I can sense he gets a touch frustrated when I have to keep asking him to repeat himself.

Emma—Mark and Louise's girl Emma—calls on me occasionally, and she once had a sandy-haired son in tow whom she'd named *Oliver Mark*. He was polite, inquisitive and chatty. Seeing his grin and the honey-amber eyes, I felt I was staring at Mark, and couldn't take my gaze off him. To the boy's horror, I insisted on hugging him close when they rose to leave. It was just so hard to let go of what I thought of as Mark's essence inside him. I asked after Louise, but Emma was evasive, said only that her mother hadn't been well and was having some tests done. I was sad about that. I'd liked Louise, for the brief time our paths had crossed. Anyway, Emma, Paul and Felicity see a lot of each other now that they're all living in Newcastle, and it's not so far away from here, so that's a delightful thing too.

• • •

What of my friends, my dearest comrades? Predictably, all of us outlived our spouses. Gabby finally divorced Frank after the children had all grown up; she must have been preparing for that not so long after that night at the wine bar. She'd married again—a sweet, younger man, a widower with two children. She blossomed after that, and with help, gained mastery over her finances. Frank, estranged from all but one of his children, died of liver disease.

Nancy, long ago, changed her plans and returned to Jack saying only, 'Maybe I truly loved him, after all.' Over time Jack developed Parkinson's disease and became very dependent on her. He hated to let her out of his sight. She arrived home one afternoon to find him unconscious on the bathroom floor after a fall and he died several days later in hospital. I'd never seen Nancy cry until then, and when she started, she couldn't stop, not for a long time. I held her close then, as she'd held me.

Eventually of course, there had to be just one woman left standing, and that would, unfortunately, be me. Nancy died last year, or perhaps it was earlier than that, I can't exactly recall. Her cane fell from her grip while she was waiting at the edge of a train platform; she leaned forward to see where it had rolled to, and she fell. It wasn't an oncoming train that killed her— she was winched to safety by some fellow travellers before it arrived—but a blood clot formed after the operation on her broken femur. Gabby died a few months later of B Cell Lymphoma; she'd ignored or not even noticed some of the earlier symptoms.

The accumulated losses—Mark's death and my mother's demise, the children and grandchildren spread around the country, and then the loss of my dearest of friends—all seemed to shred more parts of myself. Occasional letters from Marion and Jeffrey also reminded me of the loss of the family we might have been and the long-ago forfeiture of my childhood and innocence. Once again, I relied more and more on the people who populated my imagined world to keep me company. And I read—oh, did I read—about other people's real lives or fictional worlds, until my eyesight began to cause trouble. My new glasses are heavy and cumbersome.

Then I was left with thoughts and memories and meanderings, like: what would my life have been like if I'd been a boy, or been born in another country or simply hadn't always been afraid? What if I hadn't let those loops of celluloid fantasy take over? Might I have been a better person? A very different person? And what would happen if I lost all my memories? Would I still be me?

• • •

The daydreams. That parallel universe of smoke and mirrors. I kept it up for a while, to fill the void, the aching loneliness. Working out details of a fantasy world could take up swathes of my thinking time, especially because I had so much of it. When you're old, life can become a slow, daily immersion in cold discomforts and lonely reflections.

I don't know what other people did to distract themselves, but I'd escape into my invented scenarios, clichéd though they were, during the endless hours of waiting that seem to attach themselves like limpets to the elderly, whether we're sitting alone and still at bus stops, in doctors' waiting rooms or in the dentist's chair, or standing uncomfortably at the supermarket checkout, or lying in bed at night waiting for sleep. These daydreams were silly, harmless. They relieved some of the aches and the odd shooting pains that an aging body inevitably feels. While I might have appeared to be paying attention to my surroundings, time and again I'd be visiting some dazzling other-worldly landscape. Alice down the rabbit-hole. People talked to me and I'd nod and smile and take care to look into their eyes and try to listen, but soon the dilation of their pupils would pull me into that dazzling world, where things were near-perfect, and so too was I. The allure of the impossible.

And then, all of a sudden, the incessant day-dreaming stopped. I don't know why, but I remembered someone saying, 'It's important to focus on what's happening to you *now*.'

So I did. And in doing so, I left space to feel the feelings long suppressed. I cried. A lot. And in between, I laughed and exploded and gave myself over to whatever beast had scrambled furtively behind my breastbone, until it too disappeared, sated.

• • •

There's been no great epiphany, no *eureka* moment. The clock of my childhood remains frozen, set in time, readily retrieved. But the events of the last few decades are turned back to front, compressed, like when you look the wrong way through a telescope. Everything is small and just beyond reach. The clarity of the distant past contrasts with the fog of yesterday and today. And time, as with age, trickles along in steady rhythms, encounters stones and boulders, or flows with gentle or violent determination towards its destination.

Yes, I am old. Over the last decade or so, my body has morphed into an old woman's shell. My once firm, strong thighs, that had let me climb trees, run, skip and play, those sturdy, vital legs that would carry me anywhere and could wrap easily around a tree trunk or a lover's waist, have become loose, dimpled and marked with spidery veins behind the knees. My belly, once so taut and trim, that stretched to carry three healthy babies and then sprang obligingly back into shape, is now round, stubborn and has given in to gravity. My breasts, which nursed effectively and served me well as an adornment and as an instrument of pleasure for so long, are well past their usefulness and have creases and folds in strange places. My waist has thickened even further. My hair is totally grey. The skin on my arms is like soft, crinkled crepe paper; it's thin, translucent, and vulnerable to bruising. My face is narrower, with puckers and pleats in unexpected places; there are deep lines forming parentheses from nose to mouth. My lips are also thin, decorated with a crenelated fan, top and bottom. The only parts that I recognise are the very faint silver scar running lightly along my jaw line and another tiny one, unnoticed by anyone else, between my nose and upper lip; the still-arched eyebrows, grey too now, and the honey-coloured eyes with flecks of yellow that seemed to so excite some people and disturb others. It's ironic that I spent so many years wishing to be someone else, and now that I am, she seems nowhere near as interesting or as vital as the one left behind.

I miss those things I could always do but took for granted all through my younger days. The physical exertions that at the time meant nothing are now too difficult to accomplish. I wish I'd not wasted all the youth, vitality and rhythm inside me by replacing it with ridiculous daydreams. I wish that I hadn't let the weight of my flaws and other's barbs and punishments get in the way of my enjoyment of life. But that's what we do, some of us, isn't it?

I can wish all that, but in truth, the what-ifs don't matter. It's the *what is* that matters. And I made it through, this far.

• • •

'How are you feeling, Elise? Mrs H? Doctor will be here to see you soon. But dinner is here, if you'd like something. Or I can get you a snack instead.'

I'd love to lean forward and stroke this man's smooth face and his thick, black hair. Have him hold my hand for a little while. But I just nod and smile and assess what sits, congealed, on my dinner plate.

CHAPTER FORTY-THREE

When I started getting ill, I had many trips to doctors and hospitals, blood tests, x-rays and scans. When organising the maintenance of the house got too much for me, Paul helped me sell the family home and find a place in a retirement village. I cried a little, though kept the tears and disappointment, to myself.

Then, after a year in the new place, I had a fall, nothing too serious, mind, but enough for the staff to send me to hospital, where I was told that my hip was broken. When I returned to the village, and had a few more dizzy spells, they moved me into a different wing, a place for higher care needs. Though the staff promised me I'd be back in my own independent unit soon enough, I never got there. My new room is small but adequate, with a single bed, an armchair, a small wardrobe with very few clothes, a dresser, a large television on my old teak cabinet, a compact desk with the computer Paul gave me, and photos of Mark, the children, grandchildren and people I now don't recognise. I don't know what happened to the rest of my things. The walls are painted in a soft blue hue. There's a clean, white-tiled bathroom attached to my room. I can bathe myself, most of the time.

The workers here are generally pleasant. They're brisk, competent, eager to please, though more eager, of course, to get home at the end of their shifts. Some speak different languages and they're sweet but don't always understand me, nor I them. It's a multicultural crock-pot—or should that be hot-pot? Melting pot? I get confused. They treat me well, leave me be when I want to be alone, help me when I need assistance. But there's one particularly officious woman in charge, British I think, must be all of thirty-five. She's seriously lacking in charm and patience, and appears never to have been burdened by self-doubt. But all the other staff members are agreeable and kind, especially Aravinda.

My co-residents are a mixed bunch, nice enough, but some are a bit loopy; they wander into my room and think they belong here. If I try to shoo them away, they sometimes become aggressive, so I've learnt to just let them sit with me and chat or they stare at the TV or the walls until someone arrives and leads them away. In the dining room, those of us who can sit up and feed ourselves generally have wide-ranging conversations that can get us lost in a forest of half-remembered detail but are entertaining nevertheless. At night I hear the odd scream or indistinct words babbled over and over. Nights here are too warm with the thermostats set to twenty-one degrees.

It's funny, you know, in amongst all the missing pieces of my past, I remember this thing very well. When I was sixteen, after my world was turned inside out, I wrote in my journal: 'One day I will walk into my room and it will be an old woman's room with an old woman's smell.' And so it is. I'm more often than not confined to this space now, and it certainly is an old woman's room with a particular aroma. I've grown to quite embrace the combination of talcum powder and rose water, lavender and dry parchment, a vague trace of incontinence, and years of other people's quiet, honourable decay attached to every surface.

I hear subtle things as well—possibly the ghosts of previous occupants' diminished lives, their reels playing over and over on the greying walls around me. Walls anointed with people's joys, hopes, dreams, failures, dis-appointments and triumphs. I will leave my mark here too.

I know my memory and health are failing rapidly now. That's just how it is. I still like to work on my life's jigsaw, though only in my imagination now. There's a lot been completed, but the pieces that remain, the darker colours and strange shapes, don't want to fit. And that's fine. I focus on the bright scenes. Right in the centre are perfect images of Mark, Patricia and Paul, each one of them in bold relief, vibrant, sparkling, rainbow-infused. These three, my loves, who shielded me from the dark, drew me into the light and gave me purpose and substance. Various grandchildren and great grandchildren have shape and essence, though they've merged so much in my mind. A little way to the left in the picture are Lillian and Marion, bathed in pale green. They're seated, with their faces turned towards me. My mother's smile is timid but inviting. Marion looks as she did as a child—innocent, goofy, adorable. Off to the right is Simon, dusted in a grey-brown cloud with the texture of corduroy. He doesn't look directly at me but is focused on something beyond the edge of the puzzle.

Near the top edge stand my dearest of friends Nancy and Gabby, in vivid blues and reds, solid, constant, and reliable. And there, on the right, is Annie Robinson, my friend and champion from my childhood; she's smiling at me, dressed in her old navy gardening overalls and a pastel mauve shirt. Scattered throughout are random faces I can't readily identify. Emma? Louise? Samantha? Phil? Sister Bernadette? Frank? Jack? Then a series of blotches, teachers, classmates, colleagues, acquaintances—tiny but in their own ways, significant.

In a lower corner is a smudged image of Jeffrey and a distant blotted memory of our pain and reconciliation. To his left is an outline of my father. I think of Dad's tanned skin, his chocolate eyes, his thin smile, the hand on my sleeve, his gravelly voice. I stare and stare but, much as I want to pull him closer, give him more colour than the smoky greys and browns he inhabits, his face remains blurred, abstract. I want to remember more. I could wonder what might have been, if he'd not abandoned me, if I'd not abandoned him. But no, I won't think like that. What I know, from all these people and all these experiences, is that fear and grief and loss taught me a lot about love.

In another small corner of my puzzle is a tiny snapshot of Samson, my loyal canine companion. I imagine his wet nose nudging my hand, his delicate panting breath, the excited staccato of his claws on the linoleum. His lesson to me was to be curious and uncomplaining, to find joy in simply *being*. It took me a while to finally learn that.

Where in this story is the joy, the music, the laughter, the harmony? I experienced all those things, though they don't clamour for attention in the way that demons do. But now, having told the worst, I can remember the best. I'm not who I was at the beginning of my tale and the telling of it has been cathartic, has swept away anger, sadness and pain. And I've learnt that we're *all* capable of being both heroes and villains in a life retold.

This not-quite-complete jigsaw, my fragmented, ordinary, clichéd reality, with its tumbling kaleidoscope of intense delights and profound sorrows, its secrets, imperfections, knotty truths and deep regrets, its beauty, and its complicated, messy love, in all its forms, all its failures—all of that has been…enough. More than enough. I survived, I lived and I loved. I am now what I might have been, with no more regrets. *Haluna*—I am at ease.

• • •

We are such stuff as dreams are made on,
and our little life is rounded with a sleep.
—William Shakespeare, *The Tempest*

EPILOGUE

Soon after the funeral, I gathered all my mother's personal belongings together, scant though they were. It's taken weeks of heavy emotion and tears to sort through her things—her clothing, keepsakes, photos, cards, letters, scribbled notes, diaries and journals, and her address book, though there are so few of her friends left for me to notify. Sophie gave me an envelope of USBs and a folder full of transcriptions of voice recordings she'd made when Mum could no longer write or type. There's also a small box of documents and recordings that the receptionist at the nursing home passed on to me. They came from a volunteer who helped Mum tell her story in the last months of her life. I must write and thank him.

I'm not ready to hear Mum's voice yet, so I will start with organising her written words first. Looks like there's a lifetime contained in them. I'll try to pull everything together in a way that might be what she'd have wanted. Any errors of fact, time or place will be mine alone.

Paul and I are keen to finally get to know our mother.

Patricia Harrington
Sydney, June 2023

ACKNOWLEDGEMENTS

I owe a thousand thanks to all who helped me bring this book to fruition: To Varuna, the National Writers' House, for my week's residency and kick-start; to Canberra Writers, whose members provided feedback on several extracts, and to Rae Luckie and Peter Ramshaw for their encouragement and thoughtful assessment of earlier drafts. Appreciation and thanks to Laura Boyle, whose cover design was exactly what I'd hoped for, and to Laura Boon, for her careful editing and invaluable suggestions.

Special thanks go to Rosemary, for her generosity, guidance and friendship, and to Donald, for his assistance and technical expertise.

To family members and friends who read drafts and encouraged me to continue, thank you. I owe much too, to my dear friend Nina, whose quiet assurance that I had something useful to say in this novel kept me going whenever I had a crisis of confidence.

Finally, and most importantly, my love and enormous gratitude go to my husband, Kerry, and our daughters, Kate and Chloe. Thank you for your encouragement, constancy, love and endless support, in this and in all things. 'Bolly, Eddie?'

www.ingramcontent.com/pod-product-compliance
Lightning Source LLC
Chambersburg PA
CBHW071139180726
48291CB00007B/2263